First published in Great Britain in 2019 by Galdorbec
Copyright © 2019 by Frances Evelyn
The moral right of the author has been asserted.

ISBN e-book 978-1-9162496-0-8
ISBN paperback 978-1-9162496-1-5

https://bit.ly/FrancesEvelyn
https://bit.ly/FrancesEvelynNews

The Changeling Tree

by Frances Evelyn

The Book of the Challenge
Chapter 1

Whether the drums beat time for the feet, or the feet beat time for the drums, none can say. Melodies rise and fall from flutes and fiddles in all corners, overlapping, complementing, challenging one another to ever greater feats of harmony and rhythm. Servants bear silver trays of crystal glasses, shimmering with droplets of dew, for the dancers to snatch, if they can, as they pass. The dance whirls on across the candlelit splendour of the banqueting-hall, a room whose dimensions soar upward and reach outward in all directions further than the eye can easily see. What a human architect might achieve in glass and steel, stands here in intricately carved stone that defies all laws of gravity and logic.

The only fashion observed is extravagance. Gowns of deepest velvet sweep between cloud-like garments of net and lace. Skirts brush the floor, stand out wide or cling so short and diaphanous as to be barely visible. Hair is worn in every length, straight or curly, tall or broad, held stiff with powder, pearls and ribbons or flying loose with the rhythm of the dance. Faces, ranging from palest white to darkest black, from green to blue, are sweet or austere, smiling or hard, but all are striking in their beauty and joy.

Dancers in male form wear suits of silk and satin in all the colours of the rainbow and several more beside. They sport wigs, hats, masks and moustaches of splendour and wit. Where cheeks and chins are shaven, they are flawlessly smooth. Beards stand stiffly outward, hang in spikes or are draped around shoulders and waists so as not to impede the dance. Tailed coats and shimmering cloaks vie for space with the skirts that swing in sway to the music.

Spilling through open doors into the night, they whirl and caper where the dance takes them, lit by fireflies caught in nets of silken cobwebs. Sprays of clear, sweet, fountain water dance in the glow of the moon. Music and laughter reach up to the stars and away to the horizon's suspended dawn. In pairs and threes and permutations too complex for comprehension in the spin and flurry, they weave unerringly through the bewildering intricacy of the dance. Their pleasure echoes back from the snowy slopes of the Far Far Distant Hills, spurring the musicians on to ever greater feats of contrapuntal complexity.

For untold hours they turn and twirl, celebrate and laugh. The unity of their joy sustains the celebration from one day into the next, in a never-ending tumult of ecstasy. Day and night mean nothing to them.

Two alone resist the glamour of the music. The Queen dances when she wishes and observes when she prefers. She eats and drinks what she wants, laughs as she will, embraces as she desires, and delights in whomever and whatever she chooses. She shares her pleasure with them all and they give their obedience in return. Servants tend to her every need in the hope of elevation. Courtiers adapt their forms to amuse or flatter her. Today, she chooses to take the form of a white rose and many began this dance in floral tribute to her.

The fluidity of the dancers isn't immediately apparent amid so much variety, but here a waxed moustache is paired with a laced bodice, cut low over firm breasts. There a narrow waist and full hips belie a bulging codpiece. Dancers adapt their form, gender and attire to complement and challenge each other, shifting mid-leap to catch their partners off-guard. The Queen watches them change from daffodil to deer, from fish to dragonfly, from kingfisher to lion. The continual variation of limbs and locomotion challenges even the most skilled among them, repeatedly imperilling the integrity of the dance. This perpetual edge of danger heightens the pleasure of them all.

"Get off me," shrieks Lord Gine, who's currently clad entirely in denim, with a drooping moustache and ponytail.

"It's your own stupid fault for stopping to head-bang," snaps Lady Louple, disentangling his hair from her sequinned wet suit with rather less care than she might.

"That hurts," he wails with a pout. "And I'm not head-banging. My flares trip me."

"Be quiet," says Lord Wexen, flipping over them with the grace of a pre-pubescent gymnast. "And get out of the way. You're spoiling the dance."

He's rather pleased with the effect created by his trailing ribbons of fire and gives them an extra flourish in case anyone fails to notice.

"My tail," shouts Lord Skeck from across the hall. "My beautiful tail."

He's shaped as a lyrebird, and his tail is ablaze. The varnish is blistering, and he wails piteously with each string that snaps and lashes his back. Lady Flent rolls her eyes with unnecessary drama. Everyone knows that woodpeckers are the only birds actually made of wood. She draws closer. Her own form, a bouquet of origami flowers, bursts into beautiful flames and she lingers unnecessarily, as a sorry heap of ash, now armed with an amusing anecdote and an undying vendetta. She reforms herself as a phoenix and waddles off to tell of Lord Skeck's infamy before it slips her mind.

As the Queen sighs, a single, white petal falls. The beginning of the dance, the cause of their celebration, is already lost to memory and her joy is fading. She claps her hands and the candles are extinguished. The music stops. The dancers fall, robbed of her pleasure and assaulted by the weariness of days. Parched as they are, and weak from hunger, their first longing is for rest.

An unwary human, lured from a home and family who forgot him long ago, feels what he could only observe while the music commanded his senses: his blistered and bloodied feet; his legs, once so sturdy, now danced almost to the bone; his exhaustion so profound that none who see it can think themselves truly weary.

"It's all so dull," declares the Queen.

No response comes from her courtiers and servants. They know better than to draw her attention and risk her anger. Their Queen is capricious when wearied by joy.

"Does no-one hear me?" she says. "I'm bored. I entertain you royally and I deserve some pleasure in return."

Among the Faerie, the Queen shares her pleasure with the courtiers and the courtiers share theirs with those beneath them in a virtuous circle of joy. When the Queen is happy, the court is happy, and it's therefore in everyone's interests to attend to the Queen's pleasure without stint. If the Queen isn't happy, she shares her anger instead, turning them all against whoever might provoke her rage. Those who attend to the Queen's pleasure do so with great caution.

Some scholars distinguish between pleasure and glamour, though the ancient lore treats them as one. These pedants argue that while pleasure encourages underlings to behave in accordance with their superiors' desires, glamour compels their compliance. Wiser minds doubt the existence of glamour altogether, accounting it merely a convenient excuse for poor decisions and dubious taste.

Chapter 2

"Don't I deserve your gratitude?" screeches the Queen. "You," she says, pointing to the Lady-in-waiting, who incautiously catches her eye. "Do you not attend to my pleasure?"

"Of course," rasps the Lady Maven, changing her form into a snapdragon in the Queen's honour, her tongue clicking against the dry roof of her mouth. "I attend to your majesty's pleasure above all else, and it is an immeasurable honour to do so, but if I might be forgiven for the impertinence of asking …"

The Queen nods her permission brusquely.

"What might it be that your majesty desires?" asks the Lady Maven.

"Must I do everything for myself?" sighs the Queen. "Must I even tell you how to amuse me?"

Lord Skeck exchanges a fierce glance with Lady Louple. Lord Wexen looks at the floor and Lady Flent examines the walls. Lord Gine gazes up to the ceiling and Lady Brang peers out into the courtyard, each willing someone else to respond.

"Perhaps a game?" comes a male voice from the shadows.

"Oh, yes!" cries the Queen. "I do love a game."

A murmur of delight swells in response, fading as quickly as it grew, so that they might hear more of this new distraction.

"Might I propose a quest?" says the voice.

"A quest! Above all I adore a quest."

The Queen claps her hands with delight. In this delight, she forgets, or perhaps she chooses to ignore, her own decree outlawing all quests, games, challenges and bargains, which was announced in a fit of loser's pique after a particularly vexatious game of snap. She peers into the darkness.

"Who is that?" she asks. "Show yourself."

He steps forth from the shadows and bows low, his green eyes meeting hers, glinting gold with promised mischief. The Queen's lips curl in reluctant response. He wears the form that he knows pleases her most. Black satin breeches cling to his narrow hips. The feather in his broad-brimmed hat flutters as he sweeps it from his head in an unnecessarily extravagant bow that is nevertheless, by some curious means, remarkably alluring.

"Still fresh, I see, Lord Carrick. You are not wearied by the dance?"

"Your majesty, I come in all haste," he replies.

"Do you indeed?"

The Queen raises an eyebrow, uncertain how to respond to his bare-faced insubordination. The Faerie aren't bound by the laws of time. It moves around them like waves around a buoy. If they choose to untether themselves from the perpetual present, they can let it carry them or pass through it in whichever direction they choose, for as long as the whim takes them. His excuse means nothing. He's in the court when he chooses to be, and he should choose to be in the court when she desires it. But, for now, she leaves his impertinence unchallenged.

"Well, since no-one else cares to answer me," she says, "what do you propose, Lord Carrick?"

"If I may?"

He bows again, gesturing toward the gathered courtiers, who are beginning to adopt floral forms in carefully unambiguous demonstration of their loyalty. Between the flowers, wilt courtiers in other shapes, not yet sufficiently recovered from the dance to recognise their own best interests.

"Yes, yes," says the Queen, with an impatient wave of her hand.

Lord Carrick pivots to address the court, taking care not to turn his back on a queen who banishes courtiers for considerably less than that when the mood takes her. He speaks with careful courtesy and an appearance of innocent affection for the Faerie throng.

"Your majesty, my Lord Herald, Lady Maven, friends one and all. We revel in never-ending bliss. We dance, we laugh, we indulge our every whim and rejoice in the ineffable effulgence of our resplendent Queen. We are truly honoured by the gift of her joy."

He bows to the Queen again, and she nods her acknowledgement of his formulaic compliments. Servants move discreetly among the courtiers, dispensing reviving draughts in pursuit of favour and patronage. Lady Flent and Lord Gine clamour for their attention, wishing to appreciate this new distraction more fully. They reclaim their full vigour in the moment they drink and, with their self-interest and other senses sharpened, quickly conform to the present floral display. Naturally, they don't deign to notice who serves them. Patronage can be amusing enough, but it requires a certain amount of effort, and more exciting events are afoot.

Lord Skeck and Lady Louple make great show of refusing the draughts, extending their suffering to revel in the admiration of those around them. They play a dangerous game.

"Call this joy?" groans Lord Skeck from the floor, his blackened tail still smouldering.

This pantomime of suffering is undermined by his evident desire for the court's attention. The human who suffers beside him is more gifted: entirely consumed by the pain, he spares no thought for his audience. Lady Louple eyes him with resentment and bitter envy before redoubling her own anguish.

Lord Carrick ignores them all. He waits until he has the court's full attention before speaking again.

Chapter 3

"As our gracious Queen observes with characteristic wisdom and insight," he says. "Endless joy becomes – begging your majesty's indulgence – unending tedium. We take physical form and dance ourselves into the ground merely to simulate the counterpoint of joy, but fatigue is to misery what the pipe is to music. It enhances it, certainly, but the heart of any melody is the relentless beat of the drum."

"My lord is a terrible windbag," snaps the Queen.

He bows deeply, flourishing his feather to great effect.

"I do apologise for my unforgiveable verbosity. Your resplendent majesty awes me into nervous prolixity."

The Queen draws a leaf across one of her thorns, shredding it in silent menace.

"Might your glorious radiance permit me to speak succinctly?" asks Lord Carrick, his body still held in its bow.

"I do wish you would," says the Queen.

"Very well," he says, straightening his back, replacing his hat and holding his head high enough to efface all signs of deference. "We share our gift of joy with our human guests and they experience it to the full, do they not?"

"He's right," murmurs Lady Brang, in the form of a yellow chrysanthemum.

"Bloody humans," mutters Lord Gine, who's shaped himself as a red tulip.

"I quite like them," rustles the hydrangea bush that is Lord Wexen.

"Shhh," hisses Lady Flent, now a delicate spray of gypsophila. "Some of us are trying to hear what he's saying, you know."

"While it's true that our pleasure is enhanced by the humans' gift of suffering," continues Lord Carrick, "we only imagine that we feel their emotions. We see their pain and hear their groans, but we can't experience their misery as they enjoy the fullness of our bliss."

"It's a bloody liberty," mutters Lord Gine.

"Disgraceful," agrees Lady Brang.

Lord Carrick snatches his hat from his head in a movement clearly rehearsed, but no less appreciated for that. The plume swoops and flutters in an arc to the end of his arm which remains outstretched towards the human in their midst. When he speaks next, his tone matches the theatricality of the gesture.

"Well might this wretched mortal seek to creep away …"

"Look at him," hisses Lady Brang, pointing to the trail of blood smeared behind as the human drags himself across the banqueting-hall to the courtyard.

"That's disgusting," says Lord Wexen.

"Bloody disgrace," says Lord Gine.

"… for he benefits from an uneven bargain," continues Lord Carrick.

"Shame on you," cries Lady Brang.

"Bloody parasite," shouts Lord Gine.

"Leech," rustles Lord Wexen.

"My dear friends," says Lord Carrick, raising his hands for quiet.

This stage of Faerie celebrations often leads to the separation of human flesh from human bones, and Lord Carrick hopes to avoid this distraction.

"It is not their fault," he continues. "We heighten our joy by sharing – it's our nature to do so – but humans hoard their misery. If they seek communion in sadness, they only sully it with sympathy and comfort. We know this well."

In truth, the court knows little of humans, but Lord Carrick has a reputation as a great scholar, so his assertion stands unchallenged.

"What's your point?" asks the Queen. "Do get on and tell us about the quest, why don't you?"

"As your majesty commands," he bows again, though this time with greater efficiency. "My quest shall be to enter the world of humans in search of sorrow that we can share."

Now largely recovered, the courtiers gasp and rustle their approval. Lord Skeck and Lady Louple, clinging too long to exhaustion, find themselves ignored – ostentatious suffering quickly grows tiresome – and they anxiously vie for the attention of the drink-bearers. At this point, it amuses more vigorous courtiers to monopolise the attentions of the servants. Though they have no need of further draughts, unrelieved rage is tremendously amusing. The Faerie seek always to gain the upper hand. It is never wise to let them.

Lord Carrick's challenge thrills the court and some change shape in response. Petals are replaced by flowing curls and broad-brimmed hats with fluttering feathers; stems and leaves give way to pert buttocks and firm thighs encased in tight satin breeches. Trembling naked shoulders emerge from silk dresses, followed by heaving bosoms. Although the Faerie aren't always alert to the significance of alterations in their own forms, from her seat on the dais, the Queen is well positioned to observe their shifting loyalties.

"That sounds slightly interesting," she says, "but I presume there's a catch."

"Just a wish, your majesty," says Lord Carrick with a casual air. "Merely a wish to be granted should I succeed."

"And if you should fail?" she asks.

"If I should fail, your munificence, you may do with me as you will."

"I am Queen," she declares. "I rather think doing with you as I will is one of the perks. Or it may be a prerogative, but the distinction is epidemic."

"Indeed, your majesty. That is your right, within the ancient law."

Once again, Lord Carrick bows, his plumed hat sweeping the floor.

"However," he declares, "if I fail, I shall renounce all rights to Faerie."

The courtiers sway backward as one and turn their faces to the Queen. What Lord Carrick proposes is unheard of and they anticipate an equivalent gesture in response. While she hesitates, he speaks again.

"I ask but one small thing, your majesty."

"Name it," she says, unwisely rising to the extravagance of his proposal.

"Play with me."

By his words, he turns his quest into a challenge. His knee still bent before her, he puts out his hand, averting his gaze to allow her an opportunity for the abasement of indecision. He allows the silence to grow between them.

Chapter 4

Instead of speaking or taking his hand, the Queen beckons a giant panda forward, and the gathered courtiers part to allow him to lumber forth. They know to steer clear of his sharp claws and notorious digestive track wherever possible. Lord Carrick drops tactfully back too. There is nothing to be gained by pushing too hard.

"My Lord Herald," the Queen hisses, maintaining a smile for the benefit of her court. "Explain this to me."

"So bold a challenge, once publicly issued, cannot be rejected, your majesty," he explains, as quietly as a panda can.

"But I'm Queen. I can do anything, can't I?"

He nods patiently.

"Indeed so. However, a Queen who chooses not to grant her people the possibility of the gift of sorrow, which has been painted in such attractive colours by the Lord Carrick, might not long hold her throne."

She breathes in sharply. "Your words merit banishment."

"Indeed, they do, your majesty," he agrees. "However, were you to cast me out, I wouldn't be able to explain the possible consequences of Lord Carrick's challenge."

"Very well," she says. "Go on. But don't think I'm not cross with you."

"I wouldn't dream of it, your majesty."

He pauses until he's sure of her full attention.

"The ancient lore offers many protections to our Queen," he says, "but she is not invulnerable."

"Am I not?"

"No indeed, your majesty. Perhaps you don't recall, but your ascension to the throne depended upon your triumph over your predecessor."

The Queen smiles and nods enthusiastically.

"Of course, I remember. There's a tapestry."

For those who live in the eternal present, remembering is always a challenge. A Faerie Queen ensures that significant events are memorialised in the tapestries that adorn her palace, and these naturally focus on the glories of her own reign. Earlier tapestries are replaced as a matter of highest priority, and previous queens are thus forgotten with such thoroughness that any reference, mention or allusion to them is considered a significant breach of etiquette. The Lord Herald is wise to balance his unpardonable lack of tact by reference to his Queen's triumphant accession. Lords Herald who speak incautiously generally don't occupy the position for long.

"Is your majesty aware that your glorious succession, for which we are eternally grateful, depended upon another Queen's fall?"

The Lord Herald chuckles to himself. The use of past tenses is a rare skill in the court and if he doesn't appreciate it himself, it's entirely possible that no-one will. On its part, the court is united in an uneasy sense that there must be some reason why the Lord Herald is so very pleased with himself, and they generally change the subject to avoid accidentally finding out what it is. The Queen usually feels the same way, but at present she's struggling with the disturbing concept he puts before her.

"Are you saying that there are other Queens?" she asks.

"At other times, your majesty," replies the Lord Herald, with a chuckle.

He beckons a gaggle of liveried footmen and under-footmen forward.

"Let us say, for the sake of merriment, that this fellow here is the Queen of the bees."

The chosen footman blushes crimson and adapts in form to enhance the accessibility of the metaphor. Following the Lord Herald's instructions, the others imitate his shape and arrange themselves into a line.

"So," says the Lord Herald. "This fellow in the middle is the Queen of the bees. There are Queens before him and there are other Queens after him."

He gestures from one end of the line to the other to make his explanation clearer.

"I see," says the Queen.

"Let us say that this one is your gracious majesty."

"Alright," she says. "Though I wouldn't say that he's particularly gracious."

"He certainly is a wretched fellow," says the Lord Herald. "But one couldn't presume to attempt to replicate your majesty's grace. The point is that there are Queens before him, and there are Queens after him. Do you see?"

"Yes," says the Queen. "This seems entirely straightforward."

"Is your majesty sure?"

"Yes. Quite sure. It is well known that the bees have many hives and must therefore have many Queens. And footmen, apparently. Fancy that!"

The Lord Herald sighs and begins his explanation again. Although the courtiers watch for a while, they soon disperse in search of more accessible distractions. They have little interest in abstract thought and the Lord Herald's rambling can't compete with the amusing sight of the human attempting to drag himself away on his blistered stumps. His groans are most diverting, and the difficulty he's having in gaining any purchase on the blood-slicked floor is simply hilarious.

Eventually, the Lord Herald's patience is rewarded.

"Do you imply that there's a Queen-in-waiting?" gasps the Queen. "One who plots to wear my crown?"

Without smiling, the Lord Herald meets the eye of the Lady-in-waiting, Lady Maven, who shifts uncomfortably to ensure that she's out of the Queen's line of sight.

"Perish the thought, your majesty, and all those who might dream of thinking it," says the Lord Herald. "And given the impossibility of even reflecting on this matter, I'm sure the ancient lore is entirely mistaken in outlining how a Queen could be deposed."

"I'm quite sure it must be," says the Queen.

"Indeed, your majesty," the Lord Herald bows his agreement.

"However," says the Queen. "I suppose you may as well tell me what it says."

"As you wish, your majesty."

He casts a pall around them. There's no need for anyone else to hear this and, although Lord Carrick is standing back and pretending to engage in the general merriment, it is readily apparent that his attention doesn't waver. What's more, since the Lady Maven barely attempts to conceal her ambitions these days, he likes to make a point of putting obstacles in her path whenever possible. A new Queen generally banishes the holder of her predecessor's memory so promptly that the newness of her own Lord Herald is entirely overlooked in the excitement of the proclamation of her accession.

The Lord Herald speaks quietly. His words are for the Queen alone.

"The essence is simple, your majesty, though the ancient law expresses it with characteristic flummery. If the court, from the meanest servant to the Queen's nearest advisors should, as one, refuse to share her pleasure, she is no longer their Queen. According to the ancient law."

The Queen gasps. Although the Lord Herald explains this to her regularly, it shocks her to the core every time. Those members of the court who remain in attendance stir around her – they cannot hear, but they see her still – and she forces her features into an expression of calm contentment. The Lord Herald pauses to give her time to digest this troubling news.

"It is a doggy dog world," she declares.

"It is, your majesty. The ancient law decrees, or perhaps it merely observes, that the court's refusal of their Queen's pleasure must be spontaneous and unpremeditated."

"Well, I suppose that's something," says the Queen.

"Quite so, your majesty, though this may be because any such discussion or prior arrangement would inevitably be exposed by ambitious lickspittles and sycophantic lackeys, resulting in the immediate banishment of all concerned."

"Quite right too," says the Queen. "Could you just remind me why you're telling me this."

One of the greatest challenges facing a Lord Herald is communicating complexities to a Queen whose innumerable strengths, glorious and splendid as they are, do not include memory or reason. The first attempt merely prepares the ground. The second attempt, perhaps, creates a vague awareness that there's something to be known. The third attempt, if well executed, may achieve a sketchy understanding of roughly what that might be. In this way, a skilled Lord Herald builds a foundation of anxiety and curiosity to excuse, when it comes, the explanation that is brief and clear enough to be comprehended.

"Your majesty, Lord Carrick challenges you to a quest. Naturally, he seeks to improve his own position and he therefore aspires to yours."

"You can't mean that he thinks to be Queen," she gasps.

"Just so, your majesty."

Gender among the Faerie is not as it is among humans. They are timeless ethereal beings who simply have no need of it. Because of their fascination with humanity however, it often amuses them to adopt gendered forms. The ancient lore explains that ascension to the throne is marked by the temporary adoption of female appearance and terms of address, for purely ceremonial reasons. Once the initial formalities are completed, a newly anointed monarch can take whatever shape he, she, it or they choose and demand to be addressed however the whim takes her, him, it or them at any moment in time. Similarly, the distinction between the lords and ladies of the court lies primarily in the titles and forms of address that they currently prefer.

The ancient lore further explains that in the turmoil of a new accession, the court is peculiarly distracted. Following one unusually vicious coronation marbles tournament, for example, many members of the court were so excited by the pretty colours and the pleasing chink of the spheres, that they neglected their usual fluidities of form and address, with the result that many settled into whichever gender they happened to be in at the time, claiming, if asked, that they were just more comfortable that way. Naturally, courtly titles have also tended towards a greater fixity since this time. This is only of interest at the present moment because it might not otherwise be apparent to human readers that Lord Carrick might reasonably aspire to be Queen.

"But I am Queen," says the Queen.

"And most glorious you are too, your majesty."

The Lord Herald's patience is well practised.

"But, as you know," he continues. "The court may turn against your majesty at any moment and refusing this challenge could create just such a turning-point."

"You're saying I must accept his challenge."

"I wouldn't presume to tell your majesty what to do."

"Of course not. I am Queen."

"Indeed, you are," he says, "and to general jubilation. However, now that the prohibition on games is breached, we can expect more challenges, whether or not your majesty accepts this one. Indeed, were you to refuse this challenge, the next would undoubtedly be less favourable. The court might turn against a Queen who continued to deny them such pleasures."

"I see," said the Queen. "You can't mean to say that my position is unstable?"

"I wouldn't presume to say so, most splendid sovereign. But yes, your majesty, your position is decidedly unstable and refusing this challenge would make it considerably more so. However, a victorious conclusion would certainly strengthen your position. I suggest that while we explore the nature of the challenge with Lord Carrick, we take the opportunity to improve the odds in your favour."

"I see," says the Queen.

"Quite so," says the Lord Herald. "In fact, I have high hopes of the challenge proving entirely impossible, in which case, he can be banished the moment the court understands this."

"It seems to me," says the Queen, "that this challenge must be accepted."

"Indeed, your majesty."

"And what of these other challenges you mention?"

"According to the ancient lore, your majesty, none may involve your royal self until Lord Carrick's is resolved."

"Very well," says the Queen. "I appear to have no other option."

"Your majesty is most wise," says the Lord Herald.

"Queasy is the head that wears the crown," she observes sagely.

"Indeed so, your majesty."

The Lord Herald raises the pall between the Queen and her court. With an appearance of pleasure, she gestures Lord

Carrick forward, puts her hand in his and steps down from
the dais.

The Book of Michael Murray
Chapter 5

It was the longest night of the year. Mike had left the pub
buoyed by the romance of his planned gesture. He'd been
to her house plenty of times before: her mum had threatened
him with the police more than once. But this was going to
be different. This was the last time. He had to stop coming,
he knew that. He'd spent the whole of his first term at uni
moping about a girl who couldn't even be bothered to let
him know he was dumped. He understood that it sounded
stupid, he'd been told so enough times, but it just wasn't like
her. She couldn't have stopped loving him so abruptly and,
even if she had, she wouldn't have treated him this cruelly.
It seemed to him that if it really had ended this way, then
none of it had been true.

If he stayed at the edge of the garden, among the trees,
he'd have a good view of the house without being visible
from inside. This was the last time he'd come here. The days
would grow longer after this. The nights would grow
shorter. His heart would brighten, and he'd put it all behind
him. He couldn't forget her, but he wouldn't allow himself
to think about her anymore. He'd build a wall between
himself and the pain she'd caused him so he could try to get
on with his life.

This was the last time. If she wasn't here or she wouldn't
speak to him, that was it. He wouldn't come back again. He

wouldn't scan pubs and bars for her face. He wouldn't look for her on trains or in stations or walking down the street. This would be the end of it.

What he needed, what he really needed, was to hear it from her. He needed her to tell him that she didn't want to see him anymore. It didn't matter how many times he'd heard it from other people: his mum, her mum, friends at college and uni. He needed to hear it from her so that he could move on. She owed him that much.

The bare branches provided some shelter from the rain, but cold drips were finding their way down his neck and under his clothes. He was straining to see anything in the darkness of the house. There were no lights. There were no Christmas lights. Perhaps the electricity had been cut off again. Perhaps they didn't celebrate Christmas at all. But surely there'd be some sign that they were in.

A clap of thunder rolled over his head and a flash of lightening illuminated the house from behind. It loomed larger than he'd expected, as if it had crept closer in the darkness. Squatting in a dip in the ground, the house had always seemed impossibly small. She'd never invited him in to see it for himself.

In the garden that bulged around the house, he could see an indistinct dark shape. Other gardens had swings and furniture and barbeques, but this one only had tree-stumps, weeds and stones. Whatever the dark shape was, it was out of place: it was waist-high and bulky and standing alone. Mike left the shelter of the trees. He was wet already, and if he was going to speak to her, he'd have to go to the door.

He'd chosen his clothes carefully. He wanted to look good, but not like he'd made too much effort. His jet-black hair had grown since she'd seen him last, and he'd made sure no brown roots were showing through. He had just enough stubble to accentuate his jawline. His black jeans were clean but faded. He wore the over-sized leather jacket she liked and a new Sisters of Mercy t-shirt. He'd seen them at uni and hoped she'd notice and ask. Once they started talking, she'd be sure to remember how good they'd been together. Around his wrist was the braid she'd made from his broken shoelace. He always wore it, but perhaps this would be the last night.

His trainers were heavy with mud and the wet jeans clung unpleasantly to his legs. His jacket held off the rain that fell directly on to it, but cold trickles were seeping down his neck from his hair. He hoped the colour wasn't running.

The ground was slick with rain and pitted with puddles. The mud of the raised garden splashed and trickled down on to the puddled path which was advancing in muddy rivulets towards the house. If this carried on, the house would be swallowed up entirely.

The wind urged him back to the trees, but he forced his way nearer. As he approached it, the shadow in the garden formed itself into an old-fashioned black pram. The hood was up, and the opening was facing him. When he moved closer, he saw that puddles were forming on the waterproof cover, building and spreading towards the shadowed area under the hood. He peered inside to see a baby. It lay still, with its eyes closed.

His first thought was that it must be dead, and he put his hand out gingerly to touch it. The baby's face was cold, but it stirred in response to his gentle fingertips. It shouldn't be out in this weather. That much was clear. It might be dry now, but it wouldn't stay dry for long. He pushed the handle, and although the pram didn't budge, the movement caused a surge in the cold pool on its cover, first towards him and then towards the baby. He pressed down to tip the water away from the opening and poured it on to his trainers instead. His bewilderment turned to anger. This was ridiculous. It wasn't right. He splashed down into the sunken path, mud sucking on to his feet, and strode to the house to pound on the door.

No-one answered and no lights came on. He peered through the window by the door, but there was no sign of movement inside. He shouted through the letterbox, but no-one came. He waded along the narrow trench that ran around the house, one shoulder sheltered from the rain under the over-hanging thatch, the other deluged by the water running off it. Overgrown plants and bushes soaked his arms and legs when he brushed against them. In places, the trench had already collapsed, and he clambered and slipped over the mud that was beginning to fill the hollowed-out space between the house and the trees around it.

The door at the back was also locked, and no lights were showing through the kitchen window. The door through to the hall was standing open inside, but it only revealed more darkness beyond. There was nothing to show that anyone was home.

When he got back to it, the pram's cover was heavy with rain again. Mike tipped it down gently, draining the water carefully away from the baby and not caring when it splashed coldly down his legs. It wasn't as if he could get any wetter than he already was. He carried the pram to the edge of the garden and lifted it gently down to the path. He trod carefully on the treacherous mud, the muscles in his arms burning. The baby slept on as he set the pram gently down by the front door. A slanting wooden overhang provided some shelter from the rain when the wind wasn't gusting, and he used his body to block the worst of the rest.

Mike's legs were protected from the wind in the trench by the house, but the muddy rain was pooling deeper here, and he felt its chill seeping into his feet. Squeezed against the pram, he waited, arms folded, feet bouncing for warmth. They'd be back soon. They couldn't have gone far in weather like this. He watched puddles forming in the raised garden, joining and growing until they emptied their contents into the shining black pool swelling in the corners of the trench around the house. Periodically, the edges of the garden crumpled and broke away like glaciers calving.

They must have gone further than he'd imagined, but wherever they were, they'd be rushing back to bring the baby in from the rain. They must be. Mike shivered and blew into his hands. He rubbed his arms. The baby began to grumble and stir. He rocked the pram gently, hoping to keep it safely asleep, muttering assurances and pleas.

"It's fine. Shush now. Don't wake up. Please don't wake up."

The baby began crying in earnest. If they were anywhere nearby, he was sure they'd hear it and come running, despite the noise of the wind and rain. Perhaps they'd fallen asleep upstairs, not realising how badly the weather had changed. He banged on the door again, but no-one came.

Chapter 6

When Shirley Murray was on lates, she always needed to potter around for a while in her dressing-gown and slippers while she unwound. She'd had a shower, after washing away the drips from Mike's hair dye, and managed to get the smell of the hospital out of her hair. She kept it short for practicality but had enough vanity to have them bleach in highlights to hide the grey. She was proud of her trim figure and calm head in a crisis, but she'd been on her feet all day. What she needed was to flop on to her saggy sofa, its old-fashioned floral exuberance hidden by a colourful throw that no-one else ever bothered straightening. She needed to put her feet up on the coffee table that she'd cleared of mugs and crisp packets. Brian was already asleep upstairs, but she had to unwind before she could settle, and she couldn't unwind with plates on the floor. There'd been four deliveries today and another one heading towards a caesarean when the night shift came on. Shirley was dead on her feet. She just wanted a bit of something to eat and some down time. There wasn't anything she fancied on the telly, so she'd watch the Christmas tree twinkling while she drank her tea and her mind fell quiet. Then she'd go up.

She'd only just put her cup down when Mike started slamming doors and dripping mud all over her hall carpet.

"For goodness sake!" she said. "You haven't even got a coat on. Didn't you see the forecast?"

Rivulets of dye had run down his face. He'd leave black splotches everywhere he touched if he wasn't careful.

"Stay there," she said. "Don't move. I'll get you a towel."

"Can you help me, mum?" he asked.

His right sleeve was hanging empty. With his left hand, he was supporting his right arm, which was zipped under his jacket. Her exasperation turned to fear.

"Oh my god. Are you hurt?"

"No, I'm fine. It's just ..."

He gestured towards his zip and she pulled it down to reveal a baby cradled underneath. Exposed to the light and the cold, denied the soothing comfort of his motion, the baby began mewling. Shirley's mouth fell open.

"What's going on?" she asked.

She could only make out parts of it over the noise and the fuss. He'd found the baby abandoned. In this weather! He was drenched through and chilled to the bone, but there wasn't time for him to dry out and change.

"You need to go to the late-night chemist on London Road. We need a little carton of milk. For new-borns. And a bottle. It needs to be sterilised, so we can use it straight away. And some disposable nappies. The smallest size. Ask if you're not sure. But just the milk and the bottle if that's all you can get. Run. They'll be closing any minute. Go."

She shut the door after him and shouted up the stairs.

"Brian. You need to get down here."

A little sugar-water on a flannel bought quiet for the moment. Shirley turned up the gas fire to make the living-room cosy and lay the baby on the sofa beside her to check its little body for injuries. The baby was damp with rain and sweat, so Shirley put the clothes aside and wrapped her in an old towel held together with safety pins from her sewing box. It wasn't ideal, but it would have to do for the moment. With the throw from the back of the sofa, she made a cocoon to keep her warm and safe.

"Brian. Wake up," she yelled, banging on the banisters.

The baby was grizzling half-heartedly.

"I know. I know, sweetheart," she cooed, with the detached affection of a professional carer. "I know you're hungry and I promise it's coming."

She put the kettle on and found a jug and a tray. She didn't like leaving the baby on its own, but it would take her twice as long if she tried to hold her while she was getting everything done. Crying wouldn't do her any harm, but Shirley popped back to the living-room to check on her when the cries subsided.

"Brian Murray," she yelled on her way past the stairs. "I'm serious. Get yourself down here, will you?"

The baby began crying in earnest.

"I'm sorry, love. You'll get your milk soon, I promise."

She pulled back the curtain but there was nothing to see through the rain. She picked up the baby to rock in her arms.

"Shush now. Everything's alright. Mike won't be long with that milk of yours. If you'll just be quiet for a minute, I can phone the police while we're waiting."

It was a short call. She didn't have much information anyway, so they'd need to ask Mike when they got here, and it was difficult to be heard with the baby crying in any case. It didn't cross Shirley's mind that her son might have done anything wrong. He was a good boy. He always had been.

A blast of cold air rattled the windows when the front-door opened, and Mike passed a dripping carrier bag into the living-room.

"Here you are," he said. "Did I get the right things?"

She peered inside.

"Perfect. Thanks love. Go and get yourself dry now. And get your dad up, please."

"I'm up," grumbled Brian, standing back to let his wet son squeeze past him on the stairs. "What's all the fuss about?"

"Hold her for a minute," said Shirley, passing him the baby as she went back to the kitchen. "Take her into the living-room where it's warm."

Changing her tone, she turned to the baby.

"I'm just going to get your milk for you, petal. I won't be a second. I'll be as quick as I can."

"Who's this?" asked Brian, making to follow her.

"Living-room," she said. "I'll explain in a minute."

She poured the milk into the bottle and put it in the jug of hot water to warm. There was enough for three cups of tea, so she put the mugs on the tray with a packet of Hobnobs. It was likely to be a long night. When the milk was warm enough, she wiped the bottle dry and carried everything through.

"Now then," she said, opening the living-room door with her elbow. "Help yourself to tea, love. I'll take the baby. There you are. Oh, my word, you're hungry, aren't you?"

"What on earth's going on?" asked Brian.

"All I know," said Shirley, "is that Mike found her somewhere. She must have been abandoned by her mother, poor little thing. She could've drowned in this rain, let alone the cold. The police are on their way. Mike'll be down any minute."

By the time Mike came down, the baby had sucked herself into a daze. He sat down quietly and watched his mum gently rubbing and rocking her, humming a familiar tune that he couldn't quite place. The room was warm. It was late. His mum was talking in a soothing voice to the baby, and his dad was nodding back to sleep. Mike's eyelids began to droop too.

"Oh no you don't," said his mum, throwing a cushion at him. "You can't sleep yet, my lad. Wake up."

"What is it?" he asked "Is it ok? The baby?"

"She's fine," Shirley said.

"She? It's a girl?"

"Yes. Less than a month old, would be my guess. The police should be here any minute."

"Who called the police?" asked Mike.

"I did, love."

"Good," he said. "They'll have to take me seriously now."

Shirley frowned. "I'm not sure I'm following you, love. The police need to make sure the baby's safe and they'll want to look for her mother too. But what's that got to do with you?"

"She's mine," said Mike. "I'm going to look after her."

"It doesn't work like that, love. Just because you found her, doesn't mean you can keep her."

"No. Listen to me," he insisted. "She's mine. I'm her father."

"Steady on," said Brian. "There's no need to raise your voice."

Mike spoke more quietly, his teeth gritted with the effort of remaining calm.

"I found her in the garden at Tracy's house. She's mine. She must be."

It made a sort of sense to his parents. Tracy had disappeared and broken his heart. They'd heard enough about her before and since to know that it had hit him hard. It had all started so well. Shirley had spotted the tell-tale glow when he mentioned her name well before he'd found out that Tracy liked him too. Then he'd been head over heels, and it'd seemed that she felt the same. She was a lovely girl, or that's what they'd thought. And then, with no warning, she was gone. She stopped going to college without explanation. She didn't turn up for her exams and she didn't answer her phone. Mike had gone to her house a few times to try and speak to her when it first happened, but they thought he'd given up on that. The first term at uni was supposed to have put it out of his mind. He ought to have moved on by now.

Shirley Murray would have called the police anyway, but it felt less straightforward now. She was sure Mike wouldn't have done anything wrong, not on purpose, but he might have done something stupid. She'd defend him no matter what, of course, but her heart was in her throat.

Chapter 7

"Alright. Alright. I'm coming," said a voice that sounded female but without any of the softness or charm that might usually be considered feminine.

A tall figure cast its shadow against the door. It could have been a man from the size, but its contours were difficult to determine through the obscured glass in the dark hallway.

"What do you want?" she'd asked.

"My name's Mike," he'd said. "Mike Murray."

He'd seemed hardly more than a boy, though she'd known he was off to university soon. Five foot nine, maybe, or ten, and not likely to get much taller. A puff of wind could have carried him away, he was that slight. There wasn't anything special about him, as far as she'd been able to see. His hair was too long, but that must be the fashion, she'd supposed. It was straight and dyed jet-black, which probably meant something she wasn't interested in understanding. Tracy's hair had been the same. It was unwise, but she wouldn't listen.

"She's not here," she'd said, her voice dull.

"Could I just talk to you for a minute, please, Mrs Goodfellow?"

She'd opened the door far enough that he'd caught a glimpse of her shapeless brown garment and a whiff of her unwashed body and stale breath. Her joyless face was set in an expression of mistrustful determination.

"Sorry," he'd said. "I don't mean to intrude, but do you know when she'll be back?"

"She didn't tell me."

"Do you have an address for her? Or a number I can call her on?"

"No."

She wouldn't have told him if she had. She wouldn't have wanted to encourage him. Nothing good could come of it.

"She can't have just disappeared," he'd said.

He'd seemed determined to disregard the obvious: that this was exactly what she'd done.

"She's gone," she'd said.

He'd put out his foot to stop her closing the door.

"Please. Just tell me how I can get in touch with her."

"You can't," she'd said.

"Will you tell her I called?"

"Maybe," she said. "If I see her."

"I'll just keep coming back until I can talk to her," he'd said.

"That's up to you. But you'll be wasting your time."

She closed the door firmly, pushing his foot aside with her own. Over the months, they'd had many variations of that conversation. At first, Mike had accepted that she didn't know any more than he did, but he'd come to suspect that she was keeping something back. A mother whose daughter went missing without word should be frantic with worry, not indifferent and uninterested. At night, when he couldn't sleep and his mind kept itself busy with unthinkable scenarios, he convinced himself that she was hiding something: that she not only knew where her daughter was but had been involved in her disappearance. After he'd reported Tracy missing, her mother stopped answering the door to him altogether.

Chapter 8

One of the sofas had been pulled forward to make room for the Christmas tree by the window, and the coffee table had been moved out to make room for them to sit. Opposite the corner made by the two sofas was the television, but it wasn't on. Shirley sat nearest the door to the hall, still holding the baby. Mike and Brian were on the sofa by the window.

"But it all makes sense now, do you see?" said Mike. "Her mum sent her away because she was pregnant."

"That would be very old-fashioned," said Shirley, cradling the baby's warm head with her hand.

"She is very old-fashioned," said Mike. "You should see her."

"Well, ok, if that was true," Shirley said, "why would Tracy bring the baby back to her mum's? And why wouldn't she get in touch with you when she did?"

"I don't know, alright?" said Mike. "I just know it's my baby. Our daughter."

"You're sure you were the only one there?" asked Brian.

Mike turned on him, his eyes blazing.

"At the house, I meant," said Brian. "You're sure there wasn't anyone else at the house?"

"Yes," said Mike. "That's what I'm telling you. There was no-one there."

"How do you know that for sure?" asked Shirley. "Did you go into their house, Mike?"

"What? No. She was in a pram in the garden. I told you."

"But you did check there was no-one in?" asked Brian.

"Yes," said Mike. "I checked. Of course, I checked."

"Did you leave a note?" asked Shirley.

"How could I have left a note?" Mike asked. "Have you seen this rain? And I didn't have any to write with. Or on. I don't understand why you're asking."

"You took someone's baby," Shirley said, as gently as she could. "They could accuse you of kidnapping her."

"But she's mine," said Mike.

"Mike, love, we don't know that for certain. And even if she is, you can't just take her. Her mum'll be beside herself. We should ring them, let them know she's alright. In fact, let's do that now."

She passed him the baby.

"Make sure you support her head. That's right. Now then, what's their number?"

"There's no point," said Mike. "Because there's no-one there. And the phone was cut off months ago."

His frustration dissolved as he gazed at the tiny creature nestled against his chest. She had downy blonde hair and thick black eyelashes. Her cheeks were round and smooth, her little button nose speckled with white. She frowned and wriggled in her sleep, her tiny fingers stretching and curling. He loved her.

Blue lights flashed against the curtains. Car doors opened and closed.

"That'll be them now," said Shirley. "Mike. Mike, listen to me."

He tore his eyes away from the baby.

"Listen. They don't know you like we do, love. Just think about what you say, alright?"

"Just tell them the truth," said Brian.

Shirley glared at her husband. "But carefully, ok?"

Chapter 9

The neighbours would be round tomorrow, wanting to know what was going on. Even with the sirens turned off, they couldn't have failed to see the lights whirling across their walls and ceilings. Shirley hustled the police officers, a man and a woman, through the front-door as quickly as she could, keeping them busy in the hall to buy Mike some time to collect himself.

"It's foul weather today, isn't it?" she said, tugging on the policeman's coat sleeve to demonstrate her helpfulness when dealing with the law. "It's playing havoc with my carpets."

34

"Thank you," said the policeman, though he found her assistance unsettling. "So, it's Mrs?"

He was round-faced and barely older than Mike was. He seemed like the type to be bullied, and Shirley hoped he wouldn't take it out on them.

"Murray," she said. "Shirley Murray."

"Could you tell us where you found the baby, Mrs Murray?" asked the policewoman, tucking her coat over the hall radiator.

Shirley considered picking it up and hanging it on a hook, but she thought better of it. The policewoman had uncompromisingly short hair and an air of authority. Shirley thought she seemed the sort to think the worst of people, given half an opportunity.

"No, it wasn't me who found her, officer. It was my son, Mike, who rescued her. It's what he's like, you see. Caring and selfless. Community-minded, that's our Mike. He's just through here, looking after the baby, poor abandoned little thing."

The policewoman followed her into the living-room where Mike was sitting on the sofa, gazing at the baby in his arms. He hardly looked up when they came in. If the room had felt crowded before, it was over-flowing now, with two more coming in and Brian on his feet with his hand outstretched. Shirley peered around the police-officers from behind.

"Please go in," she said. "We're letting out all the warmth. Make room, Brian."

She gestured to her husband to re-tie his dressing-gown. It wouldn't do to give the police the wrong impression.

"I'm WPC Lambert," said the policewoman, shuffling further into the room. "And this is my colleague, PC Hanks."

"Is it alright if we sit down, Mrs Murray?" asked PC Hanks.

"Yes, of course. Not at all," said Shirley. "Can I offer you a cup of tea? Coffee? Hot chocolate?"

"That's very kind of you Mrs Murray," said WPC Lambert. "But we need to ask some quite urgent questions, if you don't mine."

"Yes, yes. Of course."

Shirley sat down and pulled the flaps of her dressing-gown together. She wished she'd found time to get dressed. Should they have turned off the Christmas lights, she wondered. WPC Lambert had her notepad and pen poised. She hadn't written anything yet, but she was taking it all in. PC Hanks was scribbling away furiously, noting down descriptions. They probably wouldn't need them, but he practised whenever he could. Shirley Murray. Female, IC1, late 40s, early 50s. Five foot 2. Medium build. Short, light brown hair, greying. No distinguishing features. Brian Murray. Male, IC1, early to mid-50s. Five foot 10. Balding. Distinctive nose. Mike Murray. Male, IC1, late teens, early 20s. Five foot 9. Long, black hair. Same nose. They were fleshy, those noses, with a clear division down the middle, separating them into two perfect little nasal-buttocks. PC Hanks would remember if he needed to, but you should never write anything down you wouldn't want to have to read out in court.

"Now then," said WPC Lambert. "Mr Murray, please could you tell us where you were when you found the baby?"

"Peston Forest," said Mike. "There's an old house in the spinney off Hinkley Rd."

WPC Lambert nodded to PC Hanks, who muttered into his radio.

"That's quite a way from here, sir," she said. "Could you tell us what you were doing all the way over there on a night like this?"

"I wanted to know if my girlfriend was home," said Mike.

"I see, and your girlfriend lives in Peston Forest, does she?"

"Yes," said Mike. "That's her house. The one in the spinney."

"Ok. We'll come back to that. Now, could you tell us in your own words what happened tonight?"

WPC Lambert took notes calmly, interrupting occasionally for more information. She communicated by glances with PC Hanks, who left the room several times to talk on his radio, clambering around the coffee table to reach the door. On his way back, he reported that the social worker had been held up, that a car had been dispatched to the house, that the house was empty. His inaudible conversations in the hall made Shirley uneasy. It was obvious that someone was going to take the blame for this. She wasn't going to let Mike be a scapegoat.

"He did the right thing, didn't he, officer?" she asked. "I mean, he couldn't have come away and left the baby out there on a night like this. Where's the mother, that's what I'd like to know. What was she thinking?"

"I'm sure there's a perfectly reasonable explanation," said Brian.

"What I'm saying," said Shirley, enunciating carefully, "is that her mother shouldn't have abandoned her."

WPC Lambert waited for her to finish and turned back to Mike.

"So, you're registered as the baby's father?"

"No," said Mike. "Well, I don't know."

"I see."

She caught PC Hanks's eye and closed her notebook.

"We lost touch," said Mike. "Me and my girlfriend. But she's definitely my daughter."

"PC Hanks," said the policewoman.

They exchanged another glance and he left the room again. Shirley heard him speaking into his radio and opening the front door. He ushered a middle-aged woman into the room.

"I'm sure you understand that the baby's welfare has to be our highest priority," said WPC Lambert. "My colleague …"

"Susan Thorne," said the woman, pressing her lips together in a no-nonsense smile.

"… needs to check her over, just to see that she's alright."

"Oh! Hello Shirley," said Susan. "Long time! How've you been?"

"Fine. Fine," said Shirley. "You know how it is. It's alright, Mike," she said. "You can give her to Susan."

The sofa was too low and soft to stand up holding the baby, so Mike held her up for Susan's outstretched arms.

"Careful," he said. "You have to support her head."

"That's alright love," the midwife said as she lifted the baby towards her. "Hello young lady. You've been causing a bit of a fuss, haven't you?"

She walked towards the door.

"Wait," said Mike, getting to his feet. "Where are you taking her?"

PC Hanks moved to block the door while Mike stretched his legs over the coffee table. They stood facing one another, close enough to be menacing, but without physical contact. The front-door opened.

"What are you doing?" Mike shouted. "You can't take her. She's mine."

"Calm down, sir."

PC Hanks put one hand flat on Mike's shoulder.

"Get out the way," shouted Mike, trying to push him aside.

"Mike! Stop it." Shirley held him tightly, pinning his arms down with hers. "It's alright, love. It's going to be alright."

"Thank you, Mrs Murray," said WPC Lambert. "I'm sorry sir, I really am, but until we can confirm that you're the father, social services are legally responsible for the well-being of the child. Hopefully this will all be resolved very quickly, but we won't be able to access any records before the morning."

"Is there anything else you need from us tonight?" asked Shirley. "We'll do whatever we can to help, won't we, Mike?"

"No," said WPC Lambert. "Thank you for your cooperation."

Before she left, she put a hand on Mike's arm.

"You saved her life, you know. Whatever happens, you'll know you did the right thing."

"That's right, son," said Brian.

"Alright, mate," said PC Hanks on his way out. "Ma'am, Sir."

The Book of Faerie Facts, Part J
Chapter 10

Most courtiers pursue their all-pervasive rivalries by whim and instinct, usually forgetting the wrongs that caused their last fury the moment they become enraged by something more diverting. There are only a few whose minds can encompass the notions of past and future, and this enables them to understand cause and effect, which equips them to plot and scheme on a level unimagined by the rest of the court. Comprehending time is, to the Faerie, what the sixth sense is to humans. Those who don't have it don't understand what they're missing. They consider it fanciful and little suspect the power it imparts. Those who do have it know that its value is beyond price, and they understand the importance of keeping all knowledge of this skill to themselves.

It is therefore an uncomfortable truth that one of the highest positions at court is, by both convention and necessity, occupied by just such a time-knower. The Lords Herald would be unable to advise their Queen effectively without understanding how time binds this result with that action or this outcome with that decision. They couldn't make any sense at all of the ancient lore if they didn't appreciate that it was compiled, largely with the best of intentions, by a series of previous Lords Herald, appointed by a series of deposed Queens. The uneasy relationship between the Queen and Lord Herald is necessarily one of mutual dependence and mistrust. At least one of them understands that the terms of all previous Lords Herald and the reigns of all earlier Queens ended in banishment one way or another.

The Hall of the Heralds occupies an obscure corner of the palace and is generally visited only by accident. It holds little meaning for most courtiers, who simply cannot comprehend the import of its tapestries. The evidence of their own eyes tells them that the Lord Herald is a giant panda and yet these tapestries represent Lords Herald in other forms. Any normal courtier who wanders into the Hall is swiftly driven out by the blinding headache such conundrums are prone to create. Once outside, they put it entirely out of their mind, and the resulting headache is both gone and forgotten.

The Faerie change their form at will or by whim to express their personality, their moods or their last passing thought. Imitation of the appearance of a superior is the highest – and therefore the most frequent – form of courtesy, though in the kaleidoscopic fluidity of the court, even flattery is fleeting. The promptest flatterer adopts a form as close to the Queen's as is compatible with avoiding her wrath. For example, if she adopts the form of a sleek racehorse, those around her will become less powerful racehorses bearing less pleasing white markings, or manes that are less carefully groomed. If the Queen is feeling particularly testy, wise courtiers will be conspicuously scabby or lame.

The introduction of some slight variation or obscure association is celebrated as a mark of subtlety, so that if the Queen should adopt the form of a parrot, her court will be filled with many species of exotic bird, each one reinforcing the others' appearance to create a semblance of collective stability among the flurry of feathers. A courtier adopting the form of a pirate under these circumstances is accounted a great wit and regarded with considerable suspicion. This new form may spark off a flurry of sea-goers, marine life or Halloween costumes, which might be considered discourteous to the Queen, though she's as unlikely as anyone to notice, and may don an eyepatch herself if the fancy takes her.

Such changes of form are effortless and superficial. They have no more long-lasting effect than fancy dress does among humans. No matter how many moments the Faerie spend as dragons, for example, they become no more inclined to breathe fire or hoard treasure than is otherwise natural to them. Although all dragonic activities and abilities are available to them while in dragon-form – in the same way that a human may change their gait or voice while in fancy dress – the Faerie are in no way altered by these superficial changes of appearance. Similarly, despite rumours to the contrary, it is now generally believed that a human who adopts the costume of a pirate will usually find both legs intact on resuming their normal dress.

In contrast, it's customary for Lords Herald to adopt a stable form, as selected by the Queen, on their accession to office. In addition to making them easily recognisable, this creates an appearance of gravity and reliability amid the joyful chaos of court. As among humans, although necessary, these qualities are both ridiculous and repugnant.

Lords Herald demonstrate their devotion to the office and detachment from the frivolities of court by physically becoming the form they adopt. The tapestries in the Hall of the Heralds therefore represent not Lords Herald who appear to be a badger, an oak tree, a large pebble, and so on, but a badger, oak tree and large pebble who are – or were, for the benefit of those who can appreciate the distinction – Lords Herald. It's fair to say that some of the forms selected for the Lords Herald are more successful than others.

When not attending to the needs of the Queen, Lords Herald must see to their own physical needs, whether they be snuffling, growing acorns or gently eroding. To allow for this, they're excused some of the normal duties of the court. The ancient lore explains that oak trees are not skilled dancers, for example, and that badgers tend to overheat if kept at it for too many days at a time. To allow for the limitations of materiality therefore, and to spare the court the embarrassment of praising their ungraceful attempts, Lords Herald are neither expected nor compelled to dance.

The termination of a Lord Herald's tenure is entirely at the Queen's whim and, having become their physical form, ex-Lords Herald leave the court to live out however many days may be allotted to it in the normal course of affairs. An unfortunate consequence of their materiality is that the more experienced a Lord Herald is, the more powerfully he – for by convention Lords Herald are male regardless of their previous inclinations – is influenced by the needs, desires and customs of his physical form. For example, the pebblish Lord Herald grew exceedingly wise through his patient exposure to the ancient lore, but increasingly disinclined to act upon the Queen's summons. He now enjoys the good-natured buffeting of his fellows on the bed of the River Severn, only occasionally reflecting with relief on the tribulations of his former life.

For the avoidance of undue influence, the physical needs of the Lords Herald are supplied by means of an appropriate portal to the human world. Wherever and whenever a Lord Herald may happen to wander in that world, one end of the portal is always with him. The other opens into an antechamber to the throne-room, ensuring that if the Queen calls, the Lord Herald will hear. For obvious reasons, this limits them to forms found in those parts of England, Wales and Scotland which can be reached without crossing saltwater, though this is less constricting than might at first appear. For example, the appearance of a single unicorn on the soil of this island, captive or free, at any point in time, would be enough to enable a Queen to direct her Lord Herald to shape himself accordingly. What problems this form might cause him in the human world would be no concern of hers.

The current Lord Herald spends a considerable portion of his time eating and digesting bamboo shoots. As his dietary needs are met through his portal, by the reliable ministrations of the keepers at Edinburgh zoo, he's entirely impervious to Faerie bribery. The challenge of concentrating on anything other than bamboo shoots for many minutes at a time isn't currently considered an obstacle to the performance of his office. In fact, the less opportunity he has for thinking his impenetrable thoughts, let alone for sharing them, the happier the rest of the court generally is.

Chapter 11

There's no obstacle to the Faerie wishing to spend time in the human world insubstantially – examples are well documented as tricks of the light, divine apparitions, ghosts, auras, rainbows and so on – but the novelty of physical interaction does have a degrading allure. In addition to the frequent temporary adoptions of different appearances and the permanent physical transitions required of Lords Herald, there's a third type of shapeshifting among the Faerie. They can, if they choose, become physical either in their own world or in the parallel world of humans.

Should the Faerie adopt material manifestations of their own natural forms in the human world, they suffer no consequences of any kind beyond a barely perceptible confusion on their return to insubstantiality. However, presumably cowed by their evident superiority, humans tend to run away when they encounter the Faerie in their natural forms and, for this reason, they usually manifest in human form and enjoy the added piquant thrill of their own debasement.

However, the adoption of physical form comes with a price. The body of a small boy, for instance, exerts an influence upon the Faerie who occupies it for any period of time. The ill effects of a brief visit to the human world is generally short-lived — the fascination with dinosaurs and burping passes in time, for example — but experts speculate that remaining in human form in the human world for longer would result in longer-lasting or more pronounced consequences. Since the concepts of permanence, time and experts are all challenging to the Faerie, this theory isn't widely understood or well explored. The human world is tedious in its adherence to the dictates of time and the laws of physics, so the theory is extremely unlikely to be put to the test.

Chapter 12

As a result of the Queen's prohibition on games and bargains, the Faerie spend less time in the human world than once they did. They no longer frequent groves and enchanted pools to make bargains with unwary wayfarers. Waiting around for someone to wander past was always a bit hit and miss in any case. Instead, a few join the crowds at racetracks and football stadiums in search of the elusive treasure called sorrow, though it's widely understood that they can experience human emotions only vicariously. A few come to care who wins or loses and, in the energy of the crowd, mistake their own triumph and rage for shared joy and sadness. It is this delusion which imbues Lord Carrick's quest for sorrow with an irresistible and poignant aura of possibility.

The Faerie have not only the gift of joy, but also the gift of anger. Combinations of these emotions combine to lift them from boredom, the third point of their emotional triangle. This should not be taken to imply a lack of complexity in Faerie emotion, for a considerable range is encompassed within these three. Spite and revenge are particularly enjoyable, though the pleasures of outrage, resentment, indignation and *Schadenfreude* should not be underestimated. In contrast, although jealousy, envy and other manifestations of the green-eyed monster offer little pleasure to those who feel them first-hand, they are highly valued for the amusement they offer to the rest of the court.

Although the Faerie have an emotion a little like fear, real fear depends both upon an understanding of time and the realisation that one doesn't necessarily get everything one wants. If human anger were blue and human fear were red, Faerie fear would be that shade of purple which is most difficult to distinguish from blue. It is, in any case, felt only fleetingly, in the moment before its realisation.

A bargain, game, quest or challenge feeds the entire emotional range of the Faerie. The victor's joy and the anger of the vanquished produce a sweet and bitter contrast to stimulate and energise the Faerie soul. These emotions are enhanced by sharing, downward through the hierarchy of the court. If the Queen were enraged or delighted and she chose to share her emotion, the courtiers would feel it as if it were their own, excepting only the Lord Herald, who needs to keep a clear head and is, in any case, generally preoccupied by his physical needs. Excluding him, every courtier, according to their rank, gifts their emotions to those beneath them, unless they're cunning enough to realise the power to be gained by keeping their feelings to themselves.

There is no feeling sweeter than the perfect balance of bliss and rage engendered by competition between the Faerie. The participants are temporarily elevated, if elevation is necessary, in a hierarchical cascade by which members of the court individually and voluntarily adopt a lower position than the participants that they might savour their heightened emotions. The thrill of the challenge is exceeded only by the clash of joy and wrath at its conclusion, swiftly followed by the quibbling of connoisseurs claiming to have experienced that exquisitely rare flash of fear.

Bargains and games between the Faerie and humans offer a different blend of emotion. The malicious anticipation of human failure and gleeful expectation of Faerie joy offer novel pleasures to complement the court's usual bliss, but they don't promise the partisan rivalries and the mingling of opposing emotions engendered by more even competitions.

Were the Queen to ask, the Lord Herald might opine that her prohibition on games had been unwise, though he would do so with exceeding caution, being aware that it might be the last thing he said before losing the power of speech altogether. The position of the Lord Herald teeters across the tension between the joys of the court and the promised surrender to materiality; the necessity of advising the Queen well and the inevitable dangers of doing so; the need to flatter her folly and ignorance and the irresistible desire to be a smart-arse. The period of office varies, but many an incoming Lord Herald observes a gleeful grin on the face of his predecessor in those few moments which may be available for gloating.

The Book of Plans
Chapter 13

Shirley had managed to get Christmas day off work. She'd been looking forward to making it a special one, but Mike had been quiet and fraught, and seasonal jollity had been in short supply, despite the crispiness of her roast potatoes and the moistness of Marks's best luxury pud, no expense spared. Now they were in the dreary featureless days before New Year, and she and Brian were both back at work. Mike was supposed to be revising, but he was rarely out of bed when she left, no matter which shift she was on. He sometimes sat in front of the telly with them in the evening, like normal, but it was obvious he was in a world of his own.

"I'm going to phone them," he said, cutting across an exchange of remarks about the newsreader's blouse. "They were supposed to be here an hour ago and it's driving me mad. I've got to do something."

He stood up, but there was no room to pace.

"I'm sure they'll be here as soon as they can," said Brian, sorting through the empty chocolate wrappers in the tub on the coffee-table, "Just try to stay calm, son."

"How can I possibly stay calm?" asked Mike.

"We know it's difficult," said Shirley. "And it might be even harder when they get here, love. You need to understand that they might not be able to tell you very much. It would all depend on her, you see, on what she wanted. But whatever happens, I promise I'll ask around at work. Someone's bound to know something. I'll let you know as soon as I hear anything – by phone, if it's after the holidays."

"I'm not going back to uni," Mike said, surprised that she'd thought he might.

"Oh Mike! You have to," said Shirley.

"Come on now," said Brian through his toffee.

"How can I?" asked Mike.

He was a clever lad, thought Shirley, but he didn't have the sense to see what was in front of his eyes. It was like before, when he'd messed about in the sixth form. She'd told him he needed to get his head down, but he wouldn't listen. He had to find it out for himself. It knocked him back, of course, when he saw his grades, but he didn't give up. He'd seen sense in the end. He gone to college and worked his socks off and, on the second try, he'd got the grades he needed to study law. Law! Shirley wasn't going to let him throw it all away for some baby that probably wasn't even his. When a girl gets pregnant and doesn't want to face her boyfriend, it doesn't take a genius to figure out why.

"You can't give up your degree," she said. "Not now."

"I don't see what choice I have."

"Mike, love, we don't know what's going to happen with the baby. Just say she is yours ..."

"She is!" said Mike.

"Ok, well let's not argue about that now," said Shirley. "But there has to be some reason why Tracy's kept you in the dark."

"You're saying she doesn't want anything to do with me?"

"I don't know, love," said Shirley. "I can't read her mind. But it is her choice when it comes down to it. Isn't that right, Brian?"

Brian nodded, but didn't speak.

"There must be some reason why she just disappeared, though," said Mike. "And why she left the baby. It's not like her. There must be something seriously wrong."

"Well," said Shirley, "you might be right. But unless she's turned up, they've only got your word that you're the father, love. And even if she did put your name on the birth certificate or they did blood-tests or whatever, they're not just going to hand her over to you."

"Why not?" he asked.

"Well, they know you lost touch. You've already admitted you didn't know she was pregnant."

"But I'm the father," said Mike.

"Ok," said Shirley, carefully. "But they're going to be wondering why she had to disappear. Why she wanted to hide from you."

"She wasn't ..."

"I know, love. I know. I'm just saying what they'll be thinking. You can't blame them, really. It's the obvious conclusion to draw. And as long as there's any question mark over the baby's safety, they're not going to take any risks, are they? The most important thing is to keep that baby safe, isn't it, Brian? Brian."

"Yes," said Brian.

"I can see that," said Mike. "I do understand that …"

Hoping that she might be able to help him see sense, Shirley pressed her point.

"And you've got to be realistic, love. How would you look after a baby? If you weren't studying, you'd have to get a job, wouldn't you? And either way, you wouldn't have the time."

The doorbell rang.

"I'll get it," said Shirley. "You wait here."

"Ok," said Mike quietly, his heart pounding.

"Mrs Murray," said WPC Lambert, taking off her hat. "You remember my colleague, PC Hanks?"

PC Hanks nodded a greeting from behind her.

"Yes, of course. Hello," said Shirley. "Go on through."

"Mike, Mr Murray," said WPC Lambert. "We thought you might like an update on our progress so far."

"About time!" said Mike.

"Mike!" said Shirley. "I am sorry about that, officer. It's all been rather difficult."

"Not to worry," she said. "Feelings are running high. It's completely understandable."

"Sorry, where are my manners?" said Shirley. "Would you like to sit down? Chocolate? Mince pie?"

She gestured towards the sofa as if they might otherwise have perched on the mantelpiece or the coffee-table. The

Christmas lights were twinkling away incongruously in the window and Shirley wondered again what it might say that she hadn't thought to switch them off.

They sat and WPC Lambert took out her notebook.

"We have managed to track down the mother," she said. "It turns out that she's undergoing medical treatment."

"Is she alright?" asked Mike. "What's the matter with her?"

"We don't know all the details yet, because questions are tiring for her. But she has given us permission to talk to you."

Shirley nodded. "That's something, isn't it, son?"

"That's great," said Brian.

"There you are," said Mike. "I knew there was something wrong."

"In fact," said WPC Lambert, "she asked if you would visit, sir. She appears to feel that she owes you an explanation."

Mike nodded, smiling. "Good. That's good, right?"

"I wouldn't want to speak for her, if you don't mind," said WPC Lambert.

"No, absolutely. That's completely understandable," said Shirley, patting her son's hand. "So, what can you tell us? Are you sure you won't have a chocolate?"

"No, thank you. She's at the Royal. On the oncology ward. She's been in a very bad way, but the doctors are optimistic."

Shirley nodded. "She's had cancer, Mike."

"Cancer?"

"She wouldn't have wanted treatment while she was pregnant, I don't suppose," said Shirley.

WPC Lambert shrugged apologetically. "I'm afraid it's not my place to discuss the details."

"I knew about this case," said Shirley. "I never made the connection, but Angela was talking about it at work the other day. Poor girl. How's she doing?"

"There's a good chance, they said."

WPC Lambert's intonation undercut the tenor of her words.

"I see," said Shirley. "But who was supposed to be looking after the baby? They'd have never let her go home if there wasn't someone to take care of her."

WPC Lambert checked her notebook. "Baby Rose was..."

"Rose!" said Mike. "That's her name?"

"That's right, sir. Baby Rose was left in the care of her grandmother, a Mrs Margaret Goodfellow."

Shirley lifted her eyebrows but kept her mouth shut.

"But I'm afraid we've had no success in contacting Mrs Goodfellow and Miss Watts is in no fit state to take care of Rose just now."

"Miss Watts?" asked Mike.

"That's the name of the baby's mother, yes. Alison Watts."

"Oh," said Mike. "Then it's a different person. I thought you were talking about Tracy. Tracy Goodfellow."

"It is the same person," said WPC Lambert. "She's using an assumed name for reasons which are currently unclear."

Shirley patted Mike's arm. "Perhaps she got mixed up with some bad people, love. There's all kinds of reasons why she might've changed her name."

It could have been to get away from the unfortunate local associations of the name Goodfellow, Shirley supposed.

Marriage was another possible reason, of course, but she'd let someone else point that out to Mike. Mind you, she'd changed her first name too, and she was still using *miss*, so it might not be that.

"I'm sure Miss Watts can explain everything to you herself, sir," said WPC Lambert.

"When can I see her?" asked Mike.

He was already pushing himself up from the sofa. Shirley knew he'd run all the way there just for a glimpse or a word from this Tracy or Alison or whatever she wanted to call herself these days. And now there was the baby too, and who knew what complications that might bring. She hoped he wasn't going to get his heart broken all over again, but there wasn't much she could do to protect him from himself.

"There'll be visiting hours," she said. "You can't just turn up."

"When are they?" asked Mike.

"In about half an hour," she conceded.

"I'll give you a lift," said Brian, slapping his palms on his legs and groaning himself to his feet. "Come on son."

Mike grabbed his jacket on the way out. Shirley fought the urge to go with them. There were one or two things she needed to get off her chest too, but he deserved a chance to talk to the girl privately first.

"Don't go in with him, Brian," she called. "They'll need some privacy."

"What do you take me for?" he asked.

Chapter 14

Shirley gave Alison a few weeks to sort things out with Mike before she took the opportunity for a quiet word herself. She was on earlies and nobody challenged her right to be there outside visiting hours. It was one of the perks of the uniform, and it meant that unless Alison told Mike she'd been, he need never know.

The baby was in a Perspex cot, but Shirley couldn't see her face. The name on the whiteboard confirmed that this was the right bed, but the girl in it was unrecognisable. The black in her hair had been cut out and fallen out and what was left was downy and mousy brown. She was thin and pale, as Shirley had expected, but where before she'd seemed carefree, reckless even, now she looked older than her years. Shirley hesitated, wondering whether to give her more time, though the baby would still be with emergency foster carers if her mum wasn't up to looking after her.

"Hello Mrs Murray," Alison said, taking the decision out of Shirley's hands. "I thought you might come."

She hadn't had many visitors. Her own mum hadn't turned up yet, and she'd lost touch with friends from college. When she spoke, the re-animation of her features made her look like herself again. Her green eyes glinted cheerfully, but the prominence of her cheek bones and pointed chin in her thin face made what had been sweet and youthful seem fragile and unworldly.

"How are you doing?" asked Shirley, pulling the curtain around them for privacy. "I haven't brought you any flowers or anything."

"That's alright," said Alison, pushing herself into a more upright position. "I'm ok. Better than before anyway."

Neither of them had smiled yet.

"I haven't come here to give you a hard time," said Shirley. "In case you're wondering."

"I wouldn't be surprised if you did," said Alison. "You've got every reason to."

"I know you've been in the wars. You've had it tough."

Alison shrugged. It was what it was.

"But you broke his heart, you know, dropping him like that."

"I know," said Alison.

"And then just disappearing off without a word."

"I know."

"For all those months. He never gave up hope, you know?"

"He's told me, and I am sorry."

"But he's happy now that you're back," said Shirley. "And as long as my boy's happy, I'm happy. Do you understand what I'm saying?"

"Yes," said Alison.

"But I'm not having you hurting him again."

"No," said Alison. "I understand."

They sat in silence.

"He's due back at uni soon, you know," said Shirley. "He's got exams coming up."

"I didn't know that," said Alison. "I should have realised, but he didn't say."

"No," said Shirley. "I thought he might not have. Do you know he's thinking about jacking it in?"

"Oh," said Alison. "No. I didn't know that."

Shirley sighed. "I suppose he doesn't want to put you under pressure by saying anything, but I think you ought to know what he's thinking, just in case you don't want the same things."

Knowing that she was betraying her son's confidence, she didn't meet Alison's eye.

"He's imagining that you're going to be a family," she said. "I've no idea how he plans to support you all without his degree, but is that even what you want? I mean, do you want to be with him, and if you do, do you want to be poor? I'm not trying to be offensive, but you can see how it is."

"Yes," said Alison. "I can see why you're concerned."

She paused and when she spoke again, it was careful and slow.

"I think I do want that – to be a family – or at least to try. Mike loves Rosie and he's lovely with her and I know he loves me, and I care for him, a lot, I do, and I think I'll grow to love him again. But I don't think he should give everything up for me."

Shirley nodded. The honest uncertainty gave her more confidence than blithe assertions could have done. Any fool can plan for happy ever after, but the girl understood that there was more to it, and that was reassuring.

"Ok," she said. "Well, I've got a plan that might keep everyone happy for the moment. Do you want to hear it?"

"Yes," said Alison. "Please."

The conversation that followed was practical rather than warm. For Mike's sake, and on Brian's encouragement, Shirley was willing to let them move into their house, on condition that he finished his year at uni before transferring his course to Leicester. She'd rung up to talk to them and they'd been very clear about the importance of finishing the year where he was. It would show them he was serious about his studies, they said. She and Brian would help with Rose whenever they could, but only if Alison wanted them to, and Shirley promised to give her and Mike their space and not interfere. As soon as they felt able to cope on their own, they could move out, if that's what they wanted to do.

"I think you're a sensible girl," she said, "and I'm relying on you to treat him right. I know it might not work out between you, but I need you to promise me you'll let him see the baby, even if you do split up. If that happened, it'd break his heart to lose her as well. How does that sound to you?"

Alison had been listening in silence. She couldn't rely on her own mother and, even if everything went well, it would be a while before she was healthy enough to consider coping on her own. It wasn't in her nature to rely on other people, but this wasn't just about her. It might make all the difference in the world if Rose had a family to love her.

"I'd need to talk to Mike," she said.

"Of course, but before you do that, there is one more condition."

"What is it?" asked Alison, though she thought she knew.

"I'm not going to ask you who the father is," said Shirley. "If Mike's happy to believe it's him, that's good enough for me. She's his and that's the end of it. But I can't let him love Rose – or me and Brian either for that matter – if you won't promise to keep her safe. You have to give me your word you're never going to leave her with your mother again. I'm not saying she shouldn't be allowed to see her, but you can't leave her unsupervised."

"No," said Alison. "I won't. I promise. I give you my word."

"I shouldn't wonder if the police won't want a word with her when she turns up in any case," said Shirley. "What with one thing and another."

"There's no saying when that'll be," said Alison. "She's not exactly reliable."

"Will you tell her where you are?" asked Shirley.

Alison shook her head. Shirley knew she might change her mind, and she wasn't moved by the tears. They could mean anything, or nothing at all. What mattered was her promise. She was confident the girl was old-fashioned enough to keep her word and mature enough to put her baby's safety first.

"Right," she said, standing up. "Good. So, you need to talk to Mike. He'll be mad as hell I came to see you, so I'm going to leave it to you to tell him."

"Ok," said Alison.

"You're going to persuade him to see out the year at uni?" asked Shirley, who needed to be sure.

"Yes. Of course."

"Ok. When they're ready to discharge you, I'll have his room ready for the three of you. Is there anything you'd like me to fetch from your mum's house?"

"No, not really," said Alison. "I don't have much there. I'll go over later, when I'm up to it."

"Right," said Shirley. "I'll be off then."

"Thank you," said Alison. "You're very kind."

"Don't think that for a second," said Shirley, though she softened her words with a smile for the first time. "I'm not doing this out of the goodness of my heart. I'm doing it for Mike, but I will do what I can for you."

For the first time in months, Alison felt some of the tension leaving her body. There was no reason why things couldn't work out with Mike if she set her mind to it. Perhaps things were going to be ok.

"You look after yourself," said Shirley. "Take it easy."

"I will. Thank you."

When Shirley peered into the cot at the side of the bed, Rose was lying awake, her arms and legs jerking as her green eyes took in the changes in light around her. Shirley wasn't sentimental about babies – she worked with them every day – but she did feel drawn to this one. It was too soon to discern how her features would end up. She just looked like a baby. But there wasn't anything that said Mike couldn't be the father.

Shirley hadn't planned on being a nan this soon, but now that she thought about it, it did appeal. Brian was already talking about making a dolls' house now that he had more time on his hands. Perhaps this would work out for them all.

The Book of Terms

Chapter 15

Lord Carrick takes a crystal glass from a silver tray, acknowledges the admiration of the court, and follows the Queen from the banqueting-hall. The Lord Herald, who rarely enters the throne-room without an explicit invitation, takes the opportunity for a mid-morning snack in his compound in Edinburgh zoo. Thanks to the lush vegetation, the zoo-keepers' respect for his privacy and the fluidity of his relationship with time, his frequent absences from the human world go entirely unremarked.

In the quiet of the throne-room, Lord Carrick affects not to notice the Queen's fury. She claps her hands, changing the soft furnishings from green to black. Silver threads turn to cobwebs and gleaming lamps to flickering candles that cast as much shadow as light. In the same moment, she re-shapes herself into her natural form, the better to hide her true feelings. Her blue-green skin flutters like a thousand tattered butterfly wings. Her claws flash, reflecting light which is not otherwise seen.

"Call the Lord Herald," she snaps.

Officious footmen repeat her command in all directions around the palace. It is often the Lord Herald's fate to leave his bamboo half-enjoyed, and with an appearance of hurry, he enters and bows.

"Your majesty," he says.

"There is to be a game," the Queen says, through clenched teeth, their previous conversation chased from her mind by the transition between rooms.

The Lord Herald bows again.

"Yes, your majesty," he says.

"I suppose there must be rules," says the Queen.

"It wouldn't be a game without them," answers Lord Carrick, with a smile.

The Queen nods to the Lord Herald. The Lord Herald claps his paws and a liveried footman advances with a scroll on a velvet cushion. The Lord Herald opens the scroll with a flourish, letting it unfurl to the floor in the time-honoured fashion that only he can truly appreciate, and the footman bows backwards from the royal presence. The Lord Herald glances at the Queen, who nods briskly. Lord Carrick's eyes smile throughout.

"Your Royal Highness," declares the Lord Herald, a quill poised in his right paw, "according to the ancient law, it is customary first to determine whether the same terms are to apply equally to all opponents or whether they shall play under different rules."

"The same is easier," says the Queen.

"Different can be more amusing," says Lord Carrick.

"Let it be different then," she says. "I don't care."

The Queen can't afford to lose face, and in the privacy of the throne-room, nothing is truly private. The Lord Herald speaks again.

"That being so, it is customary to determine whether there is to be parity between the rules observed by the participants."

"As the Lord Carrick chooses," says the Queen.

It's a gamble that she has no choice but to take. Any appearance of doubt or insecurity on her part could undermine the court's confidence in her to a terminal degree.

"Oh parity, I think," says Lord Carrick. "Where's the fun otherwise?"

The Queen nods her appreciation, though she suspects he seeks only to put her off her guard.

Chapter 16

Usually the courtiers disperse quickly after a ball – the Queen is notoriously unpredictable when she's bored and weary – but enough stay to watch Lord Carrick's game play out that the banqueting-hall continues to buzz with the thrill of the challenge and the pleasure of speculation about the terms. As other entertainments begin to pall, the court is drawn back in from its distractions elsewhere. The communal excitement of anticipation is building in response to every half-heard sound or imagined movement from the direction of the throne-room. Many of the courtiers are still in the form of flowers, though perhaps a few more bear wide-brimmed hats with sweeping feathers which, if asked, they would be entirely unable to explain.

The Queen sweeps back into the banqueting-hall, followed by the Lord Herald and a troop of liveried footmen, who race to join the procession along its route through the antechamber. She moves slowly to allow for their squabbles about the correct order of precedence in her wake.

When the royal presence becomes known, a tide of imitation spreads ahead of her through the banqueting-hall. Courtiers resume their own natural forms in a wave emanating from their Queen, some clad in ethereal beauty and others in remarkable grotesquery. Following behind her, the Lord Carrick notes, if no-one else does, a subsequent ripple of feathered hats and escaped ringlets.

He beams, sharing his delight with those who can feel it, and enjoys observing the guilty wave of pleasure traversing the court. In contrast, the Queen chooses to keep her feelings to herself on this occasion. She returns to the dais and acknowledges her subjects with a regal nod. Only then does it occur to the footmen that she requires a throne and they hasten to magic one for her, bickering over the significance of each leg in turn, unsure whether the greater glory belongs to those who create the leg or those who instruct them on the form it should take. Once these matters are resolved to reasonable stability, the Queen seats herself with an air of great patience and fortitude. She could magic herself a throne with no effort or fuss, but on such occasions it's necessary to observe the appropriate protocols.

The Lord Herald awaits her permission to begin, and she gives it with a curt nod.

"Ladies and lords," he says, "subjects of our gracious Queen and of her every pleasure, a challenge is issued and accepted this day. In accordance with the ancient law, the rules are agreed and set down in the scrolls. Let it be known that our illustrious Queen, in her great wisdom, retains the right to remain immaterial or to adopt physical form should she so desire. She accepts the constraints of time ..."

He pauses for a round of applause, which the courtiers dutifully supply.

"... but her majesty remains unaffected by all other physical laws. Lord Carrick, the challenger, takes human form for the duration of the challenge. He is bound by all limitations thereof, excepting only fixity of form and the constraints of time."

The court buzzes with contention as to the parity of these terms. That chronology is a burden is a matter of common consent – to wait for time to keep up with one is vexatious for those accustomed to moving through it unrestricted – but the ability to shapeshift does address many of the disadvantages of mortality. In their material manifestations, the Faerie decay at the usual rate, though they can prevent their decline becoming terminal by frequent changes of form. Faerie-questers often accept the physical restrictions of an old woman's body, for example, because appearing weak and harmless puts humans off their guard, but it's rarely long before an opportunity arises for the dramatic, alarming or witty revelation of their true selves. That this may cause any disadvantage to actual elderly women living apart from their neighbours is really no concern of theirs.

The buzz in the court is that the Queen has infinitely preferable terms. Lord Carrick is outsmarted. There's no doubt about it. The Queen can manifest as Faerie, human, animal or inanimate object at will. She can be immaterial or material according to the needs of the moment. Though she is subject to time, she has the option of sitting it out. She need only manifest as a rock or a river to minimise the inconvenience – though not the tedium – of chronology. Provided this manifestation is immaterial, she need suffer no lasting consequences of any kind.

In his weak human forms, in contrast, the Lord Carrick will feel hunger, thirst and pain. He will be subject to illness and to injury by blade or fire or any other imaginative means the humans might devise, and if he cannot shapeshift in time, escape may become impossible. Few in the court appreciate the additional risks of whatever unknown consequences might result from an extended period in human form, though this additional danger enhances his reputation among those who hold their own understanding in high regard. The fellow feeling thus created flatters them as well as him.

Lord Carrick's admirers purr their approval, each according to their own understanding, the plumes on their hats growing perceptibly longer and more magnificent to reflect their appreciation. Imagining the risks and the suffering he faces brings them great pleasure. If he succeeds, he'll bring them greater pleasure still, but that's of less importance in this moment and thus of no importance at all to most. Few of the Faerie can remember past events with any certainty; fewer still can focus on any imagined future.

For now, it is the Queen's immediate and obvious displeasure that delights them.

Chapter 17

The Faerie court is strictly hierarchical. Every courtier knows their own place in relation to every other. The Queen, of course, sits above them all. Next to her comes the Lord Herald and after the Lord Herald comes the Lady-in-waiting. The tenure of Queens and of Lords Herald end always in exile: Queens at the will of the court and Lords Herald at the whim of the Queen. Their only aspiration can be to cling to their office for as long as possible. The Lady-in-waiting's position is different. Though her banishment is also a distinct possibility, she can – and always does – aspire to be Queen.

The relationship between the Queen and her Lady-in-waiting is, naturally, an uneasy one. Under almost constant observation by her sovereign, the Lady-in-waiting must be subtle in her rivalry. Any overt challenge will lead to immediate banishment. The only reason she isn't banished as a preventative measure is that another Lady-in-waiting will be just as bad.

A well-advised Queen keeps her Lady-in-waiting busy. The Lady-in-waiting is fortunate whose Queen engages her merely in trivial and pointless activities. Less fortunate are those entrusted with responsibilities which infuriate the court.

The three highest offices – Queen, Lord Herald and Lady-in-waiting – hold fixed positions in the hierarchy for the duration of their terms. Constitutional experts observe that although holders of high office must sometimes undertake unpopular acts, the status of their official position must be upheld no matter the contempt with which its current occupant is regarded. In preference to immediate banishment, a Queen may therefore choose to retain a Lady-in-waiting or Lord Herald whose personal status has fallen below that of their office, not least because the court takes great pleasure in the opportunities for disrespect that arise from such disparities.

Below the Lady-in-waiting, the other courtiers can all say, without hesitation or fear of contradiction, where they are positioned in relation to every other. Lord Gine, for example, may know himself to be above Lord Carrick and Lady Flent but below Lady Brang and Lord Skeck. What he's less likely to know, is what positions these eminent lords and ladies occupy in relation to one another.

Whatever their positions might be, ordinary courtiers are subject to constant change from one moment to the next. Should Lord Gine issue an opportune bon mot, he might immediately realise himself to be above all four of his illustrious peers, but the churn consequent upon a witty bout of leapfrog might result in his relegation to the lowest rank before he fully comprehends the glory of his achievement. It goes without saying that wherever he might be, he resents everyone above him and despises everyone below.

That the Lord Carrick currently occupies an elevated rank is dawning upon those he surpasses one by one. Although they naturally resent his advancement, they succumb to it for the sake of the emotions he shares. In addition, his challenge delights them and draws the Queen's fury, and no-one could possibly object to that. At present, the Lord Carrick enjoys a remarkably precipitous position.

A series of bargains and treaties, known as the ancient lore
– or law – there is some disagreement as to the spelling –
place certain restrictions on the Queen's power. She may not
harm her courtiers herself, holding only the right to
withhold her pleasure or to cast them from it. The higher
rank a courtier attains, the closer they skirt the risk of
banishment at any moment, but the Queen who banishes a
favoured member of the court does so at considerable risk to
her own position.

On the edges, where the otherworld abuts the world of
the humans, the outcast Faerie, known as banishees, bewail
their unhappy and unmagical fate. They cluster around mists
of droplets and slicks of oil in the hope that enough will
gather to create a rainbow to carry them back to the
otherworld. There, they take back their magic, re-enter the
court as lowly servants and begin again their struggle to re-
ascend the hierarchy. Many banishees experience only
repeated failure in their attempts to return to the Faerie
world, with most of their endeavours disintegrating into
arguments about who is responsible for which droplet and
which colour has pre-eminence. Cooperation doesn't come
naturally to the Faerie.

More unfortunate still are those Faerie unwisely drawn
by the glitter and glimmer of a Christmas display, a holistic
healing centre or a crystal shop. It goes without saying that
manmade crystals can never grant re-entry to the Faerie
world, and the unfortunate Faerie who are drawn to them
flit endlessly between their unmagical glints like flies buzzing
repeatedly against a window. Where one comes, others
gather, and in time they flurry in rages as thick as dust motes,
each suspecting the other of some secret insight into the best

way or place to obtain their longed-for re-admission into the Faerie realm.

Any human sensitive to Faerie aura who ventures into a crystal emporium will find themselves overwhelmed by an irresistible urge to liberate these poor trapped creatures. Sadly, because there are few humans equipped to comprehend this sensation, they often misinterpret it as a desire for over-priced shiny things, and thus nourish and perpetuate the very rage they seek to dispel.

Chapter 18

Whether they're engaging in a challenge, jostling for position at court, or struggling to re-enter it, rivalry permeates everything the Faerie do. Having confirmed the terms of the challenge, the Lord Herald observes the dreamy pleasure that subsequently settles over the courtiers. Naturally they'll pick up their own petty squabbles in time, but for now they're content to enjoy the exquisite animosity of their superiors.

"Right then," says Lord Carrick, adjusting his hat to best advantage. "That's that all sorted then."

He stands back to allow the Queen to descend from the dais.

"Just a moment," says the Lord Herald. "I'm terribly sorry, Lord Carrick, but now we must set down the terms of victory."

Lord Carrick looks to the Queen, expecting to see her blue-green skin taut with fury. Instead, she smiles benignly, which naturally puts him on edge.

"I see," he says. "Well, yes. Of course, it's important to do that."

"Ha!" cries Lord Skeck, whose natural form resembles an atmospheric mist. "He's not feeling so clever now."

He looks to those around him for approval, but all eyes are fixed on the dais.

"Lord Herald," says the Queen. "Perhaps you could expand."

"It would be a pleasure, your majesty," says the Lord Herald, perhaps, it might be said, a little smugly. "There are four possible outcomes to the Lord Carrick's challenge. The most likely, of course, is that your majesty succeeds while Lord Carrick fails."

"Hear hear," shouts Lady Louple, whose natural glimmer, resembles that of a dragonfly, though regrettably her natural shape is that of a gnarled toenail.

"And clearly that is a win for your majesty," says the Lord Herald.

"Obviously," says the Queen.

"Hurrah," shouts Lord Wexen, who is, for reasons that he can't remember, in the form of an ostrich.

"Indeed," says the Lord Herald. "And in the highly unlikely case that those outcomes were reversed, the result would be likewise."

"Quite right," shouts the Lady Flent, who has no idea what the Lord Herald means, but doesn't like to be left out.

"Do I understand this?" the Queen hisses to the Lord Herald.

The Lord Herald leans towards her to whisper in reply.

"What I'm saying is that if he succeeds and you don't altogether succeed, that makes him the winner, your majesty."

"Gosh," says the Queen. "I'm not sure I like the sound of that."

"I'm afraid the ancient lore considers this a fairly standard feature of games and challenges."

"How frustrating," says the Queen.

"Indeed, your majesty."

The Lord Herald raises his voice to address the court at large.

"These two situations are entirely straightforward. However, two more outcomes are possible, and these leave the result rather less clear."

Lord Carrick frowns. It's considered good form among the Faerie not to acknowledge complexities and ambiguities until they arise, because it's often more fun that way. The Lord Herald's intervention is most unsporting and creates a rather sticky position for the challenger.

"Do they?" he says, with an air of indifference. "Well we can't have that."

"Quite so," says the Lord Herald. "In case these possibilities aren't clear to you, Lord Carrick, allow me to explain. The first is that both yourself and her gracious majesty succeed. The second, begging your majesty's indulgence, is that you both do not."

"Do not what?" asks the Queen.

"Succeed, your majesty," says Lord Carrick. "The Lord Herald suggests that we might both fail."

"Does he, indeed?" asks the Queen, bestowing a regal glare upon her Lord Herald.

"Begging your majesty's indulgence," says the Lord Herald, "as I'm sure Lord Carrick appreciates, I'm only postulating it as a remote and theoretical possibility, and speaking purely hypothetically, so it barely counts."

"Boring!" shouts Lord Skeck, whose powers of concentration are a good measure of the court's as a whole.

"Be quiet," snaps the Lord Herald. "This is important."

"Oh my," says Lady Louple, taking a step back from the dais.

"What's happening?" asks Lord Wexen.

"I don't know," she says, "but it's definitely something."

"Lord Carrick," says the Lord Herald, with a tight smile. "Since I'm sure you'll agree that our glorious Queen will undoubtedly triumph ..."

It is a curious feature of royal challenges that queens retains the right to banish their opponents at any point before its commencement, during its course or after its completion. A challenger's only security lies in queens' general inability to consider the possibility that they might need to. It is therefore unwise for Lord Carrick to do anything other than agree at this point, and he does so in sulky silence.

"... it seems hardly worth quibbling," continues the Lord Herald, "about these two possibilities which are so very unlikely to occur."

"Hear, hear," shouts Lord Skeck.

"I shall therefore set down," says the Lord Herald, "merely for the sake of avoiding tedious debate, that we are rolling these two highly unlikely possibilities in with the outcome that we're all agreed is almost entirely inevitable."

"Does the ancient law mandate this approach?" asks Lord Carrick.

"Oh yes," says the Lord Herald. "I'm sure it does."

By a remarkable stroke of good fortune, the Queen's advisor is also responsible for preserving and interpreting the scrolls of the ancient lore, of which there are a great many. They are written by countless Lords Herald with fundamentally contradictory views, and to save them from the tedious task of searching for precedents, etiquette dictates that the Lord Herald's legal pronouncements are infallible. This is in the interests of almost all concerned, because the purpose of these precedents would inevitably be forgotten by the rest of the court before they were found, necessitating tedious explanation that all right-thinking Faerie would prefer to avoid. It is perhaps less useful that the same conventional infallibility applies to the Lord Herald's ability to identify the number one is thinking of.

In short, Lord Carrick has no choice but to concede the point. He gestures to the gathered courtiers.

"If I may?"

"Be my guest," says the Lord Herald. "I mean, be her majesty's guest. If that's what her majesty wishes."

The Queen indicating her acquiescence by an almost imperceptible movement of her chin, Lord Carrick turns to face the court, his back straight and his head held high.

"My dear friends," he announces. "In order to avoid subjecting you to the tedium of an uncertain outcome, the terms are set down as follows: although there are four possible outcomes, only one – that I alone succeed – will result in my winning the challenge."

"What does he say?" asks Lord Wexen.

"Blowed if I know," says Lady Louple.

"Something about numbers, I think," says Lord Gine.

"How ghastly," says Lady Flent.

"Rather bad taste, in my view," says Lord Wexen.

"Hear, hear," shouts Lord Skeck.

The court disperses and shuffles away, taking with them a mild sense of anti-climax which they're ill-equipped to understand. Lord Carrick takes his leave with unusual bad grace.

"Someone's like a bear with a saw shed," remarks the Queen.

"Yes, your majesty," says the Lord Herald. "And I don't like to blow my own trumpet …"

"Goodness me," she says, "Then please don't feel obliged to on my account."

The Book of Fairy Stories
Chapter 19

"Look at you, all lovely and clean!"

Rose's mum was waiting for her in her pink bedroom, putting clothes in the wash or folding them back into drawers, and picking up the toys that were strewn across the floor.

"Did you have a nice bath?"

"Yes," said Rose, nodding vigorously, as if her meaning might otherwise be unclear. "There were lots and lots of bubbles and daddy played the sneezing game."

"Did he? That sounds like fun."

Rose cooperated with her pyjamas as they talked. She got herself dressed usually these days, though she sometimes needed help with buttons and zips. But there were times when it was easier to do it for her while she was standing still. Alison patted the pink bed with its fairy princess bedding, and Rose clambered up to be tucked in.

"Are you ready for a bedtime story?" Alison asked.

"Yes," said Rose.

"Yes what?"

"Please please please please please."

"Well alright then," said Alison. "Which one would you like?"

"Hmmm."

Rose always took her time choosing, but Alison could have predicted the outcome. The favourite story of the moment was *Rapunzel,* from a book Shirley bought her for her second birthday. Rose wasn't old enough to read the words, so they looked at the pictures and Alison amused herself by telling the story as she preferred it. She wasn't sure how much of it Rose took in, but it was as much about cuddling up and helping her be still for long enough to go to sleep as it was about the story.

"Right then. Snuggle down. That's it. Once upon a time there was a couple who wanted more than anything to have a baby, but for years and years no baby came, and they felt very sad. At last, a baby began growing in the mummy's tummy and that made them very happy. When it was nearly time for the baby to be born, the mummy really wanted to eat some salad, but it was the middle of winter and there was no salad growing anywhere except in the garden of a wicked old witch. This is before there were supermarkets, you see. Now, the daddy loved the mummy so much that he crept into the witch's garden and picked some lettuce for her to eat. He didn't tell her where it came from, because he didn't want to worry her, but it was so good that she asked him for more, and he climbed over the witch's wall again the next night. On the third night, just as he was putting the lettuce in his bag, the witch caught him by the neck.

'What are you doing in my garden, you thief?' she shouted.

'I'm sorry, my lady,' he said, because it never hurts to be polite. 'My wife's expecting a baby and I picked it for her.'

'I should have you thrown into prison,' said the witch.

'Please forgive me,' he said. 'I'll do anything you ask.'

'Oooooh now,' said the witch. 'Do you give me your word?'

And he gave her his word. Was that a good idea, do you think?"

"No," replied Rose, who'd known the question was coming. "You never make promises to witches or fairies."

"That's right. He gave his word without even knowing what he was agreeing to. How silly was that?"

"Very."

"You're right. And I suppose he spent the rest of his life regretting it very much because what the witch wanted in return was his daughter. When she was born, they called her Rapunzel and Rapunzel's daddy expected every day that the witch would come and take her away from him. But she didn't come, and Rapunzel grew from a baby into a little girl and from a little girl into a big girl and in time her daddy put his silly promise out of his mind. On the day of Rapunzel's thirteenth birthday, they didn't have a big party for her, because they weren't rich enough for balloons and party bags, but they did make her a special tea with lots of lovely vegetables and a nice cake. And they were just about to cut the cake when there was a knock at the door. Who do you think it was?"

Rose's green eyes were wide with fear.

"The witch!" she whispered.

"That's right. It was the witch. And she said the daddy had to let her take his daughter away because he'd made her a promise. Was she right?"

Rose nodded, twirling a strand of hair around her finger while she sucked her thumb.

"Well yes, that is what he agreed to, but it's always worth trying to bargain with fairies and witches. I suppose he can't have realised that though, because the witch did take Rapunzel away and she locked her in a tower. This tower had only one room, right at the top, and no door or stairs, only a window. When the witch wanted to visit her, she'd call up …"

Alison paused to give Rose time to take her thumb out of her mouth and join in.

"'Rapunzel, Rapunzel, let down your hair.' That's right. She's got lovely long brown hair, hasn't she, like yours? So, Rapunzel would hang her hair out of the window and the witch would climb up it. And for many years the witch was the only living person she ever saw. What do you think of that?"

"Bad."

"That's right. How do you think Rapunzel felt?"

"Sad," said Rose.

"I think you're right. If I was her, I think I'd feel angry too."

"Me too. At the mean old witch."

"You don't think she'd be angry with her daddy?" asked Alison.

Rose frowned and shook her head.

"No," she said. "She loves her daddy, not the naughty witch."

"Do you know what," said Alison, leaning down to kiss her soft brown hair. "I think I'd try to escape. I'd get bored stuck in that silly tower."

"Me too," said Rose.

"How do you think she could escape?"

"She could fly," said Rose, with a giggle.

"Maybe. But I can't see any wings. Can you?"

Rose shook her head, her thumb returning to her mouth.

"Do you think she could jump?" asked Alison.

Rose shook her head again.

"Well, I don't know," said her mum. "It is a fairy story, so she'd probably be caught by birds or land on a bed of leaves or something, wouldn't she? I don't think she'd be hurt. Though nobody would be silly enough to jump out of a window in real life unless there really was no other choice. How else might she escape? Could she scratch her way out?"

Rose considered this and shook her head.

"I suppose that might hurt her fingers," said Alison, "but she's in there for years, isn't she? She might have enough time to get used to it."

"She doesn't," said Rose. "A prince comes and rescues her. Tell the story, mummy."

"Alright. One day, Rapunzel is sitting in her tower, brushing her hair and singing and a prince rides by on his horse and hears her. He's handsome and rich, of course, but it's far more important that he's kind and clever and funny."

"Like daddy," said Rose.

"Just like daddy," agreed Alison. "So, the prince watches the tower, and he sees the witch calling up to Rapunzel and climbing up her hair, and when she's gone, he goes to the tower himself and he calls up … 'Rapunzel, Rapunzel, let down your hair.' That's right. And he climbs up her hair to the tower. How do you think Rapunzel felt when she saw him?"

"Happy."

"I'm sure you're right. She must have been pleased it wasn't the witch. But perhaps a bit nervous too, because he was a stranger, wasn't he? She didn't know him at all. If a stranger climbed through my bedroom window I'd shout and run away."

"Me too," said Rose.

"It's not going to happen, though, because your window's tight shut. Shall we have a look?"

Alison pulled back the curtain to check the window was closed. A horseshoe was nailed to the wall outside and a mobile hung inside, made of hagstones, iron bells and bags of dried herbs tied with pretty ribbons.

"Yes, that's fine. No-one can get in through your window. And anyway, you've got me and daddy just the other side of this wall and nanny and grandad over that way, so when you make a noise in the night, we all come running, don't we?"

They settled back down under the pink covers.

"Anyway, the prince visited lots of times and he was always very kind and polite and never asked her to make any promises or tried to pressure her into anything, and in the end, she had an idea. Do you know what it was?"

Rose shook her head.

"You do know," said Alison. "She cut off her hair and made a rope for them both to climb down so they could live happily ever after. But can you remember what happened to the witch?"

Rose pointed to the picture, dipping her head down so she didn't have to take her thumb out of her mouth. She was starting to give in to her tiredness.

"Rapunzel left her rope of hair hanging down from the tower and hid behind a bush until the witch visited the next day, didn't she? And after the witch climbed through the window, Rapunzel set fire to the hair, didn't she? Do you remember why?"

Rose shook her head.

"It was to trap the witch. The nasty old witch was trapped in the tower and couldn't steal any more children ever. Do you think it served her right?"

Rose nodded sleepily.

"I do too. And because Rapunzel was so brave and had such good ideas, and because the prince was such a kind and lovely fellow, they lived happily ever after. The end. Night night, gorgeous."

"Night night, mummy."

"Sleep tight."

Shirley was waiting on the landing as Alison tiptoed out.

"Am I too late for a nigh night kiss?"

"No," said Alison. "But try not to get her too excited."

"You can rely on me," said Shirley, going into Rose's room. "Here comes the nighty night tickle monster."

Rose squealed and giggled, and Alison rolled her eyes indulgently. She'd stay upstairs until Rose was settled because she had some reading to do for her course. Shirley tended to want the window open, so she'd check it was closed before she went down.

Chapter 20

Alison popped her head around the door to find Rose already in bed, looking at a picture book. Catching sight of her unexpectedly, she was struck by how grown up her daughter was looking, though she was still small for her age. With the baby fat receding, it was beginning to be possible to see Rose's features emerging: the narrow forehead, broad cheeks and pointy chin. Her hair was still light brown, where it used to be blonde, but it would darken more with time.

"Give me a kiss," demanded Rose.

"Of course!" said Alison, flinging herself on to the pink quilt. "Night night, Rosie. Daddy's on his way up to read to you tonight."

"And here I am," said Mike, bounding through the door. "Da daaa."

"Are you sure this is ok?" asked Alison. "I know it's my turn, but I do need to get this essay done."

"Yeah, definitely," he said, grinning at Rose. "Why wouldn't I want to read to my beautiful daughter? I'll probably pop out for a bit after, if that's alright."

"Of course," said Alison, "but try not to spend too much."

"It's only a pint," said Mike.

"Yeah, and the rest."

"What is mummy's problem?" Mike asked Rose, who gave a vigorous shrug in return.

"Mummy thought we were saving up for a deposit on our own flat," said Alison. "But daddy would rather go out drinking with his mates."

"It's just a quick drink," said Mike. "I just want to celebrate the end of my exams. I've been working really hard, you know."

"I know you have," said Alison. "While I've been playing with our lovely daughter and painting my toenails. The whole time. No housework or coursework or anything else at all."

"Alright," said Mike. "Alright. Just one. Two max. I promise. And I'll get up in the morning so you can finish off your essay."

"Your daddy's very lovely," said Alison. "Aren't we lucky?"

"Yes," said Rose.

"But we do need a bit more space," said Alison. "And a bit privacy, don't we?"

"I'm not arguing with that," said Mike. "A bit more mummy and daddy time, that's what we need."

"You know it," said Alison, kissing him back. "But I've got to write this essay."

She held him away with the flat of her hand as she waved to her daughter.

"Goodnight Rosie."

"Goodnight mummy."

When the door closed, Rose leapt up from the bed and put her palms together with Mike's. They began low down and lifted them into a cheer.

"Yay! Daddy story!"

"Which one would you like?" he asked. "Thomas the Tank Engine? Biggles?"

Rose put her hands on her hips. "Don't be silly daddy. I'm a girl."

"Are you?"

He put his head on one side to look her up and down, then gazed around the pink room with a frown.

"Are you sure?"

She nodded firmly.

"Ok. If you say so. And what do girls like?"

"Fairies," she said.

"Really? Why?"

"They're pretty."

"Like you?"

Rose smiled. "Yes, but they can fly and do magic as well."

"Well so can you."

"No, I can't."

He narrowed his eyes. "Have you tried?"

"Yes," she said.

"I find that hard to believe. Do you know, when you were born, your fairy godmothers granted you three wishes?"

"Did they?" she asked.

"Yes. The first wish was that you could always have a cuddle when you wanted one." He put out his arms. "So that's that one. Your second wish was for bedtime stories, and your third one was for night night kisses. Have you decided what story you'd like?"

"Rumpelstiltskin," she said, holding out the book.

Mike took it formally and bowed.

"Your wish is my command," he said. "Come on then, snuggle down. That's nice. Ok. So, once upon a time there was a miller who loved his daughter very much, just like I love you. And he boasted about her to everyone he met, just like I boast about you. One day, he got so carried away that he boasted she could spin straw into gold."

"Do you say that about me, daddy?"

"No. That would be silly. Where would you get the straw from? Anyway, his boast reached the king, who was a very greedy man and loved gold more than anything. He locked the miller's daughter in a dungeon full of straw and told her he'd cut off her head if she hadn't spun it into gold by the morning."

"That's not very nice," said Rose.

"It isn't, is it? That's the trouble with kings and queens, you see. They think they're better than other people."

"Aren't they?" asked Rose.

"No. They're usually worse, but don't tell your nan I said that. It has to be our little secret, ok?"

"Ok," said Rose.

"Now the poor girl doesn't even have a name in this story, which doesn't seem right, does it? What shall we call her?"

"Dancerella."

"Nice!" he said. "So, Dancerella was scared and sad. She knew she couldn't spin straw into gold, and she really didn't want her head cut off. She did the best she could, but it was no good at all. Just as the sun started rising, just when she'd given up all hope, a funny little man in a little red cap appeared before her. There he is. He's got a funny nose, hasn't he? All long and pointy instead of nice and wide."

"Bum nose," said Rose, with a giggle.

"What did you say?" Mike demanded, in his most imperious tone.

"Bum nose," she giggled.

"Are you casting aspersions on my magnificent hooter?"

"Your magnificent bum nose," gasped Rose, almost helpless with laughter.

"Well," said Mike, flaring his magnificent nostrils. "There's only one thing for it."

"Don't tickle me," said Rose.

"I shall have to tickle you."

"Please don't tickle me."

"Not even a little bit?"

"No."

"Do you promise to show all proper respect to my magnificent facial protuberance?" he asked, wiggling his nose.

"I promise," she said, giggling again. "But it does look like a bum."

"I'm willing to concede that," he said. "As long as we're agreed that it's magnificent."

"Yes," said Rose. "Definitely."

"Well then," said Mike, turning back to the story. "So, this funny little man with the very silly nose said he'd spin the gold for her if she gave him something in return. He said he wanted the ribbons from her hair, and that seemed like a pretty good deal, so she shook hands with him and curled up to sleep. When she woke up, the room was piled with beautiful shining gold up to her knees, and the funny little man was nowhere to be seen. Do you think the king was pleased?"

"Yes," said Rose.

"That's right, but he didn't let her go home. Oh no. He gave her some food and a nice new hat and the next night he took her to a bigger dungeon filled with even more straw. What do you think of that?"

"Mean."

"He was. He was mean, and greedy. And, of course, the girl – Dancerella was it? – she couldn't spin the straw into gold, no matter how hard she tried. Just as the sun began to rise, she gave up all hope. She put her head in her hands and began to cry. And then what happened?"

Rose pointed to the picture. "The funny little man."

"That's right. And he said he'd spin the gold for her if she gave something in return. And what he wanted was her nice new hat. Just like the night before, she fell asleep and when she woke up, the dungeon was filled with beautiful shiny gold up to her waist, and the funny little man was nowhere to be seen."

Mike watched Rose re-arranging her stuffed toys so they could listen to the story too. The pink rabbit was having trouble sitting up straight, so she leaned her against the sparkly unicorn. She sat Pumpkin the puppy on her lap because he liked to look at the pictures.

"Go on," she said.

"Ok. So, the king gave her some food and some brand-new shoes and the next night he took her to the biggest dungeon of all. This one was filled to the ceiling with straw, and the exact same thing happened. Just as she was giving up hope, the funny little man appeared and offered to spin the straw into gold for her if she gave him something in return. And she said yes."

"Mummy says she should have asked him what he wanted before she said yes," said Rose.

"That's quite right," said Mike. "But a verbal agreement without witnesses would never stand up in a court of law, would it? And do you know why not?"

"Why?"

"Because it's just his word against hers. All she has to do is say she never agreed to it. There isn't anyone other than him to say that she did."

"Why?" asked Rose.

"Because there was no-one else there. And usually you should keep your word, of course you should. But sometimes you just have to say you're sorry and you've changed your mind."

"Why?"

"So, you don't get pressured into doing something you don't want to do," said Mike. "I'm getting myself into all kinds of trouble here, aren't I? It's not ok to lie. I'm just saying you're allowed to change your mind. Alright? And maybe we should wait until you're a bit older for this conversation. Anyway, the funny little man jumped up in the air and snapped his heels together in delight. Dancerella didn't know why he was so happy, so she curled up to sleep as usual, and in the morning, the dungeon was full of beautiful shining gold right up to the ceiling. But this time, the funny little man was still there.

'Hello,' said Dancerella. 'I didn't expect to see you this morning. Is there something wrong?'

'Not at all,' he said. 'In fact, I'm feeling very pleased with myself.'

'Why?' asked Dancerella.

'You promised to give me something in return for spinning the straw into gold,' said the funny little man.

'Yes,' she said, holding out her brand-new shoes. 'Did you want these?'

He laughed. 'No. They're not even my size.'

'Would you like some breakfast?' she asked. 'A cup of coffee?'

'Pah! I can have breakfast at home.'"

"He's very rude," said Rose, sitting her pink rabbit up again.

"He certainly is," said her dad. "But anyway, Dancerella said, 'What do you want then?'

'Your first-born child,' he said, and with a cackle of laughter, he disappeared.

Now Dancerella was young and she thought babies were boring, so she didn't think that was too bad, and she was pleased to keep the shoes, which were the nicest pair she'd ever had. In the morning, the king was so delighted with all the gold she'd spun that he married her to his son, who was much kinder than the king, and terribly apologetic about the whole business. She didn't see the funny little man again, but it didn't matter because no-one ever asks princesses to do any spinning. And she was so busy with the wedding and all the balls after that, that she didn't think about the funny little man ever again. And they all lived happily ever after. The end."

Rose turned the page and jabbed at the next picture sternly.

"What's this?" asked Mike. "He came back?"

She pointed again. "He wants the baby."

"She's never going to give him her baby, surely?"

"She promised," said Rose.

The pink rabbit had fallen face down again, so she picked her up and leant her back up against the unicorn with a stern stare.

"Oh dear," said Mike. "Well, let's find out what happened then, shall we? Many years later, the prince had become the king and Dancerella had become the queen and they had their first-born baby, a beautiful little princess. That night, the funny little man appeared and insisted that the queen should keep her promise. She offered him money and jewels and castles and everything she could think of, but he wasn't interested in any of that. Which kind of makes sense, doesn't it? If he can spin straw into gold, he can buy anything he wants for himself. No, the only thing he wants is the baby.

The queen cried and begged, and in the end, he agreed that if she could guess his name, he'd let her keep the baby. He said she could have three guesses on each of three days. What's three add three add three?"

Rose counted, using his fingers when she ran out of her own.

"Is it eight?"

"That's very close. Well done. If you put three fingers up on that hand and three on this hand and I put three on mine, we can count them all up. One two three four five six seven eight …"

"Nine," said Rose.

"Fantastic," he said, with a high five. "So, she has her first three guesses. 'Is your name David?' she asks, and the little man roars with laughter. 'Is it Steven? Is it Jason?' He disappears so quickly that he leaves his laugh behind and Dancerella watches it chasing after him into the dark forest."

Rose picked up her pink rabbit and threw her off the bed. If she wasn't going to behave herself, she could listen to the story from the floor.

"The next night," Mike continued, "she makes three more guesses – 'Is it Reginald? Is it Archibold? Is it Engelbert?' – and he laughs at every single one. This time, when his laugh chases after him into the forest, Dancerella has a horse ready, and she follows it to a little house in a clearing. She creeps right up to the house and peers in through the window. Inside, the funny little man is spinning a cot and blanket out of gold and laughing to himself. 'She'll never get it. She'll never guess it. Rumpelstiltskin's too clever for her.'"

"That's his name," said Rose. "He said his name."

"He did, and Dancerella tiptoed back to her horse and rode back through the forest to the castle. When he came the next day, she was ready for him. 'Is your name Tumplequillpen?' she asked, and he laughed so much, he cried. 'Is it Bumpletrillfin?' she asked, and he laughed so much, he could hardly breathe. 'Is it Rumplestiltskin?' she asked."

"It is!" cried Rose.

"It was," said her dad. "And he was furious. He stamped his foot so hard, he fell through into the dungeons. And when he got there, they made him spin straw into gold every day for ever and ever and ever."

"Serves him right," said Rose.

"Yes, it did. And everyone else …"

"Lived happily ever after."

"That's right. Now, what about that third wish of yours?"

Chapter 21

Rose held her mum's hand as she skipped across the playground. She had her coat on, zipped all the way up, even though they'd argued about it all the way to school that morning. Alison wished she knew how the teachers did it.

"Did you have a nice day?" asked Alison.

"It was alright," said Rose.

"What did you do?"

90

"Lots of things," said Rose. "Too many to talk about."

Rose was concentrating on where she was putting her feet. If she talked, she might forget and step on one of the cracks.

"Just tell me one thing," said Alison, who found it difficult to leave her daughter at school every day and to believe – really believe – that she was happy and cared for and safe.

"Painting," said Rose. "Mia cried because Chloe said hers looked like a poo."

"Oh dear. What was it?"

"Mifty."

"That's her dog, isn't it?" asked Alison. "Does Mifty look like a poo?"

"No!" said Rose. "She looks like a dog."

"I can see why Mia was upset then."

"Look at the pigeon!" said Rose.

"Oh yes. It's only got one foot, hasn't it? Poor thing. Have you got any homework this weekend?"

"I have to do a drawing about the games children played in history times."

"That sounds interesting," said Alison. "Do you want to press the button?"

Rose held on to the spike underneath the box at the crossing. She needed to know which came first, the green man or the spike going round, but afterwards she could never remember.

"Ok," said Alison, when the green man appeared. "It's safe to cross now."

"I'm going to ask grandad," said Rose.

"That's a really good idea, but grandad's fishing with your great uncle Tony, isn't he? He won't be back until next week."

"Can't we phone him?"

"No sweetheart, he's out in the middle of nowhere. I don't think there are any phones."

"I would ask nan," said Rose. "If she wasn't dead."

"Yes," said Alison. "And she'd love to help you. It's sad that she can't. Mind that puddle."

"Jasmine says you should have two nans and two grandads. Chloe's got three grandads and I've only got one. I don't think that's fair."

"No, I don't suppose it is fair, but that's how things are sometimes," said Alison. "Actually, you did have two nans, sort of. Nan was your dad's mum and my mum is your gran. It's the same thing as a nan really. It's just another name for it."

"I didn't know you had a mum," said Rose.

"Everyone has a mum, sweetheart."

"But I don't know her," said Rose.

"Well, she's always away a lot, you know."

"Can I have some sweets?"

The stretch between the newsagents and the rides outside Tesco was always the most perilous part of their walk back from school. The important thing was never ever to give in.

"It's nearly time for tea," said Alison, which sometimes worked.

"Is grandad very sad?" asked Rose.

"I suppose he must be, some of the time, but he's got uncle Tony to keep him company and we do what we can to cheer him up, don't we? He's always very happy when he's with you."

"I wish we still lived at nan and grandad's house," said Rose.

"I know, love, but we thought it might be nice to have a bit more space, just the three of us. And we can't move back now."

"I liked it better before," said Rose. "I miss nan."

"I know sweetheart. I miss her too. We all do. But I tell you what. Shall we go and see grandad as soon as he gets back from fishing?"

"I don't like it when grandad goes away."

"I know, love. But I bet he'll have a present for you when he gets back."

They were by the park now. Usually Rose wanted to play on the swings, but Alison had a coursework deadline, so she hurried her on with a jumping game. With any luck, she'd have forgotten about feeling sad by the time they got home.

"Where does your mummy live?" asked Rose.

"Oh, quite a long way away."

"We live in Leicester," said Rose.

"Yes, that's right. We do."

"Does your mummy live in Leicester?"

"Yes," said Alison. "She lives in the house I grew up in."

"Really?"

"Yes. It's not a very nice house, though. It's cold and a bit smelly. Here we are."

The door to their block was open, as usual. Alison took it off the latch and made sure it closed behind them. She didn't understand why the other tenants were so casual about who came in and out.

"We could go and see your mummy after tea," said Rose.

"I'm afraid not, sweetheart. It's too far. Do you want fishfingers tonight or beans?"

"Both!" Rose said.

"Ok. I'll see what I can do. Do you want to call the lift?"

Rose stood on tiptoe and pressed the button with two fingers from each hand.

"Can we go tomorrow?" she asked.

"No, love. I'm sorry."

"Why?"

"She doesn't really like having visitors."

Rose frowned. Everyone liked having visitors, nans and grandads especially.

"The lift's taking a long time, isn't it?" said Alison. "I wonder what the problem is."

"We could phone her."

"Well yes, I suppose, but if she's not there she won't answer it."

"What about her mobile?" asked Rose.

"She hasn't got one, love."

"Curiouser and curiouser."

"It looks like we'll have to go up the stairs. Shall we count?"

"I'm too tired to count."

Rose took the steps two at a time, hauling herself up with the handrail. The stairs doubled as a fire escape, and although there was a waist-height barrier and a railing, they were otherwise open to the elements. Someone had used a spray-can to draw a circle round a fresh deposit of dog poo. It overlapped with other circles in a range of colours, although most of the contents had been washed away. Alison wasn't sure how many dogs and how many paint-sprayers were involved, but she had to admire their balance and persistence. Rose was trying to find a route between the pink circles and Alison was trying to be patient with her.

"Not that one," she said. "There's one there. Nearly at the top now."

"Have I ever been to my gran's house?" Rose asked.

"You lived there when you were a baby. Just for a few weeks while she looked after you."

"Where was daddy?"

"He was away at university. But then he came back to Leicester instead, and that's when we all moved into your nan's."

"Who looked after me then?" asked Rose.

"All of us: me, daddy, nan and grandad."

"Did your mummy visit us?"

Alison put her key into the front door. Rose was still asking questions, but she was losing interest in the answers. If Alison judged it right, it might be possible to divert her on to another track.

"Do you know, I think your grandad's worth two nans and two grandads all by himself, he loves you so much. What would you like for pudding?"

"Only jelly and ice-cream and sprinkles and squirty cream and chocolate sauce. That's all."

"Jelly and ice-cream and sprinkles and squirty cream and chocolate sauce?"

"Please," said Rose.

"Good girl. I don't think we've got all that, but I'll see what I can find. And, if you're good, we'll go shopping tomorrow and get some sprinkles."

"Can we ring your mummy after tea?" asked Rose.

"What? No, love. It really is best not to."

"But Jasmine said ..."

Alison squatted down to Rose's level to unzip her coat.

"The thing is, Rosie, that your gran is ... well ... she's sort of poorly, in her head, and that makes her a bit strange sometimes. She can't help it, I don't think, but it makes her difficult to be around and she might not be pleased to see us even if we told her we were coming. But I tell you what, shall we ask Kamla if you can talk to Chlo's Grandad about growing up in Jamaica? That'd be more interesting than anything about boring old Leicester, wouldn't it?"

Rosie screwed up her face. She wasn't convinced.

"And if that's not good enough for you, we'll just have to see what daddy can remember about his dinosaur-racing days."

"He did not!"

Alison looked back over her shoulder as she went into the kitchen.

"Or did he?"

"No, because dinosaurs went extinct billions and millions of years ago."

"You're so right," Alison grinned. "I always get confused about that. Now I come to think of it, they weren't dinosaurs at all. They were dragons. Silly me."

"Daddy had real live dragons?" asked Rose.

"With fire and everything."

"Really?"

"He hatched them out from their eggs, you know. He had to put them under a chicken, because mummy dragons sometimes forget to look after them, but the poor chicken kept complaining about its bottom being too hot."

"Mummy!"

Chapter 22

"I'm too old for bedtime stories, grandad. I can read to myself now."

"I know you can, Rosie, love," said Brian. "You're very good at reading. But I'd still like to read you one if you'll let me."

"Well alright then," said Rose. "But only because of how much I love you."

"Thank you, sweetheart."

She was growing up fast, but she hadn't grown out of cuddling her grandad yet. He hoped she never would. There were posters of singers between the unicorns on her pink walls these days and Brian had no idea who they were, but he knew there was no pointing asking. He'd only forget, and it might all be different by Christmas anyway. He selected a book and sat on the bed while Rose pootled about getting herself ready. Mike and Ali were too busy with work and studying to go out much, but they knew he'd always babysit when they needed him to. When they'd asked if he could do every Thursday, he'd been delighted, but it turned out to be for couples' counselling. He was sure a nice meal and a bottle of wine would do them more good, but he wasn't one to interfere.

"What about this one?" he asked, when Rose was settled under the covers.

"I do like that one," she said, smiling at the familiar illustrations.

"There you are then. I do too, so I'm going to read it, on the understanding that it's for my own benefit, and you can listen if you want to. Ok?"

"Ok," said Rose, snuggling up beside him.

"Here we go, then. Once upon a time, there was a town called Hamelin which was over-run with rats. They tried traps and they tried cats, but nothing stopped those blooming rats. They stole bread from the tables of the poor and cheese from the royal pantry. Nothing was safe from them. So, the town council put out a proclamation promising a whole sack of gold to anyone who could rid the town of rats. Lots of people tried, but no-one succeeded."

"I like that man there," said Rose. "He's putting them in a cage and they're just squeezing out between the bars."

"Oh yes. And what's this one doing?"

"She's running away because there's a rat in her hair."

"Ooh, I don't blame her," said Brian. "I wouldn't like that either."

He ran his hands over his scalp.

"You haven't got any hair, grandad!"

"So, their claws would be even more scratchy," he said. "Anyway, stop making this all about me. I'm trying to read my story. One day a pied piper came, and when he played his pipe, all the rats came out of the houses and ran after him to the river, where they were washed away downstream. The pied piper went to the town council to collect his money and the mayor said a whole sack of gold seemed a bit much for such an easy job. All the piper had done was play a tune and walk down to the river, he said. Wouldn't half a sack be fairer? Or a quarter?"

"Dad says that's breach of contract," said Rose.

"Does he now? He's a clever fellow, your dad. Well, the pied piper was very angry, but instead of calling his lawyer, he took out his pipe and began to play. And this time, it was the children who poured out of the houses and followed him out of the town. But instead of leading them to the river, he led them to a grassy green hill and the children followed him into it. All except one."

"That one," said Rose, pointing.

"Oh yes. The poor little crippled boy − I'm not sure I'm allowed to say that anymore, but anyway. That little fellow couldn't keep up with his friends, and by the time he reached the hill, they were all gone. He could hear the piper's music echoing from under the ground, but he couldn't find his way in. So, in the end he turned around and hobbled all the way back home. Is that the end? Gosh. It's a bit bleak, isn't it?"

"Yeah," said Rose. "Mum said his parents would be happy he was safe, but he looks really sad."

"He doesn't, does he?" said Brian. "Poor little chap."

"He's got no-one to play with," said Rose.

"Do you think he'd be happier if he wasn't the only one left behind?" Brian asked.

"I think so. He'd be happy if he had some friends to play with."

"That would definitely make a difference," said Brian. "Unless he just wanted to go with the piper."

"He shouldn't," said Rose. "Because of stranger danger."

"Good point," said Brian. "You should never go off with someone you don't know."

"Mum says I shouldn't even talk to strangers," said Rose. "But sometimes it's rude not to."

"I can see that it would be," said Brian. "But you know she's just trying to keep you safe."

"I know," said Rose. "I wish she'd let me walk to school with Chlo, though."

"Leave it with me," said Brian. "I'll see if I can talk her round."

"Thanks grandad," said Rose, with a big snuggle. "You're the best grandad in the world."

"No, you are," said Brian.

"I'm not a grandad," said Rose.

"Oh," said Brian. "I suppose it must be me then."

Chapter 23

Her dad had come once, but he didn't like sleeping in a tent, so he always claimed there was something more important going on at work after that. Rose enjoyed camping with her mum and the history re-enactors, though. They'd set up somewhere on a battlefield or in the grounds of a castle and the adults would spend the day showing people how to start a fire or weave or carve a wooden bowl or whatever it was they wanted to demonstrate, leaving the children free to roam. Rose enjoyed the envy of the normal children, who were spending an improving day under the eye of their bad-tempered parents. When she saw someone from school, they always wanted to know why she was dressed like she was, and it was nice being the centre of attention. They had history days at school too, and her mum always made sure her costumes were fantastic.

The evenings were best, though, when they were camping. After the last of the visitors had gone, the historical re-enactors turned inward. Most were clear that they were modern people trying to re-create authentic historical conditions, but Tom and Sarah always stayed in character and although the children all denied believing it, it seemed possible to every one of them that the couple genuinely were from medieval times. For starters, no-one ever saw them arrive or leave – a car or motorhome would have been a dead giveaway – and although their arms were tanned, there were no white marks where watches would have been. They'd never been seen on a mobile phone or holding a cup of tea or reading a newspaper.

So, after dark, when Tom pushed his lank hair back from his beard-grizzled cheeks and when Sarah began beating on her drum, the children gathered around their fire knowing that they were in for something different. They held back at first, but the story always drew them in.

"Have I told you of the time I was taken by the fairies?" asked Tom.

Sarah beat her drum to emphasise the rhythm of his call as he repeated it.

"Have I TOLD you of the TIME I was TAKEN by the FAIRIES?"

The children muttered among themselves, but no-one dared reply.

"Have I TOLD you of the TIME I was TAKEN by the FAIRIES?" he asked again.

"No," a voice replied, and the others giggled and pushed each other forward.

"Shall I TELL you of the TIME I was TAKEN by the FAIRIES?" Tom asked, the beat of the drum growing louder each time he asked the question.

"Yes," replied one of the children.

"Yes please," said another.

"Shall I TELL you of the TIME I was TAKEN by the FAIRIES?" Tom asked again, louder still.

"Yes," they shouted.

Parents were gathering now too, outside the circle of light cast by the fire, and that gave them the confidence to move forward so Tom's story could begin. Sarah accompanied quietly on her drum, adjusting her beat to the action and atmosphere of the story.

"The year was 1485," began Tom, to a military rhythm, "and I was making my way home from the field at Bosworth where I fought for good King Richard over towards the marsh that way, by Fox Covert Lane."

A few of the adults cheered and others booed good-naturedly in return. Tom waited for them to fall quiet without acknowledging the interruption.

"My friends were taken prisoner or dead and I was making my way home alone. It was a dark, quiet night as I walked along the Fenn Lanes, taking care to keep my feet on solid ground, when I saw a woman before me. She smiled and put out her hand.

'Come with me," she said.

'Where to?' I asked.

'To a place of happiness and joy,' said she. 'Far away from the fear and fury of the battle.'

I can't explain how, but I knew she was a fairy. I took her hand and she led me across the marshes to a green hill I'd never seen before, though I'd lived in these parts all my life. The hill opened and she invited me to go in. I dragged my feet, afraid to go with her, but I was also afraid to be left behind.

'Do you promise to let me come back?' I asked.

'Of course,' she said. 'If that's what you want.'"

Tom paused and drank from his wooden cup.

"And?" asked one of the children, when they'd waited as long as they could bear.

"What happened?" asked Rose.

"You can't just leave it there," called another.

"You want to know, do you?" he asked. "Well, don't say I didn't warn you. I followed the lady into the green hill, and she revealed herself as the Queen of the fairies in shining robes and crown. You've never felt such joy nor heard such music. In the distance, I could hear dancing and feasting and laughing and when the Queen beckoned me forward, I fell to my knees, for I'm no fool. She welcomed me graciously and bid me join in the pleasure of the throng. A servant brought a crystal glass on a silver tray."

He paused again and the children urged him to continue.

"I was about to drink when I saw how eagerly the Queen was watching me, and then I was afraid. I put the glass back on the silver tray and I said thank you, but I wasn't thirsty. I said I wouldn't intrude on her festivities because I needed to get home to my wife and children. She stamped her foot and shouted, but she'd given me her word I could leave. In a flash, she was gone, and I was lying in the cold water of the marsh on a winter's morning."

He paused to take another drink from his cup. No-one moved or spoke.

"Well, I took myself into Drayton along roads made of stone and every house was a castle. It was early and there weren't many people about, but strange beasts made of metal were roaring through the streets and I thought I must be in hell itself. But then I saw the church I went to every Sunday of my life and I knew I was back in this world."

He fell silent and when he spoke again, he was crying, tears streaming down his cheeks.

"Everyone I loved was long dead and buried and there was no marker for their graves."

Sarah got up to put her arms around him, and the crowd dispersed quietly. While the other parents ushered their children away, Rose's mum went over to speak to them both, but Rose couldn't hear what they said.

"Do you think Tom's story was true, mum?" she asked, as they settled for the night in their tent.

"What do you think?" Alison asked.

"No," said Rose. "It's not possible. But he seemed to believe it."

"He did, didn't he?" said Alison. "And I suppose that means it's true for him."

The Book of Faerie Facts, Part II
Chapter 24

Within the hierarchy of the court, there exist two estates: the courtiers themselves, and the servants. Those re-entering the hierarchy after banishment do so as the humblest underlings: as deputy to the third or fourth under-housemaid's assistant, for example, depending on circumstances at the time. They sustain themselves in the tedious requirements of their lowly position with the knowledge that they are part of the very same structure at whose pinnacle the Queen herself is enthroned and that, given enough good and bad fortune in the right places, they might even ascend to those heights themselves. In the lower reaches, those who succeed in their ambitions for advancement generally do so by patronage rather than skill or wit, which only increases the squabbling and spite among them.

Faerie servants would, if they were aware of them, take some pleasure in the differences between their own position and that of human servants. Since everything in the court is obtained by magic, which is effortless and instantaneous, the primary responsibility of servants is to elevate others through their own lowliness. The function of the deputy to the fourth under-housemaid's assistant is to occupy a lower position in the hierarchy than the fourth under-housemaid and her assistant. The aspiration of the deputy to the fourth under-housemaid's assistant is to supersede the assistant to the fourth under-housemaid and, the moment that's achieved, to supersede the fourth under-housemaid herself. The function of the fourth under-housemaid, apart from aspiring to the rank of the third under-housemaid, is to ensure that those who are below her jolly well stay where they belong.

Reflecting their lesser involvement in shaping the ancient law, Faerie servants enjoy few of the privileges held dear by the courtiers. The court offers them its protection from outsiders, but not from their superiors, each of whom is zealous in guarding the distinctions and rights of their own position. Since a weighty hierarchy sits atop them, servants face a daily peril of rebuke, chastisement and wanton mistreatment. This contributes greatly to the amusement of their fellow servants and courtiers alike.

Few of the courtiers have the wisdom to curry favour with the servants, but Lord Carrick is one such. He understands not only that they're invaluable sources of information and influence, but also that they aspire to be members of the court themselves one day. He does it not through consideration or respect, for which they would be quick to despise him, but by treating them with gracious condescension, thus affording them the hope that they might achieve advancement through his patronage, and winning him what little support they're able to offer.

All members of the court are drawn to their betters, and particularly to the Queen, though each one defers to the rights of their superiors to be closer still. This results in a loose series of concentric circles of descending rank which radiate out from the royal person wherever she goes and which writhe in constant reflection of the ever-changing hierarchy of the court. At the outer reaches are the lowliest servants, who generally aspire to avoid notice while remaining on hand in case some opportunity for patronage might arise. The servants' greater distance from the hubbub allows them to observe what might otherwise remain unnoticed, so the Lord Carrick's challenge comes as no surprise to them.

Lord Carrick is a little incommoded by the Lord Herald's vexatious quibbling, but the bare bones of his plan remain unchanged. There is, he notes, no agreement about when the challenge should begin, and it's his inalienable right to exploit whatever loophole he can find. Certain of her own victory, the Queen will rush in; equally confident of her failure, Lord Carrick will hold back until the odds are more favourable to him. There are shadows in the palace and in those shadows, using subtle magic, he can wait and observe.

Chapter 25

Humans are entirely repugnant to the Faerie. Their physicality is repellent and, notwithstanding any temporary thrill, occupying human form is ultimately demeaning. Their subjection to the laws of time and physics is pitiful, their biological necessities are disgusting, and their inability to perform any but the very simplest form of magic places them beneath contempt.

All the same, the Faerie are fascinated by humans. They can't comprehend the effects of time upon their physical forms, their peculiar obsessions with respiration, digestion and reproduction or the bizarre notion of death. They observe in puzzlement the laborious efforts that humans undertake to arrange shelter, food and warmth for themselves and their families. The very notions of family, love, loyalty and friendship are incomprehensible to them. It's only natural for the Faerie to overlay their own hierarchy and values upon human society and they inevitably find it sadly wanting.

For these reasons, as well as the simple assumption of their own pre-eminence, the Faerie place humans far beneath themselves. They occasionally lure them to court to fuss over them and dance the skin off their bones, but only in the spirit that humans might teach a chimpanzee to drink tea or a dog to walk on its hind paws, and only for as long as it amuses them. Taking on the form of a human is, for them, every bit as entertaining as pantomime drag is to humans, with the same necessity for frequent costume changes. No Faerie able to imagine being restricted to a single human form for an indefinite period would find the prospect at all enticing.

This unquestioned assumption of their own superiority offers the only advantage humans enjoy over the Faerie. It simply doesn't occur to them that they might be outwitted by humans, and each time it occurs, it creates fresh outrage and confusion. Were they able to link these events together and to cooperate in a collective response, humanity would have good reason to fear them. As it is, the Faerie blithely crowd into the Queen's palace with no regard for the consequences of their actions or for anything that might threaten their way of life.

The Book of the Real World
Chapter 26

Alison had painted Rose's room pale yellow when she grew out of pink. She'd hoped that a bright sunny colour would help her get out of bed in the morning, but it hadn't seemed to make any difference. Rose didn't allow her mum into her room usually, so she took the opportunity to note the new posters on the walls. Lindie Lila and Lisa Thiel. She didn't recognise the names, but the posters matched the way Rose and her friends had taken to dressing recently, in floaty skirts with their hair hanging loose. It was a style that suited Chloe better really, because she had the height for it. At five foot two, Rose couldn't really carry it off. Alison didn't have a problem with her dressing up, though: it was part of being a teenager, after all. School were strict about the uniform, so it was only for weekends and holidays. She was glad Rose seemed to have found positive female role models who didn't feel the need to expose too much flesh, though she knew better than to tempt fate by saying so out loud.

"How are you feeling now, Rosie?" asked Alison, with a hand on her forehead. "You're not as hot as before but I can get you some more paracetamol if you want it."

Rose swallowed painfully.

"Have you told dad I'm ill?" she asked, in a voice weaker and croakier than it needed to be.

"Yes," said her mum. "I've asked him if he could pop round after work."

"But I'm poorly," Rose whined. "I want him now."

"I know you do sweetheart, but he's in the middle of something big. You know he can't just drop everything. I'll see if he can give you a call when he stops for lunch. Now, will you try to eat some of your toast for me?"

She went back to the kitchen and Rose took a bite. She could hardly taste the Marmite, and the toast scratched against her sore throat. She sucked a few mouthfuls until they were soft enough to swallow and left the crusts on her plate.

"Is that all you want?" asked her mum when she came back. "Oh dear. Well, that's fine. Now then. How about if I read you a story?"

It was nice being looked after. Mum had taken the day off work because she didn't want to leave Rose on her own when she was feeling so rotten. Usually, she was busy rushing to work or shopping or cleaning, or whatever, and usually Rose just wanted to be left on her own anyway, but today they both felt like company. It was weird being babied, but it was nice too.

"Is this one ok?" asked her mum. "I know you're too old for it, but I love the pictures."

Alison held up a book of fairy stories from her bottom shelf. Rose hadn't known it was still there, but it had been one of her favourites once.

"Go on then," she said.

"Once upon a time," said Alison, "there was a king and a queen who wanted very much to have a baby. They waited and waited and after many years, their daughter was born, probably by IVF like Kamla's two, do you think? The whole kingdom rejoiced, and they invited everyone to a grand celebration where they announced her name, Beauty. That's a bit of a gamble, if you ask me. What if she'd ended up pug-ugly?"

Rose pulled her quilt down from her face and glared.

"Sorry. Obviously, she wasn't going to end up ugly because she's good and everyone good is beautiful and everyone bad is ugly. Everybody knows that. Anyway, they all put on their best party clothes – look at that one there. He can't get his hat through the door. That did used to make you laugh – and they came forward one by one to give their gifts to the baby. When everyone else had finished, it was the turn of the three fairy godmothers.

'I give the gift of love,' said the first fairy. 'Everyone who sees her will love her, throughout her life.'

'I give the gift of happiness,' said the second. 'She will find and spread joy wherever she goes.'"

Rose's eyes were closed, but Alison could see that she was still listening.

"The third fairy godmother was just about to speak when a dark shadow passed over the cradle as the wicked fairy flew into the room. The king and queen exchanged nervous glances. They'd decided not to invite the wicked fairy because she was a bit of a troublemaker, but they were beginning to wonder if that had been a mistake.

'Ah!' said the wicked fairy, 'I haven't missed all the fun, have I? I too have a gift for the child. When she reaches thirteen years old, she shall prick her finger with a spindle and die.'"

"Why didn't the wicked fairy love her and be happy because of the first two wishes?" asked Rose.

"Well," said Alison, "that's because fairies can see through that kind of magic, so it doesn't work on them. Anyway, luckily, the third fairy godmother hadn't given her gift yet. She'd been planning to give the gift of mechanical engineering, so that Beauty had something to fall back on and would be able to fix the drawbridge and invent the aeroplane. The third fairy godmother was getting a bit old for flying and wondered what the point was of a drawbridge at all if it took a whole battalion of soldiers to put it up or down ..."

"I really believed that was how the story went," said Rose, lifting her head belligerently.

"... but instead, she raised her wand and said.

'I can't undo my sister's spell, but my gift is that before she dies, the princess will fall asleep and everyone in the castle who loves her...'

She wasn't quite sure where she was going with this, and the expressions on the king and queen's faces suggested that they were already foreseeing problems.

'... but there'll be no creepy-crawlies or mice or anything like that ...'

The king had a thing about spiders.

'... and the whole kingdom will be protected by an impenetrable barrier of thorn, so everyone outside the castle can get on with their normal lives but no-one can invade the kingdom ...'

The queen looked relieved about that, the fairy godmother noted.

'... and there'll be some sort of sprinkler system in case of fires ...'

The royal chamberlain was crying. He hadn't stopped since the wicked fairy first spoke.

'... until the princess is awoken by true love's first kiss and it's all somehow sorted out so that everyone lives happily ever after.'

The court breathed a sigh of relief as one, and the wicked fairy shrieked with frustration. It really wasn't fair to mess with another fairy's spells like that."

Alison saw that Rose's eyes were closed and put down the book to leave.

"Don't stop," said Rose.

"Sorry. I thought you were asleep."

"I'm not."

"Ok. Well, the royal chamberlain thought this was all terribly romantic and the queen quite liked the idea of staying young while her sisters got all saggy and baggy, but the king wasn't having any of it. He sent out his servants to find all the spindles in the kingdom and burn them, which did irreparable damage to the domestic spinning industry and forced a great many skilled workers out of their jobs."

"You can't resist, can you?" asked Rose.

"It's cause and effect, love. There are always consequences. Fortunately, the spinners were resourceful folk and they re-trained in darning and mending so they could make a comfortable living out of patching up everyone's old clothes. The Union of Worshipful Spinners voted unanimously to boycott the king's mending in protest at his thoughtless actions, and by the time of Beauty's thirteenth birthday, the only clothes he had that were fit to wear in public were his pyjamas."

"That's not right, though," said Rose, pointing at the illustration, which clearly showed the king in full royal regalia.

"Shush," said Alison. "You've got your eyes closed. Anyway, I don't know why he didn't just wait until she was old enough and tell her not to mess around with spindles."

"Because she'd have to find one to figure out why, wouldn't she?" said Rose.

"Yeah, you're right, actually. That would never work. What was I thinking! So, anyway, it was Beauty's thirteenth birthday and everyone in the palace was busy with cooking and cleaning and decorating – and mending – in preparation for her party. They were all determined to be happy because they knew that there were no spindles anywhere in the kingdom and nothing could possibly go wrong.

'Off you go and play somewhere,' said the queen, who was wrapping Beauty's new puppy.

'I just need to take it from the top one more time,' said the king, who was practising singing with the royal band.

'I can't talk to you now,' said the cook, who was icing a cake taller than Beauty herself.

'Perhaps later,' said her fairy godmothers, who were lighting all the candles in the banqueting-hall.

No-one had time for Beauty, so she wandered off into a part of the palace that she didn't usually visit. It was old and dusty and dark, and she didn't even care if she spoilt her party dress because it would serve them right for not paying her any attention on her birthday. Through a door she'd never seen before was a winding staircase, and she followed it up, around and around, to a turret room where a ragged and startled-looking youth was sucking on his finger.

'Who are you?' said Beauty. 'What are you doing? Take your finger out of your mouth. It really is most unhygienic.'

'I'm just delivering this spinning wheel,' he said. 'It's a surprise for the princess, but this bit here is quite sharp.'

'Let me see,' said Beauty. 'This bit here? That doesn't look sharp. Ouch.'

Which just goes to show that she would have been better off with the gift of mechanical engineering after all."

"Mum!" said Rose.

"Ok, well the princess sank down to the floor fast asleep and so did the king and the queen and the servants in the palace who all loved her dearly. The only person who didn't was the ragged youth, who didn't live in the castle and whose first impressions of the princess hadn't been entirely positive. Unfortunately, he couldn't work the drawbridge on his own, so he couldn't go home. He had a great time eating the party food and playing with the royal toys, but after the first few years, he started getting lonely and bored of stale cake. He took to talking to the sleeping courtiers and most of all he talked to Beauty, mainly because she was the only person in the castle he'd spoken to while they were still awake, so that made her his best friend in the whole world. She was getting dusty, so he put her out on a balcony in a nice fresh breeze and then found her a comfortable bed. Nothing weird happened because he was a nice normal chap and he fully understood the importance of consent."

"Oh. My. God," Rose said.

She opened one eye. Her mum wasn't even pretending to read the book anymore.

"Honestly, Rose, you'd be surprised. Did you know they have to give contraceptives to women in comas? Honestly. You can't be too careful. There's a lot of freaks and weirdos out there. Anyway, more years passed, and the boy grew from a spotty oick with greasy hair to a good-looking young man. He talked to Beauty every day, telling her all his hopes and dreams and confiding that he was, in fact, a prince who'd been enslaved by the wicked fairy when he was a baby. Over time, of course, he fell deeply in love with the beautiful girl who lay sleeping before him, though obviously she was quite a lot younger than him by then, which made the whole thing a bit weird, not to mention legally dubious. Naturally, he made no attempt to kiss her."

Rose leant up on one elbow. The paracetamol seemed to be kicking in.

"Go on," she said. "I'm looking forward to seeing how you talk yourself out of this."

"We're getting there," said Alison. "Now, the prince hadn't had any kind of an education, but he was handy with tools, and one day he decided to have another go at fixing the drawbridge. All it needed was a minor adjustment and a spot of oil and after that, it went like clockwork. He picked up a big iron sword, just in case, and wandered into the village nearby, expecting there to be ruin and devastation as far as the eye could see. Instead, he found that, while the king and queen had been asleep, the villagers had developed a fully functioning liberal democracy and, out of respect for their heritage, had industrialised the manufacture of cloth. It was obviously in the interests of the workers to observe all appropriate health and safety measures, so all spindles and other dangerous components were well labelled and protected by safety guards. What they wanted more than anything, was open borders and free trade with their neighbours, but the impenetrable barrier of thorn was thwarting the will of the people. The prince borrowed a horse and rode to the wicked fairy's house in the woods."

"And?" asked Rose.

"Wait a minute," said Alison. "Ok, yes. The wicked fairy recognised the prince at once and told him to sweep the floor, which was unbelievably dirty because it hadn't crossed her mind to run the hoover round herself. Not once. Ever. And it was covered with clothes that needed washing and dirty cups, and …"

"Alright," said Rose. "I get it. Nazi!"

"But the prince said, 'No.' He said 'I won't sweep your floor unless you break the spell on the castle and let everyone wake up. And I need the thorns gone too.'

Now the wicked fairy would have told him to go away, but she had noticed his iron sword and she didn't want to make him cross. You know fairies are afraid of iron, right?"

Rose shrugged. "Whatever."

Alison continued, "Well, fairies are afraid of iron. So, the wicked fairy said, 'I'm fine with that, actually, because the princess will die if she wakes up.'

And he said, 'Ok, well you'll have to change that as well then.'

'Damn,' the wicked fairy said. 'I shouldn't have mentioned it. But anyway, what's in this for me?'

And the prince said, 'There's the sweeping.'

She said, 'Do you call that a fair bargain?'

So, he said, 'Ok, what do you want?' …"

But before Alison could give the answer, Rose interrupted.

"She said, 'I'd just like to be invited to parties once in a while.'"

"That's right," said Alison. "You remembered!"

Rose smiled. "I like your version. It's not so black and white."

"The thing about fairies," said her mum, in the serious tone she often used for nonsense. "Is that they're sticklers for bargains. You need to negotiate carefully, but they'll keep their word if they've given it. They haven't got any choice."

"If you say so," said Rose.

Her mum continued with the story. "And the prince said, 'Ok, wait here.'

He rode back to the village and he said to the villagers, 'If the wicked fairy agrees to take down the impenetrable barrier of thorns for the sake of international trade, will you invite her to your parties so she'll let everyone in the palace wake up?'

The villagers agreed, on condition that the king didn't start throwing his weight around again. They'd got used to managing their own affairs and they didn't want a return to all the bowing and scraping. They were willing to accept a ceremonial constitutional monarchy for the sake of tourism, but that was it.

'Ok,' said the prince. 'Can I borrow a wheelbarrow?'

He pushed it to the castle and wheeled the king across the drawbridge. As soon as they were outside the reach of the spell, the king woke up.

'I say,' he said. 'Who the devil are you, and what am I doing in a wheelbarrow?'

The prince introduced himself, politely ignoring the state of the king's pyjamas, and explained the situation. Luckily, the king had just about enough sense to see reason, and he agreed to everything.

'Just wait here,' said the prince, handing him a packet of mints because although he badly needed to clean his teeth, he would fall asleep again if he tried to use one of the bathrooms in the castle.

The prince ran back to the village with the wheelbarrow, jumped on a different horse – because it would be animal cruelty not to let the first one rest – and rode off to let the wicked fairy know what had been agreed. She waved her wand, broke the spell, and everyone in the castle woke up at once, without any dodgy non-consensual underage shenanigans. They postponed the princess's party for a few days while they made new food and ordered new clothes, and this gave the spinners the boost they needed to expand their manufacturing cooperatives through international trade links.

Word soon spread that the mythical kingdom behind the impenetrable barrier of thorns was now open for business – the thorns being replaced by a purely symbolic hedge maintained very neatly by the Farmers', Gardeners' and Style-builders' Union – so tourism boomed too, and the kingdom grew prosperous, with the least economic inequality of any developed nation. They had the most amazing parties and they never forgot to invite the wicked fairy. She wasn't so bad once you got to know her – you just had to be careful not to make any wishes or promises when she was around."

"What about the prince and the princess?" asked Rose.

"Oh yeah. Well, people do talk, and it all became rather awkward between the two of them. Beauty was still only thirteen years old, after all. Everyone watched them whenever he spoke to her, and the prince couldn't help blushing and stammering, so he took the first opportunity to join a trade mission back to his own country. He defeated the evil troll who'd taken over his kingdom, claimed his crown and worked tirelessly towards a peaceful transition into liberty and democracy. That took a few years, and although he never forgot the princess, he kept his feelings to himself, because he was worried about the ethics of it all and didn't want anyone to think badly of him. The End."

"That's not a happy ending!" said Rose.

"Isn't it?" asked Alison. "Ok then. A few years later, Beauty took a gap year in the neighbouring kingdom. She saw the prince working in the fields with his people, because he got bored sitting on his throne in the castle when there was work that needed doing. He knew who she was, of course, and it was awkward at first, but by the time they'd been out on a few dates, they were able to laugh about it all. Several years later, when they'd got to know each other so well they knew how to argue and didn't have any secrets left, they decided to live happily ever after."

"That's better," said Rose, blowing her nose.

"It's not very realistic, though," said her mum.

"You want fairy stories to be realistic now?"

Her mum smiled. "Shall I go away and let you sleep?"

"Yeah, for a bit."

Alison got up, but Rose spoke again before she reached the door.

"Mum?"

"Yeah?"

"You know your necklace?"

"This one?" Alison lifted the chain, making the three pendants jingle against each other. "What about it?"

"I thought you'd stopped wearing it."

"I always wear it," said Alison. "It's usually tucked away."

"Why?"

"I just think it look a bit scruffy, you know. People ask about it and I can't be bothered to explain."

"Can I see it?" asked Rose.

Alison came back to the bed. She didn't take it off, but she let Rose examine the pendants.

"What's this one? The little shield?"

"It's medieval. From a horse's harness."

"That's cool," said Rose. "Is that the one you found at a dig and the guy in charge said you could keep it?"

"Something like that," said Alison.

"He probably fancied you."

"Maybe," said Alison.

"And what about this one?" asked Rose. It was a roughly cut chunk of clear, colourless crystal, neither shiny nor particularly pretty.

"That was a present from my dad. It's the only thing I've got from him."

"What was he like?" asked Rose.

"Not as nice as he seemed," said Alison, which was as much as Rose had ever managed to get out of her.

"What happened to him?"

"I don't know, but I wouldn't be surprised if he turned up one day."

The last pendant was a blackened iron key.

"What's that one?" asked Rose.

"It's just a good luck charm," said Alison. "It keeps me safe."

Chapter 27

"What's going on?" asked Alison, pushing open the bedroom door.

Rose looked up from the black bag she was filling.

"I'm redecorating my room," she said.

"You are, are you?"

"Yeah, it's all a bit babyish now really, isn't it? And kind of tired."

It was true. Over the years, a changing rota of TV characters, vampires and bands had stickied dots of yellow off the walls to reveal the pink underneath it, and the white underneath that. In some places, there was no paint left, and there was a patch by the window where the plaster was turning back to powder. The room was badly in need of redecorating.

"Ok," said Alison. "What were you thinking of doing?"

"I'm going to repaint it, obvs," said Rose.

"There's no need for that tone," said Alison. "I think I've got some filler and sandpaper somewhere for those holes. I'll show you how it's done."

"God, Mum!"

"What?"

"I just want to do it my way, ok?"

"Yes, of course," said Alison. "I'm not trying to interfere. But it'll look a mess if you don't fill the holes."

"Aren't I even allowed to paint my own room now?"

"Of course, you are. I'm just trying to help."

"I didn't even ask for your help?" said Rose.

"Ok," said Alison, knowing that it wasn't a question despite the intonation. "Fine."

She closed the door behind her. There was no point trying to reason with Rose. She wouldn't be told, but that was teenagers for you. She needed to do it her own way first, and then she'd ask for help. It didn't matter. The walls would need at least two coats anyway, and if the state of the rest of the flat was anything to go by, there'd be plenty of damp patches that needed re-plastering before any painting could start. It wasn't going to be a quick job, that was for sure, and if she pushed too hard now, Rose wouldn't admit to needing help later.

With Rose getting so independent, it was about time for Alison to have the talk with her. She couldn't put it off much longer. Rose wouldn't be able to keep herself safe if she didn't understand what the risks were.

"Do you want any of this crap?" asked Rose, dumping a jumbled heap of stuff from her bedroom on the kitchen table.

There was a mobile made with hag-stones and herbs, a little figure made out of iron nails – their ends carefully filed down so as not to hurt little fingers – a rowan-wood bowl of potpourri, with enough sweet-smelling ingredients to disguise the fact that some of the herbs had been chosen for different qualities. Alison fingered a windchime made with enamelled bells, each painted with a flower or plant: St John's Wort, daisy, four-leafed clover, red verbena, ash, rowanberries.

"But this is your lucky windchime," she said.

"It's not though, is it?" said Rose. "Lucky, I mean. I'm too old for all of that. Look, if you want it, you can keep it, but otherwise just chuck it or take it to a charity shop or whatever, yeah?"

Rose rooted round in the cutlery drawer and took a bag of crisps from the cupboard.

"I'm just about to start tea," said Alison.

"But I'm hungry now," said Rose. "God!"

Alison sighed. Even the most basic conversations were challenging. She wondered if she'd left it too late to have the talk. If Rose wasn't willing to listen there'd be nothing she could do. Maybe if she made some notes, it would help her think it all through. Tea could wait for a while now anyway.

Back in her room, Rose levered the lid off the paint tin with the knife from the kitchen and started on the wall by the window. She probably needed a bigger brush, because it was taking a long time and the paint kept dripping. Light blue on a yellow background seemed to end up a sickly green, which wasn't what she wanted. When her mum called her for tea, she left the lid off the paint. The next time she looked, there was a thick skin on top and the brush had dried solid. It didn't matter anyway. The curtain hid most of what she'd done.

Chapter 28

It was embarrassing not being allowed out on her own. Rose was nearly fifteen years old and it had been a major battle just to be allowed walk to school with Chlo. She could go to Chlo's house after school, as long as Kamla was there, but that hardly even counted, because her mum always found some excuse to ring, just to check. When Rose thought about it, it was actually her mum's fault that she was on her own in town now. If she hadn't had to lie about the rehearsal, it wouldn't have mattered that Chlo had been off school sick. She could have just gone home instead or got her dad to pick her up early. But as it was, she had a couple of hours to kill and she didn't want to risk any awkward questions. She wouldn't put it past her mum to embarrass her by complaining to the school about cancelling the rehearsal without any notice, and then she'd be in for it.

There wasn't much point being in town without Chlo. Rose tried some things on, but she couldn't tell if they suited her. She bought a coffee, but she felt uncomfortable sitting in Mrs Bridges' by herself. She'd found a nice tea-light holder in the Lanes, but she wasn't even sure about that without hearing Chlo's opinion. In the end, she decided to text her dad to say the rehearsal had finished early and head back to school.

There were buses, but it would fill the time if she walked, and she was running a bit short of money in any case. There were plenty of people around, and it was only just getting dark, so she wasn't worried about feeling unsafe. Rose was going past Lidl on Humberstone Rd when a voice came from behind her.

"Excuse me. Hello there?"

She turned around. It was a man, youngish, dressed in bright purple dungarees and a green t-shirt. Most people walking past them were wearing their winter coats, but he didn't seem to have noticed the cold. He had curly dark hair and red-rimmed glasses with thick lenses, and he was holding out her history book.

"Is this yours?" he asked.

"Yeah," said Rose, taking it from him. "Where did you find it?"

He shrugged. "It fell out of your bag thing."

When she looked over her shoulder, she saw that her rucksack was unzipped. Other books slipped out as she swung it off and he picked them up for her and waited until everything was safely back inside, his eyes fixed on her face.

"Thanks," said Rose, swinging her rucksack back over her shoulder.

"Someone must have been trying to steal from you," he said. "You can't be too careful."

"No, I suppose not."

She wasn't particularly worried about it. The zip did come loose sometimes, but everything that was supposed to be in there still was. Her money was in her blazer pocket anyway, and she was following the map on her phone, so there wasn't anything worth nicking in her bag.

"Anyway, I should be going," she said. "Thanks again."

"I'm going this way too," he said, walking along beside her.

She turned into Kent St, and so did he. It wasn't as busy, but there were still people around. On Melbourne Rd, it was quieter, but there were people in the houses, and she was ready to shout if she needed to. She knew to shout 'fire' because her mum said people were more likely to respond if they thought their own homes were at risk.

"This is nice, isn't it?" said the man, who'd been talking non-stop despite her on-going failure to engage in the conversation.

"Look," said Rose. "I'm grateful to you for giving me my book back, but this is making me uncomfortable now."

"What?" he asked in a wounded tone. "What have I done?"

"You're following me," she said.

"I am not!"

"You are, and I want you to leave me alone."

She walked faster, but he sped up to keep pace with her.

"You're not being very friendly," he said.

"I don't even know you."

She followed the road round to the right, going faster still.

"I'm an old friend of your mum's," he said. "She knows you're coming with me. She said it's ok."

"I don't believe you," said Rose. "Go away."

He overtook her and stood in her path.

"Come on," he said, holding out his hand. "It's time."

Rose skirted around him and ran. He shouted something after her, but she didn't hear what it was. It didn't matter anyway, because she didn't want to know. When she got to the corner with Darley St, she looked back and he was nowhere to be seen, which was a huge relief. She kept running until she was past the park, then slowed back to a walk. Her phone buzzed with a text from her dad saying he was parked outside school already. She hadn't expected him to leave work straight away and it seemed like she hadn't walked as fast as her phone had predicted. She texted back that she was on her way and ran down Gwendolen Rd.

"Hiya," she said, as she opened the car door, trying to sound as if she'd just come out of her rehearsal and everything was completely normal. "Have you been waiting long?"

"Long enough to know you didn't come out of school," said Mike.

"Don't tell mum," Rose begged. "She won't let me go anywhere without her. I just went into town for a couple of hours, that's all."

"On your own?" he asked.

"No," said Rose. "I was with Chlo."

"And you definitely didn't talk to any strange men?"

"As if!"

"Look," said Mike, as he started the engine. "I know your mum's a bit over-protective sometimes, but she's got your best interests at heart."

"Are you going to tell her?" asked Rose.

"Not this time. But I don't want you doing it again, ok?"

"Ok," said Rose.

"I can try and talk to her, if you like," he said.

"No, it's alright. I'll do it. It'll be fine."

"Alright," he said. "Do you fancy pizza?"

"Yeah. Ok." Rose sighed. "I just wished she trusted me more."

"I'm not sure lying to her is the best way to win her trust."

"Whose side are you on?"

"There are no sides, Rosie. That's not how it works."

When he dropped her off at home after they'd eaten, Alison was sitting in the kitchen with the lights off.

"Are you alright, mum?" asked Rose. "It's pitch black in here."

Alison blew her nose.

"So it is! Don't mind me, Rosie. I'm just feeling a bit sorry for myself."

Rose put her arms round her. "Is it because of dad?"

"I think I'm used to that by now, love." She wiped her eyes. "Anyway, never mind me. There's something we need to talk about."

"I can't. I've got homework," said Rose, heading for the door.

"Can't you do it at the weekend?" Alison asked.

127

"I want to get it done before I forget."

"Ok, love. Can I just ask you something?"

Rose shrugged.

"Did anything happen today? Anything unusual?"

"No," said Rose, feeling sure her mum could see through her lie. "Why?"

"It's nothing. No reason. Listen, I'm going to make a phone call in my room, but just let me know if you want anything, ok?"

The Book of Her Refulgent Majesty's Glorious Quest

Chapter 29

The throne-room is decorated with bunting and banners to celebrate the Queen's imminent victory. The Lady-in-waiting is arranging a ball on the theme of conquerors, winners and champions, and courtiers are bustling themselves into appropriate forms. As is often the case, they're disinclined to engage in actual research, and instead base their choices on whatever they may happen to think they know. Outside the throne-room, Lord Skeck, in the form of a bulldog smoking a cigar, chats to Lady Brang, who's a small wooden horse, painted red. The Queen herself is in the form of Maud Watson, the first Ladies' Wimbledon champion, in full tennis whites.

"Right then," says the Queen, bouncing jerkily on the balls of her feet. "I might as well get this done."

"What does your majesty propose to do?" asks the Lord Herald.

"I'm going into the human world, finding a human, bringing them back to share their sorrow. Bosh bish. Job done," says the Queen, swishing her racquet.

She expects that Lord Carrick is already engaged in his own attempt and has no wish to be left behind. It doesn't cross her mind for a moment that he might be lingering in the shadows behind the throne, listening to every word.

"I think it might prove to be a little more complicated," says the Lord Herald. "Lord Carrick is a cunning fellow."

Lord Carrick nods quietly to himself. It's gratifying to be appreciated, even by that treacherous and monochromatic mammal.

"Do you indeed?" asks the Queen, executing a perfect backhand. "You think I can't beat him? Is that what you're saying?"

"Not at all, your majesty," says the Lord Herald. "I simply mean that it's a more difficult challenge than someone less wise than yourself might imagine."

"Pish," says the Queen, indicating to a footman that he should throw her a ball.

"Though, of course, your plan is an excellent one," says the Lord Herald. "For example, going into the human world seems a remarkably wise first step, and there's no question that the challenge could not be completed without finding a human. These stages of your plan are exceedingly well-considered. Your majesty is justifiably renowned for her strategy and sagacity."

"I am," says the Queen, retrieving the tennis ball from under the throne. "Though I hardly think it needs saying."

She puts the ball on the floor between her feet and whacks it with the side of her racquet, as if it were a croquet mallet.

"Howzat?" she cries, and the court claps its approval politely.

"Indeed," says the Lord Herald.

"Well go on then," she says, putting her racquet over her shoulder. "You might as well get it off your vest."

"Your majesty," the Lord Herald bows. "The ancient lore confirms what I have observed myself, which is that humans can't simply be abducted. They must choose to come to our world of their own free will."

"Nonsense," says the Queen. "That would be most inconvenient."

"I'm sure your majesty knows best," says the Lord Herald. "Moreover, although the humans are able to suffer most prodigiously, they've demonstrated repeatedly that they're entirely incapable of sharing their misery."

"Humph," humphs the Queen, bouncing the strings of her racquet off the toes of her tennis shoes in turn.

"If your gracious majesty might allow me to make a suggestion," says the Lord Herald. "I consider myself something of an expert on the motivations and aspirations of giant pandas. Being one myself, I believe that I could lure a giant panda into our world with very little trouble, though perhaps with some small loss of dignity."

"Look," says the Queen. "I don't mind you having a little show off once in a while, but what you're saying simply isn't interesting."

"Your majesty is most kind," says the Lord Herald. "What I mean to suggest is that spending a little time in human form might allow your majesty to develop some insight into how a human might most effectively be lured."

"I don't think I like the sound of that," says the Queen, attempting to balance her racquet upright on the flat of her hand.

"I believe it to be the strategy that Carrick will adopt."

"Well then," says the Queen as her racquet clatters to the floor.

"I beg your majesty's forgiveness," says the Lord Herald. "But I'm not sure I understand,"

"Understand what?" asks the Queen.

The Lord Herald digs his claws into his palms. Although his is a thankless task, he must remain patient.

"I'm not concerned with whether or not you understand," says the Queen. "I have a challenge to win."

With that, she steps away into the human world. The Lord Herald clears the throne-room and returns to the peace and quiet of Edinburgh zoo. Lord Carrick sighs. It's very tedious to be stuck observing from the shadows when there's nothing interesting to watch.

Chapter 30

"Get out," snaps the Queen. "All of you."

She rips down the bunting and banners and throws herself into the throne. Lady Maven, her Lady-in-waiting, lingers by the door until it seems safe to approach. Lord Carrick observes from the shadows.

"The court is delighted by your majesty's return," says the Lady Maven.

"Is that so?"

"Goodness me, yes, your majesty. Might I just ask whether our celebration ball is to proceed?"

"Of course, it bloody isn't," says the Queen. "Are you trying to vex me?"

"I beg your majesty's pardon," says the Lady Maven, and wisely leaves it there.

"Humans are stupid," says the Queen. "They don't do what they're told."

"It's most perplexing," says the Lady Maven.

"I need advice from the Lord Herald," says the Queen. "He's irritatingly wise."

"Might I make a suggestion?" asks the Lady Maven.

The Queen nods her approval.

"Your majesty is widely celebrated for her wisdom."

"That is true."

"And the Lord Herald can be just a teensy bit negative."

"You're right about that," says the Queen.

"So, might it not be wise for her majesty to take advice instead from those who agree with her?"

"That does make sense," says the Queen. "I am very wise."

"Indeed, you are," says the Lady Maven, whose words are not necessarily a good guide to her thoughts.

"Go on then," says the Queen. "Tell me what you're thinking."

"Well," says the Lady Maven. "There's no question of your majesty not winning the challenge, of course, but if Carrick were to succeed, he would win his wish."

The Queen presses her lips together.

"You are skating on very thin mice, Lady Maven," she says.

"I don't mean to imply that anyone is in any doubt of the outcome, but – and I'm speaking entirely hypothetically, of course – if he were to succeed, he might wish for your majesty's kingdom, or life, or obedience and, begging your majesty's pardon, but his wish would be fulfilled by magic. Your majesty would have no choice in the matter."

"Is that right?" says the Queen, through gritted teeth, wondering who her next Lady-in-waiting might be.

"It is regrettable," says the Lady Maven, "that, according to the ancient lore, your majesty is bound by the terms of the challenge."

She observes the Queen's quiet fury and continues hastily.

"The court wonders why the Lord Herald allows such things."

"As do I," says the Queen, wondering who her next Lord Herald might be.

"Your majesty simply must win," says the Lady Maven. "For the sake of the court and of all your loyal subjects."

"Well of course," says the Queen. "But how?"

Chapter 31

The ancient lore codifies everything that's needful to know. By convention, only the Lord Herald speaks of past events at court, and even he does so subject to the Queen's unpredictable wrath. Most courtiers regard the Lord Herald with awkward bemusement, as humans do scientists, theologians and spiritualists. They don't go out of their way to offend him, but they don't actively encourage him either.

While he certainly appears to know what he's talking about, how much they're willing to listen depends very much on whether they like what he's saying.

Experts postulate that lack of practice and easy distraction is eroding what little chronological ability the Faerie retain. The various diktats of the ancient law ensure that opportunities for the development of this skill are rare. When the last time-wise Faerie gives themselves wholly to the present moment, scholars suggest, there will no longer be very much point to it. Since this would neither matter nor mean anything to the Faerie, no-one really cares.

The Lady Maven is a time-knower, though few suspect it. She understands that if the Queen hadn't been fatigued by the dance, bored by the endless joy of the court and elated by the idea of a quest, she would have considered her promise to Lord Carrick more carefully. Lady Maven knows it was no coincidence he arrived when he did. His challenge was carefully planned and, regardless of the outcome, it will inevitably undermine the Queen's position. Lord Carrick naturally seeks his own advancement, but the Lady Maven has other plans, and, for the moment, it is the Lady Maven who has the Queen's ear.

They sit amidst the debris of bunting and streamers, disconsolately flicking party snacks at the servants, who are clearing up entirely without magic. For the greater amusement of the Queen and her Lady-in-waiting, they're permitted to grumble and groan about this as much as they like, on the strict understanding that it makes no difference whatsoever.

"I believe," says the Lady Maven, "that, for all their inferiority, entrapping humans is a more difficult matter than one might imagine."

"It is," says the Queen. "It really is."

"If only one could live in human form, one might gain some insight into how these creatures think."

"I wonder," says the Queen, "whether living in human form might give one some insight into how they think."

"It is no wonder your majesty is reputed to be so very wise," gasps the Lady Maven. "Your thoughts are indeed startling in their originality."

"They do smell, though," says the Queen. "Something awful."

"Perhaps your majesty thinks to dwell at some distance from them…"

"I think maybe if I live as a human but away from them, perhaps in a forest, I might become able to bear their stench."

"A foolish monarch might draw attention to herself by constructing a palace …" says the Lady Maven.

"I think a humble hut, or a cave, would be most appropriate," says the Queen, expressing the fondness for the idea of a simple life which is common among those who live in effortless comfort.

"Your majesty's wisdom astounds me," declares the Lady Maven, "though I hasten to add that I never doubt it. For the purposes of ensuring my own comprehension, my understanding of your plan is that your majesty proposes to live in a humble hut …"

"Or cave," says the Queen.

"… or cave, in the middle of a forest, at a distance from the humans, and to await their approach rather than scaring them by initiating contact. In the meantime, you propose to gain insight into their thoughts by living in human form. Bravo."

The Lady Maven applauds enthusiastically. With Lord Carrick apparently absent from court, his rank is already beginning to slip. If the Queen were also out of the way, a spontaneous bout of unanimity might break out in favour of a new monarch. Should that occur before Lord Carrick's challenge is completed, he remains bound by its terms though the next Queen wouldn't be expected or obliged to fulfil a bargain in which she has no personal involvement. A successful challenger alluding to a previous queen in the hope of achieving satisfaction would be both foolish and instantly forgotten. These are circumstances which could well work to the Lady Maven's benefit.

"Your majesty is particularly wise in appreciating the importance of patience," says the Lady Maven.

"Right," says the Queen. "I'm off to get this done. Keep an eye on things here for me, will you? Nose to the groundstone and all that."

"Leave it to me, your majesty," says her Lady-in-waiting. "You can rely on me entirely."

Chapter 32

An apple-cheeked old woman enters the empty throne-room with her back bent but her head upright and eyes alert. Beneath her cloak is a human. She presumes it to be a child because it's smaller than they usually are. She isn't certain, but it doesn't signify. The throne-room is dusty and cobwebbed, the throne itself concealed beneath a cloth.

"Your majesty!"

A footman, in human form and livery, drags himself upright from his slump against the wall and the Queen puts her finger to her lip. The repeated call of her name through the palace would bring the entire court running, and she doesn't want an audience until she's sure of her victory.

"Come here," she hisses.

He comes in all haste. "Your majesty."

She pulls back her cloak to reveal the human and passes it to him, glad to be rid of her disagreeable burden. Resuming her natural appearance, she prods it with a long, curved nail, and the infant cries out angrily and opens its eyes. The Queen's joy at her success sweeps through the footman, who smiles down on the child in his own natural form. Mistaking his pleasure for friendship, the child smiles back, its eyes wide. The Queen's blue-green skin and the footman's translucent feathers would certainly startle an older human, but everything is new to this child. Until it learns to distinguish between friend and enemy, good and evil, it accepts whatever comes with gummy curiosity.

"Stop that," shouts the Queen. "Stop smiling at once. I command it."

The little face tightens. The little mouth opens in a wail. The noise is most unpleasant, though the Queen observes that the liquid droplets gathering in its lashes have a certain shining beauty. If it could be managed, these drops might make an enchanting chandelier: a centrepiece to a banquet, perhaps, to celebrate her victory.

"I believe this to be sorrow," she says to the footman. "What do you feel?"

It would suit the Queen's purposes better if she could experience the child's emotions for herself, but she cannot soil her royal person with the feelings of her inferiors.

Although she condescends to share hers with the footman, there is etiquette in all matters and everyone's place at court depends upon observing the proper protocols.

In truth, the footman is feeling that type of anger which is most closely related to fear. The Queen's temper is legendary. No-one would draw her attention or stand within reach if there were a way to avoid doing so. Naturally, she doesn't want to hear about his fear, and the very fact that he can feel it is something he'd rather keep to himself. He concentrates on the child, searching for something else to report. It wriggles and screams in his arms, distracting him from the challenging task of knowing what he's feeling.

"Hold it tighter. Concentrate," commands the Queen. "Be physical. That might help."

He adopts a material version of the human form he previously occupied – his natural form not being suited to holding a baby – and experiences the restrictions of his flesh and the potential of his muscle. The tighter he holds the creature, the more noise it makes. Its little fingers do him no damage through his royal livery, but a tiny nail finds the skin of his hand and he feels it scratch him there.

The pleasure of pain is a familiar gift to those lower down the hierarchy at court. Courtly patronage necessarily involves abasement, chastisement and fantasies of retribution. Those most inventive in inflicting punishment insist on physicality in the ones they chastise and construct elaborate ceremonials to draw out the enjoyment. This tiny scratch, effaced at will, is insignificant in comparison but there's no benefit in it and that makes him angrier than the discomfort alone would justify.

"Tell me," insists the Queen. "How does it feel?"

"I don't know, your majesty," the footman says. "I'm not sure."

"Does it feel different? Is it new?"

The Queen's eyes shine with pleasure that could quickly turn to rage.

"I can't tell for certain," he says. "I think perhaps, your majesty, it may be the same. Mostly the same, I mean. The noise makes it difficult to be sure."

The notion interests the Queen. "Does the noise affect you in some way?"

The child's cries are shrill now. It beats at the footman with its feet and head, trying to force him to loosen his grip. The footman frowns, struggling to retain his hold.

"I don't know, your majesty. I can't tell."

Many footmen before him, and eminent courtiers too, have been cast out for failing their Queen in smaller matters than this, for there are many ways to fail her. He resents being put in this position and tightens his grip on the child.

The Queen stamps her foot.

"Tell me. Tell me now." She pinches the child and pulls its hair. "What does this make you feel?"

"Your majesty," says Lady Maven, her Lady-in-waiting, who sweeps into the throne-room in a high-necked white nightgown and fluffy pink slippers.

She removes her eye-mask and smooths her hair. Night has no meaning in the court, but she understands that the Queen wishes to believe she's acting discreetly.

"Forgive me," she says. "I was passing, and some slight noise caught my attention."

The Queen accepts her apology without acknowledgement.

"Tell me how it makes you feel, Lady Maven. This fool doesn't know."

"If I might be so bold, your majesty. I think perhaps he's afraid."

"Afraid, is he?" says the Queen, peering into the footman's face for the first time.

"Naturally he's afraid in the presence of his Queen," says the Lady Maven. "But that isn't what I mean."

"Make it be quiet," the Queen snaps to the footman. "I can hardly hear myself blink."

She gestures him towards the furthest corner of the throne-room. The footman bows and moves away to quieten the child's cries.

"What are you trying to say?" the Queen asks her Lady-in-waiting.

"Your majesty."

The Lady Maven dips down and bows her head.

"Yes, yes" says the Queen. "Go on. Spill the beads."

"Your noble quest is known far and wide, your majesty. Were this fellow to agree that he feels human misery, and were he to prove mistaken, he might expose you to public mockery. I believe he's unsure and seeks to protect you from the possible consequences of his own uncertainty."

"I see. Very good. I suppose that is not such a bad thing."

The Queen nods sharply to the Lady Maven and calls the footman forward.

"Well?" she asks. "Can you say yet what you feel?"

Grateful for the intervention and not objecting to the gratitude that will be required in return, the footman takes the chance of smiling at the Lady Maven, whose office affords considerable opportunities for patronage. He's rewarded with a smirk of mutual understanding. The

Queen's quest takes her away from the court these days and Faerie pleasures are less tempered than usual by the precepts of the ancient law.

"My lady, if I may," he says, bowing to allow the Lady Maven to appreciate the tautness of silk and firmness of buttock.

The Queen watches the child with distaste and doesn't observe the interplay between them.

"Tell him to speak," she says, trying to reinstate the usual protocols now that the Lady Maven is with them.

The Lady Maven nods to the footman.

"I think, perhaps," he says, "that possibly I feel only irritation at the noise, my lady. Even on its continuation, I do not experience the child's misery. Indeed, since there is no obvious cause for the uproar, it also provides little pleasure."

"I see," says the Queen. "You may tell him that his honesty and bravery do him credit."

"Her gracious majesty observes that your honesty and bravery do you credit, my good fellow."

"Thank you, my lady."

He bows again.

"It's quiet now," says the Lady Maven, peering at the bundle in the footman's arms. "I think perhaps it's broken."

"No matter," says the Queen. "This size isn't terribly robust. The smaller ones are more easily portable but they're in no way amenable to reason. I shall try a larger one next time.

"Your majesty is both wise and inventive," says the Lady Maven.

If she were paying attention, the Lady Maven might note that the Queen is already developing an understanding of cause and effect: an understanding which could be ruinous to her own aspirations. The Lady Maven is, however, engaged in sending a shiver of pleasure to the footman, down his spine and around his groin. The pleasures of physicality are degenerate and perverted in comparison with ethereal bliss, and there are those who argue that their prohibition by the ancient law is designed entirely to enhance their enjoyment.

The Lady Maven reluctantly returns her attention to the Queen.

"I imagine you couldn't bear to tarry here while your scheme remains untested, your majesty, notwithstanding the clamour of your subjects for the pleasure of your presence."

"Quite so," says the Queen. "I shall return immediately to the world of humans. The court will just have to manage without me."

Lord Carrick observes from the shadows behind the throne. It saves him unnecessary effort to learn from the Queen's mistakes, and he sees the Lady Maven's intentions clearly. He can't help feeling that there's something undignified about lurking in the gloom, though he feels honour-bound to exploit his loophole to the full.

Chapter 33

The Queen retreats to the court again to confer with the Lady Maven. Although she has passed many years in the human world, her absence from Faerie is considerably shorter. Scholars propose the possibility of leaving and returning in a single moment, but this would require a degree of skill that can only be achieved through practice and tireless dedication. Since promptness is not a quality valued by those who live entirely in the present, there's no good reason for taking the trouble to acquire it.

The Queen feels relief at leaving her human form behind for a while, allowing her to enjoy the greater freedoms of immateriality. To enhance the contrast, she adopts a non-visible form, wafting as the scent of warm cinnamon buns

"They are drawn to me," she tells the Lady Maven. "The humans, I mean. I suppose they sense my superiority even if they don't fully understand it. Because I live apart from them, they consider me something special but also an object of fear, which is an emotion they're much given to. There's also an opposite feeling, which they call hope, and they often come to me with it. They think I can help them be mothers or not be mothers or make their children well or make their rivals' children not well. They do seem obsessed with children."

"May I ask if you help them?" asks the Lady Maven, who compliments her by becoming the fragrance of freshly brewed coffee.

"Sometimes," says the Queen. "If I feel like it."

"Does time pass?"

The Queen tires of wafting and distils herself into the shape of a fox with a magnificent brush of a tail.

"Well yes. It does. Hundreds of it," she yawns.

The Lady Maven follows suit, carefully shaping herself as a weedier specimen with a less bushy tail, before continuing their conversation.

"The court is eager to hear more of your challenge, your majesty. Is your majesty able to feel the sorrow of the humans?"

"No," says the Queen. "Though there's plenty of it about. They mope and they whine on about everything endlessly, but whether I'm here or there, I can't feel any of it. It's all terribly tedious."

"The humans you bring to the court are certainly very dull," says the Lady Maven.

"So dull!" agrees the Queen.

"But does your majesty find that she understands them by sharing their form?"

"Hardly. I am only here now because they want to burn me." The Queen yawns again. "I'll give them a while and go back."

"Your majesty's understanding of time can only enhance your reputation," says the Lady Maven, in a slightly forced tone. "Your triumph over Carrick is assured."

"Well of course," says the Queen. "Though I begin to consider the challenge impossible. I'm minded to await Carrick's failure rather than making repeated attempts of my own."

In the shadows, Lord Carrick raises an eyebrow. The Queen begins to think strategically. This is not at all to his liking.

"Your majesty," says the Lady Maven, who's making some headway in the court's regard during the Queen's absence. "Perhaps there are other avenues to explore."

"What do you mean?" asks the Queen.

"It may be that your success requires consent, your majesty."

"Oh!" says the Queen, the flash of a thought glowing in her eyes. "Perhaps taking them by force cannot succeed and I must instead persuade the humans to accompany me of their own free will. What do you think?"

"Your majesty is exceedingly wise to have such a thought."

"The sharing of joy among us is an act of volition," explains the Queen. "The sharing of misery may be the same. I'm eager to put my insight to the test."

"The court misses your majesty terribly, but we understand that defeating Carrick must take precedence."

"If you could just take care of things in general," says the Queen.

"Of course, your majesty."

Lord Carrick doesn't make the Queen's mistake of underestimating the Lady Maven and he doesn't make Lady Maven's mistake of underestimating the Queen. He also understands, which perhaps neither of them does, that the Queen may run out of time.

Chapter 34

There's a sound from outside the Queen's cave in the side of a small green hill in the forest. She takes care to display enough signs of life to encourage passers-by to linger, and when she approaches the mouth of her cave, she sees a man examining the cooking pot that hangs over her fire pit.

"Begging your pardon," he says, looking up. "But have you any water to spare for a thirsty traveller?"

The man appears to be travelling alone, but he looks prosperous enough. His clothes have plenty of wear in them still, and a hungry childhood couldn't have produced a frame so broad and powerful. The Queen emerges into the light in the form of a young woman, shaping herself in accordance with her observations regarding the configuration of female parts which most invites human courtship.

"Indeed. And bread too, sir?" she asks.

"I could hardly take the food from your table," he says, blushing and stammering. "If you have a table, I mean. Though I don't intend to imply that you don't. For you may have, for all that I know. A pretty young woman needs a good table. Not that anyone would think any of the worse of her if she were without."

"I would not have you starve," she says, peeping up at the babbling fool from under her eyelashes. "A great strong man like you."

She holds out a hunk of bread.

"Will your husband not mind?" he asks.

She blushes and glances downward. "I am a maid, sir."

"Your father then?"

She sighs. "Alas no. My father died last winter."

"You cannot live here all alone and unprotected?"

Her eyes glisten bravely. "I do, sir."

"You have no family to care for you? No kin to take you in?"

"I am all alone, sir."

She invites him into her cave after he's eaten, and he comes with her willingly. They emerge into the splendour of the throne-room and he turns at once to escape but finds his own world gone.

"Naughty, naughty," scolds the Queen. "You came with me willingly and now I demand repayment for my generosity."

He is a man who never thought to see Faerie for himself, but he understands his situation well enough. Wisely, he falls to his knees and averts his eyes.

"What would you have from me, my lady?" he asks.

"Give me your sorrow," she demands.

"My lady?"

"Share your misery with me," she commands.

"I don't understand."

The Queen calls the Lady Maven and gives instructions for the man to be beaten until he complies. He must consent because it's what she wants. The Lady Maven calls the footman who serves her most particularly, swearing him to secrecy for now. Reclining upon her throne, the Queen gives in to the boredom of the sticky sounds of the footman's encouragement to misery, with physical fists and clubs.

"Nothing?" she asks.

"Nothing," says the Lady Maven, turning to the footman. "What about you? Do you feel his sorrow?"

"I'm afraid not, my lady," replies the panting footman.

"Is he gone?" asks the Queen, finding it difficult to discern anything human in what is left.

Lady Maven passes the question to the footmen with a raised eyebrow.

"I believe he is gone, my lady," he says.

The footman's bared chest glistens with the human's blood.

"How very tiresome," says the Queen. "I really do consider this challenge impossible and I'm growing terribly bored of trying. I think I'll await instead Carrick's failure."

"Your majesty," says the Lady Maven, whose own plans are not yet come to fruition. "I wonder if it might it be necessary for the humans to understand what they consent to."

"I have a novel idea," says the Queen. "I wonder if the human's consent needs to be informed."

"Your majesty is most wise," says the Lady Maven, with a smile.

Lord Carrick also smiles to himself in the shadows. The Queen is getting nowhere and learning nothing. He'll continue to keep an eye on her progress, but he feels sure there's no real cause for concern.

"The proof of the pudding is in the heating," declares the Queen. "I require you to take care of the doings of my court and such like."

"As your majesty wishes," bows the Lady-in-waiting.

Chapter 35

The Queen sighs as another traveller takes his last breath and slumps to the floor of the throne-room. She wears the simple garb of an early modern peasant woman and a form of astounding beauty.

"This whole business really is enormously tedious," she says.

"Yes, your majesty."

The Lady Maven's cheeks are flushed. Whether the humans share their misery or not, she can still take her own pleasure in their sufferings.

"This one is here entirely of his own accord," says the Queen. "I employ no trickery or deception. I say, 'come with me to the land of Faerie' and off he trots after me like a little piggy." She stamps her foot. "So why won't he share his misery?"

"It is most unkind, your majesty."

"It's bad enough that they shy away at the last moment, when they understand where I'm taking them. But this fellow," she says, kicking his unyielding physical form. "This fellow knows perfectly well, comes happily along and still disappoints me. It simply isn't fair."

"Your majesty, might I …?" asks the Lady Maven.

The Queen nods her permission to dismiss the footman so the Lady Maven can speak freely in the privacy of the throne-room, though nothing in the throne-room is ever truly private.

"I give this matter a great deal of thought, as you would expect, your majesty," says the Lady Maven, who observes the Queen's improved understanding of time and therefore appreciates the necessity of more carefully hiding her own. "Your court is in a state of mourning while you are from us."

In truth, there are few who complain, and the Lady Maven is acquiring considerable influence. A few peer at the tapestries in the ante-chamber and wonder aloud who that is who sits on the throne. In the moment they all come to believe it is the Lady Maven herself, her ambitions will be realised, and that cannot be long now. Lord Carrick, who listens from the shadows, perceives this without needing to venture from the throne-room. The Queen, it seems, has little suspicion.

"Well of course the court misses me terribly," she says. "I am Queen, after all."

"And, I'm sure it occurs to your majesty …"

The Lady Maven pauses to reshape herself into a honeybee, which hovers before the Queen.

"Get on with it," she says.

"If your majesty insists," bobs the Lady Maven. "Carrick believes, I think, that human sorrow is lessened if they share it."

"He may do."

"If one human's sorrow is lessened in this way, the sorrow of the human they share it with must surely be increased," says Lady Maven. "And I believe that sorrow is more often granted to the powerless by the powerful than the other way around."

"As joy is among us," says the Queen.

"Quite so," says the Lady Maven. "I believe that, as among us, it is demeaning to experience one's inferiors' emotions. Although your glorious majesty shares the honey of her joy for the benefit of the court without any thought of hoarding it for herself, one cannot imagine that human leaders are quite so benign."

She pronounces the last word with an increased emphasis on the first syllable.

"Well no," says the Queen, echoing her pronunciation. "I am most benign."

"Indeed, you are, your majesty."

"But what does this mean?" asks the Queen.

"I believe, your majesty, that human leaders do not share their inferiors' misery but instead farm sorrow as a bee gathers pollen. Once gathered, it's their own and they can keep it as they will but also, I believe, share it if they wish."

"An interesting notion occurs to me," says the Queen.

"I also believe," the Lady Maven adds hastily, lest the Queen should complete her thought prematurely, "that human sorrow is to our emotions what nectar is to honey."

"Which is?" asks the Queen.

"Not so nice," says the Lady Maven. "And perhaps less sticky."

"I think," says the Queen grandly, "that I shall gather humans as a bee gathers pollen and claim the honey of their sorrow as the Queen of the bees does the honey of the bees."

The Lady Maven nods her encouragement. It's all nonsense, and she has no reason to believe it will help in any way, but it will keep the Queen occupied while her Lady-in-waiting supersedes her in the mind of the court. If the Queen fails repeatedly at a complex task, she will certainly become frustrated with it, but if she succeeds repeatedly at a simple task, although it leads nowhere, she'll remain confident in her progress and keep at her pointless endeavours. Similar principles underlie many computer games and loyalty cards in the human world.

"Right then," says the Queen. "I'm off."

"Just one more thing, your majesty."

The Queen rolls her eyes. "Come on. I'm in hurry."

"I'm sure your majesty builds some kind of a hive to store these humans."

"Well of course," says the Queen. "And what form do you imagine that will take?"

"In your infinite wisdom, I'm in no doubt that you build it on the edge between our two worlds, where neither the Faerie nor the humans can detect or disturb it," says Lady Maven.

"Naturally," says the Queen, who only now gives the matter any thought at all. "It surprises me that you imagine I might do anything different. Now, I really must be going."

"If I may, your majesty," says Lady Maven. "There is just one more thing."

The Queen groans in frustration. "What?"

"Your majesty surely knows that humans who fear our kind are unlikely to come willingly."

This truly is a startling insight. The hierarchy of the court doesn't require the Queen to understand the emotions of her inferiors and the ancient law doesn't allow her to feel them. The longer a Queen occupies the throne, the less able she is to imagine how anyone else might be experiencing her reign. For any Faerie, imagining how a human might feel is a considerable challenge; for a Queen it's next to impossible.

"Quite so," says the Queen. "It occurs to me that humans who believe in the Faerie but don't have the sense to fear me are most likely to yield the desired results."

"Your majesty is exceedingly wise. If I might make so bold, I believe the humans record their interactions with us in books and that re-creating a familiar scenario might help your cause."

"It may be some time until my next return, Lady Maven."

Reading even the simplest of books is a challenge for those with limited powers of concentration. The Faerie do not enjoy the benefit of the many centuries of collective endeavour and many hours of individual practice which now enable humans to give their undivided attention to several screens at once and still engage in warm and fulfilling social interactions. Fortunately, the Queen of the Faerie has at her disposal the College of Heralds, which consists of time-knowers who have nothing better to do than win her approval in the hope of advancement.

"Your majesty knows best," says the Lady Maven.

"Well, of course, I do," says the Queen. "I am the Queen."

Lord Carrick rolls his eyes. One might almost feel sorry for her. She's no match for Lady Maven and her time is certainly running out. That idea of a hidden place between the two worlds is a good one, though, and he decides to explore it while he's waiting for his time to come. The notion of reading the humans' books to learn about them is an intriguing one too. Once again, he congratulates himself on the wisdom of learning from the Queen's attempts before beginning his own. He strikes a heroic stance, imagining the memorialisation of his actions in the tapestries of his future court. He will, perhaps, downplay the lurking.

Chapter 36

The Queen watches from above as the girl runs into the wood, chasing the rainbow. Using their own stories to trick them is proving a great success, and the Queen delights in her own cleverness in devising this plan. The colours of the rainbow are peopled by human forms ascending into the light in an inexplicable mingling of human and Faerie lore, but it has certainly proved effective in luring them in. The Queen lets the girl examine the rainbow until the sky grows dark, and she slips down to place a golden key beside her while she sleeps.

When the girl wakes, she's cold and aching. Her dress is damp and dirty, and she fears the punishment that undoubtedly awaits her at home. Her eyes fall upon the golden key on the moss beside her.

With ill-grace, the Queen takes the form of a fish with the head of a small owl. There's no conceivable excuse for it, except that it's what happens in the book she's re-creating. She swims through the air on her shining feathered fins. Keeping slightly ahead of the girl, she leads her to a cottage and shifts there into the form of a beautiful woman.

"What is your name?" she asks the girl.

"Charlotte," she replies.

"How old are you?"

"Eleven."

"You don't look it," says the lady.

"How old are you, please?" returns Charlotte.

"Thousands of years old," answers the lady.

"You don't look like it," says Charlotte.

This is the most vivid dream Charlotte's ever had and it's following the story of her favourite book perfectly. The conversation thus far is entirely familiar. What the lady says next takes her entirely by surprise.

"The point is, though, will you come with me?"

"Where to?" asks Charlotte. "To the land of the shadows?"

"What nonsense," says the lady. "No, to the Faerie kingdom."

"Begging your pardon, but what for?" asks Charlotte.

"I'm the Queen of Faerie," the lady says. "And I need you to come with me so I can defeat an impudent fellow who challenges me."

Charlotte relaxes. She should have known that a dream wouldn't follow the story properly. This one seems to have become muddled up with some other fairy tale, though she isn't sure which.

"Please could you tell me about the challenge, my lady?" she asks, remembering to be polite.

The Queen is taken aback. She hadn't anticipated any further explanation being necessary.

"Well, if you must know," she says. "It's really very simple. I just need to take back a human who will share their misery with my subjects."

"You want me to come with you to be miserable?" asks Charlotte.

"Yes, that's right. As I say, it's perfectly straightforward I can't imagine why it should take you so long to grasp the idea."

"I don't want to," says Charlotte, running out of the cottage and back through the wood towards her own garden.

"Oh, for goodness sake," sighs the Queen as she swoops after her. "I don't believe I said running away was an option."

Charlotte feels no hunger or thirst after that. She feels no pain from cramped limbs or pinched guts. There's only darkness and the sound of lonely children crying.

The Book of the Present
Chapter 37

Rose turned her key and pushed the door open. The flat was quiet. She'd popped in at Jess's with Chlo on the way home after the last of their mocks, and they'd lost track of time. They'd been messing around with henna and achieved very mixed results. Chlo's hair didn't look any different, but Jess'd had a ginger disaster that needed an emergency trip to the chemist's so they could fix it with a semi-permanent brown before her mum went completely mental. Rose couldn't see any difference in her own hair colour, which was a dark, golden brown to start with, but the girls swore it looked warmer in the right light.

She was really going to miss them. Chlo was off to Jamaica soon for the whole summer and Jess was going to France, and they'd been trying to talk Rose into visiting her dad and Ava in their new place in the Netherlands. It was easy for them to say she was mad not to go, but they hadn't seen him being all lovey-dovey with her or making a fuss over her stupid little children. Rose just couldn't face it. And they knew she'd never been abroad before. They knew she was scared of flying, so why they thought she was going to do it all by herself, she didn't understand. In the end, they'd given up and watched a film, but their hearts hadn't been in it.

It didn't matter that it was a late night, because nothing mattered now until the summer holiday started, and anyway, it was Saturday tomorrow, but the thing was that her phone had run out of charge, so she hadn't altogether told her mum where she was or when she'd be back. Kamla had turned up to collect Chlo, and Rose could have asked for a lift, but it hadn't seemed worth the bother and she'd wanted to watch the last ten minutes of the film. She thought Jess's mum would offer her a lift, but then she saw the empty bottle by the sofa and decided it was best not to ask. She just walked it in the end. It wasn't that far, and it shouldn't have been a big deal. It wasn't even dark really, but it was late, and she knew what her mum was like.

The flat was quiet and there weren't any lights on. If her mum hadn't been looking out for her, she might get away with saying that Jess's mum had dropped her home, but she'd have to wing it. Whatever happened, she'd be in trouble for not letting her mum know where she was, but it might still be possible to head off the full nuclear. Rose's skin prickled in the quiet flat. It was entirely possible that her mum was waiting in the dark somewhere, fuming. She could be anywhere right now, in the kitchen or the living-room, or in either one of their bedrooms, just building up to an almighty row. If that was how it was, avoiding it wasn't an option.

"Mum?" she called.

There was no answer. She flicked the switch and kicked off her shoes. Walking down the hall, she checked in the kitchen.

"Mum?"

She crept to the door of her mum's bedroom. If, by some miracle, she was asleep, there was no point waking her up. The yelling could wait until morning as far as Rose was concerned, and she might be able to soften it with a cup of tea in bed or something. But it would be a mistake to try and sneak to bed if her mum was awake. Rose opened her mum's bedroom door as quietly as she could.

"Mum?" she whispered.

The curtains were open and the electric light from the walkway outside shone on to the empty bed. Rose couldn't believe her luck. There must have been something on at the museum. Her mum would have told her about it, maybe even reminded her that morning, as if morning was a good time to tell anyone anything. But that didn't matter. What mattered was that Rose had got away with it.

Her mum did go out sometimes, and she was ok leaving Rose on her own if she promised not to leave the flat or to answer the door to anyone she didn't know was coming.

Usually, she'd message with suggestions about what to eat and how to heat it up, and sometimes she'd ring the landline, just to make sure her daughter actually was where she was supposed to be. Rose plugged her phone in to check that she hadn't missed any messages. Just because her mum wasn't here, didn't mean she wasn't furious.

But there weren't any. Whatever her mum was doing tonight must have been interesting enough to distract her from the usual fussing. A chilling thought struck Rose. Her mum could be out with a boyfriend. She'd definitely been hiding something lately. Rose had caught her talking animatedly on the phone a couple of times and she'd hastily ended the call and acted awkwardly casual. Rose shuddered. She hoped her mum wasn't on a dating app. It was disgusting really, when you thought about it.

It wasn't that she minded her mum having a boyfriend, in theory, but she absolutely didn't want to have to acknowledge it. It was bad enough her dad being all soppy over Ava, without her mum doing it too. It would be alright if they understood that it was up to them who they hooked up with, but she knew they wouldn't be satisfied until she said she was happy for them, and that was never going to happen. Her usual policy with her mum was just to insist that she didn't want to know. She was pretty good at heading off those conversations when her mum tried to start them. No-one could make her talk about it if she didn't want to and, as long as they weren't talking about it, it wasn't happening as far as she was concerned.

She checked the landline for messages too. It wasn't like her mum to go completely off radar. Her grandad had left a vague message about wanting a chat, but that was all. She found a scribbled note from her mum in the kitchen, saying there were leftovers in the fridge, and breathed a sigh of relief. If Rose was supposed to have known that her mum was going to be late back from work, that meant her mum hadn't realised that Rose wasn't home when she should have been. There was nothing to worry about.

Chapter 38

The landline rang a few times the next morning, but Rose didn't give anyone that number, so she never bothered answering it. Her mum would get it if she was in, and if she wasn't, they'd leave a message. The grief she got if she forgot to pass on a message or didn't get it right made it better for all concerned if she just let the answerphone pick up.

The same approach usually worked for the door – her friends never came round without arranging it first – but whoever was hammering on it now didn't seem to be giving up. Her mum would be getting another snippy email from the residents' association if she wasn't careful, and that would mean another lecture about how lucky they were to have a roof over their head, and blah blah blah. After last night, it didn't seem worth taking any chances, so Rose dragged herself out of bed and shuffled to the door in her pyjamas. The sun shone in from the open walkway and she shaded her eyes to protect them from its brightness. It was unseasonably hot for June.

"There you are!" said her grandad. "You really shouldn't open the door like that."

"Do you want to come in?" Rose asked. "What time is it?"

She yawned and stepped back to let her grandad past. He'd put on weight since nan died, and with his sticks as well, he took up the whole width of the hall. The rubber suckers on the ends left black marks along the bottom of the wall, but she didn't suppose it mattered.

"It's twelve thirty," he said. "I've been trying to get hold of you all morning and in the end, I had no choice but to come over myself."

His face was shining red and he was out of breath. The lift had been out of order for a while, and she felt bad that he'd had to walk up the stairs.

"You never came on the bus?" she asked, feeling the dampness under his shirt when she hugged him.

"I got a taxi," he said. "I was worried because you weren't answering the phone."

He hadn't been out much since his last fall. It was about confidence more than anything else, her mum said, but Rose could see that coming here had been too much for him. She squeezed past so she could open the door to the kitchen and pull out a chair for him.

"I didn't think it'd be for me," she called back to him. "Do you want a cuppa?"

Now that she was up, Rose realised she was hungry. She opened cupboards to look for breakfast and filled the kettle while her grandad completed his journey down the hall.

"Is mum expecting you?" Rose asked. "I haven't seen her this morning."

He lowered himself on to the chair with a groan and took a sheet of kitchen roll to wipe the sweat from his face. Seeing his features individually as he wiped, made Rose realise how large his nose was. She was sure it hadn't always been that big.

"That's better," he said. "There's something we need to talk about, love."

"Yeah?" said Rose, absent-mindedly.

She couldn't find a clean bowl for cereal and there were only crusts left for toast. Rose sighed. It was too hot for all this. Her mum had locked the windows, as usual, even though there were bars on the outside. She rooted through the key bowl on the counter but couldn't find the one she needed.

"Rosie, love. Sit down," said her grandad. "There's something I need to tell you."

Rose put their tea on the table and sat down opposite him. There were bananas in the fruit-bowl that looked a bit blotchy, but they were better than nothing. She broke off the bits that were alright to eat and leant over to drop the rest into the bin.

"Is everything alright?" she asked.

"Your Mum's in hospital," said her grandad. "Now don't panic."

"Oh my God! What happened?"

Her brain flooded with anxiety. Just because her mum had known she was going to be out last night, didn't mean she hadn't had an accident. She could have gone on a date with a homicidal maniac who'd drugged her and dragged her away. She could have gone shopping this morning and been run over, or she could have eaten something and gone into anaphylactic shock. Just because she didn't know she was allergic didn't mean she wasn't. Anything could have happened, and all the possibilities were roaring through Rose's mind at once. It was a struggle to focus on what her grandad was saying.

"She went in yesterday for a routine check-up and they needed to do some tests, so they kept her in overnight."

Rose breathed out. That wasn't so bad.

"Is she ok? Can I see her?"

"That's what I'm here for," said her grandad. "You've got time to have breakfast and a shower if you're quick. I'll call us a cab when you're ready. Visiting hours start at two."

"I didn't know anything about an appointment," said Rose, picking up her tea to take it to the bathroom. "Did you know she was going in?"

"I didn't know she'd stayed in until a couple of hours ago," said her grandad, "but she did tell me about the check-up."

Rose wondered how she was supposed to behave like a responsible adult when her mum treated her like a child.

"She could've told me," she said, with her hand on the bathroom door handle. "How was I supposed to know?"

Her grandad leant back on his chair in the kitchen to answer.

"I suppose she didn't want to worry you, love."

His expression was sympathetic, and his voice was calming. He didn't really do stress, but Rose could see he was worried, and that revived her anxiety. She wondered if it was bad luck that she'd been pleased her mum hadn't been home. Perhaps it was her fault the hospital had kept her in.

"I was out last night," she confessed. "Late. I didn't even know she wasn't here. And this morning, I've just been lying in my bed."

"You can't go blaming yourself for that, Rosie."

"But I should have realised."

"And I should have asked if there were any messages for me last night instead of letting the agency staff leave it until the morning."

Rose went back into the kitchen for a hug.

"It's not your fault," she said. "I'm really sorry you had to come all the way over here, grandad. I should have answered the phone."

"It's alright, love," he said, with a squeeze. "You weren't to know."

"I should have got up earlier, though," said Rose. "I should've realised something was wrong."

"How could you have?" he asked. "You have to stop finding ways to make it your fault. Believe me."

"Why didn't she tell me about the appointment, though? It's not my fault I didn't know about that."

"I'm sure your mum thought there was no need for you to know," said Brian. "She wouldn't have wanted you to worry."

Something in his tone alarmed her. She put her tea on the table and sat back down.

"Are you saying I should be worried?"

"Let's just get ourselves over there so your mum can fill you in herself, shall we?" said her grandad. "There's no point me trying to tell you things I don't properly understand myself."

Chapter 39

It was cooler inside the Royal Infirmary. Rose's grandad seemed to know his way around, and she followed him into lifts and through a maze of corridors. It was all she could do to stand still when he stopped to rest. If she'd known where they were going, she could've gone ahead and let him catch up in his own time, but she was gripped by a superstitious fear of asking which ward her mum was on.

The oncology ward was calm but busy. Rose tried not to look at the other patients as she and her grandad made their way to the desk. She was wearing denim shorts with ripped black tights and a black top. She shouldn't have worn black. It had to be unlucky that she was wearing black.

"We're here to see Alison Watts," said her grandad. "I'm her father-in-law and this is her daughter."

"She's in bed five," said the nurse, glancing up with a busy smile. "It's just up there on the right."

Alison looked tired and pale. Before they'd even reached the bed, she was telling them not to worry, that everything was going to be alright, but Rose could see for herself that it wasn't true. Her mum was nervous. Her grandad was worried. Neither of them would meet Rose's eye.

"What's going on?" she asked.

Her mum creased her forehead and took Rose's hand.

"You know I had a brain tumour when you were a baby, Rosie? And they operated and treated it, and everything was fine for years? Well, it's come back. They need to operate again, and I might have to stay in for a while."

"But you'll be alright?" asked Rose.

"I hope so," said Alison. "I mean, I was alright last time, wasn't I? For a long time."

"They're very good here," said Brian. "World class."

"Absolutely," said Alison. "This is the best place for me to be. Really it is."

She winced suddenly, her face constricting with pain.

"Are you alright, mum? Do you need me to call a nurse?"

"I'm fine, love. It's nothing," said Alison. "I just knocked the cannula."

She pulled herself to a seated position and Rose adjusted her pillows the best she could.

"Thanks love," said Alison. "I tell you what, though, I'd love a proper cup of tea."

"Ooh, me too," said Brian, rooting in his pockets for money. "And could you bring me a bacon sarnie if they've got any? I'd settle for ham."

"Sure. Ok," said Rose. "Can I get you anything to eat, mum?"

"No thanks, love. The operation's quite soon, so I'm not supposed to eat anything anyway."

Rose knew they were just getting her out of the way so they could talk, and that suited her fine. She'd need some time to herself if she was expected to put a brave face on this.

Chapter 40

The hospital café was easy enough to find, but Rose got lost on her way back, ending up on a sweltering glassed corridor that looped back towards the main entrance. She hadn't wanted to read the signs, but there was no choice in the end. The route to oncology was well marked.

Her grandad was watching her mum with a frown on his face when she got back to them. Her mum's eyes were closed.

"Here she is," said her grandad, a little too brightly.

"Thanks Rosie," said her mum. "Just put it there, would you?"

"Sure. There you are, grandad. I put your sugar in, but you might want to give it a stir."

"Thanks love."

"And they only had ham."

"That's great though. Thanks love."

He stirred his tea with the little wooden stick while Rose helped her mum to sit up again. She kept deflating like a balloon, crumpling in on herself. It didn't feel right pulling her about, but she didn't seem able to do it for herself. She looked vulnerable in her hospital robe: smaller and less herself.

Rose felt dizzy. She sat on a plastic chair. The backs of her legs stuck to the padding on the seat and she peeled them off in turn. It wasn't pleasant, but it took her mind off other things.

"We've been talking about where you're going to stay, just while I'm in here," said her mum.

"I can stay at home, can't I?" asked Rose.

She knew her mum wouldn't think so straight away, but this was her chance to prove she was capable of looking after herself. And if her mum let her off the leash a bit now, it would be hard to keep such a close watch on her afterwards. She didn't want to let the opportunity pass her by.

"I can cook for myself," she said, "and I'll make sure I switch the cooker off and I always make sure the windows are locked when I'm on my own now, don't I? It's been ages since I forgot."

Her mum frowned painfully.

"I'm sorry, Rosie. It's not that I don't trust you, but you're just not old enough."

"I'm nearly 16."

"I know love. Nearly. And I'm sure you'd be capable of feeding yourself if you set your mind to it, but there's more to it than that. If social services found out you were on your own, they'd take you into care. I've already had a nurse asking who's looking after you. And I don't want to be worrying about where you are or who you're with the whole time."

Her grandad leant forward. "You wouldn't want to worry your mum, would you love?"

"Ok, alright, I get it," said Rose. "I don't want you worrying about me, mum, but what about if grandad came to stay at ours? He could sleep in your room while you're in here. That'd be ok, wouldn't it?"

"We did talk about that," said her mum, "but I'm afraid it wouldn't work."

"I'm so sorry, love," said her grandad. "But I need help with all kinds of things these days and I can't expect you to be at my beck and call. I need to be in the home."

"I thought you were getting better," said Rose.

167

"I am, but I still need help and there are things I couldn't ask you to do, love."

"I wouldn't mind."

"I wouldn't be comfortable with it," he said firmly. "And that's the end of the matter."

She'd made excuses so far about visiting her dad in the Netherlands, but she might as well go now. It was hard to like Ava because she was too perfect and nice. It just made you want to do something mean to find out how she'd react. And Ava's children were too young to be interesting, though her dad couldn't seem to get enough of them. The way he talked, it sounded like he preferred them. Just because going to her dad's was the only option left, didn't mean she had to like it.

"Ok, fine," said Rose. "I suppose I'll have to go to dad's, then."

Her grandad frowned.

"I'm sorry, love. I had a quick chat with him this morning. He's doing some training for work in Brussels for a few weeks, but you might be able to go to him when school finishes, if you need to."

Rose pouted. "Not that Ava would want me there, anyway."

"I'm sure that's not true," said her mum. "You'll need a bit of time to get to know her and her family properly, that's all. It would probably be better to go and stay with them another time, when everything is a bit more settled."

Her grandad pursed his lips, resisting the urge to criticise Mike or his new partner. Alison would always be his daughter-in-law as far as he was concerned. It had made no difference to him that they'd never married, so it made no difference that they'd split up either. It was good that Mike was happy, really it was, after everything, but that didn't mean he had to move abroad while his only child was still at school. And it didn't matter how cheap the flights were. Holland was still foreign in his book.

"Ok," said Rose. "I'll stay at Chlo's, then."

Alison shook her head.

"It wouldn't be fair on Kamla to ask, love. Not when we don't know how long it'll be for. You can't sleep on Chlo's floor for weeks on end, can you? And aren't they off to Jamaica soon anyway?"

"Is it going to be that long?" asked Rose.

"It's hard to say for sure," said her mum.

"So where am I supposed to go if no-one wants me?"

"Don't be like that, love. You know that's not how it is." Her mum paused. "You could stay with your gran for a while."

"Who?"

"Your gran. My mum."

"I don't know your mum," said Rose. "I didn't even know I had a gran."

"Of course you do," said her mum. "I'm sure I must have told you about her."

"Not that I remember," said Rose. "This is so not fair."

She thumped back into her seat with her arms folded, and her mum closed her eyes. Brian sat quietly, waiting for someone else to speak. It was Alison who did, and she did it without warning or preamble, opening her eyes as if she'd only closed them to blink.

"So, you can stay with your gran. Just until your dad's back from his trip, and then you can go over to his for a while and see how it goes with Ava and her kids. I don't suppose it matters if you miss a few days at school now your exams are over. Grandad's going to find out whether we can claim for the taxi-fare to school from your gran's for now, but we'll make it work anyway." She paused. "It'll be fun. A bit of an adventure. It's not for long."

"Yay!" said Rose, without enthusiasm.

"And when all's said and done, your gran is family," said her grandad.

"Where does she live anyway?" asked Rose.

"Just the other side of town," said her mum.

"Seriously?"

"Still in Peston Forest, is she?" asked her grandad.

Alison nodded and Rose shrugged. She didn't know where Peston Forest was, and she didn't much care.

"Anyway," said her mum. "It's not that far from town, so you'll be able to come and see me any time you like. I'm sure your gran would probably come with you in the cab if you wanted her to."

"If you went by bus instead," said Brian, "you might be able to pop in on the way home from school and save a bit on cab-fare."

"Well yes," said Alison. "I suppose so, but it's probably better to stick with cabs just to be on the safe side."

"That's that then," said her grandad. "I'll just pop out and give her a call."

They watched him walking slowly away.

"So, your mum's been living in Leicester all this time," said Rose.

"Yes," said her mum. "I'm sure you knew that."

"How would I know that? Have I even met her?"

Her mum shrugged evasively. "Maybe not so you'd remember."

"So, how come?" asked Rose.

"Well, she wasn't a great mum to me. She was away a lot when I needed her."

"What, daytrips and stuff, like nan and grandad used to?"

"No, she just wandered off sometimes. On her own."

"Where to?" asked Rose.

"She never really wanted to talk about it, love."

"Why not?" asked Rose. "I don't get it. Your dad wasn't around either, was he?"

"No." Her mum smiled tightly. "But that wasn't a problem. I looked after myself, and it was fine, but – before you say it – it was different then."

"How long did she go away for?"

"However long she wanted to, Rosie love."

"But wasn't she worried about you?"

"I don't suppose she can have been," said Alison.

The concept was alien to Rose. She wished her mum would back off a bit sometimes and give her some space, but the idea of not having her there at all was alarming.

"But when she came back, right, she could see that you'd been alright, couldn't she? I suppose that's why she thought you'd be ok the next time? I mean, I bet she built it up gradually, didn't she?"

Her mum frowned. "She was never really herself when she got back. I think I looked after her as much as she looked after me."

"Is that why you're all, you know?" asked Rose, hunching her shoulders and stretching her arms like a mother hen.

"I suppose. I certainly wouldn't leave you on your own if I could help it."

"You did last night," said Rose, though she knew this wasn't the right time to mention it.

"I'm sorry about that," said Alison. "I honestly thought I'd be home not long after you and then everything went crazy here and I just lost track of time. I did ask the hospital to ring grandad, but I should have asked Kamla myself if you could stay over with them."

"It's ok," said Rose. "It doesn't matter. To be honest, I was late back from Jess's and I was just relieved not to get into trouble. I didn't even know you weren't home until grandad came round this morning."

"Oh, I see." Her mum paused. "Shall we call it quits, then?"

"Ok," said Rose. "But didn't anyone ever notice your mum was neglecting you, though?"

"No love. It was different then. Not so many social workers."

"Couldn't you have asked for help?"

"I didn't want anyone interfering," said Alison, with a sharp intake of breath that Rose chose not to hear. "Mum would've hated it too."

"But what about your teachers and your friends? Wouldn't they have noticed if you weren't ok?"

Her mum sighed.

"So many questions! I've told you all of this before, I'm sure I have. I didn't go to school all that much. I didn't finish my exams. That's why I had to do it all later on and that's why I'm always on at you about doing your homework." She shrugged. "I don't think the teachers were all that bothered, to be honest."

"I know how you must have felt, though." Rose sighed, "I feel like no-one wants me either."

"I'm not having that, Rose. It's rubbish. Lots of different people in lots of different places want you, so you're going to have to move around a bit for a while to keep them all happy. It won't be for long."

Rose wasn't a kid. She didn't believe that for a minute, but her mum was looking tired and she didn't want to give her a hard time about it.

"Alright. Whatevs," she said. "When am I going to go?"

"Later on today, I hope. Grandad's just sorting it out with your gran now."

"I feel like a parcel," said Rose. "Like an unwanted parcel left on the wrong doorstep."

Her mum laughed. "You always were a drama queen."

Chapter 41

Brian came back to the ward looking careworn and grim.

"Is everything ok?" asked Alison.

"Yes," he said. "Fine. She was very positive about it, actually. She's looking forward to meeting our Rosie after all this time. As it happens, she's got someone with her. A friend, who sounds like a very sensible woman. So, there's no need to be concerned."

"That's good," said Alison.

"It was reassuring," Brian said, with a tired smile.

Rose could see that her mum was tired too. The gold glints in her green eyes were the only colour left in her face. She hadn't noticed before that there was so much grey in her mousy-brown hair. Alison put out her hand.

"I want you to have my necklace," she said.

"No," said Rose. "I don't want it. It's yours."

"Just look after it for me," said her mum, and she leant forward so Rose could lift it over her head.

Rose put her hand on the table as she was leaning across, but the wheels weren't fixed, so it scooted away from her and her mum's tea toppled over. It wasn't hot enough to scald anyone anymore, but it spread across the flat surface and dribbled on to the floor and bed in all directions.

"I'm so clumsy," Rose said, trying to mop it up with paper towels. "I'm really sorry."

A nurse put his head round the curtain.

"I'm sorry to interrupt," he said, "but we need to be getting Alison here ready for theatre."

"I'll just clear this up," said Rose, trying not to notice the fear that flashed across her mum's face.

"Don't worry about that," the nurse said. "I'll get someone to see to it."

"Right," said her grandad, briskly. "I'll phone later to see how it's gone, love, and I'll make sure Rosie's kept up to date. Have you said your goodbyes? I mean, are you ready to go, Rosie?"

"Mum … will I see you again?" Rose blurted out.

It wasn't what she'd meant to say. What she meant was "When will I see you again?" She didn't know why it'd come out wrong, because everything was going to work out fine. It had to.

Alison frowned, and then smiled slowly, the golden flecks in her eyes catching the light.

"Yes," she said. "You will. I promise."

Brian came away frowning, which wasn't like him at all. They walked slowly back through the hospital without much conversation. Rose didn't mind stopping to rest now. The longer it took to get home, the better, since she'd only be packing a bag and heading off to stay with some mad old woman she didn't even know. She didn't like the idea of their flat standing empty.

They were met by a wall of heat outside but there weren't too many people waiting for cabs, and it wasn't long before they were back in an air-conditioned environment. When they got back to the flat, they hunted for keys and opened windows in the hope of creating a draught, and Brian shouted suggestions through about what Rose should pack. She could hear his sticks banging against chair-legs and cupboards as he rummaged around in the kitchen.

"Don't forget your toothbrush," he called.

"No, grandad."

"Or your toothpaste."

"I've got it," she said.

"Do you need to get anything from the chemist on the way?"

"No, I'm fine."

"You sure?" he asked. "You might be there for a couple of weeks."

"I'm fine, grandad."

"Shall I do you a sandwich?" he asked.

"We haven't got any bread."

"I'll see what else there is."

"I don't think I could eat anything," said Rose.

"There's a Twix here you can take with you. In case you change your mind."

Rose wasn't packing. She was sitting on her bed, messaging everyone she knew, sure that someone would come through for her. Someone's parents would be ok about her sleeping on their sofa, just until her mum came out of hospital.

"What's going on?" said her grandad from the doorway.

She should have heard him coming, with the bag from the kitchen bin swinging against his sticks. Through the thin plastic, Rose could see that he'd emptied the fridge.

"I'm just trying to find somewhere else to stay. It's only for a few days, isn't it? It's not worth bothering my gran. It's not like I even know her."

Brian sighed. "Rosie, love. It's all arranged."

"I know, and I didn't want to upset mum by making a fuss at the hospital, but I'm sure I can find somewhere to stay for a couple of days."

He put down the bag and came over for a hug. When she stood up, she noticed that he wasn't as tall as he used to be. If she stretched up now, she could rest her chin on his shoulder.

"It wouldn't be fair to ask," he said. "Like your mum said, we don't really know how long it'll be for."

"I can stay somewhere different every night if I need to," she said. "I wouldn't be any trouble."

"How would we keep track of where you were?" he asked. "Your mum just needs to know you're safe."

"I suppose."

"It's not just about who you're staying with, is it? It's their fathers and brothers and neighbours and friends and all the other people who are in and out that we don't even know about. Do you know what I'm saying?"

"Yeah, I know. Stranger danger. You're as bad as mum."

"We just need to know where you are and who you're with."

Rose sighed. "Alright."

"And anyway, your gran would be disappointed now, wouldn't she?"

"Yeah, right," said Rose. "It's not like she couldn't have seen me before if she'd wanted to."

"Look," said Brian. "I've never met her, and your nan never had a good word for her but, for what it's worth, I liked her when I spoke to her earlier. She sounded really pleased you were coming."

"I just don't understand why mum lost touch with her," said Rose.

"She had her reasons," said Brian. "But it's all water under the bridge, love."

There was a knock at the door. Brian shuffled to answer it, taking the binbag with him and calling over his shoulder.

"Come on, Rosie love. Get that packing done."

"Hello mate." It was a loud male voice. "Taxi to Peston Forest?"

Her grandad sounded confused. "I haven't called one yet, have I?"

"It's for Rose Murray. They told me to come up and help with the bags."

"I suppose I must have done, then. How on earth could that have slipped my mind? Rosie love, the taxi's here."

"I won't be a minute. I'm coming as fast as I can."

"Teenagers, hey?" said the driver.

"Yeah," said Brian.

He put the binbag by the front door, so he'd remember to take it down with him.

"Are you off somewhere nice?" asked the taxi-driver.

"What do you mean?" asked Brian.

"Well, I just thought, because you're emptying your fridge, you must be off on holiday."

"How about minding your own business?"

The conversation drifted back through Rose's open door, and she was surprised by the sudden sharpness of her grandad's tone. It wasn't like him at all. The taxi-driver sounded taken aback too.

"Alright, mate, keep your hair on. I was only making conversation."

Chapter 42

The driver opened the boot for her bags and Rose waited while her grandad folded himself into the back of the cab. When he was in, she handed him his sticks.

"You don't need to come all the way there with me, grandad. We can drop you off on the way."

"It's not a problem," he said.

He looked exhausted, though. He'd barely left the home since he'd moved there after his last fall. He knew he was never going to manage on his own again, and he'd put his house up for sale because he couldn't look after himself anymore. Having to run around after Rose and her mum was too much for him, especially in this heat.

"Really, grandad. It's ok."

"I'm coming with you," he said.

"No," said Rose. "You're not. It's too hot and we'll be going past the home on the way, won't we?"

She gave the driver the address.

"We can do," said the driver. "And I don't think there's any point arguing. This is one determined young lady."

"Alright," said Brian. "If you're sure you'll be ok."

"I'm sure," said Rose. "It'll be fine."

"Ok," he said. "As long as you're sure you're sure."

They got caught up in the rush-hour traffic and it took almost forty minutes to get to the home on Elm Tree Avenue.

"Do you want me to help you to your room?" Rose asked.

"No love," he said. "But could you just nip in and ask them to come out with a wheelchair? This heat is a bit much for me, if I'm honest."

"Ok," said Rose, venturing into the stickiness outside.

Brian fished awkwardly in his pockets until he found the slip of paper with the address on it and passed it to the driver.

"Make sure she gets there safely," he said. "I've got your number."

"Alright, mate," said the driver. "There's no need to be like that."

Rose stood aside helplessly as the staff heaved her grandad out of the cab and into the wheelchair, scolding him for going out without letting them know where he was or when he'd be back. He caught Rose's eye across their fuss and gave her a wink.

"Alright, Rosie love," he said. "You need to be off. The meter's running this whole time, you know."

He fetched out his wallet and counted notes into her hand.

"Grandad!" she protested.

"You'll need it for the fare," he said. "And anything that's left is yours to spend. Ok?"

"Ok, grandad. Thank you," she said.

Their parting felt final, though they both pretended it was no big deal. Rose didn't want to upset him by making a fuss when he looked so worn out and bothered; Brian didn't want to upset Rose by showing how hard it was to send her off to a grandmother who, whatever else might be said for her, hadn't made any effort to be part of her granddaughter's life. They both wished they could do more for each other but all they could do was make it less difficult by putting on a brave face.

"Goodbye, love," he called as they wheeled him away. "Let me know when you get there."

"I will," called Rose. "Bye."

She sat back in the cab feeling abandoned and bereft.

"Ready to go?" asked the driver, meeting her eye in the mirror.

"Yeah," said Rose. "Have you got the address?"

"It's in the satnav," he said. "Do you want this?"

He passed her a slip of paper with her grandad's writing on. She saw that it was an address and tucked it in her pocket. The driver didn't try making conversation, and she was grateful for that.

The Book of Her Glorious Majesty's Wise Advisors, Part I

Chapter 43

The Lady Maven is alone in the throne-room, quietly trying out decorative themes for her coronation. A tropical beach with palm-trees and steel drums is jolly, but perhaps not sufficiently solemn, and the lapping of the sea creates an air of unintended menace. With a wave of her hand, she tries another theme, and the air swims with incense and rings with choral music.

She won't have to be patient for much longer. In the fury of her quest, the Queen appears not to understand the importance of showing herself to the court in between the long absences. She's almost entirely forgotten. The Lord Herald doesn't leave his enclosure unless he's called, and no-one calls him these days. The court needn't realise it's choosing a new Queen for the succession to be achieved.

Lord Carrick, naturally, sees all. He watches Lady Maven for a time from the shadows, then steps forth with a sweeping bow.

"My Lady Maven," he says. "How goes her majesty's quest?"

The Lady-in-waiting starts and guiltily restores the throne-room to its previous state. The throne is hidden beneath a dustsheet and appliances flick on and off to simulate the room's continued occupation.

"I am a faithful servant to her majesty," says the Lady Maven. "You can't expect me to tell you that."

"Not well then," he smiles, gesturing her towards the pool of light cast by a standard lamp.

"I cannot say so," says the Lady Maven, joining him in the circle of brightness. "And how does your quest proceed?"

"Steadily," says Lord Carrick.

"Do you think it at all possible to succeed?" asks Lady Maven, raising her voice to be heard over the sound of a suddenly active blender.

"Does it matter?" he asks.

They dance around the real topic of their conversation. No-one to whom the thought occurs can doubt that Lady Maven wants to be Queen. Lord Carrick, perhaps, would be her Lord Herald under different circumstances, but his challenge suggests ambitions that are loftier still. If their aspirations are compatible, they might find ways to cooperate for a time, though they certainly can't trust one another. Either one might just as readily denounce the other to clear their own way forward. Neither would wish to ascend to a new office weighed down by tiresome commitments but, provided that making a bargain ensures one's triumph, one can fulfil it across a conveniently short period if necessary.

"Am I to believe, my Lord Carrick, that the only purpose of your challenge is her majesty's vexation?" asks Lady Maven.

The blender falls silent and they're plunged into darkness. A lava lamp glows into life nearer the door to the antechamber, casting hypnotic shadows on the walls and floor, and a microwave begins droning in the corner.

"I wouldn't presume to dictate what a Lady-in-waiting might believe," says Lord Carrick.

An alliance with Lord Carrick would be dangerous, for he's no less treacherous than she is herself, but danger delights the Lady Maven.

"I believe she tires of your challenge," she says.

"And yet her absence creates uncertainty at court."

"It does," she says. "It does."

The microwave pings and turns itself off. A brass-horned gramophone drones into life, filling the throne-room with the sinister sound of 'Teddy Bears' Picnic'.

"I hear that Lady Brang is rather self-assured at present," says Carrick, attempting to nettle Lady Maven into revealing her own ambitions.

She's too skilled a courtier to fall for this, and answers in a casual tone.

"Unjustifiably so, in my view. I believe Lord Wexen thinks very highly of himself."

Lord Carrick laughs dismissively.

"Lord Wexen is alone in this," he says.

"Indubitably so," says Lady Maven.

"Yes indeed."

The lava lamp switches off and the gramophone settles into its final groove.

"Do you have any aspirations of your own, Lord Carrick?" asks the Lady Maven, with an air of unconcern.

"Me? I aspire only to serve the Queen's glory to the best of my limited and humble ability. Yourself?"

"There is no greater honour," replies Lady Maven.

A toaster shoots hot crumpets into the air and an officious under-footman bustles to replace them. Although nothing in the throne-room can be considered truly private, Lord Carrick and Lady Maven fall silent until his task is completed.

For readers of less sensitive perceptions, it may be necessary to explain that by their daringly explicit conversation, the Lord Carrick clearly sets his ambition at a position below the throne, but that the Lady Maven does not. Neither is necessarily telling the whole truth, but that could hardly be expected.

"I believe that she acts upon your suggestions," says Lord Carrick.

He's able to speak more freely now their ambitions are clearly – but deniably – defined.

"Indeed," says Lady Maven, "though she considers the ideas to be her own."

"I have another suggestion which may amuse you," he says.

183

"I may suggest it to her if it does."

Chapter 44

It's dark, but the Queen's eyes have no need of light. The small humans are stored together and, as she predicted to Lady Maven, in her enormous and widely renowned wisdom, time is being pulled taut by the presence of so many children out of their rightful places. They stretch its restrictions to the limits as they cower and whimper in isolation. They don't know that they're cramped together with their own kind and they're entirely unable to perceive or take comfort from one another. This is marvellous to behold, and the Queen is impatient to collect their sorrow for herself. She glows her joy down upon them and they turn their faces towards her, their eyes closed against her radiance.

"I can give you this. I can give you this joy," she exults.

The joy of a queen will surely tempt them. It's more than fair recompense for the miserable suffering they're to share in return. She reaches her claws to the nearest child, a boy of seven or eight, who whimpers at her approach.

"You," she commands. "Give me your sorrow."

He cries out and strains to pull away from her. In the joy she shares, he can feel the pollution of her anger at a quest that causes her so much trouble, the bitterness of her loathing for Lord Carrick and the spite of her anticipated triumph. He keeps his eyes firmly closed and shakes his head.

"You then," she shrieks, tossing him aside and pulling out a little girl by her arm. "I command you to agree to come with me and share your sorrow."

The girl struggles to escape, preferring to be alone in the darkness.

"Be sad," roars the Queen. "Are you not filled with sorrow?"

They are, all of them, but fear overwhelms it.

"Share it with me," she demands, ignoring all courtly protocol in her quest to succeed.

In the absence of their sorrow, she feels only her own rage. She wants nothing more than to destroy them all for their defiance.

"How many of you must I collect to distil a single drop of misery?" the Queen howls, ripping their flesh with her claws. "Tell me. Tell me at once."

Chapter 45

A footman slumping to attention in the antechamber is startled by the Queen's call from the throne-room.

"Call the Lord Herald and my Lady Maven."

He obeys her command, and cries of "Call the Lord Herald," and "Call the Lady Maven," echo around the palace, finding their intended recipients in the weak sunshine of Edinburgh zoo and the splendour of the Lady-in-waiting's sumptuous chambers, which are filled with cast-off gowns and jewels that she leaves lying around to create the impression of regal opulence. The Lord Herald reaches the throne-room first, brushing specks of semi-masticated bamboo from his fur as he enters.

"Your majesty," he bows. "May I say what an enormous pleasure it is to enjoy again the scintillating grace of your munificent presence?"

He is wise to speak carefully, for the Queen is in the form of a granite pestle and mortar the size of an armchair. She grinds continuously as they speak, and although it would be unseemly to peer too obviously, the Lord Herald catches a glimpse of what appears to be a small human skull being broken and crushed to dust.

"Tell me everything I need to know," she demands, her pestle pounding.

"Everything, your majesty?" he asks. "About everything?"

"About Carrick, of course, and his quest. What is he doing? What does he achieve?"

The Lord Herald nods his panda head. Although it would be considerably wiser not to, he can't help chuckling as he gives his report.

"Your majesty, the palace guard are under orders to monitor all movement across the boundary between the worlds, and there's no evidence that Carrick has so much as set foot across the edge."

"He remains in court all this time?" asks the Queen.

"Unfortunately, your majesty, it isn't entirely possible to confirm that he's in the court either."

"This is most peculiar," says the Queen, stopping her grinding.

"Indeed, it is, your majesty."

"What's he playing at, do you think?"

"I'm not yet in a position to hazard a guess, your majesty."

The Lady-in-waiting joins them, pausing to courtesy before approaching the throne. She wears the black dress and white apron of a waitress but without the white cap. Her aim is to appear attentive and subservient, but not suspiciously so.

"Do you hear that, Lady Maven?" asks the Queen. "The Lord Herald tells me that Carrick cannot be located."

"Much as I respect the Lord Herald and his position," says Lady Maven, "he's talking nonsense. Everyone knows that Carrick is absent from court and that he therefore must be in the human world."

"When did you see him last?" asks the Lord Herald.

As is well known, the Lord Herald's position allows him to deploy the past tense. He rarely bothers because few at court appreciate the skill involved. However, he has suspected for some time that the Lady Maven may be one of those dangerous individuals who does. If she is wise in the ways of time, she's working hard to conceal it, and this naturally causes him considerable concern.

"Not since the ball, I believe" says Lady Maven, focussing on the lie and neglecting to appear baffled by the question.

The Lord Herald notes her easy reply with concern. A Lady-in-waiting who understands cause and effect is a far more effective schemer than is customarily placed in that position. Should she succeed in becoming Queen, there's no question that she would appoint a new Lord Herald. No Queen could want her court to be haunted by so physical a reminder of her predecessor's reign, even if she didn't have her own rivals to elevate out of contention. He quietly weighs up the benefits of his current position against the opportunity to eat without interruption, and shrugs. At this point, there doesn't seem to be much in it. What comes will come.

Chapter 46

In the shadows behind the throne, Lord Carrick raises an eyebrow. He's long been aware that the Lady Maven is a time-knower, but now the Lord Herald knows it too. Given the danger she poses to the Queen and the Lord Herald himself, she may soon cease to be a threat to his own ambitions.

"Where can Carrick be?" asks the Queen, reshaping herself as Lord Nelson and raising her telescope to her eyepatch.

"He must be in the human world," says Lady Maven, still shaped as a humble waitress. "I mean this with all due respect, to the Lord Herald, who is clearly wrong."

"I most certainly am not," says the Lord Herald. "Intending no discourtesy, the Lady Maven is evidently something of a moron."

"Never mind that now," says the Queen. "It's of no help to me if you're at each other's stoats. Is there any way that Carrick could pass between the worlds without detection?"

"Your majesty is wise to put the Lady Maven's stupidity to one side," says the Lord Herald smoothly. "As long as I am monitoring movements between the worlds, Carrick cannot pass unnoticed."

"Begging your majesty's indulgence, the Lord Herald is an idiot," hisses the Lady Maven. "Because if Carrick were in the court, we would sense his presence."

"Unless he hides himself with subtle magic," says the Lord Herald. "As any fool would realise."

"When her majesty passes to the other world, can you be sure that she does so alone?" asks Lady Maven.

"Well no," he admits. "But he would hardly be standing by at all times in case of an opportunity to pass through with her."

Lord Carrick nods in agreement. Although he is usually close by, his attention often wanders, and the tedium of the idea repels him.

"He need only do it the once," says Lady Maven, "and I wouldn't put it past him."

"Well I would," says the Lord Herald. "Your majesty, Carrick is skilled and devious, but he isn't patient."

Lord Carrick purses his lips. Patience isn't a quality he's ever valued or aspired to, but he resents the comment all the same. He'll show that impertinent panda. If he can be bothered.

"Do you see?" asks the Lady Maven. "The Lord Herald is withholding information from you."

"While a Lady-in-waiting might witter on about any trivial thing that crosses her mind," says the Lord Herald, "a Lord Herald could hardly expect her majesty to listen to everything he knows about the ancient lore."

"I should think not," says the Queen, unpinning her empty sleeve to let it hang loose. If she sways from side to side, she can make it twirl like a tassel and the effect amuses her.

"Indeed," says the Lord Herald. "The whole point of a Lord Herald is to relieve her majesty of that burden and to advise her of the ancient lore, as and when it's relevant. The ancient lore includes numerous philosophical models which suggest a great many theoretical possibilities about more or less everything, and a Lord Herald must make judgements about which it is useful and possible to explain. And also when."

"I have great confidence in her majesty's intelligence," says Lady Maven, who has nothing of the sort. "I'm quite sure she'll have no trouble grasping anything you might wish to tell her."

The Lord Herald pauses slightly too long.

"Does my Lord Herald think me stupid?" asks the Queen, flipping up her eyepatch to observe him through two narrowed eyes.

"No indeed, your majesty. Goodness gracious me, no. Your majesty is famed the length and breadth of the palace for her wisdom and insight."

He pauses again to think and, when he speaks, it's with a chuckle in his voice.

"Very well. And purely for the sake of proving my point. There is, for example, a particularly abstruse theory described by the ancient lore as thinning. The idea is that time can bear only so much disruption. Imagine that time is a dance, your majesty. Should an individual, particularly one who is ordinarily subject to time, happen to move across the dance instead of with it, the dance will part around the obstruction, correct itself and move on but there's a limit to the disruption the dance can bear. If too many individuals are dancing against it, the dance itself loses shape, do you see, your majesty?"

"Yes, yes, of course," says the Queen, attempting to observe him through the wrong end of her telescope. "I've seen time stretching for myself and I can't think why you would bother telling me something I already know perfectly well."

"How fascinating," says the Lord Herald. "I should certainly like to note down your majesty's observations for posterity. That is to say, prosperity. For the prosperity of the court. Anyway, this theory is based on a certain amount of reality already. We can monitor Carrick's movements, for example, because whenever anyone crosses between worlds or across time, it causes a temporary weakness. We simply don't know what might happen if too many weaknesses were to occur for an extended period or in the same place or at the same time and that's where your majesty's observations would be particularly useful."

"Place and time are different, are they?" asks the Queen.

The Lord Herald pats her hand with his panda paw.

"Your majesty's understanding is justifiably legendary," he says.

Lord Carrick rolls his eyes. When he's Queen, he'll have no truck with such bare-faced flattery. He'll surround himself with courtiers who tell him the truth. Rebels and malcontents will be more use to him than lickspittles and sycophants. He pauses to wonder just how sycophants are related to elephants and loses focus on the Queen's conversation.

Although it isn't necessary for him to pass into the human world unnoticed, he does like the idea of unnerving them. It will amuse him to outsmart that insufferably self-satisfied panda. He only hopes he needn't be patient very much longer. If the Queen can't be said to have failed soon, she may run out of time altogether.

The Book of Unwelcomed Guests
Chapter 47

Traffic was at a standstill on the outer ring-road. The driver edged around the Scudamore roundabout slowly, affording Rose a 180° view of the wilted flower display: 'Sponsored by Dumblewash. Building a Better Tomorrow.'

Despite the heat of the sun, the sky was a heavy and luminous grey, poised for a storm, and Rose was feeling uncomfortably sticky against the seats of the taxi. They crept around to the next roundabout, with each stop and start punctuated by the driver's mumbled complaints. He was having problems with the air-conditioning and not keeping his eyes on the road, which made him impatient with anyone who tried to change lanes. When they turned on to the Hinckley Rd, the traffic sped up and warehouses and showrooms flashed by on the left, giving way, further from town, to houses that gradually increased and then decreased in size.

Rose spotted the sign for Spinney Hills Rd when they turned the corner, but the driver couldn't seem to find the house. He drove up and down three times, turning his cab more impatiently each time, and eventually asked, "Are you sure this is the right address, love? What number is it?"

She leant forward to check the address on his satnav as she retrieved her grandad's note from her pocket. The satnav said, 'Spinney Hills Rd, Peston Forest', and that matched what she'd been given.

"I don't think there is a house number," she said. "It just says 'the old cottage'."

"Don't you know?" he asked.

"I've never been here before," said Rose. "Not that I can remember."

The driver sighed. He'd been on the brink of packing it in for the day when this call came in. Just one last pick-up, it was supposed to be. All he wanted was to get home and pour himself a cold beer. He hadn't asked to be sent on a wild goose chase with a minor who didn't even know where she was going. He didn't want to end up having to take responsibility for her safety if he wasn't able to drop her off. That really was the last thing he needed.

Rose peered through the window. It wasn't what she'd imagined. From what her grandad had said, her gran's place was surrounded by trees, not modern brick-built houses like these, with their neat little postage stamp gardens. She remembered her dad talking about her gran's house once, though she hadn't understood at the time that it was just the other side of town. He'd made out it was practically crumbling to dust. It was supposed to be really old. This couldn't be the right place.

"Is this definitely Spinney Hills Rd?" she asked, though she knew that it was.

"Yes. This is the right road … Hang on a minute," the driver said, slowing down as another car pulled away from the kerb. "There it is! No wonder I didn't see it before!"

A hand-painted sign indicated, with a peeling arrow, that 'The Old Cottage' was down a narrow alleyway that was fenced off between two of the modern houses. Rose paid the driver and he handed her bags over from the boot.

"Are you going to be alright with those, me duck?" he asked.

"Yes … thank you," said Rose.

"Here's your receipt."

It was printed on card, with a picture of a convict behind bars. 'We can't get you out of jail,' read the slogan, 'but we can help keep you out. Don't drink and drive.'

"Put that somewhere safe, love," he said. "You never know when you'll need it."

He waited for her to do it, so she tucked it into her phone case to avoid seeming rude. It obviously mattered to him. When he pulled away, leaving her at the end of the alleyway, she regretted not accepting his help with the bags. Her rucksack was sticky on her back and her shoulder-bag kept slipping down her arm. She picked up the smaller suitcase in one hand and pulled the larger one on its casters with the other hand. It couldn't be all that far. She'd just have to manage.

The alleyway was squeezed in between two houses, narrowed by meter boxes and a telephone pole. It was a job getting through with all her bags. There wasn't any tarmac or gravel: just mud, baked hard. The big suitcase twisted and bounced over the ridges, and Rose's shoulder-bag slipped and tangled itself round her legs. The smaller suitcase was heavier than she'd realised and the handle bit into her fingers. She stopped to rearrange the bags and wipe her forehead. The alleyway stretched the whole depth of the houses and right down to the bottom of their gardens.

A little girl on a trampoline watched impassively through a trellis fence on Rose's right. She was licking an ice lolly and bouncing with a regular and joyless rhythm. Rose made a half-hearted attempt at a smile, but she didn't smile back. The girl's eyes followed her until the path turned to the left, stealing a few feet from the end of the opposite garden, and took her out of sight.

It was darker now, but no cooler. A tall and unlovely fence on Rose's left faced a high shaggy hedge, buzzing ominously, on her right. With the sound of traffic blocked by the buildings, the insects were the loudest noise she could hear. Between the fence and the hedge, the alleyway was blocked from view and cast into shadow, despite the brightness of the day. But it was a muggy, hot shadow without any movement of air to carry away the heat. The hedge was interrupted by a tall wooden gate with peeling black paint. It bore a hand-painted sign. 'The Old Cottage. Keep out.' Tempted though she was to do what she was told, just this once, Rose raised the stiff latch and pushed the gate open.

The house was beamed like a country pub, but it was dark brown and light brown rather than black and white. Patches of light brown had fallen off to reveal a muddier brown underneath. The house was lower down than the garden, and a track had been beaten from the gate down to the door. The garden rose up around the path on either side, so that the ground floor windows were only partly visible. The roof, whose overhang cast the upper floor into shadow, was an uneven mass of grey reeds, weighed down by moss and pulled from below by ivy. An upstairs window was boarded up, and broken glass glinted among the weeds beneath it. A red and black graffiti tag had been sprayed in several places on the walls and across the door. No-one had cared about this place in a very long time. If it weren't for the two old women hacking away at the garden, Rose would have believed it was uninhabited. She would have turned around and called a cab to take her home.

Chapter 48

The shorter of the two women stood with her legs spread wide, bending from the back to avoid risking her knees. Her bottom was facing Rose and she didn't look up when the gate opened or when Rose banged it shut. From the back, Rose could see her sunflower-patterned shorts and the varicose veins on the backs of her sturdy legs. Her navy-blue blouse was riding up at the waist and her armpits were ringed with sweat.

The taller one was kneeling on the ground, side-on. She was sharp-featured and bony and dressed all in brown, as drab almost as the house. Her ankle-length dress, made of rough material, was baggy and shapeless. A sacking bag was slung across her chest and her tired, grey hair was held back from her long, thin face in an untidy bun. She was chopping and pulling at the plants around her, apparently without distinction.

In the heat of the summer, the only plants thriving were weeds, and Rose assumed that's what they were removing at first, but when the taller woman stood up, she saw that there were plenty of weeds within reach that she hadn't touched. Instead, she gathered an armful of foliage from the ground and dumped it into a black sack. Two more sacks, already full, were baking in the early evening sun and bees fretted around the flowers, their buzzing amplified when they ventured inside. There was an overpowering smell, which Rose recognised it as lavender: old ladies' catnip, her mum called it. No matter how much they might like it, Rose couldn't imagine why the two old biddies would decide that it was important to harvest it so industriously on such a sweltering day.

The shorter one pressed her hand into the small of her back while she straightened it. Her hair was cut short with tufts of bright colours sprouting within it, apparently without care or planning. Streaks of pink, purple, blue, green and orange of different lengths and brightness mingled among the grey. She stretched and clenched her tired fingers.

"Hello," said Rose. "Am I in the right place?"

"And here she is," said the tall one, dryly.

Her face was deeply lined, and there was little indication that she'd ever used it for smiling. Her hair was dry and unkempt and badly in need of conditioning and a trim. Rose wondered why she didn't just cut it short if she couldn't be bothered looking after it.

"Well I wasn't expecting that!" exclaimed the short one, giggling.

Now that she'd turned around, Rose could see her face too. It was as wide as it was long, dominated by a broad smile and engraved with lines radiating out from her mouth and down-turned eyes. Her cheeks were reddened by the sun as well as by the exertion of gardening, and her multi-coloured hair was slicked around her wide cheeks and forehead. When blowing it out of the way didn't work, she pushed it back with both hands, smearing the garden's dust into the moistness of her forehead. She was beaming and Rose didn't understand the cause of her delight.

"There's some more just there," said the tall one, pointing to a clump of lavender.

"Whoops. I must have missed that," said the shorter one, waddling over, stiff-legged, to set back to work.

"We'll need it all, you know," said the taller one. "There won't be any second chances."

"I do know that," said the colourful one. I'm doing the best I can."

She mopped her face again and turned back to the plants.

"Not that I'd expect a thank you or anything," she muttered.

"Excuse me," said Rose, and they both turned to look at her. "I'm not sure if you've noticed that I'm here. I'm looking for Margaret Goodfellow."

"We know that!" bubbled the short one, tucking her blouse energetically into her shorts.

The tall one looked Rose up and down, apparently unimpressed with what she saw.

"Well, you're here now," she said, pressing her lips together when she'd finished using them for speaking.

"You did know I was coming, right?" asked Rose. "Only my grandad – Brian Murray, his name is – he said he'd phoned to sort it out. I'm quite happy to go back home if you don't want me here. It's not as if I wanted to come in the first place."

The tall one rolled her eyes.

"There's no need to make such a fuss," she said.

She turned away and tugged off her gardening gloves.

Rose was hot and tired, and she didn't actually want to be here at all. The mean-faced one was treating her like she was dirt, but at least the short one looked pleased to see her.

She was beaming and giggling like an idiot, her big red cheeks glowing.

"Are you my grandmother?" Rose asked her.

"Oh no no no," she giggled. "That's Margaret."

She pointed towards her companion, the gesture pulling her blouse loose from her shorts. Margaret raised her chin in curt acknowledgement and walked away, speaking over her shoulder.

"Maureen, would you show her to her room?"

"Do you want to lie down?" asked Maureen, flapping her blouse in sympathetic ventilation. "You look a bit pale. All this lavender is a bit much, isn't it? What must you think of us?"

Rose chose not to say, but she did follow her inside. The house was dark and damp-smelling, despite the heat.

"Don't worry about your bags," Maureen said. "We'll just leave them in the hall for now and bring them up later."

Rose left her suitcases and rucksack by the front-door but kept hold of her shoulder-bag. Shadows of pictures that no-one had loved enough to keep had left brighter spots on the stained and faded floral wallpaper in the hall and alongside the creaking bare wood staircase that Maureen was trudging up. Rose followed her, looking at the pictures that remained in case there were any embarrassing ones of her mum. When she put her weight on the third step, the board tipped up and scraped against her other ankle.

"Just press it back into place," said Maureen. "That's the ticket. You'll learn to avoid it soon enough. Just watch where I put my feet."

Rose followed carefully after her, avoiding each step that Maureen stretched to step over. They reached a landing and then, surprisingly given the size of the house from the outside, turned to ascend another staircase, this one narrower, steeper and less sturdy.

"Mind your head," Maureen warned, but not soon enough. "Bloody stupid place for a beam, if you ask me," she giggled, sheepishly. "Here you are, then."

Her ankle and head smarting, Rose looked around the attic-room. Beyond the smell of damp, she detected the odour of something long dead. It might still be here, desiccated in the thatch, or it might have been taken away after its juices had seeped into the fabric of the room. The floor was sloping and uneven and Rose made her way across it only cautiously.

There was no carpet, just a faded, dirty rug made of rags and disfigured by scorch-marks. An ugly, square, dark-wood cupboard filled one wall to about the height of Rose's shoulders, and the ceiling slumped down to within inches of its top. Even at its highest point, the ceiling was lower than in a normal room, and the beams made it lower still. A full-length speckled mirror on a stand should have reflected light from the window, but no brightness seemed to penetrate the gloom thrown by the overhanging thatch. Under the cobwebbed window was a lumpy bed, and on the bed was a stained and soft cardboard box, overflowing with tired Christmas decorations. There was no bedding. There was no sign that any effort had been made to make Rose feel comfortable or welcomed or cared about.

"Sorry it's a bit dusty in here," said Maureen. "I'll open the window, shall I?"

She strained against the handle.

"It ... just ... won't ... Ah, there we go."

A shower of paint flakes dropped off the frame and fell into the garden, joined by dusty fragments knocked off the low-hanging thatch. The handle hung uselessly in Maureen's hand. Where there should have been a catch there was only a scar in the wood.

"I'm not sure what to do with this now," she said. "Let me see ..."

She settled for propping the handle against the window-frame and gave it a little pat as she turned away.

Opening the window brought little relief. It was sweltering outside, and the atmosphere was heavy. The house was cooler, but the air in the attic was thick with the smell of damp straw, dust and decay. A pigeon fluttered on to the thatch, followed by two others, their calls sounding as loud as if they were inside the room. Their movements dislodged an old wasps' nest from the dark centre of the roof, and it crashed to the floor, shattering into papery fragments. Rose watched dust trickling down from the thatch as the pigeons flapped lazily away.

"Well," said Maureen, nudging what she could of the wasps' nest through the door with her foot. "I'll leave you in peace."

She bustled out of the room and Rose overheard her conversation on the way down the stairs.

"Ooh, that's nice of you, Margaret."

"You take it," said Rose's gran.

"I've got my hands full with this," said Maureen. "Besides, don't you think it'd be better if you did?"

Chapter 49

With a sigh, Rose's gran came through the door backwards carrying two glasses and a plate of biscuits on a tray stained with brown circles. Rose was relieved to see that she was trying, if only belatedly, to make an effort for her long-lost granddaughter. She knew that old people weren't always very good at expressing their emotions because they'd been brought up to be repressed, so she was willing to give her gran the benefit of the doubt if it seemed worth it.

Stooping to avoid the beams, her gran balanced the tray precariously on top of the cupboard but, instead of passing a glass to Rose, she pretended to trip, and deliberately drenched her with the sticky lukewarm liquid.

"Oh dear," she said, in an indifferent tone.

"What the hell?" said Rose.

"There's no need for language," said her gran. "I suppose you'd better take your wet things off now and put this on."

She took a piece of material from over her arm and threw it on to the bed. It was a dress: long, shapeless, and apparently made from a sack, like the one she was wearing herself.

"What is this, a cult?" asked Rose.

"Don't be ridiculous. It's a dress."

"There's really no need," said Rose. "I brought my own clothes with me."

"Put it on," said her gran.

"I don't want to."

"I didn't ask if you wanted to," her gran snapped, then paused and tried a softer approach. "I'm sure your mother must have told you to behave yourself while you're here, and that means doing what you're told. If you don't mind."

Rose shrugged and muttered 'whatever'. She'd go down for her own clothes in a minute. There was no way she was putting that thing on.

"Give me your wet things," said her gran.

"It's fine," said Rose, feeling increasingly uncomfortable. "I was thinking I'd just give them a quick rinse. They'll dry off quickly enough."

"I'd really rather you gave them to me," said her gran.

She put out her hand, but Rose didn't move.

"Come along now," she said.

Rose wriggled out of her wet clothes and handed them over, covering herself self-consciously with her arms. Her gran rolled her eyes.

"Put it on then."

Rose pulled the sack-dress over her head. A quick look in the mottled mirror confirmed that she looked ridiculous. It was itchy against her bare and sticky skin. The sleeves hung loosely from her shoulders, and the whole weight of the heavy dress dragged backwards on the neck. There was a hood, she realised, that was pulling it down. All she needed was a cushion and a bit of rope round her waist and she'd pass for Friar Tuck. She could already feel the heat gathering beneath her skirt.

"Are you having a fancy-dress party, or something?" she asked.

"What on earth are you talking about?"

"Never mind," said Rose.

"That's much more practical," her gran said, leaving the door slightly ajar. "I'll find you a belt later."

Rose pushed the door to with her foot, muttering, "I wonder why we lost touch", but before it was quite closed, it opened again, and her gran threw a grubby looking quilt and pillow towards the bed. The pillow rattled against the box of Christmas decorations, and the quilt slithered to the floor. Rose heard Maureen making her heavy way downstairs.

"That'll do for now," said her gran. "Get some rest."

She took the tray, leaving the second glass of tepid home-made lemonade and the plate of biscuits where they were. Rose toyed with the idea of a hunger strike but decided it would be a pointless gesture if nobody even cared. The lemonade wasn't as unpleasant as she'd expected, and the biscuits were surprisingly good.

She opened the door and crept down to the landing to peer into the hall. Her bags weren't where she'd left them at the foot of the stairs. On a normal day, she'd have crashed down shouting until she got them back, but she wasn't sure whether normal was a thing around here. Throwing a strop might make things worse and put them on their guard, which was the last thing she needed. The first chance she got, she was going to grab her bags, put some decent clothes on, and be off. Sofa-surfing for a couple of weeks would be better than staying here. Her mum would understand once she'd had a chance to explain. She was sure of it.

She checked her phone, but the signal was weak. When she tried her grandad's number, the call was disconnected before he answered. It was probably better this way, she thought. She was rubbish at lying anyway, so she'd just send him a message instead. She didn't want him worrying about her unnecessarily. He had enough on his plate. She'd call him properly as soon as she'd found somewhere to stay.

Well I got here in the end! Thanks for everything today. You looked really tired. I hope you're ok.

You're probably resting now so I'll ring tomorrow. If you call me, use this number. Gran's landline is out of order. Rose xx

If he didn't call the landline, it was possible she'd be able to let him know she was ok before he found out from her gran that she was missing. After her grandad, she messaged her mum, Chlo and Jess together, and her dad:

I'm here. Everything's fine and there's nothing to worry about. Have you had your operation? How RU? xxx

OMG! Talk about shitholes! Can I stay at either of yours tonight? GGF x

Hey. You already know that mum's in hospital and I'm at my gran's. It's bare rank. Can I come to you instead? I won't get in your way. Rx

While she waited for the replies to come in, Rose had a poke around. She rooted listlessly through the Christmas decorations and peered into the mirror, barely able to make out her own features in the gloom.

Close up, she saw that the cupboard was decorated with carvings of people, plants and animals. There was a swirly knot made of dragons or snakes. It was kind of Celtic looking, and she'd be interested in it if she wasn't so hot and angry. She took a photo in case she felt like looking at it later, when she was safely out of here.

She gave the cupboard door a half-hearted tug. It didn't open and she decided against trying harder. It might be noisy, and she didn't have a good reason for prying. There was unlikely to be anything interesting inside anyway. On top of the cupboard was a calendar, showing a faded view of a fat man prancing along a beach and the words, 'Skegness is so bracing'. Underneath the picture was a dusty Perspex rack of tiny cards with days, numbers and months on. They were supposed to be changed every day, but when she picked it up, she discovered that they'd been glued in place on today's date. It was weird, but there wasn't much about her gran's house that wasn't, so she shrugged and took another photo to show to Chlo and Jess later, wiping the dust off her screen against her dress. She turned away and picked up the quilt to put it back on the bed. It slipped straight back to the floor, as if reluctant to contribute to her comfort in any way.

Maureen and her gran were working away in the garden again. Because it was raised above the level of the ground floor, they weren't all that much lower than Rose was, and their voices carried clearly in the still air. Rose peered through the window, snapping a few more photos while she watched them. The girls would never believe her otherwise.

Maureen was red and sweating. Hard physical labour on such a hot day couldn't possibly be a good idea at her age and in her condition.

"I'm sure you told me a different name," she panted, wiping her face.

"There may have been some confusion."

"Margaret Goodfellow! Even you couldn't forget the name of your own granddaughter. How could you not have known it was her, for goodness sake?"

"Alright, alright," said her gran. "I knew. Are you happy now?"

"Why on earth didn't you keep in touch with them? Why didn't you tell me?"

"Because of this, Maureen. The third degree. Now, are we going to do this today, or not?"

Maureen sighed.

"It wouldn't hurt you to make a bit of an effort with her, you know."

She waited for a response that didn't come.

"Would it?" she asked.

Again, there was no answer. Maureen shook her head with a noisy sigh and bent back over the lavender.

Rose put the box of decorations on the floor and flapped the quilt in the air, to remove any spiders that might be lurking. She spread it over the bed and lay on top of it. It smelt musty, but that was one of the least bad smells this house had to offer. She wasn't going to be able to make her escape until they came in from the garden, so she might as well rest. There was nothing else to do.

Rose understood perfectly well now why her mum hadn't wanted to keep in touch. Her gran was cold and mean and really weird. It made complete sense that they'd become part of her dad's family instead. What didn't make sense was that her mum had sent her here now, unless she was on some drug or other that was messing with her head. That was the only rational explanation Rose could come up with. She was sure her mum would see things differently if she was in her right mind. Once Rose had a chance to explain how hideous it had all been, her mum would be glad she'd found an alternative.

Her grandad had said her gran was looking forward to meeting her. He'd said she sounded nice and it wasn't like him to tell lies. He'd probably been giving her the benefit of the doubt. He always did try to think well of people. But he'd be on Rose's side too, when she'd had a chance to explain it to him properly. There was no way her gran wanted her here. She and her sweaty friend obviously had more important things to do anyway. Rose was going to have to take responsibility for herself.

She plugged her charger into a socket and snatched her hand back from the electric shock. She flicked the switch off with a biro from her shoulder-bag, afraid to touch it again, but worried about starting a fire if she left it plugged in. She was probably best off keeping her phone to hand in any case. They'd already taken the rest of her bags off her, after all. If she couldn't re-charge before she left, she'd need to save what charge she had for later. She touched the plug gingerly with the tips of her fingers before pulling it out again. This place was a death-trap.

The Book of the Terms of Defeat
Chapter 50

The Queen sends away her courtiers and servants, growing tired of their expectations and dissatisfied with their advice. She transforms her throne-room into a lakeside beach and herself into a tanned and sun-bleached young woman in cut-off shorts and flipflops. She lies in a hammock under the shade of the trees, enjoying the distractions of physical form. When one is hungry, one eats, for example. It's a simple equation for pleasure.

"I'm so tired of it all," she says aloud. "I'm just so bored of the court."

"I could help you with that," says Lord Carrick, stepping out from among the trees. "Do you want to concede?"

She shades her eyes from the sunlight that dazzles around him.

"Oh, you're here, are you?" she asks.

He's bronzed too, his stubble sun-kissed. His hair is fair and, where it hangs below his faded sunhat, it's being ruffled by a light breeze. He wears pale-coloured shorts, frayed at the legs, and a flower-patterned shirt hangs loose, held together by two buttons half-way up. He smiles a smile that curls her toes with pleasure: he has shaped himself to fit the needs and desires of her physical form.

"It is a wretched place by all accounts," he says, handing her an opened beer-bottle.

He leans against the tree at her head to drink from his own. It unsettles her that she can't see him, which is surely his intention.

"It is," she says. "And they're wretched people. Nasty, brutish and short."

She sits up, putting her feet on the floor, and Lord Carrick leans over to clink his bottle against hers.

"I had no idea they were so tiresome," he says.

"You've been there then?" she asks.

"Oh yes," says Lord Carrick, though he made his challenge after only a few brief visits and hasn't been to the human world since it began.

"They're quite impossible," says the Queen, tipping her head back to drink.

"Entirely," says Lord Carrick, carefully mirroring her actions.

"They obey no orders," she continues. "They have no respect. They're selfish and rude."

He puts out his hand to help her stand as he eggs her on.

"They think themselves intelligent," he says, "but they behave entirely without reason."

"They do," she agrees. "One might begin to wonder if your foolish quest were even possible."

"Indeed, one might," nods Lord Carrick. "Does your majesty consider conceding at all?"

"I do not."

She stands, drawing herself up to her full height.

"I shall continue this contest until you're defeated," she says.

They walk to the water's edge and kick off their sandals to let the waves lap around their feet. The lake is large enough to seem a sea, with sanded beaches fringing its edges.

"How will you know?" he asks, his voice even and gentle.

"What do you mean?"

"It seems to me that, in the excitement of the challenge, the Lord Herald focuses on what form victory takes. Unfortunately, he neglects to set down the terms of defeat."

The ancient lore observes that the Faerie don't negotiate. They struggle to distinguish negotiation from bartering, begging or invoicing, all of which are unutterably vulgar. Eradicating ambiguity and foreseeing loopholes are similarly unseemly, though no less essential for that. To avoid the appearance of incivility, the terms of a challenge are, by convention, set down rather than agreed, allowing for a certain amount of seemly discussion about how they should be expressed, which is clearly distinct from the impropriety of quibbling about what they should be. Given the limitations of Faerie memory, the accuracy of the written record is crucial. An impartial observer might well comment that, in practice, discussions about how something is written inevitably shades into negotiation about what is agreed, but there are no impartial observers at court, so this is rarely a problem.

The Queen presses her lips together, understanding that this omission wasn't accidental. Neither it is a coincidence that Lord Carrick is here now, when she's losing hope in her quest and her advisors are not to hand. She has no confidence in the Lady Maven's loyalty, of course, but it shakes her to realise that the Lord Herald also advises her badly. If he were present, he would already be banished, but as she reflects, she understands that this would serve Lord Carrick's purpose well. For now, she will deal with Lord Carrick without advisors: she has time-knowledge of her own now to ensure he won't best her. Once that's done, she can consider the Lord Herald's fate at her leisure.

"As Queen, I alone shall determine if I'm defeated in this challenge," she says.

He bows.

"As befits your gracious majesty. And my defeat?"

She hesitates, knowing he seeks to trick her.

"What would you suggest?" she asks.

"It would be impertinent of me to suggest anything to your gracious majesty," he says, taking another swig of beer. "But since you ask, there are a range of alternatives. I might be allowed to determine my own defeat, for example, or that power might be yours alone. Or my defeat might be subject to the clamour of the court or to a pre-agreed limit of some kind."

The Queen doesn't deign to respond. At least, that's how she hopes it seems. In reality, she dares not speak. He lists the alternatives rapidly to confuse her and she fears falling

211

into his trap unawares. She wishes the Lord Herald were with her now but can't think how to call him without losing face. While she hesitates, Lord Carrick selects flat stones from the beach and skims them across the surface of the lake, which is flat and smooth beyond its fringe of waves.

"Of course, your majesty knows better than I whether the quest can ever be completed," he says.

She nods. He's right about that. With all the time she's spent in human form, she knows more about them than anyone else. Since she hasn't been able to complete the challenge, there's no reason to assume that it can ever be achieved. In this instance, she does know better than the Lord Herald and the Lady Maven. She feels confident, once again, that she can reason every bit as well as her advisors these days.

Chapter 51

If the Lord Herald were so very wise, the problem that Lord Carrick raises – the failure to set down their terms of defeat – would not have arisen in the first place. On this basis, the Queen decides to make her own decision for a change. She realises, of course, that Lord Carrick will attempt to sneak in a choice he wants her to select, but all she need do is identify and avoid it.

"Talk me through the alternatives again," she says.

They stand in the lakeside shallows, the waves lapping around their ankles. The longer they remain here, the deeper their feet sink into the sand. Naturally, they see this as a competition, though neither admits their determination to outlast the other. The one who remains steady when the other stumbles will consider themselves the victor. If it's Lord Carrick, he'll keep his triumph to himself. The Queen, of course, won't.

"That I determine my own defeat…" says Lord Carrick, pressing down the index finger of his left hand with the neck of the beer-bottle he still holds in his right.

This, she is sure, she cannot allow. Clearly Lord Carrick will never declare himself defeated and it would diminish her power to give him the right to do so. A wave reaches behind them almost to the sandals they left by the water's edge. The tide is coming in.

He continues, pressing down his middle finger.

"That you alone determine my defeat …"

Tempting though it is, she knows this to be an unwise choice. It would give her the power at any moment to declare him the loser and cast him from the court, but she can cast him from court already and nullify the challenge, so she wins nothing by choosing this option. If her decision were unpopular, it would embolden other challengers to follow thick and fast, and the temptation of his destruction might blind her to these dangers in the heat of the moment.

"That would be somewhat mean-spirited," she says, and he raises his bottle in a silent toast to the nobility of her self-sacrifice.

Lord Carrick swallows his frustration at her failure to leap at a choice that appears so obviously in her favour. His plan, necessarily without delay, was to reveal these unbalanced terms to a court which is already bad-tempered and bored. The court would undoubtedly prefer a dashing and debonair challenger to an absent and unsporting Queen, and he's confident he could generate enough bold excitement to obliterate any support the Lady Maven might have secured in the meantime. Technically, he would ascend to the throne still bound by the terms of the challenge, but with the commencement loophole still in play, that needn't cause him any real trouble. In time, the court could be induced to believe that his lack of failure was the same as success, and the unfulfilled challenge would have provided on-going protection from his own future challengers.

The waves are now reaching her calves and the Queen feels the sand trickling away beneath her feet. She digs in with her toes, determined to keep her footing.

"Well?" says the Queen. "Is this all there is?"

"Not at all," he says, pressing down his ring finger. "We might agree that my defeat is determined by the clamour of the court ..."

Absolutely not, the Queen tells herself. Once given the right to condemn him, the court will want also the power to acclaim his victory. In any case, no matter how incontrovertible his failure, she can't rely on the court to denounce him. They're as likely to celebrate his daring or an opportune witticism as to damn his failure, foolish sprites that they are. A wave splashes above her knees, dampening the royal shorts.

"These cannot be all," says the Queen.

"No indeed," says Lord Carrick, pressing down his little finger. "We might also agree some pre-determined limit."

"Explain," says the Queen.

"Well, humans frequently choose a period of time during which a challenge must be completed. Indeed, some of their challenges are entirely focussed on the matter of time."

"How so?" asks the Queen.

"They often challenge one another to traverse an agreed distance by an agreed method of locomotion in the shortest time," he says. "Or to perform some other pointless feat most quickly."

"How peculiar," says the Queen. "And this amuses them?"

"I believe so," says Lord Carrick. "But now I come to think of it, although those of us who have dwelt among them might understand what that entailed, we could hardly expect the rest of the court to grasp it."

He chuckles indulgently. He's right. She knows he's right, and she feels sure his preferred outcome is approaching. Droplets from the next wave splash her chest, sticking her clothes to her torso. A few yards out, the lake remains calm and smooth.

"So, what do you suggest?" she asks, her voice a little louder now.

"One might perhaps set a limit on the number of attempts that might be made," he shouts back, above the roar of the pounding waves and the clatter and hiss of their retreat.

The Queen considers this. Having made innumerable attempts to complete the challenge, she begins to suspect that she's made no progress at all. If the number of attempts had been limited, she would already have been forced to concede defeat. The idea of applying this constraint to Lord Carrick so late in the game is appealing, but if the number of attempts is restricted, he'll have to be more cautious. As he approaches his final chance, he'll become increasingly unwilling to fritter it on uncertainty. On reflection, this doesn't seem too bad. She likes the idea of him suffering from indecision, knowing his chances are running out. Her court will have no patience with a challenger who hesitates. There's no glory in waiting until one is sure to succeed.

Chapter 52

Each wave threatens the Queen's balance now. Under cover of their assault, she moves her feet to brace herself against them. She turns her face sideways to avoid the impact.

"How many attempts have you made?" she shouts, in a gap between waves.

"So far, your majesty, none," Lord Carrick concedes.

"None?"

She doesn't trouble to contain her laughter. While she's been so busy, he's done nothing at all. He bows his head, acknowledging her disdain.

"I hear, your majesty, that you're more active."

A wave slaps into his face and he wipes his eyes, spluttering. The Queen smiles.

"That may be so, but I'm interested to know which of my courtiers keeps you so well informed."

He shakes his head, scattering droplets in every direction.

"I'm sure you understand, your majesty, that I can't risk having so powerful an enemy among your closest advisors."

"Tell me at once," she says. "I demand to know."

"Unfortunately, your majesty might hesitate to believe that, notwithstanding her proximity to your royal person, she could plot against you so treacherously."

The Queen is pleased that she sees through his evasions. Feeling her pleasure and the anger with Lady Maven that follows, Lord Carrick is content to change the subject.

"Would you consider three attempts a proper number?" he asks.

Three is traditional in such matters and considerably fewer than the attempts she's already made herself. Lord Carrick seems confident he'll succeed. Arrogant, even.

"One," she says. "To avoid boring my devoted subjects, you may make one attempt. You may bring one human back to my court and if they cannot share their suffering, you fail, and I triumph."

"But your majesty …" he protests.

"I have spoken."

She gestures him into silence, confident the upper hand is hers. The next wave knocks him off balance and, although he windmills his arms energetically, he topples with a satisfying wail. Smiling smugly, the Queen returns to the beach the better to observe his soggy emergence, and the lake falls glassily still.

She understands that even if she's victorious in their game, her position can still be undermined by it. If there's any sense that she hasn't won well, the next challenger will step forward quickly and offer less favourable terms. A court without Carrick is a pleasurable dream, but she wouldn't be allowed to enjoy it uninterrupted. On the other hand, as long as they are engaged in this quest, there can be no other challengers for her crown. The continuation of their game perpetuates the moment they're in and, she reflects, this moment is not so bad.

Lord Carrick wades grumpily back to dry land. The Queen slips her feet into her dry flipflops. His sandals are embedded in damp sand and he complains loudly about the discomfort to his toes. The Queen can barely contain her delight at his failure and fury and dismisses him at once so she can recount her triumph to the Lord Herald.

As he slips back into the shadows, Lord Carrick is also smiling. He has no doubt of his own ultimate victory. If needs be, he can spend centuries in the human world and return the moment after he left the Faerie court. He can take all the time he needs in that world in the blink of an eye. But the Queen's position is more precarious than she imagines, and that is a thought that troubles him. If she's overthrown before he claims his victory, he may be forced to complete the challenge without any hope of his prize. He needs this Queen to remain on her throne until he's ready to depose her, and their agreed terms of defeat should reassure the Queen that she can safely remain at court, thus frustrating the Lady Maven's ambitions. This alone, he reflects, justifies his wisdom in delaying the commencement of his own quest. How clever it was of him to foresee all this.

The Book of Curious Discoveries
Chapter 53

Rose opened her eyes, not sure whether she'd slept or not. The attic-room seemed darker and cooler, but the air was still close. She could hear the pigeons squabbling on the thatch and a lawn-sprayer was on somewhere nearby, the sound of the droplets lazily swishing from side to side, though a storm still felt imminent. Realising that she couldn't hear her gran and Maureen outside, Rose sat up quickly. This might be her chance to sneak away before dark.

When she stood up, the floorboards creaked, and she remembered the loose board on the stairs. Getting out of the house quietly was going to be a challenge. She wondered if going out the window might be an option. It was big enough and although she was on the second floor, it wasn't all that far to the ground. She peered out. To land on the raised garden, she'd have to clear the trench around the house, and the window was too small to do that in a single bound. The idea of hanging outside the window to make the jump didn't appeal at all. She wasn't sure she could rely on the window-frame to hold her weight. Perhaps, she could tear up sheets for a rope, like they did in films. Climbing out would be quieter than jumping too. There weren't any sheets on the bed, but there might be some in the cupboard.

She was on her way across the room when she heard a noise coming from inside the cupboard: a scrabbling sound, like a mouse, maybe, or a rat. The house was probably crawling with vermin, she realised. Sighing, she went over to listen at the door, putting her hand on the handle for balance. Without warning, it burst open, and Rose backed away. From inside the cupboard, came a girl. She was skinny, but not in a good way. Her broad forehead was framed by long, dark hair that needed washing and combing and then probably washing and combing several times more before any self-respecting hairdresser would be willing to try repairing the mess of split ends and the too-short, uneven fringe. She was wearing chocolate-brown flared trousers and a paisley-patterned smock top, and when she straightened up, her bony ankles and wrists protruded grubbily in all directions.

"Hello Rose," she said. "I'm Tracy."

Rose's expression made her laugh. Her pointed little chin lifted in an impish, open smile.

"You're wondering what's going on, aren't you?"

"Well ... yes," said Rose.

"Come with me, and I'll show you."

She went back inside the cupboard, leaving Rose reeling in confusion. No-one had told her there was another girl, of about her own age, in the house. She couldn't understand why her gran and Maureen wouldn't have mentioned it. Perhaps they didn't know Tracy was here, but in that case, how could she have known Rose's name? Had she hidden in the cupboard while Rose was asleep, or had she been there all along? If she'd been there all along, could she have overheard Maureen or her gran using Rose's name? Rose wasn't even sure if they had.

Tracy pushed the swinging cupboard door open with her foot. She was sitting inside, frowning.

"Did they tell you not to?" she asked.

"Who? Those two? Please!"

Tracy shrugged, and gave a mischievous smile. "Well, if you're not allowed ..."

"As if!"

"I dare you!" said Tracy, her green eyes glinting.

"Whatever!" said Rose. "Shove up and make room."

Chapter 54

"Where are you?" asked Rose.

It was dark in the cupboard and she felt around cautiously with her fingertips at first. She held her arms outstretched to touch the wood on either side and moved them back and forth. It didn't make sense, but there wasn't any doubt about it. Tracy wasn't in there. There must be a trick of some kind – a false back or something – and Rose didn't feel like being messed around after the day she'd had. She pushed against what she thought was the door, but there was no give. She turned and tried again, then pushed at another side, beginning to feel panicky, but knowing that panicking wasn't going to help. She'd become disoriented, that was all. She forced herself to take deep breaths and worked her way around the sides of the cupboard, counting aloud before making the next quarter turn.

When she got to 'four' and the door still didn't open, there was only panic left. Rose was trapped. Her sack-dress was tangled round her legs and pulling on her throat. She couldn't breathe. It was hot and stuffy and dark, and she was going to suffocate. They'd think she'd run away, and it would be years before anyone found her rotted corpse, like in the stories. They wouldn't even notice the smell in their stupid stinky house.

She tried one final push with her back against one of the longer edges, bracing her feet against the side in front of her. The door burst open and she fell backwards into the room, to find Tracy, sitting on the bed, reading. She put the book down and pulled her knees up tight to her chest, watching Rose cautiously.

She was wearing different clothes now: a dress covered in a pink and purple pattern of tiny flowers and swirling leaves. The waist was high, and the skirt was long and full, pleated with tiers and trimmings of mismatched lace. Over the dress was a thick bottle-green cardigan several sizes too large. Rose wondered when Tracy had had time to change and why she needed a cardigan in the middle of summer. As if in answer, wind rattled bare branches against the window, and Rose shivered. That made no sense, so she focused on what she did understand.

"Ha, bloody, ha," she said. "Very funny."

"What are you on about?" asked Tracy.

"Shutting me in the cupboard. Tremendously witty. You must be enormously proud."

"What are you talking about?" asked Tracy, sitting on the bed and twiddling at her necklace. "Who the hell are you?"

"So now you're pretending you've never seen me before."

"I have never seen you before," said Tracy.

"What kind of game is this?" asked Rose.

"I'm not playing a game," said Tracy. "I'm reading a book. See."

She held it up to demonstrate that she was speaking the truth.

"Why don't you shut up and tell me what's going on?" asked Rose.

Tracy laughed nervously. "Which?"

"Which what?"

"Do you want me to shut up or to tell you what's going on?"

"What's going on?" asked Rose. "What are you playing at?"

"I don't know what you mean."

"For goodness sake!" Rose took a deep breath to hold back her frustration. "Why did you lock me in?"

"In where?" asked Tracy.

Rose gestured furiously.

"In the cupboard?" asked Tracy. "I didn't!"

"Of course, you did. Do you think I shut myself in there?"

"I think I'd know if I'd done it," said Tracy.

"You think I wouldn't know if I had?"

"And yet there you were, shut in the cupboard."

"What's that supposed to mean?" Rose snapped.

"Well, you're the one who was stupid enough to get stuck in a cupboard," said Tracy, her knees still drawn protectively to her chest. "How about if I ask you some questions? What with you being in my house and everything."

"You might as well," said Rose. "I'm not getting any sense out of you."

"Well, let's start with what the hell are you doing in my room?" asked Tracy.

"What do you mean your room?"

Tracy sighed and answered with elaborate patience.

"A room is part of a building, usually with four walls, a floor, ceiling, door and windows. These buildings are often called houses. This is a room. It is my room. In my house. It's up to me who's allowed in it. I don't know you. I didn't invite you and you shouldn't be here. Why are you in my room?"

She gesticulated sarcastically as she spoke, and her necklace caught the light. The pendant was a roughly cut crystal.

Rose leant forward to see it better. It looked a lot like her mum's.

"Where did you get that from?" she asked.

"What?" asked Tracy, forgetting for the moment that she was the one asking the questions.

"The crystal," said Rose.

"It was a present." Tracy's tone was defensive now.

"I don't believe you." Rose put out her hand. "Give it back."

"Get lost. It's mine. And stop trying to change the subject. Who the hell *are* you? And what are you doing in my house?"

They glared at each other.

"Give … it … back!" ordered Rose.

"N O spells no," said Tracy. "It's not yours."

"Well it's certainly not yours. Give it here."

Rose made a lunge, but Tracy was too quick for her. She jumped off the bed to the other side of the room, ducking to avoid the ceiling beams.

"If you don't tell me who you are right now," she said. "I'm going to phone the police."

Tracy was bluffing. They didn't have a phone and she was alone in the house, but it didn't occur to Rose to challenge her. The calendar on the cupboard caught her eye and she went over to examine it. It said Friday, December 22, 1978.

"How did you change the date?" Rose asked.

Tracy stuck her tongue behind her lower lip. "Dur! The bits of card move."

"But they're glued down."

"What?"

"They're glued together," said Rose, picking it up. "You can't change the date."

She shook it, scattering small pieces of card across the carpet.

"Oh, well done!" said Tracy. "What did you do that for?"

She collected the cards together, keeping a careful eye on Rose, who was rubbing her thumb and forefinger and looking confused. She held up the calendar for closer inspection and ran her finger across the top of the cupboard, checking for dust. She looked around the room, gradually taking it in. Tracy took the calendar from her while she was distracted and returned it to the top of the cupboard.

The room looked different. It looked brighter even, though the day was darker. The windows were cleaner, but it was more than that. It looked newer. Less old, at any rate. There were posters that hadn't been on the wall before, and the walls looked less dingy: the paint was whiter, fresher. Rose checked, but it wasn't wet.

She frowned, looking at the posters. She'd seen the remake of Starsky and Hutch, so she knew who they were, but this poster was for the original. The others showed singers with fluffy hair and dreamy eyes and there was a band as well, in tight-fitting tartan. It all seemed to fit with Tracy's clothes and hair and the date on the calendar. Someone had gone to a lot of trouble to make it look like it was 1978.

"Could this be a reality show?" she asked, not expecting a reply.

She knocked on the wall to see if it was a stage set. You could change scenery quickly if there were enough people to move it. A reality show that could put together a set this convincing would have plenty of people involved. If Tracy's costume was Velcroed at the back, she could have put it on over her other clothes, so that wouldn't have taken long either, and the baggy cardigan would hide the extra bulk. Rose looked around for more evidence. The room would be smaller if this was a set, or maybe bigger if the room she'd seen before was the set. It might have been the other set that was moveable. Or maybe the two rooms would be same size if they'd just replaced one set of scenery with another. There were too many possibilities and she wasn't sure what size it had been to start with, so thinking about it wasn't going to help her.

"Turn around," she said to Tracy.

"I'm not turning my back on you."

"Look, either you're messing with me, and there's hidden cameras filming this whole thing …"

Tracy's response seemed genuine. "Are you completely mad?"

"… or this cupboard is some kind of a portal."

"What?"

"You're going to make me say it out loud? Ok. Then I'd like to make it clear that I don't believe this cupboard is a portal for travelling in time. What I believe is that you've gone to a lot of trouble to mess with my head. And I really don't appreciate it."

Tracy's eyes and mouth opened wide.

"You're the sign!" she said.

"The what?" asked Rose.

She laughed and shook her head.

"Never mind."

The view from the window caught Rose's eye and she leant over the bed to look outside.

"Where've the houses gone?" Rose asked.

"What houses?"

"The other houses," said Rose. "The ones that are supposed to be out there."

"There aren't any – well, you can see some over that way if you lean out, but I wouldn't recommend it."

Rose was determined not to be made a fool of. She knew they edited these things to make them more entertaining and that meant, among other things, making people look more stupid.

"Ok. So, this is '1978'. Very good."

She made the inverted commas audible as well as visible so they couldn't make it seem like she'd fallen for it.

"Why don't you show me around a bit?" she asked, to call their bluff. "Shall we go and have a walk outside in '1978'?"

"Alright," said Tracy. "I suppose so, but I'm not going out with you dressed like that."

She reached into the cupboard and pulled out a brown corduroy dress.

"Here. Put this on," she said. "I never liked it much anyway."

The cupboard, Rose noticed, was now full of shelves and clothes.

"I know there's a false back," she said, for the benefit of the cameras. "Someone's put those things in there from the back while I wasn't looking. In fact, that's probably how you did it, isn't it? This isn't the same room at all."

She knelt to push at the back of the cupboard but couldn't make it move. Tracy rolled her eyes and held out the dress. Rose shrugged. It looked less scratchy than the sack dress she was wearing and going outside had to be the quickest way to prove this was all faked.

"I'm not getting changed with people watching," she said.

"There's only me here, and you needn't think I'm covering my eyes," said Tracy. "I'm not that stupid. You could be the Yorkshire Ripper, for all I know."

"Do I look like the bloody Yorkshire Ripper?"

"I don't know, do I? And anyway, you still haven't told me your name."

"Taylor," said Rose, watching for a flash of disbelief. "My name's Taylor Swift."

Tracy shrugged.

"Alright. Don't get your knickers in a twist. It's not my fault."

In the end, Rose stepped into the corduroy dress and pulled it up under cover of the sack she was already wearing. She looked out for cameras the whole time, but she was pretty sure they couldn't have seen anything.

"Would you look at that?" she said, standing in front of the mirror.

"Yep," said Tracy. "It's bad."

"No, I mean, even the mirror looks newer. I can't believe the attention to detail that's gone into this."

"This old thing?" said Tracy, peering at it in bemusement.

They stood side-by-side looking into the mirror. The corduroy dress was tight around Rose's chest, and the skirt started practically under her armpits. The sleeves were puffed out at the shoulder and elasticated at the wrist with purple trimmings. Her legs stuck out at the bottom like skinny sticks.

"You look worse in that than I do!" said Tracy, not bothering to hide her delight. "Here." She handed over a pair of green woolly tights.

"Seriously?"

"Unless you want the wind whistling round where the sun don't shine."

Rose put them on and pulled them up, not forgetting the cameras.

"Shall we go then?" asked Tracy.

Chapter 55

They went down two flights of stairs and into the hall. While Rose tried to adjust her sagging tights without exposing herself, Tracy compared their feet and nudged a pair of scuffed brown lace-ups towards her.

"We won't go far," she said. "There's not much to see."

She zipped up a tight-fitting waist-length anorak, light blue with a broad dark-blue stripe half-way up. It was shorter than her dress and cardigan, and none of the colours matched. She handed Rose an old green coat with big plastic buttons.

"It's my Mum's," she said. "You'd better not get it dirty."

As Rose buttoned it up, she looked around the hall. The floral wallpaper was faded, but not as grubby as it had been. It seemed as if some of the shadows on the paper in her gran's hall were covered up by pictures of corresponding sizes and shapes, though she couldn't be sure. Someone really had gone to a lot of trouble to make this convincing and she couldn't imagine why they'd have bothered.

In a sudden flash of insight, she realised that her mum and her grandad must have been in on this too. No-one would've gone to all this trouble if they hadn't known she was coming. This would've taken weeks to set up. The old woman probably wasn't even her real gran. If that was how it was, that must mean her mum wasn't actually ill, and the thought lifted her spirits.

Tracy was absolutely right, in one sense: there wasn't much to see. The door opened on to the same trench, though a sloping path made of broken concrete slabs now led up to an area of scrubby grass and weeds that could be the same garden for all Rose could tell. Past it, there were leafless trees, followed by back walls. They walked through an alleyway on to a street, and a few streets further on, there were some shops.

"It's Sunday, so nothing's open", said Tracy, as if none of it was at all out of the ordinary.

Tracy was a good actor and it put Rose on edge. The streets were as convincing as a film set and she couldn't make sense of it. She was braced for the big reveal, where someone would appear with a huge smile and a microphone and ask how she felt. But she couldn't understand how they'd done it. There'd been houses and gardens and fences all around her gran's house, and they weren't there anymore. How was that possible? Rose looked around her as they emerged from the trees. There were people around too, and the clothes and the haircuts and the cars, all just looked right, but they would, wouldn't they? If you were going to do this, you'd do it well.

She looked around for cameras attached to lampposts or buildings but couldn't see any. They must be well hidden. The cars were really smelly, which was a nice touch. There weren't very many of them, and Rose wondered if that was because of health and safety – air-pollution and all that – or whether it was just to keep down costs. But even so, this was an extraordinary amount of effort for a prank they'd only be able to stretch to a few minutes of telly. She glanced at the trees and the sky, forgetting to appear unimpressed. They'd changed the weather, the season even. How had they done that?

Down the hill on the main road, a cream-coloured bus went past, with an open door at the back. It moved away just as a passenger reached the stop, and he ran after it, grabbed hold of the pole and jumped on. Rose couldn't believe they'd allow that, even in a reconstruction. He must be a stuntman. The windows upstairs were covered with condensation, but a waft of cigarette smoke mingled with the exhaust fumes as it drove past.

There were children in front gardens, playing on the pavement and spilling over into the road. Quite little kids too, with no adults keeping an eye on them. A gang of girls about her own age shouted as they went past.

"Hey, Oddfellow, did you find your midget friend in a jumble sale?"

"Just ignore them," Tracy hissed. "You'll only make it worse."

The girls followed them part of the way, shouting and hooting, until they were distracted by a little boy with an Afro and a packet of sweets going in the opposite direction. Rose listened to their conversation as it faded into the distance.

"Oi, give us a Rolo."

"We'll be your friends forever."

"She'll let you see her bra if you like."

"I bloody won't! That's disgusting."

"What was that about?" asked Rose. "Who were they?"

"Oh, just some girls from school," said Tracy.

"Not friends then?"

"No. Definitely not friends."

Rose felt sorry for her. She was obviously being bullied, and that might explain why she was so aggressive.

"Have you thought about talking to a teacher about it?" she asked, forgetting momentarily that none of this was real.

"About what?" asked Tracy.

"About being bullied, of course."

Tracy snorted, but didn't answer. They walked on in silence, turning by a school to go back up the hill. Rose was feeling stupid. If she wasn't careful, she'd get sucked into this whole thing.

"Watch where you're walking!" Tracy said, too late to be helpful.

"That's disgusting," said Rose, scraping the bottom of her shoe against the edge of the curb. "That's taking it too far."

"What are you on about?"

"Never mind," said Rose.

"Try and look where you're going," said Tracy. "If it's not too much trouble."

The next turn took them back into the wood, and Rose poked at the sole of her shoe with a twig.

"You need to get it all off," said Tracy. "We'll never get rid of the smell if you tread it in with you."

She waited while Rose wiped her shoe on some ferns. She seemed to be building up to something.

"Can I come with you?" she asked, with uncharacteristic enthusiasm. "Please."

"Where?" asked Rose.

"In the cupboard, of course. For the time travel."

Perhaps this was the pay-off moment. They'd go back into the cupboard and end up on stage in a theatre full of people. Rose's mum and her grandad would be in the audience. Probably her dad too. She hoped it wasn't Michael McIntyre. She didn't want to have to sing. Derren Brown would make more sense: he could have hypnotised her and taken her somewhere else entirely.

"Yeah, sure," she said.

Tracy grinned. "Brilliant."

"I haven't forgotten that you've been in it already," said Rose, not wanting to look gullible.

"No. Well, yeah, all the time when I was little, but not since it came over all Narnia."

"No, that's not right," said Rose, pleased at catching her out. "You came to 'my time' to get me, remember? That's why I went into the cupboard in the first place."

"I've never been anywhere in that cupboard. I swear it!"

"Yeah. Whatever," said Rose.

"Cross my heart and hope to die," said Tracy.

It was unnerving that she sounded entirely genuine, and it made Rose doubt her own understanding.

"So, let me get this straight. You're saying you didn't come out of that cupboard and dare me to get in it?"

"Swear to God," insisted Tracy. "I can see why you were so mardy now, if you thought I was messing you around."

"Me mardy? You're unbelievable, you are."

They carried on through the wood without talking. Tracy was trying to find a way to understand what had happened, but Rose was walking faster, just wanting to get it over with.

"Ok, hold on," said Tracy, coming to a halt. "Maybe I haven't done that yet – maybe that's still in the future for me."

"Ok," said Rose. "Whatever. Very clever."

"It's got to be good in a way, hasn't it?"

"How do you mean?" asked Rose.

"Well, if I, in the future, think you ought to go into the cupboard, that must prove that nothing bad happens, mustn't it?" said Tracy.

"Unless you needed me to 'rescue' you or something," said Rose, adding the inverted commas with her fingers as an afterthought.

She didn't believe it, of course, but it was difficult not to get caught up in the narrative. Perhaps it was one of those immersive experience things, like an escape room. She was still expecting a big reveal, but she didn't mind engaging with the story if it would help get this over with, as long as it was clear that she hadn't fallen for it.

"Or I could be luring you into a trap," said Tracy, leading the way through the trees.

"I suppose," said Rose. "But why would you?"

"I don't know," said Tracy. "I wouldn't necessarily know the reason yet, would I?"

"You should have been acting upset or angry or something, then."

"If I wasn't, I suppose it must be alright," said Tracy.

"There's always the evil twin option," said Rose, as the house loomed in front of them, apparently out of nowhere.

"I don't think that would be the least believable thing about all of this."

Tracy made a noise like a laugh.

"Nope," she said. "There's only ever been me. Though I wouldn't mind having an evil twin. She could go to school for me. She'd fit right in."

She opened the front-door and called out before they stepped in.

"Anyone home?"

There was no answer.

"Go on," Tracy said. "I know you don't believe it's real, but we could just see where we end up. What do you think? It can't be worse than this."

Rose examined Tracy's expression. She seemed serious. Either she was an amazing actor, or she really believed Rose had travelled through time. For a moment, she wondered if Tracy wasn't in on it either, but then remembered that if she wasn't pretending to live in 1978, she actually believed she did. Whatever was going on, getting back in the cupboard seemed to be the way to get to the bottom of it.

"Yeah. Ok," she said. "Fine. Let's do this."

"Magic!" said Tracy.

Chapter 56

When they opened the cupboard door again, the shelves and contents were gone. Rose and Tracy climbed inside, all elbows and knees. Rose pulled the door to behind them and they waited, though neither of them knew what they were waiting for.

"What do we do now?" asked Tracy.

"I don't know," said Rose. "I'll have a look."

She pushed the door open and looked out.

"We're still here," she said. "Nothing's happened."

"Did you do anything differently before?" asked Tracy.

"I did close the door properly last time," said Rose, "but I couldn't open it, so I was trying to avoid doing that."

She wasn't going to admit it, but what she really wanted was to be able to open the door without warning and catch them mid scene-change.

"Maybe getting stuck in here's part of it," said Tracy. "I think you should try it."

Rose wasn't going to fall for that. She tried again without fully closing the door, but when she opened it, they were still in Tracy's room. If they were determined for her to close the door properly, it could go on like this all day, so she decided to get it over with and see what happened. Without an inside handle or anything to hold on to, it was hard to get any kind of purchase on the door, and Rose wondered how she'd closed it so easily before. Eventually, Tracy wrapped a hanky around the outside handle, and, after a few failed attempts, she managed to slam it shut by holding on to the corners.

Everything was quiet. Rose put her ear to the door, listening for sounds of movement on the other side. They'd been too noisy to hear anything up until now, and she realised she must have been making a lot of noise the last time too, but they wouldn't catch her out again.

"What now?" asked Tracy.

"Shhhh! I'm listening."

"What for?"

"Shhhhhh!" said Rose.

Tracy waited for another few minutes.

"Can you hear anything?" she whispered.

"No," said Rose.

It was possible that the cupboard was sound-proofed. It would make sense not to cut corners on that when they'd gone to so much trouble with everything else. Rose realised that the longer she left it before opening the door, the less chance there was of catching them red-handed.

"Right," she said. "Let's go."

The door was too stiff to open quietly, but they both pushed at once and it fell open, propelling them into what was unmistakeably the same room. The windows were hung with thick black cloth, which stopped any light getting in or out, and there was a gas light hissing on the wall. The rug, the bed, the mirror and the cupboard were all still there, less shabby but to all appearances the same. The calendar was missing from the top of the cupboard and the posters were gone.

"It's you!" cried the girl on the bed, clapping her hands with delight.

Her voice was precise and clipped, like someone from a black and white film.

"Well, I never expected that!" she laughed. "Hullo Rose. Who's your friend?"

Rose's heart sank. No reality show had this kind of budget. No-one could have changed sets so quickly or so quietly. She looked at Tracy, who was beaming and gazing around the room in delight. This must be real. It genuinely did seem as if they really had travelled through time.

The girl on the bed had thin shoulder-length hair in an unremarkable shade of brown. An attempt had been made to curl it, but without any great success. She wore it with a side-parting and a bow that matched the darker seams on her faded blue pinafore dress. Her face was long and thin, and the hairstyle accentuated the length without doing anything to soften it. Her clothes and hair were those of a little girl, but Rose didn't think she could be much younger than she was herself. It was hard to be sure, while she was sitting down, but she looked to be about five foot seven. While the other two gaped at her and around the room, the girl was bouncing slightly on the bed with barely contained excitement.

"Who are you?" asked Rose. "If you don't mind me asking."

"I'm Peggy, you goose."

"Peggy. Do you know me? I mean, have we met?"

Peggy roared with laughter. "Oh, I see. I see how it is!"

"What?" asked Rose. "How what is?"

"This is *your* first time, isn't it?"

"What do you mean?" asked Rose.

"It is!" Peggy threw her head back. "It's your first time, isn't it, Rose?"

"What are you talking about?" asked Tracy. "And why are you calling her Rose?"

"It's her name," said Peggy.

"No, it isn't," said Tracy. "Her name's Taila something. A bird's name. Swallow or starling or something."

"Swift," said Rose. "Taylor Swift. But it's not, actually. That was kind of a joke, but it's hard to explain. Sorry. It is Rose really. Rose Murray."

"You told me Rose Watts," said Peggy, with a laugh. "How many names do you have?"

"That's weird," said Rose, wondering how she could have known. "Watts is my mum's name."

Tracy frowned. She folded her arms, and scowled, pretending not to listen. She was used to people cutting her out of conversations at school. It was best to pretend not to care.

"So, you've never done this before," said Peggy. It was a statement rather than a question. "This is your first time."

"Sorry, you've lost me," said Rose. "My first time doing what?"

"Jumping, of course! Through time. Parachuting from one time into another."

"Yeah," said Rose. "Bloody hell!"

"There's really no call for that," said Peggy, getting up from the bed.

"You can't be serious!" said Rose.

"I'd forgotten how small you were," said Peggy.

"Rude," said Rose.

"I need you to come down and talk to mother," Peggy said. "She thinks I made the whole thing up."

She fell quiet.

"What's the matter?" asked Rose.

"It's confusing," she said. "Mother sent me to a doctor who helped me make sense of it all, or that's what I thought. It seemed as if he was the only one who understood me, but perhaps he was wrong."

"Look, I'm sorry," said Rose. "But I have no idea what you're talking about. Are you saying that you've already met me? Because I've certainly never met you before."

Peggy hesitated.

"Oh. Yes. I see. No. I can't take you to see mother, can I? Even if you do exist, she'd just think you were barking mad as well."

Tracy tried to catch Rose's eye to share her estimation of Peggy's sanity. Rose ignored her.

"I'm Tracy, by the way," she said. "In case anyone cares."

"Yes," said Peggy. "I know."

"So, what happened with us before, then?" asked Rose.

"I can't tell you," said Peggy. "It could be very dangerous."

"Why?"

Peggy frowned, trying to remember.

"It could be disastrous to cause a rapture in the space time continuing."

She beamed proudly.

"Oh, ok then," said Tracy, twirling her finger next to her head without any attempt at subtlety. "We certainly wouldn't want that to happen."

"No. I think we ought to listen to her," said Rose. "I think things can go wrong if you mess with time."

"You're some kind of an expert time-traveller then?" asked Tracy.

"No, not really. I mean, not at all, no. But I've seen it in films and on TV and stuff. All I know is you have to be careful not to change history. Especially your own timeline. Like, if you killed your grandad, or whatever, you'd end up never having been born. That kind of thing. There's something about butterflies in China too, or it might have been Brazil, but I can't remember what it was."

Tracy and Peggy nodded uncertainly. If they were struggling to get their heads round that, Rose decided, raising the possibility of parallel alternate realities would completely blow their minds. She wasn't sure she understood it well enough to explain anyway.

"So, when is this?" she asked.

Peggy smiled, delighted to be on safer ground. "Today is Monday, the 17th of May, 1943."

"Oh my god!" said Tracy. "We're in the middle of the war!"

"It's actually nearly over," said Peggy. "That's what mother says. She says the tide has turned."

"Have the Americans joined in yet?" asked Rose, trying to look on the bright side,

"Yes," said Peggy. "Ages ago."

"Oh! Maybe this is a different timeline then," said Rose.

"What do you mean?" asked Peggy.

"Nothing. It doesn't matter," said Rose. "Anyway, is there rationing, and all that?"

"I'll say! I can't remember the last time I tasted real butter. Or proper bread. Oh, or cake …"

"What about bombs?" Rose interrupted.

"Not so many now, but there were quite a lot before. That's why we were evacuated, but nearly everybody's back now, of course, what with everything."

"It must be frightening," said Rose.

"Being bombed? Not half!" said Peggy. "But there's no use in making a fuss about it. We're all in the same boat and it makes it harder for everyone else if you get yourself into a tizzy. You just learn to stay calm even though you're shaking inside. It's not so bad now really, apart from the rationing. I suppose we're all used to it."

"And do people really paint their legs with gravy browning?" Rose asked.

"People do some funny things," said Peggy. "Though that would be a waste of good gravy browning, if you ask me."

"Fascinating as this is," said Tracy. "I'm going out to have a look around."

"There's not much to see," said Peggy, "but I don't see why not."

"I wasn't asking for your permission, thank you very much."

Rose saw Peggy bristling. They seemed to rub each other up the wrong way. She wasn't sure why that was, but she didn't want to get caught in the middle.

"Could we go out?" she asked. "I'd like to have a look around too."

Peggy put her finger to her lip and opened the door cautiously.

"This way," she hissed. "Shhh."

They tip-toed down to the landing and waited until Peggy beckoned them down to the hall. While she selected a coat for each of them from the hooks by the door, Rose glanced at the wallpaper. It was already past its best, but she could see now that it must have been quite nice when it was new. The yellow and orange flowers made the hall look brighter. There weren't any pictures missing and she glanced at the black and white photos that hadn't been there before, but there wasn't time to examine them in detail. Peggy hurried them into old pairs of wellies and out of the front door, where she edged between a vegetable patch and a chicken run and made for the trees at top speed.

Chapter 57

"Who are we hiding from?" asked Tracy, as they joined Peggy in the safety of the trees.

"Mother," said Peggy, panting.

"Are you grounded?" asked Rose.

"Grounded?"

"You know, as a punishment. Kept in and not allowed to see your friends."

"What for?" asked Peggy.

"I don't know," said Rose.

"Well I certainly don't." Peggy shook her head in bewilderment. "No, I just don't want to have to make any introductions. I'm not sure everyone knows how to behave."

She tipped her head in Tracy's direction and gestured towards her with her eyes.

"You can shut your face," Tracy snapped.

"Oh please," said Rose. "This is really getting on my nerves. Is there something you two need to talk about?"

She waited for a reply, but neither of them spoke.

"No? Then do you think, perhaps, you could try to make an effort to get on with each other?"

Tracy shrugged. Peggy pursed her lips.

"I'm not saying you have to like each other," said Rose. "But if you could just, please, stop bickering, ok?"

"That's perfectly fine with me," said Peggy. "I don't suppose there's anything to be gained by being childish."

Tracy rolled her eyes.

"Don't let her get to you," said Rose. "It's just the way she talks. I don't think she's doing it on purpose."

She noticed Peggy looking hurt.

"I didn't mean it like that," said Rose. "Honest."

"You need to button the coats up," said Peggy. "You can't wander round looking like that."

Tracy muttered mutinously, but they both began buttoning their heavy macs.

"All the way," said Peggy. "You need to cover yourselves up."

"Which way shall we go?" asked Rose when she'd finished.

"This way," hissed Peggy. "Follow me."

She led them through the wood, in the same direction Tracy had taken Rose earlier. At the edge of the wood was a grassed area where small boys were chasing a brown leather ball as if their lives depended on it, though it was almost too dark to see.

"That seemed further," said Rose.

"It was," said Tracy. "Look – that's the far side of Empire Road. Commonwealth Avenue can't have been built yet."

One side of the road was missing. There was just a row of terraced houses, all with their windows blacked out, facing the open ground. A few girls were playing hopscotch in the road between the houses and the football game, and two women stood on the pavement with headscarves tied under their chins, cigarettes in their mouths and their arms folded. They were surveying the scene and chatting with one another. They yelled at the boys when the ball strayed too near the houses but paid no attention whatsoever to the children playing in the road.

Tracy marched out of the wood towards them.

"No," hissed Peggy. "Come back."

"Make me," she called over her shoulder.

"You probably should come back. Just for a minute," called Rose, but Tracy took no notice.

"She needs to be more careful," said Peggy, watching Tracy with a frown. "People will think she's a spy."

"She does look like a spy in that mac, doesn't she?"

"The mac's fine," said Peggy. "But they've only to look at that queer hair to know she's not from round here."

"She is," said Rose. "Just not yet. Tracy, please come back," she called after her.

"I can look after myself just fine, thank you."

"We have to go after her, Peggy. We can't just leave her. What if she's arrested? What if they shoot her?"

"Calm down," said Peggy, "and stay here. There's no point in your making a spectacle of yourself as well."

She marched across the grass. Tracy had already drawn the attention of one of the head-scarfed women, who was nudging the other and nodding towards her. The first woman spoke from the side of her mouth, but loud enough for Rose to hear, despite the distance between them.

"What *does* she think she looks like?"

"Do you think her mother knows she's parading around looking like that?" asked the second woman.

"Mind your own business," said Tracy. "Silly cow."

The second woman took her cigarette out of her mouth to show she meant business.

"I'll give you a clip round the ear if you're not careful, madam."

"Yeah, I'd like to see you try," said Tracy.

"What's your name?"

"Like I'm telling you!"

"Hello Mrs Green," cried Peggy, a little too loudly. "Hello Mrs Murray. Lovely day, isn't it?"

She covered the rest of the distance between them at a trot.

"I see you've met my cousin. I do hope she hasn't been behaving oddly at all."

The two women glanced at one another and nodded, as if it all made perfect sense.

"You want to get her along home," said the first woman. "Keep her out of trouble."

"I will do. Thanks Mrs Green. And I'm terribly sorry."

Mrs Green nodded her acceptance.

"Say hello to your poor mother," she said.

"I will do," said Peggy. "Thank you. Goodbye Mrs Murray. Goodbye Mrs Green."

She pulled Tracy by the arm back towards the shelter of the trees.

"Get off," hissed Tracy. "What was that all about?"

"Don't you know there's a war on? You can't just wander around drawing attention to yourself."

"What are they going to do? Arrest me?"

"Well, yes," said Peggy. "They might."

She shook her head and laughed.

"What are you laughing at?" asked Tracy.

"That must be the first time it's ever been useful that everyone thinks I'm cracked in the head. They'll gossip about this, but they probably won't ask mother any awkward questions."

"What if they do?" asked Rose.

"Then I'll catch it," said Peggy. "But probably they'll just talk behind her back, as usual." She paused, glaring at Tracy. "Well?"

"Well what?" Tracy snapped back.

"Aren't you going to say thank you?"

Tracy rubbed her nose and sniffed. "I wasn't going to bother, actually."

"The manners of some people!" said Peggy. "I almost wish I hadn't gone to the trouble now. What difference does it make to me, after all?"

"So," said Rose. "Shall we go back to the house, then? I mean, if we can't really explore, there's not much point staying out here, and we do need to figure out what's going on."

"Yeah. I thought it was bad in my time," said Tracy, "but it's even more of a dump now."

They trudged back through the dark woods and crept up to Peggy's bedroom.

"Now what?" asked Tracy, peering at the bed as if it didn't deserve to be sat on.

"Well, let's look at our options," said Peggy, getting ready to count on her fingers.

"Sod that," said Tracy. "I'm going back in to find somewhere better."

She climbed into the cupboard and put her face back out, pointedly addressing Rose alone.

"Are you coming, or what?"

"Wait a minute," said Peggy, peering into the empty space. "Where are my things? What have you done with the shelves?"

"Never mind that for now," said Rose, standing in the way of the door, so Tracy couldn't leave without her. "They'll turn up again later, I think. Look, I don't understand what's happening, but it's obvious you're a part of it if you've already met me. I can't tell you what's going to happen if you get in this cupboard. We could end up anywhere. Any time, I mean. Do you want to come with us?"

Peggy grinned. "Do I?"

"Don't mind me," said Tracy. "I wouldn't want anyone worrying about what I want."

Chapter 58

Outside the cupboard, it was still unquestionably the same room, but now the walls were newly white. It was plain, not luxurious in any way, but it looked cleaner than Rose had seen it before. There was a jug and bowl on a stand and an embroidered sampler on the wall that read 'At the time appointed, I will return unto thee. Genesis 18:14'. There was a knitted blanket on the bed, and a chamber-pot next to it. The mirror was gone, but there was a fireplace instead, with a bright and cheerful rag rug in front and a bucket next to the grate. Lying next to the bucket were a little pan and brush from which a small quantity of soot had fallen on to the rug. The room smelt of coal and smoke.

"What's going on here?" asked Peggy.

"Oh, this?" said Tracy. "This is the past."

Peggy rolled her eyes. "I have done this before, you know. What I wanted to know is why someone has dropped these things here. It's not safe at all."

She began sweeping up the ash on the rug, revealing a glowing ember underneath. The smouldering was quickly stamped out, but it had scorched a black mark into the rug. Tracy scowled again. Peggy was a bossy know-all who wasn't content just muscling in on this whole thing: she had to be right all the time so she could take charge. It was a shame really. Rose had started to seem alright for a while there.

Rose shrugged.

"Just untidy, I guess," she said.

"I don't think so," said Peggy. "That doesn't make sense. Look."

She pointed to a mesh fireguard, which had been set to one side.

"I think someone was clearing the grate," she said. "Maybe we scared them. They might still be here."

She began looking around the room.

"So, what's it like in the seventies anyway?" asked Rose, trying to snap Tracy out of her sulk.

"It's rubbish," she said.

"I bet it's not as bad as 1943," said Peggy, glumly.

"Bloody hell, you have to outdo me at everything, don't you?" snapped Tracy.

"We are going to win the war, you know," said Rose, trying to smooth over their differences. "In the end. And there was some bad stuff going on in the seventies as well, child abuse and casual sexism and racism, but that gets better too. Oh, and there's the homophobia of course."

"You'd know," said Tracy.

"Of course, we're going to win," said Peggy, who was still poking around the room. "Though I suppose it is good for morale to say so once in a while."

"Not until 1945, though," said Tracy, perhaps a little spitefully.

Peggy looked to Rose for confirmation. She nodded ruefully.

"I'm afraid so."

Peggy's face fell.

"That's two more years! Do you know what month?"

Rose shrugged and shook her head. It might have been November, but she wasn't sure, and it seemed important not to get it wrong. Peggy was quiet for a while then, and Rose couldn't think of anything to say.

"Still," Peggy said brightly. "I'm sure daddy's capable of looking after himself. He's managed so far..."

Her voice trailed off, and Rose patted her arm. It sounded like her dad was in the army or something. It must be awful not knowing whether he was going to come home.

"I could probably google him," she said. "We went on this website at school ..."

The blank looks from the others weren't at all surprising really, but it brought home to Rose with a bang how far away she was from everything that was familiar.

"I've just realised something," she said. "We keep going back in time. How are we supposed to go forwards? I mean, we're not in control of this at all, are we?"

She felt her heart rate speeding up.

"No, wait," she said. "Tracy's done it. She came forward in time to me. It's alright. No need to panic."

"So, we know it's possible," said Tracy, enjoying having the upper hand. "Rose only got into the cupboard in the first place," she explained to Peggy, "because I came forward to her time and showed her how. But I haven't done that yet, so ..."

No-one was listening, so she stopped talking.

"We need to find out how to do it," said Rose, still lost in her own thoughts. "Because we're all trapped in the past if we don't."

She went back to the cupboard and opened the door to peer inside, and then looked around the room, muttering to herself.

"Stupid, stupid, stupid."

Preoccupied, she started hunting through her bag for her phone. Her grandad would be cross with her for getting herself into this mess, but he'd lived longer ago than anyone she could think of, so he might have some idea what they could do. She should still have a bit of charge yet.

"No signal," she said aloud.

She moved to the window, holding her phone in the air in case there was anyone nearby with unsecured Wi-Fi.

"Of course, they haven't," she said. "How could they?"

Tracy was staring in wonderment.

"You've got a communicator! Can you get them to beam us up?"

"It's just a phone," said Peggy, authoritatively. "Are your batteries fully inflated?"

"What?" asked Rose, bewildered.

"You said before that if your batteries weren't flat you could show me some photographs."

"I did?"

"Yes," said Peggy.

"Oh, ok then."

Rose brought her most recent photos onto the screen.

"Who's that?" asked Peggy.

"That's Maureen. I don't really know her," said Rose. "And that one's my gran. Who I also don't know, actually."

"May I?" asked Peggy.

She held out her hand and Rose passed the phone to her. She stared at it intently, her brow furrowed. She shook her head slightly.

"Can I look?" asked Tracy, overcoming her instinctive desire to appear uninterested.

"Sure," said Rose. "It doesn't work here, though. As a phone. I mean. And obviously there's no internet yet."

Tracy took it from Peggy and turned it over and over, looking for the wires. She held it up to her ear to see if there was a dialling tone, and then peered at it again. The screen had timed out.

"It's just hibernated," said Rose, leaning over to draw her security squiggle.

Tracy grinned, and Rose showed her how to page through the photographs.

"Who's the darky?" asked Peggy, over Rose's shoulder.

"I beg your pardon?" asked Rose.

"This one here. She's certainly got a touch of the tar-brush."

"You what?" asked Rose.

"Oh look, that's you with her, isn't it? What are you doing there?"

She was looking at a photo of Rose and her friends. Chlo's face was lit up with tea-lights and it made her look mysterious and powerful. She'd cropped it to use as her profile picture, it was that good.

Compared with Tracy, who didn't have a good word for anyone, Peggy had seemed alright, but Rose was shocked by her blatant racism. She knew she ought to challenge it. She couldn't just let it go. But if the past was another country, like they said, did that mean she ought to respect their racist culture?

"Can you take a photo now?" asked Tracy.

"Yeah, alright," said Rose, glad of the opportunity to park her outrage until she could decide what to do about it. "Hang on a minute."

She arranged them next to one another, held up the phone, and took a quick selfie. They huddled round to see it.

"It's just there!" said Tracy. "Straight away! No wait at all. That's incredible."

"Look at us," said Peggy. "You can tell we're related."

Rose and Tracy peered at it again. They all had brown hair, with Rose's the darkest and Tracy's the lightest, but brown hair was hardly distinctive in any case. Their faces were entirely different shapes. Peggy's was longer, Tracy's forehead was broader, but her chin narrowed to make a triangle. Rose's chin wasn't unlike Tracy's, but she had a narrower forehead.

"Wait a minute," said Rose. "What do you mean?"

"We've got the same eyes," said Peggy. "Look."

Rose looked again. They did have the same eyes, almond-shaped, perhaps slightly bigger than average, though it was hard to be sure. What was really striking was their bright bottle-green colour.

"Bloody hell," said Tracy.

"Don't swear," said Peggy, but without conviction.

"What?" asked Rose.

"I've just worked it out," said Tracy.

"What?"

Tracy stared at Peggy, and then at Rose, frowning.

"What?" asked Rose again. "What is it?"

"Don't say it," said Peggy. "I shouldn't have mentioned it."

"Don't say what?" asked Rose.

"You really shouldn't," Peggy insisted. "It's dangerous, isn't it? You're not supposed to tell us anything we can't already know."

Tracy took a deep breath.

"It's obvious really, isn't it?" she said. "When you think about it."

"What?" demanded Rose. "What's obvious?"

"What's your name again?" asked Tracy.

"Rose," said Rose.

"No, your surname."

"Murray. Rose Murray. What's yours?"

"Goodfellow. Tracy Goodfellow."

Tracy turned to Peggy.

"And yours is Lightborne," she said. "You're Margaret bloody Lightborne. It's bloody typical that you'd be here now."

"What's going on?" asked Rose.

She knew the answer, but it didn't make sense. If Peggy was Margaret Lightborne, that meant Peggy was her sour-faced gran.

"Unfortunately, what that means is that she's my mother," said Tracy.

"I most certainly am not your mother!" exclaimed Peggy.

"Not yet!" said Tracy. "But you're going to be. And I'll tell you something for nothing: you're going to make a bloody awful job of it."

"Well, I don't appear to have succeeded in teaching you any manners," said Peggy.

"You'd have to actually be around to teach me manners, wouldn't you?" said Tracy.

"Well perhaps I don't want to be around you," said Peggy.

"You think I want you to be?" retorted Tracy.

"Hang on a minute," interrupted Rose, hoping desperately that the parallel universe option was still in play.

"What?" asked Tracy.

"Well, she isn't Margaret Lightborne, is she? She's Peggy."

"Peggy's what my dad calls me," said Peggy. "I prefer it."

"Oh," said Rose. "But if you're my gran, and Tracy's your daughter, what does that make her to me? She's not my mum."

"One would certainly hope not," said Peggy, looking between the two of them as she thought it through. "Could she be your aunt?"

"I don't think I've got any aunts," said Rose. "Though, to be honest, I didn't know I had a gran until today."

"Well I definitely haven't got any sisters," said Tracy.

"There we are then," said Peggy. "I'm afraid she must be your mother."

"Just stop there," said Tracy. "It's bad enough that my bloody mother's here. I'm not having a sodding daughter too. No offence intended."

"Don't worry about it," said Rose. "You can't be my mum anyway because her name's Alison. Maybe there's an aunt somewhere you don't know about, who was adopted, or whatever. There might be all kinds of secrets I don't know because mum lost touch with my gran."

"Well," said Peggy. "It seems like no-one likes me."

She wandered over to the bed, which was still strewn with the contents of Rose's bag.

"It's not really any wonder, is it?" snapped Tracy to Peggy's back.

"For goodness sake," said Rose. "Please don't start that again. It's not getting us anywhere."

"Where exactly do you want to go?" asked Tracy.

"I think I want to go home," said Rose. "I don't want to be here at all anymore."

"Fine," snapped Tracy.

"Is this chocolate?" asked Peggy, holding up Rose's Twix, taking them both by surprise with the intensity of her question.

"Errm, yes," said Rose. "Would you like some?"

She nodded. "Would I!"

The Book of Her Glorious Majesty's Wise Advisors, Part II

Chapter 59

"Call the Lord Herald," calls the Queen from the door of the throne-room.

The words echo around the palace on the lips of footmen, under-footmen and under-footmen's assistants, all of whom are eager to be conspicuously useful. To repeat her command in this way is entirely unnecessary, on one level, because when the Queen raises her voice in the throne-room, the Lord Herald can hear her perfectly well through his portal. On another level, however, it is gratifying to have the Queen's need for him telegraphed throughout the palace so that the Lady Maven might also know of it.

The Lord Herald completes a hasty comfort stop and enters the throne-room with a bow and a hearty, "Your majesty."

"Shhh," says the Queen. "Carrick may still be nearby."

"He was here, your majesty?" asks the Lord Herald with a chuckle.

"I begin to suspect he's always nearby," says the Queen, glancing suspiciously around them. "Halls have ears, you know."

She reshapes the throne-room as a khaki tent. A map table stands redundantly to one side and the Queen, in camouflage combats, throws herself into a canvas folding chair with more force than seems altogether wise. Her face is smeared with lipstick and her lips blackened with camouflage-paint.

"My Lord Herald," she says. "I'm in need of your advice."

"It's an honour to be at your service, your glorious majesty," says the Lord Herald, who sees that she's troubled and understands the importance of flattery at such times.

For the Queen both to realise that she needs advice and also to admit it is extremely unusual. She speaks slowly, concentrating on the past tenses, which still don't come naturally to her.

"Carrick was here, just now, and he and I have established the terms of defeat."

If pandas had eyebrows, the Lord Herald would be raising them, but a twitching of his ears conveys a similar meaning.

"Indeed, your majesty. Well, that is refreshingly independent," he says.

"You needn't think I don't know my bunions," says the Queen.

"Perhaps I might record your agreement in the ancient lore without any further delay, your majesty?"

Faerie quests, challenges, bargains and wishes are not so much enforced as realised by magic. Whether or not they're written, once the terms are met, the agreed outcome comes to pass without delay. In the continuous present, the agreement and completion of the bargain are simultaneous and thus agreement to take part is the same as consenting to the outcome, so there's no need for further negotiation or appeal.

Although the completion of a Faerie bargain is remarkably straightforward, remembering the terms of the bargain is exceedingly challenging. This is where the ancient lore comes in. Were a Faerie Queen to forget the terms of an agreement before her Lord Herald had recorded them, ambitious members of the court could, and undoubtedly would, claim that she'd agreed to all manner of things, and her Lord Herald would be powerless to advise her otherwise. Knowing that the completion of the bargain occurs the moment the terms are met, the Queen would be hemmed in by any number of uncertain dooms.

Given the intrusion of time into agreements with mortals, bargains involving humans are more complicated. The consent of both parties is required for the fulfilment to take effect, and the human party can generally overturn the bargain at the moment of its consummation, merely by claiming some chronological inconsistency. The Faerie are, on the whole, incapable of contesting this and any resulting legal proceedings would be unbelievably dull. To avoid entanglement, the ancient lore advises that Lords Herald should insist upon humans giving their clear consent to the completion of a bargain before the magic takes effect. When humans foolishly concede that they're bound by the terms set down, the bargain takes effect without delay. If, however, they have the sense to quibble, the Faerie are often unnecessarily flexible just to get things over with. This is another reason why the Faerie prefer to make bargains among themselves these days.

"Carrick noted that although our terms of victory are agreed, our terms of defeat were not," says the Queen, pointedly using the past tense.

"I see," says the Lord Herald.

"I'm rather cross with you about that," she says. "I can't help feeling it's your job to think these things through."

He can't argue with this. She's right. He'd left the banqueting-hall after the challenge feeling quietly pleased with himself for outsmarting Lord Carrick on the terms of victory. It now seems, in reality, that Lord Carrick had outsmarted him. Or perhaps they'd both outsmarted one another, just a bit. It didn't matter: it wasn't something he could take credit for anymore.

Under normal circumstances, bad feelings caused by imprecise agreements among the Faerie are only realised on the conclusion of the challenge, at which point the bested party merely rolls their resentment into the on-going rivalry that probably gave rise to the challenge in the first place. Whether or not this is acted upon depends entirely on whether something more interesting arises in the meantime. Challenges ending in banishment are resolved rather more neatly and it's entirely likely that the ancient lore advises this approach somewhere. However tempting it might be to issue a Heraldic decree to that effect, the Lord Herald faces the rather more pressing issue of his own imminent and permanent mortality.

"I do apologise, your most gracious and glorious majesty," he says. "Such unforgiveable laxness on my part is, well, it's unforgiveable. Though if …"

"You can grovel all you like, but it's not much use to me, is it?" asks the Queen.

"No, your majesty," he says.

"I should banish you."

"I can certainly see the merit of that view, your majesty."

The Lord Herald bows his head, awaiting the release of banishment.

"But I've decided not to," says the Queen.

"Gosh," says the Lord Herald. "May I ask why, your majesty?"

"Because I know Carrick's up to something, but I don't know what it is. I've taken advice from Maven before, and it didn't do me any good. I think I need your help to make sense of it all."

"Thank you, your majesty," stammers the Lord Herald, taken aback by this unprecedented display of wisdom, self-awareness and forgiveness, but unsure how to put his appreciation into words without dwelling on the folly and petulance he'd anticipated instead.

"Which is not to say that I may not banish you later," says the Queen.

"Understood," says the Lord Herald. "And rightly so, your majesty."

"Yes," says the Queen. "Right."

There's a pause, in which the Lord Herald understands that he's to take the initiative but isn't sure what initiative is required of him. His own priority is to write down the terms of her agreement with Carrick before the Queen forgets them, but she may consider some other thing to be more important. A Lord Herald must always tread carefully, but his current situation is more than usually delicate.

"I wouldn't be surprised if your majesty insisted upon setting down the terms of her agreement with Lord Carrick without delay," he says.

"Yes," she says. "That. Go on then."

The Lord Herald retrieves a scroll from under his fur and waits, pen poised between his claws.

Chapter 60

"So," says the Queen, having recounted her discussion with Lord Carrick. "What does it all mean?"

The Lord Herald rubs his chin with his paw. A cork noticeboard is separated in two, with a sheet of paper marked 'the court' pinned on one side and another, marked 'the human world', on the other. On smaller scraps of paper are the names of the main actors, which are pinned in the appropriate locations. Lord Carrick's name is, for the moment, gripped between the Lord Herald's teeth.

"Might I speak frankly, your majesty?" he asks, setting Carrick's name flapping.

"Yes," says the Queen. "You may go at it like a bull in a Chinese shop if you consider it useful."

"Quite so," says the Lord Herald, placing the Queen's name tag in 'the court' and his own close beside her. "Well, it seems to me that Carrick, wherever he may be, seeks to keep you in court."

"Is it because his challenge requires me to be out of it?"

"I think it's a little more complicated than that, your majesty. It's possible that he suspects the motives of the Lady Maven."

The Queen nods. "As do I."

"Indeed, your majesty," says the Lord Herald, "though it seems to me that Maven's intentions are rather too clear for suspicion to be at all necessary."

"What can you mean?" asks the Queen.

"I believe that Maven seeks to be Queen, your majesty," he says, drawing a crown on the Lady Maven's name tag and crossing it out firmly to avoid misunderstanding. "If you'll forgive me for saying so. We don't need to suspect this, because we know it to be true."

"But I am Queen," she says, with a frown.

"Indeed, you are, your majesty."

The explanation of the process by which one queen is replaced by another is less involved than usual, thanks to the current sovereign's improved understanding of time, but the shock of the news is undiminished.

"You cannot mean that Carrick wishes me to remain in court to thwart Maven's ambitions for my throne but only so that he can win the throne for himself?"

"Your majesty's wisdom does her great credit," says the Lord Herald.

"It would appear that I am caught between a rock and a hard plaice," says the Queen.

"Quite so, your majesty."

"I shall banish them both," she says.

The Lord Herald intervenes hastily.

"Might I advise holding off on that option for the moment, your majesty?"

"But what else can I do?" she asks, moving her name tag indecisively between the human world and the court. "It seems that engaging with either one of these traitors opens me to a greater challenge from the other."

"I wouldn't presume to tell your majesty how to proceed," says the Lord Herald. "But I believe that you must attempt to defeat Carrick without too protracted an absence from court."

"But how? The task of collecting children is somewhat hands-on, you know."

"Your majesty, perhaps it might be possible to put some enchantment in place to achieve the same effect. The ancient lore outlines a theory that may be applicable in this case …"

The Book of Going Back
Chapter 61

It is a truth universally acknowledged, that even if you're stuck in the wrong time with a couple of bickering strangers who turn out to be your own family, chocolate will go some way towards making everyone feel better. It turned out that Peggy had had a tiny taste of chocolate last Christmas, in a parcel her uncle had sent from Canada, but none since. It was hard to stop her talking about it once she got going.

"We were all together: mother, my aunt Flossie, her mother and I. It was quite the celebration. Aunt Flossie shared her chocolate with us, and uncle Frank had sent some lemons too. Everyone had been saving from their rations for ages, and it ended up being a proper feast." Her smile faded. "There was a row actually. Aunt Flossie said daddy could have come back on leave to help look for me if he'd wanted to. Mrs Wentworth said he probably preferred the fleshpots of Cairo, and mother told them to get out, to leave, just like that, even though there weren't any buses or trains until the morning. I didn't know Egyptians were still cannibals, did you?"

Rose shook her head. She had a pretty good idea what a fleshpot was, but she didn't want to be the one to explain it to Peggy.

"I've got a photograph of him," said Peggy. "Would you like to see it?"

She lifted the corner of the mattress, searching for her photo, which wasn't there, of course. She lowered the mattress and stepped carefully back.

"What?" asked Rose.

Peggy pointed to the space underneath the bed and gestured to Tracy to move to one end and Rose to the other. Her instructions were so emphatic that even Tracy did as she was told without arguing. They bent down as one and there, under the bed, was a thin, grimy boy of about eight. His eyes were shut as tightly as possible.

"Hello," said Rose, but there was no reply.

"Come on out," said Peggy. "We know you're there."

He didn't come out. He didn't move, speak or open his eyes. He seemed determined to pretend he couldn't see them or hear them because, if that were true, there was a chance they weren't there.

"It's ok," said Rose, "we're not going to hurt you. If you'd let us know you were here a bit earlier, you could have had some chocolate."

The boy opened his eyes for a second and clamped them shut again. He pulled in his arms and legs as close to his chest as he could.

"Honestly," said Rose. "Really. We aren't going to hurt you. My name's Rose. And these are Peggy and Tracy. Don't mind them arguing. They're alright really."

"Ghosts," whispered the boy, through gritted teeth, "you're come to take me away."

He began to hum a tune, muttering the words he remembered. "... When other helpers fail and comforts flee, Help of the helpless ..."

"No, no, no," Rose tried to reassure him. "We're just girls. Humans, like you. That's all. What's your name?"

"Cowardy custard," said Tracy, conditioned by years of being bullied herself to have little sympathy for the weak.

"Scaredy cat," said Peggy, and they both sniggered.

"Hey," said Rose, "that's not fair. Of course, he's scared. Wouldn't you be?"

She turned back to the boy under the bed.

"But there's no need to be," she said. "Honest. Please tell us your name. We won't hurt you."

"Dick," the boy said.

This time it was Rose and Tracy who laughed. Dick closed his eyes again, humming fiercely and trying to block out the noise.

"Sorry," said Rose, trying to stop herself. "Sorry ... Dick." She snorted again. "We're not laughing at you, honest. It's just a funny name. It's hard to explain. Why don't you come out?"

"No."

He knew he shouldn't have given up his name to the ghosts. He'd given them power over him.

"Come on," said Rose. "We won't hurt you."

"No."

"Dick!" came a voice from downstairs. "What are you doing?"

Footsteps came closer, doors banging as they checked the rooms on the floor below.

"Dick! Dick!"

"We should go," said Peggy, leading the way back to the cupboard.

"Should we ask him if he wants to come with us?" whispered Rose, gathering her possessions hurriedly.

"Just leave him," said Tracy.

"I expect he wants to stay here," said Peggy. "Not everyone is cut out for this sort of lark, you know."

Chapter 62

They closed the door and sat quietly inside the cupboard. It was cramped with all three of them, and none of them had washed for a while. The experience wasn't frightening exactly, but Rose felt more nervous now that she'd accepted it was real. She didn't have any control over what was happening to her, and that was a sobering thought.

They sat huddled together quietly, each lost in their own thoughts. Rose felt impatient with herself and with the others. She was scared instead of enjoying this amazing adventure. She was actually travelling in time and all she could do was worry about how to get home. And the other two were worse. They were at each other's throats the whole time. She supposed they must all be experiencing the culture shock in different ways. It shouldn't be surprising, really, that it was so hard for them to communicate.

"It's no wonder he was so scared," said Rose. "He's never seen TV or even films, maybe, or phones or any of that stuff."

"What's TV?" asked Peggy.

"Oh," said Tracy. "Don't you know that? Televisions are sort of box things with moving pictures and sound. Like a cinema in your house."

"I know what television is," said Peggy. "I read about it."

"Well, why did you ask if you already knew?" asked Tracy.

"Never mind that now," said Rose, though she did see Tracy's point. "What I was thinking is that it's no wonder that boy thought we were ghosts. He didn't have any other way of making sense of us just appearing like that."

"Well, quite," said Peggy. "I don't suppose I could have made any sense of it if I hadn't already known you. I imagine I'd have been as confused as Tracy was about the whole business."

Rose could feel Tracy bristling, and spoke before she had a chance to erupt.

"But what I mean is that maybe we're doing the same thing. We're trying to make sense of this, but we can't because we're missing something important."

Tracy and Peggy remained silent, which was a result in itself.

"So, maybe," said Rose, "it would be a good idea to focus on the things that we can't make sense of, if you see what I mean. Because the temptation is to focus on what we think we do understand, like he did."

"Like, how is this cupboard big enough to hold us all?" asked Peggy.

"Like the TARDIS," said Rose.

"Like what?" asked Peggy.

"It's a time-travelling machine that's bigger on the inside than the outside," said Tracy.

"Is that possible?" asked Peggy.

"No," said Rose. "It's not real."

"So how exactly does that help?" asked Peggy.

"I didn't say it did," said Tracy. "I'm just saying it's in a telly programme. Dr Who."

"Ah!" said Peggy, nodding at Rose meaningfully. "Tracy, go to the doctor."

"You're the one who needs a bloody doctor," said Tracy.

"Look," said Rose, determined to focus on what mattered. "What we need to figure out is how to go forwards again. Back to our own time. Times, I mean. And once we've figured that out, we can maybe make the most of this whole experience while it lasts, ok?"

"Agreed," said Peggy. "And we're not going to find out how to go forward by sitting in here doing nothing."

"Alright," said Rose. "We're going to have to open the door again. But I don't think we should all burst out at once. It's just going to freak out whoever's outside."

"Softly, softly, catchee monkey," said Peggy.

"What?" asked Rose.

"It's just a saying," said Peggy. "Softly, softly, catchee monkey."

"Er, ok. Meaning?"

"Errm … that we shouldn't all burst out of the cupboard at once."

"Like she just said," said Tracy.

"Ok, we're all agreed then," said Rose, moving the conversation on. "So, who's going out first?"

No-one replied.

"I'll do it," said Tracy, impatiently. "If you're both too scared."

"I'm not scared," said Peggy. "I'll do it."

Rose was glad it didn't have to be her, but she could see that this would escalate into another argument if she didn't intervene.

"Let's let Tracy do it," she said. "Because she volunteered first. It can be your turn next time, Peggy. And then mine, I suppose."

They seemed to accept that, and Tracy held on to the hanky around the handle while the other two pushed at the door. Between them, they managed to get it open without falling into the room.

"You'd better not close it," hissed Tracy, as she stepped through and straightened up.

"Of course, we won't," said Peggy, though her intonation wasn't entirely clear.

"We're not going anywhere without you," Rose reassured her.

"You'd better not," said Tracy.

"We will keep the door open," said Rose. "Honest."

Tracy climbed out and Peggy hooked her fingers around the door so it couldn't fall open by accident. She peered through the crack.

"I won't pretend I'm not tempted, though," she muttered.

Rose laughed and tried to peer through the gap at the hinge side of the door. She couldn't see much at all, only occasional movements of shadows and light.

"Hello?" said Tracy. "Hello? Are you awake?"

Chapter 63

There was a sound of creaking and rustling and a cross voice said, "Who are you? What are you doing in there?"

It was the voice of a child, of a girl.

"I'm Tracy. Don't be scared."

"Scared of you?" the girl scoffed. "Don't be ridiculous. Tell me how you got here."

"I know this seems strange," said Tracy, "but we ... I ... I've come here from the future."

"Tell me more."

"The cupboard," said Tracy. "It's some kind of time-travelling machine."

"Is it now?"

"Yes. And we need to work out how to get back to where we all came from, because we keep on getting further and further away. We just need some time to think really. We won't be any trouble. I promise."

"No," said the girl. "You won't."

From inside the cupboard, Peggy could see Tracy, but not the girl she was talking to. Rose could only hear them.

"Did I say my name's Tracy?"

"Yes, you did."

The girl must have held out her hand, because Peggy saw Tracy reaching forward to shake it.

"Charlotte," she said.

"She doesn't seem scared at all," whispered Peggy.

"Shall we go out too?" asked Rose.

"We may as well," said Peggy.

By then, Tracy was leading Charlotte across the room to the cupboard, so Peggy put a hand on Rose's arm to tell her to wait. If they emerged unexpectedly it might give Charlotte a fright. Peggy caught a glimpse of her as they approached. She was about eleven, with blonde ringlets. She had a pretty face, innocent and trusting, and was wearing a long blue dress with a full skirt.

"Do you want to have a go?" asked Tracy. "You can if you like, but I can't promise to get you back."

"That's very kind of you," said Charlotte, "but I'd rather you came with me. I've got a feeling you're rather special."

Her words merged into a screaming, gnashing snarl, like nothing Rose had heard before. There was the sound of a struggle.

"What's happening?" Rose hissed. "I can't see."

"Me neither," said Peggy.

There was a bang, as something hit the outside of the cupboard door.

"Ouch!" Peggy yelled. "My fingers!"

She gritted her teeth and pushed with her knees to take the pressure off them.

"I don't know what's happening," she said. "But we need to find out. Help me with the door. One, two, three."

Tracy hadn't been scared when Charlotte first grabbed her. She didn't think she'd have any trouble fighting off a little girl with ringlets. But Charlotte was stronger than she looked. As they struggled, Tracy caught a glimpse of their reflections in the mirror. She saw herself, looking as she had when she got dressed that morning, in her flowery dress and her mum's green cardigan, but instead of Charlotte's sweet features, she saw a blue-green face, shiny as mother of pearl and tattered like rags, claws out-stretched. It breathed in deeply, smelling Tracy's fear and, when Charlotte turned to meet Tracy's eyes in the mirror, her monstrous reflection grinned, showing large pointed teeth.

"You're mine now," she hissed.

Her claws dug into the flesh of Tracy's arms, so that the ends of Charlotte's little pink fingers were stained with blood. The claws dug deeper, pulling Tracy down to the floor.

At that moment, Peggy burst out of the cupboard, with Rose close behind her. Charlotte, in her ankle-length blue dress, stood with her back to them, leaning over Tracy. Between the ringlets hanging down over her face, Rose could see Charlotte's pretty pink cheeks.

"Is she ok?" asked Rose. "What happened?"

Before she'd had a chance to answer, Peggy leapt onto Charlotte's back, hands in her hair, giving Tracy a chance to crawl towards Rose. Charlotte threw Peggy back, so that she hit the cupboard with a hollow thud, while Charlotte grabbed Tracy's ankle to prevent her escape.

Peggy was lying still. Her eyes were glazed. Tracy was sobbing helplessly and struggling to free herself, as she was dragged back across the floor. Rose couldn't think. She didn't know what to do. She couldn't think. She had to focus, but she couldn't think. That snarl. What was it? Where was it coming from? It sounded like a tiger or a lion, but it couldn't be. She heard it again. It sounded like a monster, a predator, but she couldn't see where it was coming from.

"Do something!" whimpered Tracy. "Help me!"

She was clinging to the floorboards with her fingertips, bracing herself with her foot against the floor, but it wasn't working. Charlotte was hauling her back, without apparent effort. Could it be Charlotte snarling? Rose wondered. There wasn't a monster or a big cat in the room to make that sound. There was only Charlotte. Lion-tamers used chairs, didn't then? But what good was that? There weren't any chairs. As if her body was waiting for her mind to catch up, Rose took two steps towards the fireplace. She snatched out a stick that was glowing at one end and the movement of air brought it back into flame. She was like Mowgli with the tiger, or Indiana Jones with the snakes. Charlotte would do well to be wary of fire in that dress. She'd go up in smoke before she could get it off. Rose wasn't going to set fire to her really, she didn't think. Definitely not. It was only a threat to make her let go of Tracy. But Rose wouldn't have taken that chance if she was Charlotte. She held the fire out towards her, jabbing forwards to make her move back.

"Let her go," she said. "I mean it."

Charlotte did let go. She lifted her hands in the air, though a raised eyebrow suggested her surrender wasn't what it seemed. Tracy scurried away from her to the cupboard and crouched outside, leaning against the open door. She was scared to go in on her own; scared to stay outside where Charlotte was. She stared wildly around the room until her eyes focused on Peggy, who was lying nearby. She leaned over to pull Peggy towards her, and half tipped, half pushed her into the cupboard. Then she squatted, waiting, half in and half out, holding the door open while Rose sidled across the room towards it. Rose kept her eyes on Charlotte, her fiery brand held between them. Charlotte smiled. The smile didn't look right on her face, with its evil shining through her innocence.

"What are you looking so happy about?" asked Rose, to keep her at bay rather than because she expected an answer.

"You'll see."

She took a step towards Rose.

"Stay back," Rose shouted, jabbing with the flame. "Get in the cupboard, Tracy."

But Charlotte didn't stop coming. Rose threw the burning wood towards her, lunged for the cupboard, and slammed the door, but she couldn't make it shut without the hanky to hold on to, and that was nowhere to be found. It must have fallen off, outside in the room. All they could do was scrabble with their fingertips to stop the door opening. From the other side, they could hear the scratching of fingernails on the wood, and then the sound of Charlotte's breath. There, in the chink of light that still remained, were Charlotte's lips.

"Welcome," she whispered, and the door thudded shut, followed by the unmistakeable sound of a key being turned.

"There wasn't a lock was there?" asked Rose. "I didn't see a key. Did you see a key?"

"I don't think so," said Peggy, still confused by the knock on her head.

Peggy had spent a lot of time in her room with that cupboard in the last year. Her mother liked to know where she was at all times, and being upstairs was better than sitting across from her mother's anxious face in the sitting-room. Peggy could also admit now that she'd been waiting for Rose, hoping that she wasn't completely mad.

"There might have been one once," she said, struggling to think clearly. "There's a patch on the door of a different coloured wood, just where a lock would have been."

"We're really in trouble now," said Rose. "How long are we going to be stuck in here? At this rate, we could open the door and find dinosaurs outside!"

"I don't think dinosaurs had cupboards," said Peggy, apparently recovered enough to be a know-all again.

"That's a good point," said Rose. "If we go back far enough, we'll get to when the cupboard was made, and we can't go back further than that, can we? When do you think that was? How old is it, do you think?"

Tracy was sobbing.

"Did you see her? Did you see her?"

"It's alright now," said Peggy. "She's gone. Don't be a cry-baby."

Rose tried to open the door, but she couldn't shift it.

"What are we going to do? What if we're stuck in here forever?" Tracy sobbed, her breath coming quicker and quicker. "I can't breathe. I can't breathe!"

"Calm down," instructed Peggy. "Deep breaths. Deep breaths. Head between your knees."

Tracy did as she was told, though it wasn't easy in the cramped space.

"We won't be stuck in the cupboard forever," said Peggy, as practical as ever. "We can't be. Someone must have opened it sometime in history, otherwise what would be the point of it?"

"But what if they didn't?" asked Tracy, her anxiety mounting again. "What if they never did? What if Charlotte threw away the key? Then we'd be stuck in here forever, wouldn't we? Are we just going to sit here while we suffocate?"

She began kicking at the door.

"Now look," said Peggy. "Stop it. That simply can't be right. We're going back in time. It doesn't matter if Charlotte threw away the key in whatever year that was – we're going back to before she threw it away. It's probably in the lock right now just waiting for someone to turn it."

"Ok, ok," said Tracy, though she couldn't stop herself sobbing. "That makes sense. I think that makes sense."

"That's right," said Peggy. "Pull yourself together. Getting yourself into a state won't help anyone."

"She's right," said Rose, in a more sympathetic voice. "Somebody made this cupboard sometime, and we'll get out then if we haven't managed it before. We're going to end up scaring some poor carpenter out of his skin!"

"You promise?" asked Tracy.

"I promise," said Rose. "It's going to be alright."

Tracy took some deep breaths and they all fell quiet for a while. Eventually, it was Tracy who spoke.

"Thanks for saving me, Peggy."

"You're welcome," said Peggy.

"I've just thought, though," said Rose. "If we go back to before the cupboard was made, how are we supposed to go forward without it?"

The Book of the Base and Perfidious Lady Maven

Chapter 64

Lady Maven sees, perfectly clearly, that her time is running out. The Queen is back in court, and she's closeted in the throne-room with the Lord Herald. A battalion of footmen appear to be committed to preventing the Lady-in-waiting's entry and this can only mean one thing.

Still in her waitress-form, she haunts the banqueting-hall anxiously, attempting to catch a glimpse through the antechamber and into the throne-room. Noises of banging and sawing, clanging and tapping issue forth, but the hordes of footmen won't permit her to investigate.

"This is an outrage," she shouts. "I am the Lady Maven, Lady-in-waiting to Queen Annis herself."

"And I'm telling you," says the head chief über-butler, "that you can't go in."

"You'll pay for this," she shrieks, turning on her heels.

Time, she knows, is against her. That wretched panda has succeeded in exposing her to the Queen. Or Carrick has. If she's to make an attempt on the throne, she must win the court's favour quickly. The time for subtlety has passed. Without hesitation, she fills her arms with assorted puppies.

"Lady Brang," she calls. "Look at these little cuties."

"Ooooooh," coos the Lady Brang. "They're such sweetie-weeties."

"Choose one," says Lady Maven. "Lord Wexen. Would you like a puppy?"

"Aaaaaah," cries the Lord Wexen, pointing to a collie with black and white markings. "That one looks like the Lord Herald."

"You're very welcome to him" says Lady Maven.

"Might I have one?" asks the Lady Flent.

"But of course," says Lady Maven. "Here. Take two."

Word quickly spreads across the court and soon every courtier has as many puppies as they could possibly desire. The moment they lose interest, the puppies are gone, leaving them with a feeling of satisfaction unsullied by tiresome responsibility.

"Lady Brang," calls Lady Maven, now shaped as a clown. "Do you see these bubbles?"

With a bubble-wand the size of an oar, she creates life-sized models of whatever the courtiers desire: animals, people, mythical creatures and shimmering buildings. Instead of rising to the ceiling, the bubbles hover gently at eye level, catching the light and dancing in the breath of the courtiers' excitement.

Whenever they grow tired of their bubble-creation, it pops, and Lady Maven is ready to enchant them anew.

"Lord Wexen, would you like an ice-cream?"

Their cries of delight are enough to drown out all sound from the throne-room. Only Lady Maven still hears the banging and sawing, the clanging and tapping.

Chapter 65

Lord Gine is giggling fit to burst. Lady Flent's pug puppy is furiously snapping at his bubble-bear, retreating with a whimper and a mouthful of soap after each attempt. The more excited Lord Gine becomes, the more fiercely the bear defends itself until, with a bubbly roar, it tosses the puppy up in the air and swallows it in one.

Lady Flent, in a pug onesie, stands horrified, her hand to her mouth. Lord Gine, shaped as a clown, is laughing so heartily it's a struggle to maintain his form. Lady Flent turns on him, enraged.

"How can you?" she shrieks. "Poor little Popsy."

"Popsy!" laughs Lord Gine. "It's too bloody much."

"Get her out," shouts Lady Flent. "Rescue my poor Popsy."

Lord Gine falls to the floor, his legs disintegrating beneath him. Lord Wexen wanders over to see what's going on.

"Lord Wexen," cries Lady Flent. "Thank goodness you're here."

"What's up with Lord Gine?" he asks.

"My dear little Popsy's inside his horrid bear," says Lady Flent. "And Lord Gine is finding this terribly amusing."

"I say," says Lord Wexen, licking his ice-cream. "That's rather rum."

"Is it?" asks Lady Flent.

"What?" asks Lord Wexen, their conversation already forgotten.

"Is it rum?" she says, pointing to his ice-cream. "And raisin? I like that."

"I don't think so," he says, licking it to check. "No. It's strawberry, but do you see Lady Maven with the bicycle over there? She has all manner of flavours."

Lady Flent wanders off for an ice-cream and little Popsy and the bubble-bear puddle to the floor and are gone.

"Lord Gine," calls Lady Maven. "Are you well?"

"Oh yes," says Lord Gine, regaining his feet. "I feel remarkably cheerful, actually."

He pauses as her pleasure floods into him.

"Oh, you do too, don't you?"

"I do," says the Lady Maven. "Do you know, there's nothing that gives me more pleasure than the pleasure of the court."

"Well fancy that," says Lord Gine.

"Can you think of anyone else who shares their pleasure with the court as generously as I?" she asks, watching intently for any sign of remembrance.

"No," says Lord Gine. "No-one at all. Chocolate for me, please."

"There you are," says the Lady Maven. "Do you want sprinkles or sauce, or anything like that?"

"The whole, bloody lot," says Lord Gine. "And a flake. Two flakes."

"I believe the Queen shares her pleasure with the court too," says Lady Brang. "Tutti frutti, please, in separate scoops."

"Gosh," says Lord Gine. "Well, yes. You may be right."

"Though not recently," says Lady Brang. "Or so I hear."

"That's a bloody good point," says Lord Gine. "Still, I suppose it doesn't much matter where one's pleasure comes from."

"Well, as long as you're happy," says Lady Maven, handing Lady Brang her towering cornet. "That's all that matters to little old me. Ah! Lord Wexen. Are you well? Another scoop?"

From the direction of the throne-room, the endless sounds of banging and sawing, clanging and tapping play relentlessly on her mind.

Chapter 66

"I say," says Lord Wexen. "I hear you're bad-mouthing the Queen."

He's shaped as a giant cornet, though he can't remember why. Lord Gine is a chocolate flake. The banqueting-hall is now a giant fun-fair, with ghost trains and halls of mirrors, big wheels and dodgems.

"What?" asks Lord Gine, looking up from the ducks he's attempting to hook. "No. I don't do that. I consider her majesty entirely gracious and bloody regal, and what not."

"All the same, everyone says you have a high opinion of Lady Maven."

Lord Wexen leans over and picks up a duck, which he hands to Lord Gine. He can't think why he's bothering messing about with sticks and hooks when this way is so much easier.

"Well," says Lord Gine, leaning his stick against the stall. "I suppose it may be possible to have a high opinion of Lady Maven and still respect and honour someone else."

"I suppose," says Lord Wexen. "Though I can't think who it would be."

They reshape themselves as clowns and walk, in flapping strides, to the candy-floss seller.

"Lady Maven is bloody marvellous," says Lord Gine, his voice rendered slightly nasal by his red nose.

"Why do you say so?" asks Lord Wexen, startled by his bow-tie spinning of its own accord.

"I'm not sure," says Lord Gine. "It's just how I feel."

"Me too," says Lord Wexen. "I don't know why."

"I imagine we must be right if we both feel the same way," says Lord Gine.

"That does make sense," says Lord Wexen.

The flower in his buttonhole squirts water into Lord Gine's face, and they both laugh. Candy floss in hand, they go their separate ways and Lord Gine approaches Lady Flent, who's trying to dislodge a ball of bubble-gum from the bottom of her plastic cone.

"Lady Flent," he says. "I trust you're well."

"Oh yes, my dear Lord Gine," she says.

"Are you feeling well-inclined towards the Lady Maven?" asks Lord Gine, offering a tuft of candy floss.

"Well yes," she says, as it melts in her mouth. "I am rather."

The sound of banging from the throne-room interrupts their train of thought.

"The Queen, it seems, is not often with us," says Lady Flent.

"The Queen?" muses Lord Gine.

"I hear Lord Wexen thinks her days are numbered."

"Goodness me," says Lord Gine. "That's a bold thought."

"That's what I think," says Lady Flent.

Lady Flent shapes herself as a Pierrot while they watch Lady Brang hobbling towards them from the hall of mirrors. She's coated in a thin layer of real milk chocolate and is finding it difficult to walk.

"Lady Brang," calls Lady Flent. "Do you hear that Lord Wexen considers the Queen's days to be numbered?"

As Lady Brang joins them, she takes the form of a clown in multi-coloured patchwork clothes and a blue wig. With each step, a car-horn sounds from her over sized shoes, but over this noise, the sound of sawing can still be heard, rising to a deafening pitch.

"I hear that Lord Gine suggests overthrowing her in favour of Lady Maven," shouts the Lady Brang.

"I'm sure that must be right," says Lord Gine. "Bloody good idea."

The Book of Yore

Chapter 67

Rose felt more comfortable than she had before, though she felt the remnants of a lingering headache. She seemed to have more room. The bottom of the cupboard felt softer beneath her, and there was a different smell. It was fresher than the smells of mothballs and lavender and dust that she'd become used to. She breathed deeply, filling her lungs with oxygen.

"Oh, the door's open," she said. "How did you get it open?"

She peered outside. It was dark. As far as Rose could tell, there was no-one around, but there were noises everywhere:

twigs snapping, leaves shuffling, owls hooting, dogs barking. She could feel the wind moving across her skin. In the darkness behind her, she could hear the others breathing.

"Bloody hell," she said. "We're outside!"

She nudged the others awake with her foot, not wanting to reach out with her hands without seeing what she might touch.

"Tracy. Peggy. Wake up."

When she'd woken up enough to understand, Tracy breathed a sigh of relief.

"Now this is real," she said. "This makes sense."

"What do you mean?" Rose asked.

"This," said Peggy, leaning back.

The moon came out from behind the clouds and Rose stood up. There was light only to one side of her and when she moved aside, she saw that she'd been sitting in the opening of a huge, hollow tree.

"We've come right back to before the cupboard was made," said Tracy, following her out.

"So, you think this is the tree the cupboard's going to be made from?" asked Rose.

"I suppose it must be," said Peggy, stretching her back as she emerged from inside it. "I wonder when that was … will be."

"We should go and find out when this is," said Tracy. "It looks like there's people over there and I don't want to wait until they find us."

The light of a campfire flickered between the trees in the distance, though they weren't near enough to hear the flames. Tracy set out towards it, acting braver than she felt, and Rose was torn between a desire to stay by her side and an urge to crawl back into the safety of the hollow trunk.

After hesitating for a moment, she stepped after Tracy, who was already disappearing into the darkness of the forest.

"No. Wait a minute," hissed Peggy, her back still pressed to the hollow tree.

"What?" asked Rose.

"We need to be able to find this tree again," said Peggy. "If we all wander off, we might not be able to tell which one it is."

Tracy came back, scowling.

"Keep your voice down," she said, largely out of the habit of opposition.

"Oh my God!" said Rose. "You're absolutely right. That was so close!"

"I suppose the easiest thing is for someone to stay here," said Peggy, choosing to let the blasphemy slide for once. "Shall we draw straws?"

"I'll stay," volunteered Rose. "If that's ok with you guys, I mean."

"I want to go," said Tracy. "It's fine with me if you two are too scared to. You can both stay here, if you like."

"No chance," said Peggy, trying to sound brave. "I'm not going to miss out on an adventure. Are you sure you'll be alright staying here on your own, Rose?"

It wasn't what she'd planned, but she could see the sense in it.

"Ok," she said, "but don't be long."

"I don't think the fire's all that far off," said Tracy. "We'll be back soon."

"Right then," said Peggy. "We'll go closer and have a scout around. Maybe whoever's there will be able to help us. But they might be hostile, and we shouldn't reveal ourselves until we're sure it's the right thing to do. Alright?"

"You're not in charge," snapped Tracy.

"I was just making a suggestion," said Peggy. "What do you think we should do?"

"I think we should keep ourselves hidden until we know it's safe to come out."

"Which I think is what I said," said Peggy.

"Yeah, well, you can think that if you want to," said Tracy.

"I shall," said Peggy.

"Go on then," said Tracy.

"I do," said Peggy. "That's what I think."

"Why don't you both shut up?" asked Rose. "You've got no chance of sneaking up on them if you're bickering the whole time. Have you?"

Peggy pursed her lips and Tracy shrugged a half-agreement as they set off towards the light of the campfire. Rose stood with her back to the tree, watching their silhouettes merge into the shadows. The small sounds of their movement through the trees were soon submerged in the louder noises of the forest nearby.

Time passed, but it was impossible to know how long they'd been gone. A cloud moved over the moon and, except for the distant flickering of the fire, it was completely and utterly dark. This wasn't the darkness of a bedroom with lights shining through the curtains, a phone charging on her bedside table and a light-switch a few steps away. This was a primal untamed darkness: a darkness beyond control. Rose fought to stay calm as it bore down on her. The moon would be back soon, she told herself. Then it would be fine. The nice bright familiar moon. And there must be some stars somewhere. She looked up, but the canopy of trees obscured her view of the sky. Only the glow of the fire broke the blackness. It seemed further away than it had before. She heard something moving. She heard a twig snapping, some leaves rustling, and her mind connected those small sounds into something coming towards her. She could hear it creeping closer, pushing branches aside and trampling the undergrowth. Were there wolves in olden times, she wondered? Were there bears?

Out of the blackness, from the direction of the fire, came a sound, a snarl, that made Rose's blood run cold

Chapter 68

Tracy and Peggy had grown up surrounded by trees. Rustling leaves and creaking branches were normal background noise for them. They knew they wouldn't be able to move through the wood silently, so they didn't try to. As long as they didn't crash around too carelessly, the crackling of the flames and the talking and laughter of the men sitting around the fire should provide cover for the noise of their movement. As they drew closer, they moved more carefully, but no-one noticed them coming.

One of the men was leaning over the fire, stirring a pot. In the shadow of the trees, Peggy breathed in its tempting smell.

"Did you hear that old Geoffrey Carter died?" said the man with the spoon.

While he stirred, he held the skirts of his off-white tunic bunched in his left hand to keep them clear of the fire.

"Aye," said a younger man who was facing them full on.

He was gangly without being particularly tall, his thin face marred by spots and patches of red raw skin. He took off his cloth hat and placed it carefully on a rock beside him.

"Three weeks since," he said.

"Day before Whitsun," agreed the first man.

"God rest him," said the third man, who was seated at a little distance from the fire.

He spoke quietly, in the voice of one accustomed to being heard. A hood sat across his shoulders, casting his face into shadow. The younger man drank from his water-skin, nodding.

"He knew his time was coming, they say," said the cook.

"There were omens," said the younger man, to a snort from the man in the hood.

"Gilbert heard them too," he protested, his voice leaping back to its original childish pitch.

Gilbert continued stirring the pot, apparently unwilling to be drawn in.

"Omens, were there, Matthew Dorley?" asked the older man.

A wiser man would have held back from expressing his belief in them, but Matthew Dorley wasn't a wise man.

"That's right," he said, defiantly.

"So, they say," said Gilbert, who was wiser than his companion.

"Tell me about these omens," said the older man.

"He heard the screeching of an owl," said Matthew.

"An uncommon sound indeed!" said the older man.

Gilbert laughed and nodded.

"The Shuck," Matthew persisted. "He saw the Black Shuck."

"A dog," snorted Gilbert, startling Matthew by banging his spoon against the side of the pot. "He saw a wild dog."

"Some fools like to be scared," said the older man, putting down his hood. "Some like to be scared near to death. They don't know what fear is."

"Go on," said Gilbert. "Tell Matthew one of your ghost stories, Walter."

"Ghost stories are for children," said Walter.

Gilbert looked disappointed and Matthew looked relieved.

"I will tell you a tale fit for grown men," said Walter.

Gilbert laughed raucously and the old man leant closer to the fire, waiting for him to quieten. In the flickering light, Tracy caught sight of his wrinkled face as he looked around him. His eyes seemed to fix on hers and she drew back a step.

"Have you heard tell of Black Annis?" asked Walter.

"I have," said Gilbert. "The old wives say she's a witch who lives in these woods."

"She lives in these woods still," said Walter. "In an underground cave scratched into the rock with her own fingernails, they say. Or in a hut deep in the forest that a man only happens upon when he's alone."

"Aye, that's right," said Gilbert. "She hides in trees, they say, like a great black cat."

"She takes many shapes," said Walter.

"I have heard of her," said Matthew. "She pounces on children who wander in the forest alone."

"And they're never seen again," said Walter.

"This is no tale for grown men," snorted Gilbert. "Begging your pardon, Walter, but Black Annis is a tale to scare children into holding their mothers' apron strings."

"When I was a child," said Walter. "I lost myself in these woods with my brother, William. I was old enough to know better. Seven winters maybe, or eight. William was four and followed me wherever I might go. That day, I wanted blackberries, or mushrooms, might have been, and I was searching for them without caring where my search took me. When I saw that night was drawing in, I couldn't find my way back."

He fell silent, and his companions waited for him to continue.

"I know this forest like the back of my hand," said Walter. "It's been my livelihood and my home these many years, but I had never seen that grove before, and I have never seen it since. There was an old stump covered in ivy and a fairy ring on the ground. William went to the ring. I should have stopped him, but I let him step inside it."

The old man stopped talking again. This time the pause was longer.

"And then what happened, Walter?" asked Matthew. "What next?"

"I heard a sound behind me. A wild boar, or so I thought. I turned and watched for it but there was nothing there. When I looked back, my brother was gone."

Gilbert smiled knowingly, sure the tale would end in humour, but Matthew's eyes were wide. Walter took a deep, sad breath.

"I shouted for him, but no answer came. I hunted for him in that grove and further afield, and then I happened upon my way home. My father and the other men searched the rest of that night and through the next day. I searched with them, but no-one could find that grove, and we never saw William again."

He paused and they waited for him to speak again.

"I look for him still, when the forest is quiet," said Walter. "For little William and for that grove."

Gilbert's smile had frozen on his lips. Neither he nor Matthew broke the silence. Walter spoke with conviction and there was no doubt his tale had shaken them both. No-one offered comfort to the old man who was wiping away tears at the memory of his long-lost brother. In the stillness that had fallen, Peggy became aware of her own breathing and tried to quieten it.

From just behind her, with no warning, came a blood-curdling snarl. It was a cruel cry that took joy in old Walter's misery. The men leapt to the far side of the clearing, putting as much distance as they could between themselves and the savage sound without risking the terrors of the darkness behind them. Peggy froze, her mouth dry and her skin pimpled with fear. The creature was right behind her. She could feel its breath, but she didn't dare turn around.

From the snarl emerged a voice.

"Black Annis is hungry now for more than children."

The men fled into the forest, crashing through the trees, shouting in their attempts to stay together, until their cries faded into the distance.

"Quick," said Tracy, "let's take this pot before they come back."

"What?" stammered Peggy. "Where is she? Where's Black Annis?"

"I'm here," snarled Tracy, doubling over with laughter. "It was me, you idiot."

"You scared the living daylights out of me."

"You should see your face."

"It's not funny," said Peggy. "I thought Charlotte had followed us."

"I tell you what," said Tracy. "If Charlotte's throat feels like mine when she does that, she'll be wanting to give it a rest for a while before she does it again."

Chapter 69

Rose was waiting by the tree, ready to jump inside if she had to, but determined not to leave without the others. There'd been a ruckus of some kind: a wild animal and people shouting, and her heart was racing. When she heard someone coming, she moved her back foot into the comforting shelter of the hollow tree, poised to escape. She recognised Peggy and Tracy's voices as they approached through the darkness. They were arguing again.

"It's just not right," said Peggy.

"I didn't ask your opinion," said Tracy. "And I don't much care what you think."

"What's the problem?" Rose asked.

"Tracy's a thief," said Peggy.

"Oh, for goodness sake," said Tracy. "We have to eat, don't we?"

"That doesn't make it right to steal."

"I suppose you think we should just pop to the shops."

"We could bargain with them," said Peggy. "We could barter."

"With what?"

"I don't know. Beads or something. Or shells. But that's not the point. We can't just take what's not ours."

"You're such a prig!" said Tracy.

"Well, at least I'm not a criminal."

"Hang on just a minute," said Rose. "What are you talking about? What happened?"

"There were some men telling each other spooky stories about a witch who steals children," said Tracy, "and I scared them off by pretending to be her."

Feeling confident Rose would be impressed by her ingenuity even if Goody Two-Shoes wasn't, Tracy thumped the heavy pot on to the ground, followed by some waterskins she'd hooked over her shoulder.

"And here's our reward," she said.

"The man telling the story lost his brother in the forest when he was a child," said Peggy. "He thought he'd been taken by the witch."

"Oh, the poor man," exclaimed Rose. "He's probably scarred for life now."

"Yes!" said Peggy. "Good point. I hadn't thought of that."

"Fine," said Tracy, stirring the pot with the big wooden spoon. "So, I'm the only one who wants anything to eat, am I?"

"Well … it's not as if we can give it back to them," said Rose, breathing in the smell. "Not if they've run off."

"True enough," said Peggy, "and I suppose there's nothing to be gained by letting it go to waste."

Despite her moral reservations, Peggy took a swig from one of the waterskins, before passing it to Rose.

"I don't think that's water," she said.

"It's beer, I think," giggled Rose. "Oh well, I don't suppose there are any licensing laws around here."

"This one's beer too," said Tracy. "I don't think there's a lot of alcohol in it, though."

"It was safer than drinking the water," said Peggy. "I learnt about it at school."

Even if it weren't for the weak beer, the excitement and the relief of being safe, at least for the moment, and of having something warm to eat would have been enough to make them merry. Before long, they were reliving Tracy's raid at the top of their voices and laughing without a thought for the darkness around them.

In the dark of the forest stood three men, watching them quietly.

"Are they witches?" whispered Matthew.

"Fairies, more like," replied Gilbert.

"Could be spirits of the dead," hissed Matthew, fear running cold down his spine.

"Whatever they are," said old Walter, "I want my brother back."

"Don't go out there," hissed Matthew.

"You can't do that," whispered Gilbert.

"Please don't," pleaded Matthew.

But Walter had lived long enough to know that no man can be sure of waking to see the next day. He'd been waiting for this chance his whole life, and it was a chance that wouldn't come again. He took a deep breath and stepped out from the shadows. The three sprites leapt to their feet.

"I greet you worshipfully," began Walter, "and with all due reverence …"

He got no further: the three spirits moved as one into the hollow of an old oak tree, and when he followed them, they were nowhere to be seen.

Chapter 70

"What happens now?" asked Rose, squeezed in against the others inside the hollow tree, with her heart thumping.

The tree was widest at the bottom. Though there'd been plenty of room for them all to sit on the ground, there was less space for standing up. There wasn't enough light to make out each other's faces but facing one another in the enclosed space felt uneasily intimate. No-one had brushed their teeth for a while and by unspoken agreement, they turned their faces to the sides. Perhaps it was because of this that their conversation took a more theoretical turn.

"I suppose we keep going back," said Peggy. "And I'd appreciate it if you could move your elbow please, Tracy."

Tracy tutted loudly but did as she was asked.

"Do you think we have to go right back to the beginning?" asked Rose.

"What do you mean?" asked Peggy

"I don't really know," said Rose.

"What choice do we have?" asked Tracy. "I mean, it's not as if we're actually in control of any of this, is it?"

"What if someone else is in control?" asked Rose. "There could, I don't know, be some kind of sinister top-secret government organisation playing mind-games with us."

"I hardly think they'd waste their time experimenting on schoolgirls," said Peggy.

"For once, I agree with her," said Tracy. "If they'd worked out how to do time-travel, they'd be sending scientists back, wouldn't they? Or historians. Not us."

"Not if it was too dangerous," retorted Rose, who didn't like having them united against her.

When they fell silent, Rose became aware of the sound of movement. Perhaps it was the movement of air, perhaps of time. Whatever it was, it was racing, growing faster and louder.

"What's happening?" she shouted. "What's going on?"

"Are we falling?" shouted Peggy.

"Hold on," yelled Tracy, bracing herself against the trunk.

"Move over," shouted Peggy. "You're squashing me."

"I can't," Tracy shouted back. "There's no room."

"We're going to be crushed," yelled Rose.

The pain of co-existing with the pith and the bark of the trunk was too intense for speech or rational thought, but by the time Rose had understood what was happening, the tree had passed through her.

"Hold on," she yelled. "Hold on to the trunk."

They clung to the slender oak, first with both arms, their faces pressed against the rough bark, then just with their hands, as it shrank smaller. The noise was deafening: a shapeless, meaningless rushing of air, punctuated by bursts of sound which passed too quickly for comprehension. The light flickered on and off so rapidly it made Rose nauseous and she closed her eyes. She could feel the ground sinking beneath her feet.

The tree was now just a slender sapling. It shrank down into the earth and then they could only hold each other and cling to the ground itself. Rose clenched her muscles, trying to make it stop. Tracy's fingers tightened around her wrist; Peggy's arm clutched her waist.

The Book of Her Gracious Majesty's Wise and Glorious Plan

Chapter 71

The throne-room is in the form of a large shed. At its centre is a woodworking bench. Chisels, planes and saws hang on the walls, each drawn in outline in white paint to ensure their proper replacement, though most of the tools are lying on the bench and those few that are hanging aren't in the right places. To one side hangs a pair of red velvet curtains. A golden cord dangling next to them implies that their opening will be a matter of some ceremony. With a heavy clunk, a giant searchlight switches on, its beams focussed on the closed curtains. It shines brightly enough that any glimpse of Lord Carrick might be dismissed as a shadow on the retina, and he loosens slightly the subtle magic that hides him, just for the fun of it.

The Queen wears a brown overall, unbuttoned, over tight-fitting jeans and an open-necked shirt. Her chest hair is lush and dark. She has a pencil tucked behind her ear and a pale drooping moustache. Over-sized mirrored shades are propped in her gelled brown hair. When the floodlight comes on, she disentangles the shades and pulls them down on to her nose, baring her bright teeth in response to its gleam. A footman sweeps the beam energetically around the walls and ceiling.

"So," she says. "You're sure this will work?"

The Lord Herald isn't, but he understands this to be a moment when certainty is required.

"Absolutely, your majesty."

"I have complete confidence in you," says the Queen, taking comfort in the knowledge that she can banish him at once if he fails her.

"I have asked our dear Lord Gine to join us," he chuckles.

"Ah, yes. Of course. Lord Gine," she says.

The Lord Herald nods to a footman who stands at the door. He nods to an under-footman standing on the other side of the doorway, in the antechamber. The under-footman nods to his assistant, who stands in the doorway leading out of the antechamber. The under-footman's assistant nods to his apprentice, who's standing in front of a mirror in the banqueting-hall holding a shaving-brush. Lord Gine sits in a barber's chair with a cape around his shoulders. His hair is liberally foamed, and he's entertaining himself by swaying gently from side to side.

The apprentice nods back to the assistant under-footman. When nothing happens, the assistant under-footman shoots a furious glare at his apprentice.

"What?" mouths the apprentice.

"Send in Lord Gine," hisses the assistant under-footman.

"Lord Gine," says the apprentice. "The Queen awaits."

Lord Gine leaps to his feet and snatches off the cape. The foam pyramid on his head is dislodged by the motion and he gazes forlornly at his reflection as it trickles down his face.

"Chop chop," says the apprentice.

Lord Gine is rendered so anxious by the Queen's summons that no other vexations can possibly gain purchase upon his mind. Any insult or assault he experiences in this state will be forgotten instantly, and it's only natural for servants to take advantage. He dashes through the doorway into the antechamber, tripping over the extended foot of the assistant under-footman. The under-footman helps him into the throne-room with a roundhouse kick, and the footman, with rather more subtlety, undermines what confidence remains with an overly formal manner and a hissed reminder that the Queen should only be addressed in the plural.

The footman bows stiffly and gestures, unnecessarily impatiently, that Lord Gine should already be approaching the workbench.

"Oh, yes. Yes. Of course," splutters Lord Gine, and turns to face the spot-lit Queen, in her brown overalls, and the Lord Herald, whose fur is adorned with curls of wood and dusted with sawdust.

"Lord Gine?" says the Lord Herald, blinking into the beam of the spotlight. "This way please."

"Thank you … youse," says Lord Gine.

"Ah," says the Queen. "There you are."

"Your majesties," he said, bowing deeply.

"Turn off the light," says the Queen. "We can't hear ourselves think."

"Of course, your majesty," says the Lord Herald. "Unless you think perhaps it creates a proper sense of occasion."

"No," says the Queen. "I don't."

"Right-o," says the Lord Herald, miming a throat-cutting gesture to the footman, who responds with alarm. "Switch the light off," he explains.

Lord Carrick ducks from view and reasserts his subtle magic. Lord Gine catches a brief glimpse of him but, in the excitement of his private audience with the Queen herself, forgets to mention it.

"Lord Gine," says the Queen. "We're working on a project to enable the defeat of Lord Carrick. And your help is required. Are you up for it?"

"Yeses," says Lord Gine, whose anxieties are mounting. "Whatevers are necessaries. We're entirely at youse guys's services, O gracious Queens."

The Queen frowns but lets it pass.

"Lord Herald, would you explain ..."

He blows a curl of wood from his fur and gestures Lord Gine nearer to examine his creation.

Chapter 72

"This," says the Lord Herald, pulling a golden cord to part the velvet curtains. "Is a cup board."

The Lord Gine nods, entirely failing to rise to the occasion.

"I've been meaning to ask," says the Queen. "How does one bore a cup?"

"I'm afraid I don't know, your majesty," says the Lord Herald. "Though I'm sure the College of Heralds will be honoured by the task of finding this out for you."

"Never mind," she says. "Carry on. Tell him what it does."

The Lord Herald smiles the smile of a panda who's entirely confident in his own cleverness.

"This cup board automates the task of gathering children," he says, anticipating an eager flood of questions and admiration.

"I see," says Lord Gine, nodding. "I mean, we see. I mean, we mean, we see ..."

"This cup board enables her majesty to remain in the court, notwithstanding the demands of Lord Carrick's challenge," explains the Lord Herald, correctly judging that waiting for Lord Gine to finish talking wouldn't increase the likelihood of his saying anything of any sense or value.

"Ah," says Lord Gine. "Yes."

"It's beautifully decorated," says the Queen, running her finger over the carved representations of her ascension to the throne and of assorted triumphs since.

"Yes," says Lord Gine. "We see."

"Tell him how it works," says the Queen.

The Lord Herald makes his usual deliberations about how much detail is required and how much might be retained. He concludes, as he generally does, that the disparity between the two is probably irreconcilable.

"Perhaps you observed my portal on your way through the antechamber?" he asks with a chuckle.

"We're afraid we don't …," says the Lord Gine, with a frown of concentration.

"Quite so. Never mind," says the Lord Herald. "The point is that one end of that portal remains here in the palace at all times, while the other follows me wherever I may happen to go in the human world."

"Hmm," says Lord Gine, deciding that sounds are less trouble than words. "Ah."

"This cup board is the same in many respects. First, it is a portal. Second, one end of the portal leads to an enchanted cave on the borders between the human world and our own, in which her majesty's collection of small humans is housed. Third, the other end of the portal roams through time looking for small humans to add to that collection. Fourth … well … three is plenty. It's a good number."

"Now," says the Queen. "I have to confess that this is the part I don't entirely understand. Having seen it in action for myself, I know that it works, but why would children climb into it if I were not there to chase them in with my awe?"

"Well, your majesty," says the Lord Herald. "The College of Heralds tells me, on good authority and after considerable research, that small children can't resist tight spaces. Wardrobes, rabbit holes, nostrils, and so on."

The Queen shrugs. There are some things one cannot hope to understand.

"Jolly good," she says. "Well then, Lord Herald, off you go and pop it into the human world."

It would be easier had the Queen not brought the cup board back with her after their initial test, which resulted in the capture of three smallish humans, but the Lord Herald judges it best not to say so. Given the machinations of the Lady Maven, he considers it wise for the Queen to remain in the court until the very moment of her triumph.

"I'm afraid that I am unable to go beyond my enclosure, your majesty. And it's rather rare that humans enter it. It's possible that a large cup board appearing there for no apparent reason might give rise to a certain amount of suspicion, which may be counterproductive. But this is where Lord Gine comes in, do you see?"

Lord Gine nods sagely.

"So, we're all agreed then?" asks the Lord Herald. "You'll do it?"

Strictly speaking, the Lord Gine is within his rights to say no, on the understanding that the Queen is entirely within her rights to banish him at any moment, should the fancy take her.

"Well ... yes. Of course," he says. "Of courses?"

The Queen squeals with delight and bounces on the balls of her feet, clapping her hands in a manner somewhat less macho than her form might merit.

"Though," continues Lord Gine, "and I hope youse don't mind us asking, but would youse guys mind explaining what *it* is?" He slaps his forehead with the palm of his hand. "They," he says. "What they are. If youse wouldn't mind."

"Of course, dear fellow," says the Lord Herald, with a puzzled frown.

"We just need you to take this cup bored and pop it into the human world," says the Queen. "And Bob's your ankle."

"We're afraid we don't quite ..."

The Lord Herald lays a heavy panda arm across Lord Gine's shoulders to draw him aside for further explanation. The poor fellow is clearly over-awed by his unaccustomed proximity to the Queen and is finding it harder than usual to concentrate. In fact, the weight of a panda arm and the length of panda claws can be somewhat distracting in their own right, but the Lord Herald is less aware of this.

"The thing is, old fellow," he says. "All you need to do is pop into the human world, pop it down, then pop back here without it. We have the perfect spot for it already."

"That doesn't sound too difficult," says Lord Gine, relieved to be back in the singular. "Though the cup board does appear to be rather large, if you don't mind me saying so."

"Not at all," says the Lord Herald. "Don't you worry yourself about that. It folds up, you see."

He demonstrates by pushing the ornamented button above the doors. The cupboard deflates like an unloved bouncy castle and folds itself, layer by layer, into the densely packed form of an acorn. The Lord Herald leans over and twists the lid closed.

"There you are," he says, delighted by his own ingenuity. "As soon as you get there, just turn the lid the other way and it'll fold itself out again."

"Gosh," says Lord Gine, straining to pick it up. "It's rather heavy."

"Well, of course it is," says the Lord Herald, not a little offended by the criticism. "It's a bloody big cup board."

"Off you go now," says the Queen, and Lord Gine vanishes at once. "Do you think he's up it?" she asks the Lord Herald.

"Absolutely, your majesty," he says. "Without a shadow of a doubt."

The Book of Getting Back
Chapter 73

Without warning, the noise stopped, and they were still. Rose raised her head to look around and found that they were in a forest, surrounded by bare-branched trees. Peggy and Tracy were lying prone, their faces pressed into the leaf-litter.

"We've stopped," Rose said.

Tracy looked up and started to her feet. Peggy sat up more slowly. Their faces were stained with mud, and leaves fell from their hair and clothes. Tracy searched the undergrowth and trees for any signs of danger. Rose and Peggy sat silently, trying to comprehend what had happened.

There were no paths, no signs or bins. Dead trees leant and slumped and, where the earth had finally released their roots, lay horizontally on the ground or hung propped against branches which strained to withstand their weight. Moss and ivy and brambles were swallowing the fallen trunks. Ferns filled the gaps between trees and trunks. Dead branches hung above them, waiting for the wind to rise and crash them to the ground. This wasn't a forest made for humans.

"We're safe for the moment," said Tracy, returning from her search. "There's no-one nearby. No wild animals that I could see."

She paced back and forth, circling between the trees around them but never letting them out of sight.

"Well that's done it," said Peggy, standing up to brush the dirt and leaves from her clothes. "I do hope we're not going to be stuck here."

"We might not be," said Rose. "Maybe there's another tree somewhere that would ..."

Her voice tailed off as she looked around. In all her life – in all the lives that had ever been recorded – no-one had ever mentioned another tree like theirs. It was unique and it was gone. She felt stupid for thinking it and stood up as an excuse to stop talking.

"Tracy," Rose shouted. "Where are you?"

"I'm just over here," Tracy yelled back. "I'm looking for weapons."

"Don't wander off," said Peggy.

"No," said Tracy. "Because I'm not a complete idiot."

"I didn't say you were," shouted Peggy, adding in a quieter voice, "but I do think it."

"Stay there," shouted Tracy. "Don't leave that spot."

"Ok," replied Rose. "She's got a point," she said to Peggy.

"I know," said Peggy. "I didn't need telling."

She rubbed her face and bent down to shake off the browning leaves and seedcases that had attached themselves to her hair.

"Right," she said, when she'd finished. "We need to come up with a plan."

"Ok," said Rose.

Peggy looked up at the branches over them and down to the ground. Rose watched her, with her own mind completely blank. After a while, Tracy re-joined them, holding a thick branch, about three feet long.

"What are you doing?" she asked.

"We're working on a plan," said Peggy.

"And how's that going?"

"Peggy?" asked Rose, hopefully.

"Well," said Peggy. "We need to work out when this is. If we're going to be stuck here for a while, we'll have to figure out how to keep warm and dry. We'll need food and water too. And we'll need to decide whether to stay here in the forest or go to find help."

"It's not exactly a plan, is it?" said Tracy. "It's more a list of things to keep ourselves busy with."

"I'd like to know what you've been doing that's so much more useful," said Peggy.

Tracy hefted her stick with a sarcastic expression.

"Marvellous," said Peggy. "We'll eat that then, shall we?"

"Please stop it," said Rose.

"Yeah," said Tracy.

"Both of you," said Rose. "Just stop it. Don't you get it? We can't get back now. We're probably going to die here."

"Now steady on," said Peggy. "I'm not sure that sort of thinking is going to help us."

"I think she's right," said Tracy. "We need to be prepared for the worst."

"Right," said Peggy. "Let's say we're all agreed that we can't get back and we're going to die here. How exactly does that help?"

"Fine," said Tracy. "Let's say everything's going to work out fine and just hope for the best, shall we?"

"Fine," said Peggy.

"In fact," said Tracy. "Why don't we whistle a happy tune and see how much that helps."

"I might just do that," said Peggy.

"Good," said Tracy.

"Yes," said Peggy. "It is good."

"Well isn't that great, then?" said Tracy.

"Fine," said Peggy.

"Shut up," shouted Rose. "Shut up. Shut up. Shut up."

They fell silent. Tracy thwacked her stick against the sole of her foot and glanced about in case of hostile wildlife. Peggy drew lines in the dirt with her toes.

"Look," said Rose fiercely. "Whatever happens to us, I think we're better off sticking together. What do you think, Peggy? Do you want us to split up?"

"No," said Peggy sullenly.

"Tracy?"

Tracy shrugged.

"Well do you?" asked Rose. "Do you want to stay with us or are you going to wander off on your own?"

"Stay together," muttered Tracy. "I suppose."

"Ok then," said Rose. "Good. At least we're all agreed on that. And if we're staying together, we need to find a way to get on, don't we? So, can you please just stop arguing?"

"It's not me," said Peggy.

"It bloody is," said Tracy. "She just keeps niggling at me."

"You're doing it again," said Rose, raising her hands in despair. "You're as bad as each other."

"Sorry," said Peggy.

"Yeah," said Tracy. "Sorry."

"Alright," said Rose. "Now, we ought to make sure we know where the tree's going to be. Just in case."

Peggy pointed to a cross she'd drawn in the dirt with her foot.

"Great," said Rose. "Well done, Peggy."

"Look," said Tracy, pointing to a large tree nearby.

"What?" asked Rose.

"It's an oak," said Tracy.

"Oh yes," said Peggy. "Well spotted."

"I don't understand," said Rose, not sure whether Peggy was being sarcastic.

"The cupboard was made of oak," explained Tracy.

"So maybe our tree came from that one," said Peggy. "Or another one nearby in any case."

"Acorns don't move far," said Tracy. "Not like hazel."

"Or ash," said Peggy."

"So, we should look for acorns," said Tracy.

"We need to find the one the tree grew from," explained Peggy, seeing Rose's bewildered expression.

"Let's start here," said Tracy, scanning the ground. "Near where the tree's going to grow."

"Though it might be that we moved the acorn to put it there," said Peggy. "Since we're earlier now than when the tree grew."

"Good point," said Tracy. "That's a very good point."

Rose wanted to be positive, but it didn't seem likely that they'd be able to find the right acorn in a forest full of trees. And even if they did, she wasn't sure how it was going to help.

"Come on," said Peggy. "Don't just stand there."

Rose shrugged and joined in. At least they were working together. That had to be worth something.

Chapter 74

Between them, they'd gathered a decent pile of acorns. Rose hadn't contributed as many as the other two because she hadn't wanted to move too far from Peggy's cross on the ground. Tracy returned from one of her wider-ranging expeditions to empty her skirt on to the pile.

"How do we know which acorn is the right one?" asked Rose.

"It doesn't matter," said Peggy, adding more to the heap.

"As long as it's there," said Tracy, peering up to see how far the oak tree's branches extended.

"Which means the more we find, the better," explained Peggy. "If you're going over there, Tracy, I'll go this way."

Rose added her handful of acorns to the heap on the ground.

"Yeah, but," she called after them. "How do we know when we've found enough?"

Peggy and Tracy exchanged a frown.

"I'm not sure," said Tracy, walking back towards Rose. "How do we know?"

"I don't know," said Peggy, joining them by the pile.

"How do we even know that's the right tree?" asked Rose. "I mean, there must be animals that move acorns around, like squirrels or whatever. We might have to do this for years before we find the right tree, let alone the right acorn."

"That sort of talk isn't going to keep up our spirits, is it?" said Peggy.

"Ha!" shouted Tracy. "That's it."

"What?" asked Rose.

"Well, we know the tree is going to grow here, right?"

"Yes," said Rose.

"So, that means that whenever we stop, we'll know the acorn we need is already there," said Tracy triumphantly.

Peggy nodded. "I suppose that makes sense."

"In fact, we can stop now," said Tracy, throwing away the acorns she was holding. "We don't need any more."

"It's already there," said Peggy, though she didn't sound entirely convinced. "But what if something goes wrong? If they're disturbed by a squirrel or whatever, like Rose said. What then?"

"It doesn't matter," said Tracy. "If a squirrel takes them all but one, it'll be the one that's left that grows into our tree."

"Are you sure about this?" asked Rose.

"Certain," said Tracy. "The tree's going to grow here, isn't it?"

"I suppose," said Rose.

"In fact," said Tracy. "We only need one acorn."

She bent over to select one acorn from the heap. When she'd found one she liked, she pushed the others away with her foot.

"There we go," she said. "This must be the one."

"Good show," said Peggy.

Peggy found a sharp stone and Tracy used her stick to break up the ground so they could bury the acorn under the leaf litter. Rose watched them, still unsure.

"How long will it take, do you think?" she asked. "I mean, how long before it's big enough?"

"I don't know," said Tracy. "It brought us all the way back here even though it was just a shoot at the end, so maybe it just needs to have started growing."

"Yes," said Peggy. "That must be it."

"But why?" asked Rose. "I mean, if it's a magic tree, why isn't it a magic acorn?"

"That's a good question," said Tracy.

"It is," said Peggy. "And we are going to make this work, aren't we? Because if I don't get back home, neither of you could be here, don't you see? Because without me, you won't be born. And it seems to me that when I get safely back to my time, my most important priority will be figuring out how to make sure we all get out of this alive."

"And if you've already seen me later on, does that mean I must get out of this too?" asked Rose. "Because that hasn't happened to me yet, has it?"

"I think so," said Peggy.

It made sense to Tracy that they should both survive. Her mother would certainly live long enough to give birth to her and on into old age, if what Rose said was true. And if Peggy had already met Rose after this, then Rose had to survive too. The prospects weren't so good for Peggy's forgotten daughter, Rose's unknown aunt. After this, her mum would have another daughter, called Alison, who she wouldn't bother telling about her lost sister. Tracy had sometimes thought of death as revenge: as a way of showing them all how they'd failed her. But she'd never gone further than thinking about it, and she didn't think she ever would have. Now it was out of her hands, and it wouldn't be long before the other two worked that out. If this was the end, she'd rather get it done without suffering their pity as well.

"Shall we see if the acorn works, then?" she asked.

Rose nodded. There was no reason not to, as far as she could see. They had nothing to lose.

They couldn't get inside the acorn, so instead they cupped their hands together, holding it between them over the hole they'd dug for it. They closed their eyes.

Rose felt a drop of rain on her hand. Wind blew coldly across it. She opened her eyes. Nothing had happened.

"It hasn't worked," she said.

"Maybe we have to try harder," said Tracy. "Were you trying as hard as you could?"

"I was just waiting for it to work," said Peggy.

"Me too," said Rose.

"Ok," said Tracy. "Maybe there's more to it than that. You should try this time. Think about where you want to be."

Chapter 75

It was dark. Rose could smell the mothballs and damp of the cupboard. Outside there was a noise of claws scrabbling against wood and stone.

"What's that?" asked Tracy. "Is it Charlotte?"

"I've still got the acorn," said Rose.

"Don't worry about that now," said Peggy. "What can you see?"

Peggy already had the door slightly open and she pushed it wider so Rose could peer out. They were back in the attic-room in her gran's house. It looked like her own present, but Christmas decorations were strung around the walls and furniture, twinkling and glittering. There were crystals hanging from the ceiling and the window, their captured light splashing rainbows on the walls and floor. The floor was scattered with a thick layer of lavender, its scent so strong it made Rose want to sneeze.

In between the silvered flakes that were missing, the mirror was gleaming. In it, Rose could see Charlotte, as Tracy had described her, green and blue and tattered. She was scratching at the floorboards in the corner of the room, and she seemed excited.

"I'm coming," she hissed. "Reach out to me."

And then she was gone. She re-appeared at the fireplace without seeming to travel between the two points. Rose saw her by the door, then back at the fireplace. Like a fly, she could only be seen clearly when she was still.

The scratching noises were coming from all around the room, regardless of where she was. Out of the corner of her eye, Rose caught sight of something flickering, but when she looked at it, it was gone. It happened again, always at the edge of her vision.

"What's happening?" hissed Peggy.

"She's here," whispered Rose. "Just wait."

"When do you think it is?" asked Tracy. "Did it work?"

"Back in my time, I think," whispered Rose.

"I do think it's going to be alright," whispered Peggy. "I'm sure I'll have spent my whole life getting ready for this."

Rose tried staring straight ahead, concentrating on not moving her eyes. From the corner of her eye, she saw something flickering again. It looked like a tentacle, perhaps, or a finger. She saw a claw – that made sense of the scratching noise – and understood that the claws were trying to scratch their way into the room. Once she'd seen the first one, Rose became aware of claws all around her peripheral vision. Everywhere the walls joined each other, or the floor, there were claws. Around the outside of the window and the door, claws were scratching their way in. She didn't understand what was happening, but it seemed obvious that keeping everything together depended on stopping them.

There was a hole in the floor. It looked like a cave, with its edges scoured with scratch marks. There was no logical way for there to be a cave made of rock under the floor of an attic-room. There was no rational explanation for it having been scratched there by claws from another world, but there it was. From the cave came the sound of crying and whimpering.

"Give it to me," the blue-green creature hissed, reaching down into the cave with one clawed hand.

With ease, she pulled out a girl, about six years old, covered in dirt and as thin as a rake. She dumped the girl on the floor beside her and reached in for another. Each time she pulled one out, the claws ripping at the edges of reality became easier to make out. Through the spaces they were making, Rose began to see eyes and mouths, and to hear the voices hissing.

"Come to us. Come to us."

By the time the cave was empty, arms were stretching through, reaching for the frightened children.

"Peggy," Rose whispered. "I don't think you've got this organised at all. I can't see any sign of my gran."

The creature lifted its head and looked towards the cupboard. It sniffed and smiled. In a single leap, it crossed the room, and took hold of the door.

"How kind of you to join us," it said, reshaping itself into the form of Charlotte, an evil light glinting in her sweet, thick-lashed eyes.

Tracy shouted, "No!" and burst out of the cupboard, pushing Charlotte with the full weight of her body.

Taken by surprise, she fell backwards, into the now empty cave in the floor. Rose's gran and Maureen burst in through the door, scattering children on all sides as they dragged a metal mesh behind them. They dropped it over the opening and Rose's gran sat on it while Maureen set to securing it to the floor with a staple gun.

"Wait a minute while I take the safety catch off," said Maureen.

"Don't even think about it," Rose's gran said to Charlotte, brandishing a nail gun. "Just give me an excuse and I'll shoot one of these lovely iron spikes right in your eye. And then another one."

"Twenty a minute, isn't it?" crowed Maureen. "Or did we get the one that did thirty a minute in the end? Can you remember, Margaret?"

"It doesn't matter, Maureen," snapped Rose's gran. "The important thing is that this one behaves herself."

The creature snarled and cowered at the bottom of the cave in its blue-green form.

"Yeah," said Maureen. "And don't forget it."

"Is it trapped?" asked Tracy.

"This will hold her for a while," said Margaret, recognising but not acknowledging her daughter. "She'll scratch her way out eventually, though. There's no time to waste."

The claws around the edges of their vision were working frantically. The gaps were growing bigger. The hissing and the whispers were becoming louder.

"Time's being stretched," explained Maureen, over the heads of the children, who were anxiously milling around the room, trying to find a place of safety. "Everyone who's out of place is helping them make it thinner. Black Annis – that's her ... it ... down there – she's been taking children away from where they belong for centuries and keeping them trapped in her cave. We think she was waiting until there were enough to stretch time thin, so the rest of them could break through. Isn't that right, Margaret?"

"And then you lot went gallivanting off into the past," said Margaret, gesturing towards Peggy, Rose and Tracy, though she wasn't looking at them. "And you did her job for her."

"What do you mean, us lot?" snapped Tracy, spoiling for a fight. She pushed Peggy forward. "This is you, you know, and I can't tell you what a prissy, bossy know-all you are."

"Now hold on …," said Peggy.

"No offence, Peggy." Tracy turned back to her mother. "You look awful, by the way. I honestly didn't think you could look any worse."

Margaret stopped scanning the crowd and turned a cold glare upon her.

"I see you made another brave hair decision," she said. "How's that fringe working out for you?"

"I tricked you," hissed Annis, scratching at the walls of the cave. "Fools. Cave of stone, cave of wood, it's all the same to me."

Her words were accompanied by a sound like sulphur bubbling through mud, and Rose realised she was laughing while she worked away with her claws at the rock at the side of the cave.

"You didn't trick us actually," Rose said, trying to appear calmer than she felt. "I went into the cupboard of my own accord."

Annis cackled and changed into the form of Tracy.

"I dare you," she said, in a perfect imitation of Tracy's voice.

"It wasn't you," Rose said to Tracy. "It was her all along."

Tracy clutched Rose's arm, pointing behind her. When Rose turned, she saw a girl, her clothes torn and dirty, her face thin and her hair matted. At first, she didn't recognise her, but the dress was the same colour as Charlotte's, and it dawned upon her that that's who the girl was. In a panic, Rose looked back at the pit, but Annis was still there, scratching and cackling.

"You're Charlotte?" she asked. "The real Charlotte."

Charlotte nodded, surprised that this stranger knew her name.

"Ok," said Tracy, pulling Charlotte over to the mirror to study her reflection. "It's alright," she muttered. "You're not her. That makes sense."

She raised her voice about the hubbub.

"It was her all along," she shouted. "It wasn't me at all."

"There's really no need to state the obvious," said Peggy. "And please don't shout. All we need to do is work together and I'm sure we can get through this."

"Not now, Peggy!" said Tracy.

"I see what you mean about her," said Margaret, her lips pressed tight. "Do be quiet, won't you?"

Annis shrieked with laughter. "Such fools you are!"

"Never mind that, said Maureen, "we have to get everyone back where they came from."

She was lining the children up in front of the cupboard, mostly with confidence, but occasionally a little more hesitantly.

"I've been studying my whole life for this," she announced over her shoulder. "It's amazing what you can tell from buttons. Is there a war on?" she asked a small boy, who nodded. "Who with? Oh blimey, France, that doesn't help much …. Errm, do you know what the king's called? Henry? Well done. Ok now, I don't suppose you know the number? Henry the what? His wife's name, maybe? Has he had any other wives, do you know? Come on, Margaret. Help me!"

Margaret was sorting through the children too, but apparently with a different purpose. She grabbed at the ones nearest to her, peered into their frightened faces and pushed them aside, muttering furiously. When she reached the line, she carried on regardless, taking them out of the order that Maureen was carefully putting them into. Backing away from her in fear, the children undid the rest of Maureen's work for themselves. Rose didn't blame them.

"You see," said Tracy, catching her eye. "She doesn't care about anyone else. She's in a world of her own."

"Margaret," snapped Maureen. "Stop it Margaret. There isn't time. We have to send them back."

Margaret glared but carried on.

"Stay in the line," she snapped at the children. "Stay exactly where you are."

"Alright," said Maureen in an unnaturally cheery voice. "Everyone back where you were please. Don't mind her. She isn't going to hurt you."

She went along the line, touching each child as she went.

"Anglo-Saxon, late Norman, early Norman, I think. You two need to switch round. That's it. You're fourteenth century, aren't you my love? But you're much earlier, aren't you? Earlier than Anglo-Saxon even? Iron Age? Bronze Age? Goodness me. I'm out of my comfort zone with you, my lovie. Anyway, you stand here, at the front, and we'll see how it goes. That's right. Now, what about you? Reformation, I think. That's what your hat's saying to me. Restoration, Civil war. No, that's not right. Civil war, Restoration. Whoops! That's a lovely bonnet, my dear, or probably was once. Eighteenth century? Seventeen something? Yes. Good. Ok, now we're on a roll. George the IV or Victoria? Oh, my word. Alright. Who's seen a railway engine? Splendid. You come and stand here, my duck. Has anyone heard of the Great War? Marvellous. I bet you know what year it is, don't you?"

Calmed by her authority, soothed by her kind face, but sometimes baffled by what she was saying, the children shuffled into order.

"Now then, do you know what a potato is? You do? Clever boy. Could you go and stand just in front of that girl there, what's your name darling? Abstinence? Well ok then."

The group of children waiting to be sorted gradually grew smaller. The line lengthened until it snaked around the full circumference of the small room, looping back on itself to avoid the metal mesh over Annis's cave. Tracy was at the back, angry, uncomfortable and impatient to be away from her mother. As the last few children were inserted into the line, the others had to shuffle forward and backward to accommodate them, and Tracy was being edged closer to Margaret, who was now gripping the shoulders of a wriggling boy in a sailor suit.

Without jostling or arguing, the children obeyed Maureen's instructions as if they no longer had wills of their own. They'd been trapped in the darkness for so long that they didn't know how to hope for improvement or fear anything worse. If Maureen had been lining them up to jump out of the window one after another, they would probably have followed the person in front without question or complaint.

"Right, I think that's done," said Maureen. "Now this might get a bit confusing, so I want you over here, Rose, behind the cupboard door."

Rose edged past Annis's pit to stand where she was told.

"That's good," said Maureen. "We wouldn't want to put you through by accident."

She penned Rose against the wall with the opened door and gestured the first child towards the cupboard. He was a boy, perhaps Rose's own age, but smaller and dressed in animal skins. Rose nodded her encouragement to him, and it seemed to help. He bent his head and got into the cupboard. It might seem like a cave to him, Rose thought, and perhaps that would make it less frightening.

Annis screeched in pain and anger as the door was shut, and when it opened again, the boy was gone. The children registered this in a slight wave of alarm, which ruffled the line, but it didn't stop them shuffling obediently forwards.

"There's nothing to worry about," said Maureen. "He's gone home and that's where you're all going to go. Back to your families and friends. Won't that be lovely?"

Annis continued to screech with each departure and Maureen's reassurances increased in volume each time, though she kept her tone calm and her face cheerful.

"Everything's fine," she yelled. "Nothing to worry about. You're next, my darling."

Chapter 76

It seemed to be working. Although the children were becoming increasingly distressed by the unearthly howls from Annis, they focused on the cupboard as their only hope of escape. They were moving forward eagerly, and the line was picking up speed with each child that departed.

Rose scanned the children as they advanced towards her. There was a small boy near the front now, perhaps four years old. She could see from the streaks in the dirt on his face that he'd cried a lot, but he wasn't crying anymore. Perhaps he'd learnt that there wasn't any point: that no-one ever came.

The piercing eyes in his pinched little face took in everything around him, but he reacted to nothing except Annis's screeches, each time dipping his head into his shoulders as if to avoid a blow. He wouldn't have stood out among all the others, if Tracy weren't staring at him from her position at the end of the line.

"Hang on," she said. "Is that William?"

She stepped towards him.

"It is, isn't it?"

She bent closer.

"Are you William?"

He nodded, his eyes searching her face for signs of familiarity.

"Don't be scared," said Tracy. "Walter's waiting for you. He's never given up on you."

Tracy smiled, and he took her hand as she led him to the cupboard and closed the door. This time Annis made a different sound, as if her throat was constricted by bubbles of mud.

"What did you do that for?" snapped Margaret.

"I sent him back to his own time," said Tracy. "That's what we're doing, isn't it? I thought that was what we were supposed to be doing."

"It is what we're doing," shouted Maureen, beckoning the next child forward and moving the line on. "You did the right thing, dear. It's what we have to do now, Margaret."

"What's her problem anyway?" asked Tracy. "She's not helping at all. What's she doing?"

"Tell her," yelled Maureen. "Margaret, you should tell her. She has a right to know."

"There's no point," said Margaret, her teeth gritted. "It's too late anyway."

"It might be your last chance."

"Not now, Maureen."

Annis shrieked again as another child left. The next departure was greeted with the sound of fetid air blupping through thick mud.

"I think she's laughing," shouted Rose.

"Why, though?" shouted Tracy.

"It's possible that they aren't in completely the right order," admitted Maureen. "To be honest, I was hoping the cupboard would sort it all out, but I've done the best I can."

She held two girls at arms' length as she re-evaluated the sequence.

"I think it's you first," she said, encouraging one towards the cupboard and holding the other one back by the arm.

Her decision was confirmed by an angry screech from the pit.

"Don't go so quickly!" said Margaret. "You have to give me time."

She was grasping children impatiently now, holding them tight as she peered into their faces. A grimy little boy caught her attention as he neared the front of the line, and she gripped his arm and scrubbed at his face with spit and a hanky. He tried to break free and she shook him angrily.

"Stop it," she hissed. "Stay still."

"Leave him alone," said Rose. "You're frightening him. It's alright, it's alright. Come here."

The boy knew that strangers trapped you in the dark or held your arm so tightly it hurt and rubbed spit in your face. He had no reason to believe this stranger would be any kinder. Rose felt in her pocket for something to tempt him with.

"Here, have some mints," she said, rattling the box.

He hesitated.

"They're a present. For you."

He came forward and snatched them quickly before she changed her mind.

"There, that's better. It's alright now."

She gave him a little pat on the shoulder, but he pulled away uneasily. Maureen opened the cupboard door, and he darted in. Annis gurgled foul bubbles of joy, scratching at the walls of her cave without concealment now.

"I think we need to speed up," said Maureen warily, "she'll be out of there soon. I'm sorry, Margaret."

Margaret threw her hands into the air. She turned away and gave up. As Maureen coaxed and pushed the children into the cupboard, one by one, the claws around the edges of the room receded. Imperceptibly at first, the gaps closed. The hissing voices grew fainter but Annis's screams grew louder. Through the chaos of noise, Rose thought she heard a telephone ringing downstairs, but it was impossible to be sure.

"Peggy," said Margaret, as her younger self came to the front of the line. "Listen to me. This is important …"

"There's no time," said Maureen, pushing Peggy towards the door.

"Look at the date," Margaret shouted. "Look at the date on the calendar."

Peggy turned to look, as did the girl behind her, and Rose caught a glimpse of a younger version of Maureen's round face.

"It's alright. It's alright," Maureen told her younger self, urging her towards the cupboard. "You've been very brave. You should be really proud of that and don't let anyone tell you otherwise."

Soon there was only Tracy left.

"Wait a minute," Rose demanded. "I need to know for sure who she is. Is she my aunt or what?"

Her gran didn't answer. She was staring out of the window.

"Did you even hear me?" asked Rose.

The phone was ringing again.

"Come on," said Maureen, tugging Tracy away. "You need to go while you still can."

At that moment, Annis burst out of her cave in the floor and reached out towards Tracy with the claws of both hands.

"Give me one," she snarled. "Just this one."

Tracy jumped for the cupboard. As the door slammed shut behind her, Annis threw back her head in an ear-splitting scream.

"I have scratched and gathered and trapped. I have planned and schemed and plotted. And now you scatter them like mice in a field."

"Shut up," said Margaret.

"How dare you?" hissed Annis.

"How dare you!" said Maureen. "How dare you trap those children like animals, worse than animals, and keep them in the dark, all alone? What sort of monster are you?"

Annis reshaped herself into Maureen, and they faced one another, hands on hips, their red faces shining.

"You call me a monster?" asked Annis, gesturing down at herself. "You?"

"I said shut up," said Margaret. "She may not look it, but Maureen's an angel."

Maureen's face lit up as Annis turned away from her, reforming herself into Margaret's reflection and echoing her voice.

"I know you," she said, only now realising. "I know who you are."

"That's enough," snapped Margaret. "Do you want to go back or what?"

"I don't need your help," she snapped, in the same cold tone.

"Why don't you just go then?" asked Margaret.

Annis gave a smug smile, closed her eyes and struck a pose suitable for dissolving into thin air. Nothing happened. She opened her eyes.

"You distracted me," she said. "Be quiet. I command you."

She tried again, but she wasn't smiling this time. When she opened her eyes, she shrieked in frustration.

"What's happening? How are you keeping me here? I demand that you let me go."

"You think we want you to be here?" asked Margaret.

Annis's eyes narrowed. Self-interest she could understand, but it didn't mean the human was speaking the truth. Everyone knows they seek to trap and enslave the Faerie.

Maureen stepped forward.

"I give you my word that we will do whatever we can to send you back, but we need your help. Will you help us?"

Annis hissed fear and contempt, but her head moved in what might have been a nod.

"You have to give me your word that you'll leave," said Maureen, "and that you'll never come back to this world."

Annis snarled.

"I do need you to say it," said Maureen, her tone still even.

Annis spoke slowly, deliberately, her face taut with rage.

"I give you my word that I'll leave and never come back to your wretched world," she spat. "But you needn't think you've heard the last of this."

"Right then," said Maureen, pulling down fairy lights from around the window. "Come on Margaret. Buck up."

Rose's gran threw a stained blanket over the mirror and went around the room pulling down the crystal mobiles that hung from the ceiling and window. Maureen unplugged another set of lights and bundled them into the cupboard. From the landing, she fetched a stained cardboard box, and the two women piled crystals into it so they could no longer catch the light. When it was full, they put the box in the cupboard and closed the door.

"Well?" asked Margaret. "What are you waiting for?"

Annis eyed her suspiciously as she adopted her disappearing pose, but this time it worked. The metal mesh was still stapled to the floor, but the hole beneath it was gone.

"Thank goodness for that!" said Maureen, giggling into the silence. "I don't know what we would have done if that hadn't worked!"

"So, it was just the crystals and fairy lights stopping her?" asked Rose, her mouth hanging open.

"Well, why did you think they were called fairy lights?" asked her gran.

The cupboard was still there, just as it had always been. Rose stepped forward and cautiously opened the door. The things that Maureen and her gran had shoved in it were there, at the bottom, but above them were shelves filled with sheets and towels.

"Do you think we should …?" asked Rose.

"What, go inside?" chortled Maureen. "I'm up for it if you are."

"It really doesn't work like that," said Margaret. "As you're well aware, Maureen."

The Book of Queen Annis's Famous Triumph
Chapter 77

The Queen and the Lord Herald are ensconced in the throne-room, following her somewhat precipitate return from the human world. In the interests of privacy, it's shaped as a bank vault and lined with polished cabinets of locked boxes, leaving no place for servants to hide. The Queen perches on a table in the centre and tries to focus on the Lord Herald's explanation of her situation. She's shaped in her natural form, her blue-green flesh rippling like tattered butterfly wings. She's dimly aware that her time-wisdom is already beginning to seep away and feels obscurely irritated by the suspicion that she won't miss it when it's gone.

"The ancient law explains that Faerie bargains are enforceable to the letter, but not necessarily the spirit," says the Lord Herald. "Nothing in your majesty's agreement with Carrick prevents your remaining in court and doing nothing at all to further your challenge. If, for example, there were anything that prevented your return to the world of the humans …"

"Which I don't admit," says the Queen.

"Naturally," says the Lord Herald. "But were that the case, it would have no bearing whatsoever on the terms of his challenge."

"My triumph in the challenge doesn't depend on my actually succeeding, I believe," she says, in a hypothetical tone.

"Your majesty is quite right," says the Lord Herald. "Even if we were to agree that you hadn't entirely pulled it off …"

"Which I do not concede," says the Queen.

"Indeed, but even so, it wouldn't mean that Carrick had won, and he wouldn't therefore, in a very real sense, be any nearer to winning than he ever was."

"And must all recent events be set down in the ancient lore?" asks the Queen.

"Not at all, your majesty. As I say, the terms of your agreement aren't altered by them. Were Carrick to make his move and either succeed or fail…"

"Certainly, he will fail," says the Queen, though she's dimly aware of having learnt something troubling about his plans while she was in the human world.

"But of course," says the Lord Herald. "And when that occurs, the fulfilment of the agreement between you will be effected without anyone becoming any the wiser."

"Alright," says the Queen. "So, I needn't mention any of this to the court?"

"No, your majesty. There's absolutely no need for that. And I can assure you that if any other outcome were to occur, things would resolve themselves without any embarrassment to your entirely glorious self."

The Queen frowns, wondering what other outcome might be possible, but dismisses the problem as too taxing and the answer as probably uninteresting.

"And the courtiers we enlist to aid me?"

"I'm confident that all but two of them have already forgotten all about it," the Lord Herald says, with a reassuring chuckle.

She nods thoughtfully.

"And those two?"

The Lord Herald chuckles again.

"I'm sure your majesty will find some pretext for banishing them in the coming days."

"Make sure that I do," says the Queen. "I'm going to see what Maven's up to."

"Your majesty," says the Lord Herald. "Might I just observe that the Lady Maven is currently held in rather high regard."

The Queen nods and, still in her natural form, goes out of the vault and passes back into the antechamber. Through the door, she sees that the banqueting-hall is scattered with deflated balloons and crushed popcorn. The Lady Maven sits in splendour, just across from the Lord Herald's portal, on an elaborately carved chair which looks very much like a throne. On her head is a jewelled crown, and several courtiers lie about, stupefied by her pleasure. The Lady Maven leaps to her feet and sinks into a deep courtesy.

"Your majesty," she gushes, swiftly reshaping her gown to sackcloth and ashes to suggest the necessity for a period of suffering lengthy enough that her planned banishment might be forgotten. "What an unexpected …"

"Pleasure?"

"Well, yes. Of course."

"So, I see," says the Queen.

Although there's no question that a Lady-in-waiting wants above everything to be Queen, the continuation of her hopes depends entirely upon pretending very hard that she doesn't. Trying to maintain her composure, Lady Maven performs another deep courtesy. Having defused the Queen's immediate wrath, she gradually reshapes into her natural form, which is misty and sparkling and prone to be underestimated. With this distraction and a redirection of the conversation, the Queen may forget what she's seen. As an innate time-knower who rarely adopts physical human forms, the Lady Maven is ill-equipped to anticipate the Queen's new-found understanding of time and ability to focus.

"Your majesty is gracious is all things," she purrs. "I don't want to spoil the surprise, but I'm planning a new tapestry to celebrate your majesty's innumerable qualities and I'm just seeing how it might look from your perspective."

"I do have many qualities," says the Queen. "And, Lady Maven, perhaps one that you underestimate is my power of recall. I have seen you enthroned and crowned. I do not forget this."

"Your majesty, I can …"

"You think to talk your way out of this?"

"No, your majesty."

The Lady Maven casts down her eyes.

"Is there any good reason why I shouldn't banish you?" asks the Queen.

"No, your majesty."

Banishments usually occur without warning or discussion. Negotiation, as is well known, is unseemly, and begging, though more entertaining, is both demeaning and doomed to failure. When it occurs to the Queen to banish someone, she banishes them, that being how the Faerie mind works. For this reason, the Lady Maven is confused by their conversation. Naturally, she hopes to distract and divert the Queen until all thought of banishment escapes her, but she begins to suspect that Annis is merely drawing out the pleasure of her own anticipation.

"No indeed," says the Queen, "for you are guilty of the highest treason, are you not?"

"Well, yes, your majesty, but I think …"

"I have little interest in what you think."

"No, your majesty." The Lady Maven waits. "What is your majesty's pleasure?"

"You are Carrick's ears in my throne-room," says the Queen.

She waits to see if the Lady Maven will attempt to deny it. Wisely, she doesn't.

"So confident am I of my success in his silly challenge, that I shall allow Carrick to make his move first. From this day forth, I choose to stay with my court. You will tell him this."

She holds up her hand to forestall interruption.

"Though I observe the terms of our game in every respect, my place is at court."

"Your presence brings joy to your subjects, your majesty," gushes the Lady Maven. "We joy in your pleasure and abase ourselves to its furtherance. We …"

The Queen has no interest in her flattery. Though she has no reason to think it's not true, she does wonder if the Lady Maven is being altogether sincere.

"You shall see to it that the court has no further interest in Carrick's petty challenge. The longer he delays, the more you will mock and belittle him. When he fails, there will be no sympathizers. If you please me, I may permit you to retain your place. Do you understand?"

"Your majesty is most gracious," says Lady Maven.

"Indeed, I am," says the Queen. "I shall be observing you, Maven, and I advise you not to forget that."

Lady Maven backs out into the courtyard to engage Lord Wexen in a loud conversation about how very uninspiring Lord Carrick's challenge is turning out to be. Several underfootmen and their assistants relay her conversation to the chief footman without any pretence at discretion. The chief footman represents these conversations in an ever-changing tapestry, so that the Queen need never abase herself by asking for an update.

The Queen smiles, sharing her pleasure with the court. Maven may stay for as long as she's useful. While Carrick delays, the Queen will distract her courtiers with joy and petty quarrels. When he fails – for fail he must in the end – she will take the greatest of pleasure in casting him out forever. It is only now, and perhaps only fleetingly, that she fully understands what this means.

Chapter 78

"Announce me then," says the Queen. She's arrayed as a peacock, her feathers shimmering and shivering in anticipation of their full display.

"Her gracious majesty, Queen Annis," announces the Lord Herald.

It isn't usually necessary to use the Queen's name, there being no possibility of confusion. Indeed, there's a real risk of banishment if she's feeling more than usually sensitive. However, the use of the royal name adds to the sense of ceremony on special occasions, and this is certainly one of those.

The court bows and courtesies and strains to catch a glimpse of their Queen. They can't quite explain the feeling, but it seems like a novelty that she's here. Those who are nearest shape themselves as peahens, pheasants and grouse. At the particular request of the Queen, the Lady Maven soars overhead in the form of a red kite. Courtiers shift nervously as her shadow passes over them.

"Greetings. Greetings," says the Queen, opening her tail.

This display of her magnificence elicits coos and gasps of admiration from the court.

Whispering to the Lord Herald under cover of the noise, she asks, "Who is it I need to be banishing?"

"Over there," says the Lord Herald. "Lord Gine. He's the buzzard. And up there on the rafters. Lady Louple. The barn owl."

The Queen nods.

"And the Lady Maven?"

"Perhaps not quite yet, your majesty," he says with a chuckle. "As we discussed, you may want to undermine her position first. We did think perhaps a ball?"

"Ah yes," says the Queen, raising her voice to address her court. "My dear lords and ladies. I am come to announce a ball."

The court cheers lustily.

"The theme shall be boredom," declares the Queen, apparently plucking the notion from thin air. "My dear Lady Maven will sort out all the details."

The Lady Maven swoops down, and a small puffin colony scatters to clear a landing space. This ball is news to her, as is her responsibility for it.

"Your majesty is most gracious," she says, bowing her head.

"I am rather, aren't I?" says the Queen. "Now off you go to instruct the servants, unless you want to do all the magic yourself."

She turns back to the court.

"I confess that I'm a little perplexed by Lady Maven's theme, but I'm sure she'll pull it off, like a rabbit out of a cat. She promises me the most splendid ball in woven memory, and I suggest we all hold her to that. In the meantime, Lord Gine? Lady Louple?"

They look up, startled to be addressed directly. Before anyone else is able to locate them in the crush of the court, they're gone. And the moment they're gone, they're forgotten. That is how it is among the Faerie.

"Lord Herald," mutters the Queen. "While I'm at it, is there any news of Carrick?"

"I'm afraid I don't know, your majesty. No-one is speaking of his leaving our world, but no-one can say where he is. For the moment, they do discuss his whereabouts, but I suspect this interest will be as short-lived as any other."

"Perhaps he realises it's his destiny to fail," says the Queen.

She raises her voice for the benefit of Lady Flent, who passes as a duck, followed by a growing family of ducklings.

"Do you suppose Lord Carrick hides somewhere, thinking we'll forget his silly challenge?"

"It's entirely possible, your majesty," quacks Lady Flent. "And about time too."

Her ducklings quackle their agreement and the Lord Herald chuckles. His amusement no longer causes Annis any unease. For once, she gets the joke. Lady Flent mentions time, and that really is very funny, because she has no idea what it means. The Queen joins in with the laughter and shares her pleasure with the court.

The Book of Cocoa and Understanding
Chapter 79

Margaret Goodfellow's kitchen was basic, but cosy. There were no shelves of cookery books, no shining juicers or mixers, no state-of-the-art gadgets of any kind. There was a metal sink, a bleached Formica work-surface with shelves beneath it, an old gas cooker in front of a blocked-off fireplace, and a free-standing cupboard whose door had to be rammed closed and jerked open. There was a knack to it, Maureen assured Rose.

If Rose leant back on her chair, she could see a little, old fridge in a walk-in cupboard, lined with shelves filled with tins and packets. At the kitchen window were curtains, faded, but clean, and patterned with bright pictures of teapots and jars of jam. They were open, despite the darkness outside. Another pair in the same cloth hung over the shelves under the worktop, their lower edges frayed where the seam brushed across the floor. The red Bakelite clock on the wall said it was already half past two in the morning, but time didn't seem to matter in the same way anymore. Although nothing matched in the kitchen, everything that could be made to gleam was gleaming, and Rose was sure that must have been Maureen's work. Her gran didn't strike her as the house-proud type.

Maureen was bustling around chatting and making mugs of hot chocolate for them all. Rose was sitting at the table with her gran, who was staring at her gnarled knuckles.

"I didn't know if we were going to get around to eating these," Maureen said, retrieving a tray of hot biscuits from the oven, "but it seemed a good idea to get them ready, just in case. I popped the oven on to heat up before we went up."

She put the baking tray down on the top of the cooker and carried their drinks to the table. Rose's gran took an experimental sip from her green jadeite mug. Rose's cup was more delicate and patterned with pink flowers, and she was surprised to see that Maureen's, which was child-sized, bore a picture of a golliwog in a bow-tie and yellow waistcoat. All three were chipped. Maureen's was missing its handle.

"Only you, Maureen, would think about making biscuits at a time like this," said Margaret.

"You don't have to have any if you don't want to," said Maureen, putting a plate in the middle of the table.

The plate was white, with a geometric pattern of blue hatching and black feathery lines around the rim. It didn't match anything else that Rose could see in the kitchen.

"But it's only fair to tell you," Maureen continued, with a wink at Rose, "that these biscuits have seen me through many of life's challenges."

They were delicious: chewy and fruity, with a hint of spice. Still warm, they melted in Rose's mouth and she wondered how long it had been since she'd eaten last. Centuries, certainly, but she didn't know how many hours. Peggy would have loved these, Rose thought, remembering her raptures over a fragment of Twix. In the same moment, she remembered that Peggy was still here, and watched her gran collecting crumbs from the table with her fingertips and brushing them off on to the plate. Her lips were tight and her eyes cold. Rose couldn't see any trace of Peggy in her face.

"Perhaps you could clear something up for me," Rose said. "Was Tracy my mum's sister, or what?"

"No," said her gran.

"She said she was your daughter."

"Yes," said her gran.

Maureen leant forward to pat her hand.

"Tracy was your mother, Rose."

"No," said Rose. "I'm sorry, but I don't see how that can be right, Maureen. My mum's name is Alison."

Her gran sighed. "I never liked that name."

"Oh," said Rose. "So, she changed her name. She never told me that."

"Why doesn't that surprise me?" said her gran. "Your mother always was one for secrets."

"She ran away when she was a teenager," explained Maureen in a stage whisper. "More than once. When she came back one time, she'd changed her name."

"The name I gave her wasn't good enough, apparently," said Margaret.

"Does anyone want more cocoa?" asked Maureen. "I'm going to have a spot more, but I can always put more milk on, if that's what everyone wants."

"From what she told me," Rose said, bristling on her mum's behalf. "You weren't around that much yourself when she needed you."

Her gran shrugged and turned away.

"I'll just keep it coming, I think," said Maureen, pouring milk into the pan and relighting the hob.

"Do you know where she went?" Rose asked, but her gran didn't respond

She looked to Maureen for an answer.

"I don't know, love," said Maureen, holding up the pan in offer of more cocoa, which Rose turned down. "And you don't know either, do you Margaret?"

When Margaret didn't respond, Maureen offered Rose an apologetic biscuit instead.

"I sort of knew it was her," she said to Maureen. "I think I did, anyway, but I couldn't make sense of it."

"It's natural that you're confused," said Maureen. "You've had a lot to deal with."

"I think the thing that confused me most was that they got on so badly. They were bickering all the time. Tracy was so angry with her. And just angry generally, actually."

Her gran tutted and rolled her eyes.

"What's that supposed to mean?" demanded Rose.

"She never stopped being angry with me," said her gran.

"But what for?" asked Rose.

Her gran pushed her chair back from the table.

"Nothing that I'm willing to talk about now."

"Why did she fall out with you?" asked Rose. "Why did you lose touch? Why have I never seen you before and why did she send me to you now? What did you do that was so awful she wanted nothing to do with you?"

Maureen patted her hand helplessly, and Rose turned to her instead. It was obvious her gran wasn't willing to talk.

"The thing is," she said to Maureen. "I liked Peggy. She was bossy and judgey, but she was cheerful and kind too. I don't think I could have kept it together without her. And then Tracy, my mum, was bitter and angry and nothing like how she is in real life. I just don't get how different they both were. It doesn't make sense."

Her gran was standing at the sink, looking out into the darkness. Rose raised her voice to address her.

"And if my mum knew what was going to happen, why did she send me here? Why didn't she keep me safe somewhere else?"

"She can't keep you safe," said her gran. "You're no less safe here than you would be at home."

"What do you mean?" asked Rose. "We're safe now, aren't we?"

Her gran snorted but didn't respond.

Rose turned to Maureen. "I can't remember when Tracy left. Do you think my mum saw enough to know it was going to work out alright?"

"Maybe, love," said Maureen.

"She couldn't have done, though, could she?" Rose tried to recall what had happened when. "She wasn't there when you sent that thing back."

"She always did look after herself first," observed her gran.

"That's not fair," said Maureen. "You can hardly blame her for that."

Rose didn't know what to think. Her gran had a point: as far as Tracy knew, she'd left them all in danger, and that meant that her mum had sent her to her gran's without knowing what the outcome would be. But that didn't make sense when her mum wrapped her in cotton wool the rest of the time. Why would she gamble with her daughter's safety when the end of the world was at stake but not let her get the bus on her own?

"And why the hell didn't she warn me?" Rose asked.

Her gran pulled a 'What did you expect?' face.

"Maureen," said Rose. "Perhaps you can explain. Why didn't my mum tell me what was going to happen?"

"There are lots of possible reasons, love, but it might be that she didn't think you'd believe her."

"Well, ok," said Rose. "Probably I wouldn't have. But she could have told me something, like 'don't get into the cupboard', couldn't she? Without all the details?"

"If you're anything like your mother, nothing would be more likely to guarantee that you did exactly that," said her gran.

It was irritating that she was right.

"But she could have prepared me for it all in some way, couldn't she?" said Rose. "She's had my whole life to get me ready for this."

"I'm sure she did the best she could, love," said Maureen. "It's all anyone can do."

"I need to talk to her," said Rose, pulling her phone from her bag.

Her mum didn't answer, so she left a message before her charge ran out.

"Mum, I don't suppose I need to tell you what just happened because you were there," she said. "What the hell? I can't believe you didn't talk to me about this. My phone's nearly dead, so you'll need to call me on the landline when you get this. Oh, and I hope the operation went well."

She disconnected and took another biscuit.

"Why didn't she tell me?" she asked aloud.

"How many people would believe you if you told them about Black Annis?" asked Maureen. "No-one could believe she was real unless they'd seen her with their own eyes, and some of them not even then. They'd just dismiss it as a delusion. I suppose that's how she became an old wives' tale."

She paused, interrupted by Rose's confused expression.

"Weren't you ever told the story?" she asked.

Rose shook her head.

"Do you want to tell it, Margaret?"

"Be my guest," said Rose's gran.

"Well," said Maureen. "They always used to talk about her round here. I didn't live in this part of town, but when I was a child, I used to visit my auntie Ethel in Empire Rd."

She gestured vaguely towards the front of the house.

"She used to bring me over when she visited Mrs Goodfellow, Margaret's mother; your great-grandmother, come to think of it. Now, I was scared of that wood. Ethel always told me that if I wandered off, Black Annis would catch me and eat me, you see, so I stayed near the house."

"How did your aunt know about Black Annis?" asked Rose.

"She didn't really, love. It was just a story people told to keep their children safe. It must have been passed down through the centuries so that Black Annis became just a kind of bogeyman. Mind you, the danger was in the house, wasn't it? Not in the wood. You can't imagine what it was like in that cave."

Maureen looked into the distance and munched her biscuit. Shaking herself, she changed the subject with a nervous laugh.

"I wonder why they called her Black Annis, when she wasn't black at all. I wasn't sure I'd remembered it right, but she was a sort of bluey green, wasn't she? I can't make sense of it."

"Wasn't it just racism?" asked Rose.

"Oh, I don't think so, dear," said Maureen. "I don't see how it can have been. We didn't really have it in those days."

Chapter 80

"So, were we always in the same place?" asked Rose. "Is this where the forest was?"

"Yes," said Maureen. "The wood still covered this whole area until quite recently. It was all cut down for this blessed housing estate."

"I supposed you'll be wanting to tell that part of the story," said Margaret, sourly, still facing the window.

"What happened?" asked Rose after a pause, as much to teach her gran a lesson as anything else.

"Well," said Maureen, nudging the biscuit plate towards her. "You saw me there, when I was a child? After Black Annis got me?"

Rose nodded as she took another biscuit.

"I didn't remember it for a long time," said Maureen. "I just completely blanked it out, I think. I couldn't tell you how long I was away for – years and years it must have been – but I ended up exactly where I'd been when she took me – in the attic-room upstairs – and no-one had had time to miss me. It was all very confusing."

"Tell me about it!" said Margaret, drily.

"Well, I was all of a flutter, of course, and I got no end of a telling off because of the state of my clothes. It was quite a new dress, you see, and it was completely ruined. It made things worse when I tried telling the truth, so I suppose I just carried on pretending it had never happened until I didn't believe it either. I did a pretty good job of putting it out of my mind. But then – and this is years later – I was having some counselling, after my Colin died ..."

Rose's gran snorted. "Counselling!"

"I know you had a different experience, Margaret, but I found it very useful," said Maureen. "And, anyway, it just sort of came back, this thing that I was supposed to have imagined, but the memories seemed too real. I thought maybe it was an hallucination or a message of some kind, or I don't know what, but I had to find out. I tried all sorts – you wouldn't believe it."

"You tried mediums, hypnotism, all manner of nonsense, didn't you Maureen?"

"I did. Yes, well. Getting in touch with Margaret took longer than it should have done," said Maureen. "But that was because she never answered the phone or replied to my letters. I assumed she was dead for a while, but in the end, I did a bit of digging and found that she was still listed as living at the same address. Eventually, I came here myself. To the house."

"Oh Maureen, do get on with it," snapped Rose's gran.

"That's what I'm trying to do," said Maureen. "So, I came here, after I'd tried everything else, because it seemed as if she was never going to reply to my letters or calls. And, well. You wouldn't believe the mess and the noise. There was a metal fence and there were all these chainsaws and bulldozers and wood-chippers. You've never heard such a racket!"

She glanced at Margaret.

"Anyway, there was a passageway from the road, between the barriers, and when I went down it, I saw a notice on Margaret's door. It said they'd made every effort to contact the owner, but they hadn't been able to. They were going ahead with the housing estate and once they'd done all the groundwork for that, there was a schedule for knocking down the house. Well, I marched over and shouted to some fellow with a clipboard and he told me the site was going to be made into a playground for the kiddies. He said they were waiting as long as possible before demolishing the house, just in case the owner did turn up, like it was the most reasonable thing in the world to knock down a person's house when her back is turned."

Margaret sighed impatiently.

"So, where were you?" Rose asked her. "Where were you when all this was going on?"

"I was away."

"Oh. Yes," said Rose. "I've heard about your disappearing act."

She turned back to Maureen.

"It sounds like it was lucky you were around, Maureen. What did you do?"

Maureen smiled and took in a deep breath.

"I went to the library and found all the information I could about the history of this area, and I fought to get the cottage listed so they couldn't knock it down..."

"Which is costing me a fortune," complained her gran.

"Really?" said Rose.

"... and I pretended to be Margaret until she got back," finished Maureen.

Rose laughed. "Didn't anyone notice the difference?"

"It's fortunate that Margaret has never been particularly sociable," said Maureen. "There weren't any close neighbours before, and the new ones didn't know any better. I suppose there must be people around who go way back, but I didn't bump into them. I was mostly just dealing with the council, and of course they had no idea who was who. I had all of Margaret's papers once I managed to get into the house and that was all it took ..."

"After you wrenched open a window with a crowbar," said Margaret.

"Well how else was I supposed to get in?" Maureen retorted. "So, anyway, they had no reason to doubt me. I fitted right in, actually. The children in the new houses started calling me a witch. It's ironic really, when you come to think of it."

"I've no objection to being called a witch," said Margaret. "If it keeps them out of the garden. They can call me Black Annis for all I care."

"They do," mouthed Maureen, and Rose laughed.

"Anyway," continued Maureen, "the important thing was that we were ready for Black Annis when she got here."

"Who glued the calendar?" asked Rose.

"That was me," said her gran. "I was determined not to forget, no matter how hard they tried to make me."

"Who's they?" asked Rose.

After a pause, Maureen offered the plate again.

"Any more biscuits anyone?"

Chapter 81

"I'm just glad it's all over," said Rose, taking another biscuit. "I honestly didn't think we were going to be able get back."

"Oh my," giggled Maureen, and Margaret sighed deeply.

"There are some things I need to explain to you," she said, turning back from the window, the lines on her face deepening into their well-used expression of despair.

"Ok," said Rose. "Whatever. Fire away."

"Well, the chances are that it might happen again, that sort of thing."

"How can it?" Rose frowned. "Black Annis can't come back again, can she?"

"No. She can't," her gran answered wearily. "At least I hope not."

"The cupboard's back to normal, isn't it?" asked Rose. "And you could always get rid of it, if you wanted to. Chop it up, or burn it, or whatever."

"That's not how it works," said her gran. "As I believe I've already said."

"Time travel," said Maureen with a squeal of excitement. "You're so lucky!"

Her gran dismissed Maureen's perspective with a scowl.

"Regardless of what we do with the cupboard, there's a chance it might happen to you again," she said. "In some other way. It's likely, actually. That it will."

"It's not guaranteed for everyone," said Maureen, her lips pursed tight together.

"No Maureen. That's right," Margaret snapped. "Some people it only happens to once. As if that even counts. And they should consider themselves lucky that's all it is. But we know that Rose travels through time more than once, so it seems entirely possible that she's like me."

"Like you?" asked Rose, not considering it an appealing prospect.

"Time can't hold on to me," her gran frowned. "I just can't stay where I'm supposed to be, no matter how hard I try."

"It's so exciting!" burbled Maureen.

"Oh, for goodness sake, Maureen. Don't you know enough to understand that it's nothing of the sort?"

"Yes. No. Of course not. Sorry Margaret."

The phone rang and Rose's gran got up and walked into the hall. The sound of her voice drifted back through the open door.

"Can I ask who is speaking please? ... Well you can talk to me, I'm her grandmother ... Yes. My daughter ... Oh ... Oh, I see ... When was this? ... Well, thank you for letting us know. We'll come in first thing."

She hung up and re-entered the room.

"I'm afraid I've got some bad news about your mother."

Rose knew what it was with a certainty that surprised her.

Epilogue

Lord Carrick lounges, with legs slightly too long and blond hair slightly too perfect, on a battered blue futon, which sags in the middle and threatens to unfurl and tip him to the floor. Having slipped into the human world under cover of the Queen's fiasco, outsmarting that insufferable panda, he might add, he's adopted human form for the duration of his quest, according to the terms agreed. He's already learnt a great deal from his observations of Annis's numerous failures, and he's created this room between to enable him to move from one world to the other without detection.

To his right is a tall, wooden bookshelf dividing the room in two. In front of him is a coffee-table and in the corner is a television, which picks up everything being broadcast now, as well as in the past and, up to a point, into the future. In between the Faerie and the human worlds, he finds, there's a charming degree of fluidity.

Beyond the bookcase, which he plans to fill with numerous impressive-looking and interesting books, are two doors, facing one another, on either side of the room. One leads to his dressing-room, complete with racks of clothes from throughout the ages and full-length mirrors so he can see himself from all angles. None of this is necessary because he can change by magic, but he believes that he might gain some insight into the peculiar workings of the human mind by doing it the hard way. Besides, the physical authenticity amuses him, and the tapestry will be a marvellous talking-point.

The other door leads to a short corridor. There's a door on either side and one in front of him, the last of which is entirely ceremonial. He will make his grand entrance through it when he returns in triumph to the court. The one on the left opens on to a secret passageway that takes him into the shadows of the throne-room. It'll be fun to unnerve them by slipping back and forth undetected. In homage to Annis and her cave, he's carved this secret passageway in stone. On the right is a portal to the human world, its other end tethered to one of Annis's children, snatched from the crowded room while no-one was looking.

Carrick was there, of course, in the throng in the attic-room. He's not too proud to learn from Annis's mistakes, though he is certainly too proud to admit it. With so many frightened children milling about, it wasn't difficult to watch and learn, and to take one for himself. That child will keep open his portal, and it will be the first of many. Carrick may be in human form for the duration of the challenge, but he isn't restricted by the constraints of time and he can reduce the inconvenience he suffers by moving through it with greater precision than the Faerie can normally achieve. Using portals to pass between specific moments in time through this corridor in between the two worlds has the added advantage of causing no ripples for the Lord High Panda to detect. Lord Carrick will show him the meaning of patience.

He flicks through his many television channels. He deserves a little distraction after his great fortitude in the shadows of the throne-room. For all he knows, there may be more to learn about the extraordinary oddness of the humans' way of life, and sitting here in his bedsit is a more convenient way of doing that than any other he can think of.

Observing Annis has confirmed what he'd suspected all along. Humans can't be made to share their misery, no matter the pressure or the inducements offered. It simply isn't in their nature. It really is very clever of him to see this. Perhaps he hadn't fully understood some of the other complexities of the challenge to begin with, but that doesn't matter because no-one need ever know. Following Annis's failure, it merely remains for Lord Carrick to succeed.

He chances upon a documentary about the history of sanitation, a subject which holds a horrible fascination for the Faerie. Drains are important, apparently, in keeping down unpleasant smells and nasty little germs that cause diseases. And soap is a good thing too, whatever that may be. He learns about hospitals and mortality rates. Children, it seems, are particularly fragile. This is all information that will be useful to him.

The documentary moves on to advances in sanitation during the First World War. The Faerie can't cross saltwater, so he has no interest in the muddy soldiers cowering in holes in foreign fields, but the disruption of it all appeals to him. Having all those young men out of the way will surely create opportunities for the pursuit of his plan.

He selects an outfit from the rack in his dressing room, amusing himself by fiddling with the buttons by hand. He pulls on dark green trousers, a white shirt and khaki jumper. He bends down and laces sturdy boots to his feet. Standing back up, he runs his fingers through his hair, turning it as he does so from blond to brown, the better to match the soldiers on his screen. He watches his reflection as he modifies his form to blend into the time. He adjusts the length of his body and legs until they match the proportions he's seen in the documentary and, on second thoughts, decides he may as well be taller than average, in case that gives him any kind of advantage.

"You," he says to his reflection, "are quite the looker." The golden flecks in his green eyes twinkle their merriment back.

Sources and acknowledgements

The cover shows a detail from a tapestry from around 1500, called *Narcissus*, which is in the Museum of Fine Arts in Boston and photographed under Creative Commons for Wikipedia. The book is typeset in Bembo, with XalTerion (under licence from Pia Frauss) for the headings. The cover fonts are Gabriola and XalTerion. Galdorbec's rose and thorns logo is by Gordon Johnson from Pixabay.

The advice the Lord Herald receives from the College of Heralds in chapter 72 suggests that they've read C.S. Lewis's *The Lion, the Witch and the Wardrobe* and Lewis Carroll's *Alice in Wonderland*, the first of which is an obvious influence on my story. Annis's entrapment of Charlotte in Chapter 36 is based on a fairy story called 'The Golden Key' by George MacDonald, first published in *Dealings with Fairies* (1867). It's really odd and well worth a read if you're interested. The other fairy stories are my own versions, based on traditional tales, rather than being from any specific source, though it's possible that I've accidentally incorporated details from versions I've read or illustrations I've seen. If so, please accept my apologies and let me know so that I can update these acknowledgements for future readers.

Fairy stories often contain some kind of lesson – don't try to engage big bad wolves in conversation or don't wander off in the forest – but the legal lessons Mike attempts to read into them are influenced, if only loosely, by the work of Dawn Watkins on 'Children and the Law' at the University of Leicester.

Black Annis is real, in the sense that she genuinely features in local legend. Parents in Leicestershire really did, and perhaps still do, tell stories about a witch who stole children and scratched herself a cave in Dane Hills. It was Peter Coley who told me about her first (thanks Peter!).

Annis's mis-interpreted proverbs were inspired by Dave Gorman's *Modern Life is Goodish*, on Dave. A few of them are ones that Dave Gorman found in use, including *doggy dog world*, but most of them were invented for Annis. I'm still looking for an opportunity to use *escape goat*.

I'd like to thank my first readers, Paul, Claire and my Mum, Margaret (with apologies for using your name for a character so very unlike your lovely self), for their willingness to subject themselves to a book that's really not their kind of thing, and for their patience with my questions and self-absorption. The answer to your obligatory vehicular question, Paul, is that, according to the Local History Library (http://www.lthlibrary.org.uk/library/PDF-089-1.pdf), they did indeed have open-backed buses in Leicester in the late 70s.

I'd also like to thank John (for the bees in chapters 4 and 35), Patrick, Lynn, Susan Newton, Jane Deane, Mark Peel, Maureen McLoughlin (clearly a different Maureen), Sarah Bailey and Sam Harvey. All of you, in your own ways, helped me believe that this wasn't a completely crazy way to be spending my time. So, in a way, you've really only got yourselves to blame.

Finally, I made a promise, a long time ago, to dedicate my first novel to Taj Dhaliwal. To be honest, I can't remember the circumstances, but it was something about bus stops and knights. All the same, a promise is a promise. Taj, this is for you.

The Time Before
by Frances Evelyn

Alison Watts is dead, but Alison Watts was a time-traveller, and her daughter is too. Rose is determined to change her own history, and on her first day at her mum's old school, she's sure the opportunity will arise.

Held by her promise in the Faerie world, Queen Annis sees her rivals circling the throne. If Lord Carrick succeeds in his quest, he'll win the only wish he needs to take her place. But if she banishes him too soon, the court may turn against her, allowing Lady Maven to claim the crown.

In the summer of 1914, Agnes Fletcher enjoys an outing with her friends and brothers. In the dappled sunshine of that perfect afternoon, she meets Robin Lightborne, the man who changes everything.

March 2020

Sign up to my mailing list for a free book:
https://bit.ly/FrancesEvelynNews

Printed in Great Britain
by Amazon

59529377R00215